Thorn turned the key in the ignition. He was immune to personal fear, but not to horror. And he supped full on horror in the next moment, when he heard the strange reaction, and sensed the hellish fire of the bomb blast, blowing backward and upward at him from the engine . . .

Mary was no longer there. Her mortal form, or what was left of it, had been blown clear of the vehicle on its far side. It was obvious from the first look at her that she was not going to survive. Unless . . .

Thorn closed his eyes, crouched lower over the girl, bending till his lips touched her charred flesh . . .

THORN

THORN

FRED SABERHAGEN

SF
ace books
A Division of Charter Communications Inc.
A GROSSET & DUNLAP COMPANY
51 Madison Avenue
New York, New York 10010

THORN

An ACE Book

First printing: September 1980

2 4 6 8 0 9 7 5 3 1

Manufactured in the United States of America

Prologue

The runaway fled gracefully through the smooth white tunnel, her small bare feet moving with quick darting strides. Her slight, girlish body, completely naked, was splashed by a quickly shifting disco spectrum of fantastic light that followed her from the room she fled. Music, loud rock music, followed too, throbbing with the light. Like the light, it lost its violence only partially and slowly as it increased its distance from its origin.

As if the music had caught up with her in midstride, the girl's graceful run changed abruptly, halfway through the tunnel, into a dance, but a dance that still carried her rapidly forward into the large, white room at the tunnel's end.

It was a long room, like something out of a museum almost, and the windowless white walls were angled and rectangular. The white carpet was immaculate and thick. On the walls hung many paintings, drawings, prints, and all of them were hard to see in the bewildering, reflected disco rainbow that came through the tunnel to provide the only illumination. There were carvings hanging on the walls too, and statues large and small stood everywhere. The girl's dance moved her in and out among them, as if she might be looking for another way out. But the tunnel was the only entrance, and the only exit visible.

The girl's dance was a performance meant for no one but herself. Her face was a lovely mask, utterly unlined, looking very young, and looking too calm to be a dancer's face. Around it, long brown hair swung wild and dark, dirty and uncared for. Her dark eyelids were half closed, the full lips parted levelly over white, slightly uneven teeth. The skin of her body was childishly smooth, and gleamed lightly in the strange changing light, as if she might be sweating despite the coolness of the air. Her feet were tiny and arched, grained here and there with dirt, and she set them precisely and silently down in the thick whiteness of the floor.

The driving music had less and less to do with the dance as it continued. Its movement shifted to a slower rhythm, becoming almost courtly. Then halfway through a pirouette the girl's eyes opened wide. Her balance, perfect through all the movements before this one, abruptly broke, and she went down on one knee on the rich ivory carpet, stunned into awkwardness by something she had seen.

She stared with wide eyes for a long moment into the dimness straight ahead. Then, bare shoulders heaving with a great sighing breath, she slowly turned her head. Hardly did she dare to try to see again what she had seen a moment earlier.

It hung there on the wall, amid the hundred other paintings. Conflicting emotions struggled in the girl's face; and then presently her face became tranquil again, but on a different level. She was gazing outward now, away from self. She stayed crouching there on one knee, almost exactly as she had fallen, becoming almost as motionless as one of the surrounding statues. Now even her breathing appeared to stop.

"There you are." The voice of the approaching man was slurred and gleeful, and it contained hostility. The light coming through the curious white tunnel was modulated by his approaching shadow. He moved into the girl's range of vision now, but she ignored him completely. He was as naked as she was, and looked to be a few years older. Perhaps he was twenty-two or twenty-three. Reddish hair with a tendency to curl fell damply to his muscular and freckled shoulders. He was only a few inches taller than the girl. And he was breathing heavily, as if he too might just have finished a dance or some other physical exertion.

The girl was still down on one knee. She had regained grace in her pose, but otherwise had not moved since turning her head to look back over one shoulder. She had not yet taken her eyes from the sight that had made her fall.

The young man followed her gaze for a moment. Nothing but a row of old paintings, mostly in wood frames, hanging on the white wall and, like everything else in the room, hard to see in the odd pulsing light. He was not really interested; he was used to being around people who stared at nothing. He walked toward the girl until he was standing close beside her, but still she gave no sign of being aware of him at all. Not even when he buried the fingers of one strong hand in her wild hair and tugged.

"Hey," he said, trying to turn her face toward his body. As he spoke the music in the other room cut off abruptly. Still the mad light continued to pulsate through the tunnel.

Abruptly the girl thrust out one slender arm in a graceful shove. The young man, who had no dancer's balance, went staggering back. He reeled helplessly into a towering marble statue, which rocked on its base and settled back. Mumbling something, the man tried to recover, clawed at a wall, then sat down on the white carpet with a soft thud.

Again the multicolored light wavered with approaching shadows. Another naked man was coming from the far room. The legs that bore him round the white curve of tunnel were moving trunks of bone and muscle, well designed for his great weight. The torso above the legs had once been heroic, but now sagged grossly with advancing age. Still the clean-shaven face, its chin held high, was alert, controlled, imperious. Only a fringe of hair, all white, remained around the massive head; and gray hair grew matted thickly on the chest and belly and on the heavy, still-powerful arms.

This man advanced a little way into the room and halted, looking with displeasure at the scene. "There are some very valuable things in here," he announced in a bass voice, "and both of you are evidently crazy, or completely freaked out, or whatever the word for it is this year. Therefore I am not going to let you make this your playground. Got that?"

The last words trailed off just a little. The aging man had at last taken some notice of the extreme rigidity of the girl's gaze and the strangeness of her frozen posture. The arm she had used to shove the youth away was still extended. Her head was still turned, eyes looking back over her left shoulder.

The only sound in the room, besides the violent music, was the labored breathing of the young man. He still sat on the floor, and now he was glowering angrily at the girl.

The old man said, in his bass voice: "If that on the wall really strikes your fancy, little girl, then you have good taste. Better than some people who have entered this room fully clothed and supposedly in their right minds. Well, I have good taste too, and you doubtless don't know what you're staring at anyway, and I appreciate your round little ass. In fact, out of all the orifices available tonight, I may just choose to end my evening there. But I want to do it back in the other room. So get up."

Now through the tunnel behind the old man three more naked figures were approaching, pushing before them an extensive interplay of shadows. Slightly in the lead there walked a leanly muscular man of about thirty-five. His sun-tanned body was marked with the pale outline of absent swimming briefs. Just after the man came a boy who appeared to be in his mid-teens, small and slightly built, pale-haired, blinking lost eyes at the world. The boy supported himself every few steps by leaning a frail arm against the white curve of the tunnel wall. When he emerged from the tunnel into the room and the wall flattened, he stopped, leaning his back against it for support. A step behind the boy, another dark-haired girl strolled in casually. In size, and build, and coloring, she fairly closely resembled the girl who had been dancing. The brown eyes of this newly-arrived girl were keen with interest—but they were focused on the empty air an arm's length before her face. She paid no attention to anyone else. Her full lips mumbled soundlessly, then smiled.

The red-haired man who sat on the floor ignored them all, all except the girl who had danced. Now in his throat a low murmuring of rage and humiliation had begun, and grew in loudness. On the second try he struggled back to his feet. His right hand went out to a small white cube, and from its flat surface he grabbed up a small but heavy artifact of silvery metal. Raising this, he lunged straight for the crouching dancer as his right arm swung the lethally compact weight straight for her skull.

The old man's was the only voice to cry a warning, and his yell did no one any good. It sounded simultaneously with a sharp, dying scream.

The thin young boy still leaned back tiredly against the flat white wall. His blinking eyes, completely lost, were looking somewhere on the far side of the dim room. The dark-haired girl who had come with him through the tunnel stood quietly beside him now. She was thoughtfully probing with one finger inside her own mouth, as if intent on making sure her teeth were all still there. She took no account of what had happened to the white carpet just a few feet away.

The athletic man, who was alert and could move very fast, was already a step in front of the huge old one. But there he halted his swift advance, warily astonished; his move had obviously come too late, and he had no wish to step into the fresh blood.

The huge, gray old man was astonished too. Then, because he was no stranger to sudden violence and it did not particularly upset him, and because he possessed a quickly penetrating mind, he was immediately struck by circumstances even more amazing than the mere fact of abrupt murder. Inspiration of a magnitude extremely rare grew swiftly behind his clear blue eyes. Slowly he put out a massive hand, to take his wiry companion by the shoulder.

"Gliddon," the old man said. He used the careful tone of one who wishes to wake a sleeper gently, not to startle.

"What?" The attention of the wiry man was still warily absorbed in the scene before him. Hell of a mess to be cleaned up, at best, he was thinking. The killer was now standing, swaying, as if dazed. The silver artifact lay on the floor, near something else.

"Gliddon. These two kids behind me. I want you to get them out of here. They're both stoned blind, and I don't think this has made any impression on them at all. I doubt that they'll remember seeing a thing—but anyway we'll cross that bridge when we come to it. Right now get 'em out of here and put 'em down to sleep somewhere. *I* want to deal with this." He nodded at the red spectacle before them.

"But."

"Oh, you can take charge of the cleanup later. But right now just get those two put away." The old man, an expression in his eyes befitting the discoverer of a new continent, was moving forward slowly, his gaze shifting from the dazed, spattered killer to the demolished victim, and back again. "I want to handle this, alone. I have my reasons."

One

In my opinion I owe the breathing legions of humanity no explanations of any of my affairs, no apologies for any chapter of my life. And I consider this judgement to apply with particular force to my role in the events surrounding the recent and much-publicized disappearance of one of the world's noblest works of art. Let those breathing folk who in financial anguish claim rights to the painting recover it if they are able, or get along without it if they are not. Nor do I consider that it is up to me to interpret for them those strange and violent events, mystifying to so many, which like red parentheses enclose the painting's vanishment. By the standard of objective justice it is rather I who deserve an accounting from the breathing world, I who am entitled to some reparations . . .

Bah. At my age I should know better. And in fact I do. I press no formal claim.

Only this much do I insist upon: you will understand that almost my sole purpose in setting down this history is to please myself. *Almost*, be it noted. Mina, my true great love, my delight now for almost a century, accept these pages from me as my humble effort to explain some things you must have wondered at; and be assured, my dear, that none of the breathing women mentioned here could ever begin to mean as much to me as one look from your eyes, one touch from your sweet hand. In addition, I would like to think there are a few other readers who will be able to appreciate the story, as a story, as I tell it on my own terms, in my own way. And part of my pleasure shall be to use my informed imagination to create for those discerning readers some scenes at which I was not present and could play no role. I warn you—if it is not already too late—that in these scenes it amuses me sometimes to be accurate and deceptive at the same time. You may accept those portions of the story or not, just as you choose. Indeed—do I need to say it?—you may think what you like about the whole business.

It is my decision to begin upon a certain warm spring night, not long ago. It was a night through which the smell of orange blossoms spread, to bless the Arizona air. More than five hundred years had passed between that night, and the last time I had seen my treasure. Time had marked my long-sought masterpiece, and I too was changed . . . very much changed. And yet, merely seeing it again awoke in me such things . . . one look and I was back in the City of Flowers, where winters are too cold to tolerate orange trees and palms but where nevertheless the pungent summer atmosphere bore and still bears the blended fragrance of a thousand blooms . . .

This is she, Signore Ladislao. An excellent likeness, if that is what you wish. From this you may know her. Pray Jesus and San Lorenzo that you may bring her safely out . . .

An excellent likeness; oh yes indeed. When at last I stood before that panel of polychromed wood again in Arizona, I could feel its craquelure of centuries like a net of painful scars on my own skin. I thought for a moment that my eyes were going to fill with tears. And who will believe that of me, now, no matter how solemnly I write it down?

But this history is so far getting off to a very rambling start.

Consider Phoenix, Arizona. Consider wealthy suburban Scottsdale, to be precise, as it was upon that recent warm spring night. Palm trees of all sizes and several varieties mingled everywhere with the ubiquitous orange. At dusk the streets were busy, in part because of the natives' habit, bred into them by their summer temperatures, of putting off, as much as possible, business and pleasure both till after sundown. One tourist who was present on the evening we are talking about found himself in particularly hearty agreement with this practice. He was registered at his downtown Phoenix hotel as Mr. Jonathan Thorn, permanent address listed as Oak Tree, Illinois.

At sunset a taxi took Mr. Thorn from Phoenix to Scottsdale. The street where he debarked from his taxi was wide, not too busy, and lined on both sides with expensive shops. The shops' signs were all small, discreet. Rows of expensive vehicles were parked diagonally in front of the low buildings. The plank sidewalks, partially blocked from the street by imitation hitching posts made of real, weathered wood, were roofed with more planks against the summer sun. Beyond these wooden cloisters, the low-built expensive shops were modern, though constructed in part of real adobe brick.

The building that Mr. Thorn approached was typical, being grilled on all its doors and windows with thick bars of black wrought iron. The front door was intermittently open to the plank sidewalk, admitting a trickle of people in elegant but open-throated warm weather attire. As he passed the hitching post in front, Mr. Thorn took note of an incongruous old Ford sedan, inscrutably battered and unrepaired, waiting there between a Mercedes and a new luxury model Jeep. He took note, I say, but only barely; at that moment he had other things to think about.

Just inside the door, a security guard in business suit and tie took note of Mr. Thorn, classified him as acceptable, and offered him a light smile and a nod. Thorn found himself in a moderately large, efficiently cooled room where a dozen or so folk, mostly middle-aged and prosperous, to judge by appearances, milled slowly about or sat in folding chairs. Under bright lights at the front of the room, high wooden tables already held some of the lesser items from the Delaunay Seabright collection on display. The overall decor was determinedly Southwestern, with the massive, rough-hewn ceiling beams exposed and Navajo rugs hung on the white, rough-plastered walls. Set up to face the front of the room were many more folding chairs than seemed likely to be necessary. In theory this pre-auction viewing was open to the public, but it appeared that few of the public were going to intrude upon what was in fact a pasttime of the rich. A month earlier, and the notoriety attendant upon the killings of Delaunay Seabright and his stepdaughter would probably still have drawn something of a crowd. But the auction had been well timed. By that spring night, the spectacular murder-kidnapping was already fading from the popular memory.

There were only two people present, a couple, who looked as if they might be thrill-seekers. Quite proletarian in appearance, they were being watched with vague, discreet apprehension by the auctioneers, smooth men in business suits who looked as if they might just have flown in from New York. Mr. Thorn, catching a little of that watchfulness, observed the couple too.

At one end of the rear rank of folding chairs sat Mary Rogers. (Thorn was not to learn her name until a little later.) Mary's long hair was sand-colored, somewhat curly, and usually disheveled. Her age was twenty-one, her face freckled and attractive, her disposition choleric. Her body was all shapely strength, superbly suitable for work and childbearing, and would have made an ideal model for some artist's healthy peasant—though Mary would not have made a very good peasant, or peasant's wife, or, for that matter, a very good artist's model either. She planned to use her strength in different ways, in a dedicated lifelong selfless service of humanity. She always visualized humanity as young, I am quite sure, and as eternally oppressed. Well, there are billions of youth in the world, after all, more or less oppressed. Probably cases exist even in Scottsdale. But in that auction room, alas, were none at all; Mary had to have some other reason to be there.

The auctioneers, as I have said, were a bit uneasy about this young, comparatively poorly dressed couple. What bothered them was not the fact that Mary wore blue jeans—so did a couple of other women in that small crowd. But Mary's jeans were probably of the wrong brand, and their fadedness suggested not some manufacturer's process, but utilitarian wear. Successful experts in the world of fine art can be amazingly sensitive to subtle differences in color and texture, not only in the merchandise but in the customers.

But mainly I think it was that the faces of Mary and her escort stood out in that little gathering.

Their countenances were not filled with thinly
veiled greed for the treasures (so far only quite
minor ones) displayed, nor with calculation as to
how to bid on them. Oh, it was evident enough
from Mary's face that she had some keen purpose
in that room—but what could it be? That she
might try to buy anything seemed highly unlikely, considering the prices that were certain to be
asked and bid. If she and her companion were
really wealthy eccentrics who simply enjoyed
dressing in the style of the non-wealthy, then who
belonged to that old Ford out front? Anyone who
drove that car out of eccentricity would probably
be staying at home anyway, in rooms filled with
piled garbage and a thousand cats.

Whatever apprehensions the auctioneers may
have developed regarding Mary—that she might
be contemplating some mad attempt at robbery, or
an even more hopeless effort at social protest—
these doubts must have been at least somewhat
allayed by the face and attitude of the young man
seated at her side. He was a bearded young man,
with his arms folded in his not very expensive
checked sports shirt. His look was not one of
fanaticism, but of uncomfortable loyalty. He was
bracing himself, perhaps—but not for bullets,
only for boredom or embarrassment.

Also present, to define the opposite end of the
auctioneers' spectrum of respect, was Ellison
Seabright. When Seabright entered the front door,
a few minutes after Mr. Thorn, the salesmen gave
him the warmest welcome they could manage
without seeming to be effusive about it, without
drawing possibly unwelcome attention to his
presence: the greeting for a celebrity, but one who
temporarily has more attention than he wants.

Seabright was about fifty years old. In general
appearance, he reminded Mr. Thorn strongly of
Rodrigo Borgia. Mr. Seabright weighed about
three hundred pounds, Thorn judged, and if the
tales of the family wealth were anywhere near
accurate he might have balanced himself in gold
and had enough left over to purchase any painting
or sculpture that he might desire. According to
the publicity that had begun to appear since his
brother's kidnapping and strange death, it was a
family trait to desire a good many.

Ellison Seabright, from where he stood in quiet
conversation with the auctioneers, once or twice
shot a hurried, grim glance in the direction of
Mary Rogers—as if he knew her, which was interesting. Mr. Thorn, from his chair in the front
row, could not tell how the young woman in the
rear reacted to these glances, if at all.

The other potential bidders in the room all
glowed in their not very distinctive auras of material wealth. The auctioneers, when they conferred
privately (as they thought) among themselves in
the next room, had voiced hopes that a local record was going to be set. They were daring to
compare themselves tonight with Christie's, with
Sotheby Parke Bernet. This time, even leaving
aside such relatively minor treasures as Mimbres
bowls and Chinese jade, this time they had a
probably genuine Verrocchio to put on the block.

Mr. Thorn was doubtless among those they
were counting on to run the bidding up when it
officially began tomorrow night. Although they
had never seen or heard of him before, it was
surely apparent to such artistically expert eyes
that Thorn's dark suit had been tailored at one of
the best London shops, and that his shoes were a

good match for the suit. He wore, on the third finger of his right hand, a worn-thin ring of ancient gold. His general appearance was at least as elegant as that of Mr. Seabright.

The height of the two men was about the same, somewhat above the average. Thorn's weight was considerably less—though not so very much less as it appeared to be. He looked to be Seabright's junior by ten or fifteen years, but that comparison was deceptive too. Their faces were both striking, in different ways: Seabright's for massive arrogance, Thorn's—in a way not nearly so massive. As for their relative wealth—but Mr. Thorn had not really come to Scottsdale to bid and buy.

"No, I'm sure it's going to go to Ellison," Mary Rogers was whispering to her dour young companion with the sandy beard. "The old bastard probably has more money than all these others put together. And he wants it, I know how he wants it. After what he's done already he's not going to let mere money stop him."

There were several rows of chairs between Mary and Mr. Thorn. The room was abuzz with the noise of other conversations. And her whisper was really more discreet—that was the key word of the evening, up to now—than her misfit appearance promised. So Mary's words could be heard only by her friend seated beside her, and by Mr. Thorn, whose ears were wonderfully keen. Also it is a fact that Thorn was constitutionally unable to ignore either of the two women in the room he found genuinely attractive.

The second genuinely attractive woman was dark and slender, somewhere in her mid-thirties, and sheathed in a gown that you might think had been designed expressly to wear while inspecting expensive art. She was physically young for her years, but not as young as she wanted to be or tried to be. Probably to no one's surprise, she was clinging to Ellison Seabright's right arm. Certain subtleties of body language in her pose suggested to Thorn that she was clinging there in order to avoid having to swim elsewhere. At the moment her massive escort was standing at the right end of the front row of chairs, in conversation with the head auctioneer, and with one who must be a fellow collector, a bearded elderly gentleman wearing another New York suit. Seabright was turning his massive head, looking round him in irritation. "Where's Gliddon?" he was inquiring of the world in general, though his voice was hardly more than whisper-loud. A voice not in the least Borgia, but thoroughly American. "Got as far as the front door with me, and then . . ."

A bodyguard even taller than Seabright, and almost as wide, stood nearby teetering on his toes. He was not very obtrusive, handling at least the passive aspects of his job quite well. The dark woman clung to Seabright's arm, smiled brightly, and seemed to attend closely to his every word, meanwhile wistfully wishing that she were somewhere else. Mr. Thorn could tell. He had hopes of soon discovering her name.

"Then you might as well give up, hadn't you?" the young man at Mary Rogers' side was whispering into her ear. His tone was quietly despairing, that of one who knows full well that argument is folly, but feels compelled to argue anyway. "You think he's going to listen to any kind of an appeal now?"

"No." Mary's monosyllable was quietly ominous.

"Then why the hell did we come here? I thought . . ."

At that point every conversation in the room trailed into silence.

Through a curtained doorway at the front of the room, between the two large tables, two armed and uniformed men came into view, rolling a mobile stand between them. The stand was draped with a white cloth, completely covering the upright rectangle that was its cargo. The rectangle was about the size of the top of a card table, somewhat larger than Mr. Thorn had been expecting. Then he remembered the frame. According to the news stories and the sale catalogue, a frame had been added to the painting, probably sometime during the eighteenth century.

With the stand position on the dais between the tables, the two armed men stood still, alert, on either side of it. An auctioneer came to join them, placing his pale hand on the white cloth. He let his showman's hand stay there, motionlessly holding the cloth, while in a low voice he made a brief and scrupulously correct announcement.

"Ladies and gentlemen, as most of you know, Verrocchio has signed this piece. But in the time and place in which he worked, such a signature often signified no more than a master's approval of work done by an apprentice. What we can say with absolute certainty is that this painting is from Verrocchio's workshop, and that it is in his mature style. The minimum bid tomorrow night will be two hundred thousand dollars."

With one firm twitch, the showman's hand removed the cloth.

Mr. Thorn forgot even the live and lovely flesh of the two genuinely attractive breathing women in the room. He rose from his folding chair and like a man in a trance stepped forward, closer to the painting. It of course shows Magdalen, not as she came to Christ, but as she must have looked when rising from His feet with sins forgiven. Yes, of course, painted in the mature style of Verrocchio. But by an imitator—though transfiguration would be a better word than imitation for what the creator of this painting had accomplished. How could they all fail to see the truth?

And of course at the same time the face is that of the model who posed for it, that young runaway girl of more than half a thousand years ago. *An excellent likeness, if that is what you wish . . .*

Incipient tears in the eyes of Mr. Thorn were stopped by harsh cries of alarm. Another sort of liquid, flung from behind, struck him on the shoulder, and scarlet droplets spattered past his ear to mar the cheek and hair of Magdalen.

He turned with a snarl. The girl in unfashionable blue jeans was on her feet, holding in one hand a small plastic bag almost emptied but still drooling red on the expensive carpet. Vindictive triumph ruled her face. Closer at hand, Ellison Seabright had been incarnadined from head to foot, Rodrigo Borgia skinned alive, standing in stunned disbelief. His bodyguard, galvanized too late, came pushing forward in a fury. Men and women in uniform, springing from the walls and woodwork, were all around the triumphant girl, about to seize her. You are under arrest, they cried, and in a moment they would manacle her wrists . . .

Two

Quite early in the game, long before our long marching column approached Buda, the chains of hand-wrought iron were unlocked and taken from my wrists. At the same time, my ankles were untied, and I was given a better horse to ride. To my thinking all this served as an early confirmation of my own good judgement in deciding to throw myself upon the mercy of King Matthias. Of course with the Turks close at my heels and the remnants of my own outnumbered army fast dissolving, there had been little real choice.

The king, when he accepted my surrender, had been angry with me—mainly as a result of certain false accusations, lying letters planted by my enemies for him to intercept, a whole devious chain of circumstances that I do not mean to go into here. But evidently His Majesty soon realized the truth. I did not have another chance to talk to him during the march to Buda, but his officers must have been given orders to treat me well. When we reached Buda they put me into a cell high up in the fortress, a stone chamber better ventilated and cleaner than many of the free houses of the time.

My food also was good, by the standards of the time and place, and plentiful enough. This was, you understand, more than twelve years before I fell under the treacherous swords of would-be murderers, stopped breathing, and acquired my present idiosyncracies of diet. And when cold weather arrived I was allowed a fire. Guards took me out each day for exercise in a courtyard. There I sometimes walked under the noses of papal legates—I recognized Nicholas of Modrusa once—ambassadors from here and there, some other important men and curious ladies whom I could not identify. None of these ever spoke to me, but observed silently, from balconies where they usually chose to remain half concealed. Even then, you will understand, my reputation was under construction, by German enemies who employed Goebbelsian thoroughness in their attempted destruction of the truth. Now, for important folk visiting His Majesty at Buda, the in thing to do was evidently to ask to see the monster caged. Well, at the time I enjoyed my walks despite observers, and perhaps I should now think more kindly of them. Some were doubtless sympathetic to my cause, and they may have expressed their feelings to Matthias. Still, I spent a year in that first cell.

From time to time I was given brief audience by the king, who limited himself for the most part to looking at me keenly and inquiring how I was. Matthias was then only twenty years of age, but had already spent four years on the throne of Hungary. He had come to power by what amounted to popular acclamation; and time had already begun to vindicate the confidence thus shown him by his people.

At the end of a year I was suddenly moved about fifty kilometers up the Danube to Visegrad Palace, where Matthias was currently spending a good deal of his time. A good deal of money, also, which he extracted mercilessly from the wealthy landowners of his realm, and not all of it was going to feed and equip his formidable army. Scholars and artists from across Europe were beginning to assemble there at his invitation. Already they had started to put together the magnificent library that would be known as the Corvina, and only a few years later the palace would house the first printing press in all that region of Europe . . . but I am beginning to stray from my story.

At the Palace of Visegrad I was again incarcerated. Just as the history books of the twentieth century will tell you—they do now and then get something right, at least—I was put into a cell in what was called the Tower of Solomon. My cell, or perhaps I should even call it a room, was even more comfortable than before, and the conditions of my confinement still more lenient. The thought of attempting to escape from Matthias had never struck me as a very good idea, and now even the faintest tendencies in that direction quite vanished from my mind. All signs tended to reassure me that my instinct to trust the king had been correct. Escape, even if it succeeded, could hardly get me anywhere, for I had literally nowhere to go. But patience would reveal what plans that wise, just prince was formulating, in which he meant me to play a role.

I felt increasingly certain that the king's plans, whatever they might be, must offer me something better than mere confinement, however mild its terms. I had never been more than technically Matthias's foe; his anger at me was due more to the conniving of my enemies than to anything that I had really done. And, if I may say so myself, I was too good to be wasted. Sooner or later the king would determine the right place in which to use me, and when that happened I could not fail to be restored to a position of power and official honor.

As you will see, my thinking in all this was basically correct. Even if never, in my highest flights of fancy, did I guess correctly just what the king would ultimately decide my right place was to be . . .

What you will find set down in today's history books is that the Tower of Solomon remained my prison for the next eleven years. The historical experts, who in other respects often behave as if they are perfectly sober, relate that during that time I was often granted the special boon of having small animals brought living to my cell, that I might entertain myself by torturing them and impaling them on miniature stakes. This quaint behavior must have so impressed the humanist Matthias that it was during this very period that he decided to arrange my marriage to his sister. At the same time, to punish her for consorting with such a beast as Drakulya, he had her name obliterated from all the family records. (And it is true, that historians can now find out hardly anything about her, save the mere fact of her existence, and our marriage.) When eleven years of this idyll had passed, Matthias decided for unknown reasons that it was time for a change, abruptly brought me out of my cell—whether my bride had meanwhile been locked up with me is left to the imagination of the reader—and in due course restored me to my former eminence as Prince of Wallachia.

Now, I ask you. Does it require prolonged reflection, penetrating intelligence of the first order, to infer that the above scenario lacks something, that it might perhaps profit by correction?

Truth is hard to attain. But let me at least try to restore to the record a little sanity. After the move to Visegrad, the king saw me more frequently. At each audience he probed me deeply with searching young eyes, eyes rapidly growing wise beyond their years with the experience of statecraft. At each meeting now he asked me many questions. What did I think about this particular military problem? Supposing I were the king's chief adviser, what course would I recommend in that political difficulty? What was George of Podebrady up to, and how about the Germans? Should women be encouraged to read and write? He interrogated me in areas philosophical and moral, he sought to know my mind on matters of theology and art. Always I strove to answer truthfully, weak though my knowledge was in many fields. I wanted to appear to His Majesty as neither more nor less than what I truly was: loyal and capable, yet prone, as all men are, to human imperfection.

The key conversation between us took place one sunny day in the early spring of 1464, when I had been about six months at Visegrad. My guards, whose gradually improving courtesy had fed my hopes, on that day positively bowed as they came to escort me from my now well-furnished cell. I was led into a part of the palace that I had not previously visited, through rooms where some of Matthias's growing legion of painters and bookworms were at work. The king himself was waiting for me in a large chamber, magnificently furnished. Its broad shelves contained more books, all hand-copied of course, than I had ever seen before in my entire nonbookish life.

At this meeting the king for the first time dismissed his soldiers completely. We were for all intents and purposes alone, there remaining in our sight only a couple of graybearded researchers at the end of a long gallery, doddering the remainder of their lives away over manuscripts.

The young king's smile lay thinly across his prominent jaw. "Drakulya, we have heard it said that you are a completely fearless man. Nor have we ever seen evidence of dread in you, not even on that first day when you stood before us in chains."

To my surprise, His Majesty had spoken not in Hungarian or Rumanian, our usual vehicles of discourse, but in Italian. His slow, mechanical pronunciation gave me the impression that he might have learned the little speech by rote.

Puzzled, I bowed to him, and made shift to answer in the same tongue. "My life's ration of fear was used up, Majesty, before I had a beard to shave."

Smiling, evidently pleased by my reply, the king relaxed the conversation into Hungarian. "The Turkish prison, yes. Well, it is the Turks who fear you now, *Kaziklu Bey*. I remember well the bags you used to send me, Lord Impaler, stinking to high heaven by the time I got them, filled with Turkish noses, ears . . . but never mind that now." He paused. "There are certain Christians who dread you also."

"A few may have good reason, Majesty. Most certainly do not."

"And, by the way, we have sometimes wondered why it is that you have never presumed during these talks to remind us of our father's friendship for you. It might be expected that a

man in the position of a prisoner could hardly fail
to do that."

I bowed again. "It had never occurred to me that
such a friendship could possibly have been forgotten by Your Majesty."

"Ha. And some say you are no diplomat. Well."
And Matthias stared at me, thoughtfully, as only
kings in the age of kings could stare, his eyes a
regal gray above his still almost beardless cheeks.
"Of diplomats we have enough at present. Of
army officers too, it seems. Although rumor has it
that the Sultan himself intends to lead his armies
this year, in Bosnia, as I mean to lead my own
against him . . . you see, I trust you with a military secret. Though I suppose it can hardly be a
secret any longer. Oh, you are an excellent field
commander, Drakulya. But if I gave you a command old jealousies would come to life again, old
enmities would be rekindled. I have a lot of Germans in the Black Army, you know. In adding one
fine leader, yourself, I would be bound to lose
others, in one way or another . . . no, our army is
not for you. Not right now. Yet we are loath to see
you wasted in a cell."

I spoke impulsively. "Sire, I hear from my
guards that the Holy Father is still preaching a
Crusade, and still means to lead it in person. That
the Emperor and Philip the Good have both
pledged their support. If Your Majesty were to
release me, secretly perhaps—"

"You would follow the Pope?" Matthias immediately seemed interested, and my hopes
leaped up.

"I am a Christian, if no Catholic. The Pope has
my respect. I will follow him if he will have me.
Any attack upon the Turk should work at least

indirectly to Your Majesty's benefit."

But I had misinterpreted the king's interest, which at the moment was not centered on the Turks. "Is it then not beyond the bounds of possibility, Drakulya, that for sufficient reason you might abjure your Orthodox faith and accept Catholicism?"

I had no idea why the king should put such a question to me, but I could see that he was very serious. And of course it was not a question to be answered lightly. But after giving it some thought, I nodded my assent. "If that were how I might best serve my king—it would not be impossible."

Matthias gripped my arm. "Drakulya, it rejoices our heart to see your loyalty! Those intercepted messages, that sowed such enmity between us, and caused your imprisonment—I can see now that they were, as you said, a vile trick of your enemies. And now we will unfold to you our wishes, regarding your own immediate future."

Here the king paused, eyes fixed on mine. With my own heart rejoicing perhaps even more than his, I waited to hear his plan.

When he went on, he was obviously choosing his words with great deliberation. "The service we have in mind requires a man well born, utterly loyal, and of the most solid judgment. He must be able to—how shall we put it?—inspire respect. He must also be able to follow orders. And to hold his tongue. To be utterly ruthless when the need arises. And he should have skill in arms—yes, that may prove to be of importance."

"I am honored that Your Majesty thinks I—"

"But not in this so-called Crusade. That is a great folly. You hear garbled rumors about it from your guards. But we are informed by shrewd observers everywhere. No one is going to follow the Pope. What we have in mind for you, Drakulya, is something altogether different. It is not only an important matter of state, it also concerns our own family very closely."

The king, gesturing for me to keep up with him, began to walk, as he was wont to do when weighty matters were to be decided. I remained in close attendance. His voice fell to a whisper now, so that I had to bend my head to hear.

"Drakulya, do you know how many sisters I have?" Of course everyone knows such things, and more, about his reigning monarch. But before I could fall to naming siblings, Matthias silenced me with a raised finger. Suddenly he was not so much a ruler as simply the young, worried head of a family.

"I have a younger sister, Helen, whose name has not been mentioned in my family for two years. Her age is now seventeen. At fifteen she was betrothed to a Sforza. That would have made a valuable alliance. But she behaved with great folly, so that the engagement had to be broken off. She ran away with an artisan, if you can believe it, rather than marry into one of the great houses of Italy. When she was found, we had her put into an Italian convent, until we could decide what to do next. But it was the wrong convent, as it proved, so gentle a place that she had no trouble getting out of it and running away again.

"A few months ago some Medici traders brought me the latest news of her. Quite unpleasant news, and they were too diplomatic to tell it to me directly, realizing that I must not be put in the position of having to take notice publicly of her scandalous affairs. But their report placed her in Venice . . . you can and must hear the sordid details later, and I will give them to you myself, if you agree that you are the man I need. As I think you are. I need one who will restore the honor of my crown and of my family—in one way or another—"

Three

"Because he's a bloody murderer, and I want the world to know him for what he is. That's why I did it. I waited till they brought the painting out so all the guards would be concentrating on it. I knew he wouldn't press charges against me, he doesn't want any more publicity."

Outrage and enjoyment made a heady mixture in Mary Rogers' voice, and she talked as if she were familiar with their blended taste. At the moment she was seated in an awkward armchair in Mr. Thorn's expensive Phoenix hotel suite, sipping from time to time at a can of beer. Her sturdy legs were crossed in their tight blue jeans.

It was evening again, almost exactly twenty-four hours after Mary's dye-throwing outrage. Over in Scottsdale, just a few miles away, the auction should be getting started just about now, doubtless under a heavily reinforced guard. Mr. Thorn was going to miss the bidding, which was all right with him. He had seen the painting, and he was virtually certain who was going to buy it. And even if by some chance the Magdalen should be bought by someone else, he could easily find out whom. It was not going to get away from him again.

So he felt that he could afford the time to indulge his curiosity regarding Mary and her motives. He had the habit of thinking, whenever anything bizarre happened nearby, that it was somehow meant for him. Quite often he was right.

Lounging near the window now, he glanced out

through his new polarizing sunglasses at the last fading tinges of a gory sunset. Clouds were hung theatrically above a distant reach of desert, studded with a few Hollywood mountains. From the twentieth floor, a lot of distant scenery was visible beyond the smoky metropolitan sprawl.

"You can bet I didn't know what she was going to do." This was the voice of Robinson Miller, Mary's young man from the auction room, who had turned out to be her lawyer also. He and Mary, Thorn understood, had encountered each other on some pathway of the legal jungle into which she had been parachuted by her accidental connection with the infamous Seabright murder-kidnapping; and they had been getting better acquainted ever since.

"Completely irrational behavior," Miller added now, drilling Mary with a stern look that she did not seem to feel at all. From what Thorn had seen of her lifestyle so far, it was hard to estimate whether she needed friend or lawyer most.

Last night as Mary was giving the police her name, address, and phone number, Thorn had been nearby, although she had not seen him. Today Thorn had called her up—Miller answering the phone—and had invited her up to his suite for this evening chat, saying there were matters of mutual advantage to be discussed. Yes, certainly, she was welcome to bring a friend along to the hotel lair of the mysterious stranger; and so it was that her legal adviser and probable lover sat beside her now in another chair constructed like hers at disabling angles, sipping a glass of ginger ale and ice and puffing at a large-bowled pipe.

"What I really wanted," Mary announced now, "was to get hold of some blood."

Mr. Thorn, who had been paying only desultory attention, forgot about the scenery and took off his glasses long enough to give her an intense look. It took him a moment to realize what she had meant.

"At first I thought maybe I'd use beef blood. But then I realized that it wouldn't be appropriate to throw anything real on *him*. Except maybe some real acid." Mary gave a bright giggle. "So it was just that stuff they use in movies, harmless. A friend of mine who works in a studio got hold of some for me."

"The dry cleaner found it interesting," commented Mr. Thorn. "A type of stain with which he had never had to deal before. But it came out of my suit quite easily."

"Your—?" In a second Mary's mood changed to regret and horror. "Oh, I'm sorry! I hadn't realized that any of the glop hit you. Is that why you wanted me to come up here? No, of course not. Look, I really am sorry."

"Your apology is accepted. Think no more of the matter, I was not harmed. And it is fortunate that the painting sustained no damage either."

"Yes, fortunate," concurred the lawyer. Taking his pipe from his mouth, he made fencing motions in the air with the curved stem. "Ah, you mentioned some matters of mutual advantage?"

"I did." Thorn smiled at them both, then addressed himself mainly to Mary. "It is to my advantage to learn more about Mr. Ellison Seabright. It may be to your advantage to help me do so."

"Whom do you represent?" Miller asked quickly, before Mary could respond.

Thorn turned to him. "Only myself. Therefore any information you may give me will go no farther." After a pause he added: "You may be confident also that none of it is likely to be used to Mr. Seabright's advantage."

His visitors exchanged a cautious glance, and slight shrugs. Then Mary asked: "What sort of things do you want to know?"

Mr. Thorn moved a little closer to his guests, taking a seat on a sofa opposite their chairs, his lean hands clasped before him. "To begin with, whom do you accuse Mr. Seabright of having murdered?"

"Mary," Robinson Miller cautioned, shaking his beard at her.

Mary took another sip of Coors and ignored legal counsel. "He killed his half-brother, Delaunay Seabright. And Helen, his own stepdaughter. You must have heard and read about those killings, they made news all over the country. Oh, I don't mean he did it with his own hands. But you can bet he was involved."

Thorn allowed himself a pained frown, and objected gently: "Were not the police of the opinion that Helen was killed by men trying to abduct Delaunay for ransom? And that Delaunay himself died almost accidentally, though while he was in the unknown kidnappers' hands?"

Mary brushed back her wayward hair. "I bet they weren't unknown to Ellison. I was there that night, when Del and Helen were killed—was I ever there. And I know what I saw. And I know that Ellison's no good."

"Kid," warned Miller, hopelessly.

Thorn nodded to Mary. "When I learned your name, I of course could place you as the escaped hostage of the news stories. But your claim that Ellison was implicated comes as a surprise to me. Have you any evidence that will support it?"

"No, if you mean legal evidence," said Mary, dismissing the idea. "Do you know the family at all?"

"Only through the news accounts."

"Well." Mary looked at her lawyer at last, then back to Thorn. "Excuse me, but just what good is all this going to do you?"

Thorn was not at all sure of that himself, but he was interested. He said: "I find myself in the position of being Mr. Ellison Seabright's rival. Therefore I wish to learn everything of importance that I can learn about him. If, as you say, he is really involved in murder, that is certainly an important fact."

"You're his rival as an art collector?"

"Exactly. Now can you explain to me just what he stood to gain from his brother's death? Or from the girl's?"

"His half-brother," Mary corrected, as if she thought the difference had significance. "What did he gain? The chance to buy up Delaunay's collection, at least the part of it that he really wanted. That's what he's doing over in Scottsdale right this minute. Look, poor old Del hated Ellison. He wouldn't have given him the sweat off . . . so according to Del's will, Helen was to get it all. She was the closest family he had, that he cared anything about. Del's own wife died years ago, and they were childless."

"You say he left all to Helen. His half-brother's step-daughter."

"Yes. I don't suppose she ever knew about the will. He was always nice to her but I don't think she appreciated him very much. In some ways, I have to admit, Helen could be a snotty little bitch." It was said much more in affection than in anger. Mary gulped beer audibly. "She was still a minor, only seventeen. So everything was to be held in trust. Right, Robby? And if Helen predeceased Del, or died at about the same time, which was the way things turned out, then everything in the collection was to be sold at auction, proceeds going to a charitable foundation Delaunay was setting up. Except—"

Here Mary broke off with a sigh, an unexpected, hopeless sound. Miller was shaking his head again.

"What?" Thorn prompted.

Mary said: "The Verrocchio, that's what. It's really mine."

Miller said quickly: "I think Mary is quite right, I mean I believe what she tells me. But of course legally, again—"

Mary interrupted him. "You see, Mr. Thorn, I lived there in the Seabright house for a couple of months before the night of the killings. And two weeks to the day before he died, Delaunay Seabright stood there with me in the midst of his collection, and told me that Verrocchio was mine. I didn't know what to say, how to react. Then he got sick, and that meant there was a delay in making the gift official, and evidently he never mentioned it to anyone else before he died. Or if he did, no one is going to admit it now."

Thorn made no attempt to hide his doubts. "You say he simply gave you the Verrocchio."

"I know it isn't the easiest thing in the world to believe, that anyone could be so generous. 'This is yours now, Mary, I want you to have it.' Those were his words."

"You told this to the police?"

She glanced at Robinson Miller once more.

"Yes. Or I tried. For all good it did me. We've never tried to file any kind of legal claim, since I have nothing to support it."

Thorn could not tell whether she was fantasizing or not. He felt sure she was not simply lying. He asked, in curiosity: "What would you have done with the painting, Mary? If it had actually come to you?"

Her laugh was surprisingly gentle. "Why, hung it over Robby's Salvation Army sofa. No, I'd have sold it, of course. I would have hoped to be able to sell it to some museum, where everybody would be able to see it for a change . . . Del didn't care for museums, you know, he thought they were more arrogant and greedy than anybody else. The people who run them . . . did you get a chance to look at the painting closely? It's really so beautiful."

"I agree."

"I certainly wouldn't have sold it to that creep who's got it now. I'd have made sure he never got his hands on it, and I'm sure he knew I felt that way."

There was a little silence. "May I refresh your drinks?" Thorn offered.

"You see," Mary explained suddenly, "I got to know Del because I helped out his niece when she was a runaway. I met Helen in Chicago, when she was ready to give up being on the road. I was a kind of official social worker then."

"You were a nun," her lawyer interjected.

Mary gave him a glance. "I hadn't taken my final vows. Anyway, I was able to help Helen get her head together somewhat. Delaunay appreciated that, and at his request I wound up living with them here in Phoenix for a couple of months. Helen's parents came along too, at his urging. The old man was grateful to me for helping Helen, that's all there ever was between us."

"I see." Mr. Thorn considered Mary's lush figure, the full veins in her throat. He was unsure whether he ought to envy the young lawyer with whom she was apparently living now, and/or feel regret on behalf of the dead old man who had been only grateful. There wandered into his mind the image, thin and dark, of the other attractive woman who had been at the auction room. Stephanie Seabright, mother and sister-in-law respectively of the two victims. A woman desperately wanting to be young, to start over, perhaps, somehow . . .

Mary had paused for a full breath. "Excuse me, Mr. Thorn, but you're not an American, are you?"

"I am not. Though I have made my home in America for the past year. I like your—"

"You see, we have in this country a very serious and tragic problem, of teenagers, some kids even younger, who find their homes, if you can call some of them homes, just completely unendurable. So the kids take off, hitchhiking or what have you, and quite a number of them, more than you'd think, wind up as murder victims. Nobody's done a really good study yet to demonstrate how many." Mary smiled eagerly, giving the impression she enjoyed either the lack of that crucial study or the prospect of reading what it would someday reveal. "The others, the relatively lucky ones, are sexually abused, robbed, molested. They wind up in jail, on dope, in prostitution." Mary continued to smile. No doubt it was unconscious.

Mr. Thorn said: "I see the problem. It is not a

new one." Several floors below his suite, a radio was softly playing a lament that concerned, if his old ears were to be trusted, the fate of a limestone cowboy. Very little surprised him any more.

"There are official means of attempting to deal with the problem, of course. Courts, agencies, juvenile homes. They all can do some good but it's not enough. I intended to sell that painting and use the money to show what can be done. I intended to set up a halfway house for runaways."

"Ah." Mr. Thorn appeared to be giving the suggestion his most thoughtful consideration. Then he nodded. "That sounds like a most worthy plan."

Mary, who had perhaps not expected such quick and unqualified agreement, blinked at him and slowed down. "I really can't think of anything that's needed more."

"Amen," said Robinson Miller.

Thorn asked: "This plan of yours, I hope, has not been abandoned?"

"No. Not at all. We've had to postpone things, of course, but—"

"Then you would be willing to accept a contribution?"

The sudden, innocent joy in Mary's eyes realized some of the potential beauty that her habitual fierce smiling tended to obscure. She looked at Miller. "We could at least start an account, Robby . . . I'm very grateful, Mr. Thorn."

Only grateful. "I was wondering," asked Mr. Thorn, meanwhile slowly drawing out a checkbook, "if you intended to return to the Seabright house for any reason? I assume you have moved out."

"I haven't been back since that night. Except

once for a police re-enactment. But I do still have a few things there, if Ellison hasn't had them burned. They'll have to be picked up sooner or later, I suppose."

"Might I come with you when you do that?"

"Why?" asked Miller bluntly.

Thorn opened the checkbook on his bony knee and drew a pen from his breast pocket. "I have been trying to arrange a meeting with Mr. Seabright, in his late brother's house. I have phoned several times and have been told that he will see no one. He has not returned my calls. I hope to arrange, somehow, a simple invitation to cross the threshold of that dwelling. No more than that."

Miller opened his mouth, glanced at Mary, closed it again. His eyes came back to the open checkbook on Thorn's knee, the pen poised over the blank check. At last he repeated Mary's earlier question. "You're his rival in the sense of—collecting?"

"Yes. Precisely. I should like very much to get a look at his collection."

"He's not very likely to give any friend of mine the grand tour, you know," said Mary doubtfully. "In fact I don't think he'd let either of us in the house. More likely he'd just have my things thrown out the front gate, and us with them."

"I ask only that you do what you can to help me cross the threshold. After that I shall manage for myself. Agreed?"

"Agreed." She was still doubtful.

"As for your projected charitable home—" Thorn wrote, tore out a check with a crisp noise, handed it across. "Something on account, shall we say? I hope to be able to continue my support of the project once it has begun."

Mary's eyes widened, looking at the small piece of paper. "Thank you! Jeez, what can I say? Oh, Rob, this is a start, a real start."

Miller looked, made as if to whistle, then raised puzzled eyes to Thorn. "I'll say. Thanks. You must have a real affinity for lost causes."

Four

The Vicar of Christ lay dying in a tent on the lonely, rain-sogged beach at Ancona, where he had had himself brought that he might keep a personal watch for ships. Inside his fevered brain, phantasmagorical armies of Crusaders had been embarked, and he did not want to miss the first sight of their rendezvous here, at the place he had ordained—the hosts of the Emperor, the massed cavalry squadrons of Philip the Good.

I arrived overland, to find the coastal town swarming with churchmen. But as I had expected, there was no sign of any military or naval force of consequence. A Swiss mercenary escorted me to the Pope's tent, and waited by my side till word came out that His Holiness would see me. Inside, a pair of gray-robed monks were in absent-minded attendance upon the old man propped up with pillows.

The Holy Father, looking clearheaded enough at the moment, beckoned me close to him. "You are welcome," he murmured in Italian as I knelt to kiss his ring. "And your companions? Men at arms? How many have you brought?"

I was sure he recognized my name, but it did not seem to have alarmed him. "I am alone, Holiness," I answered, standing as he motioned for me to rise. Actually of course my presence had nothing to do with Pius's call for swords about the cross. The trail of King Matthias's wayward sister had led me to Venice, and in that city I had been told she had come here. According to my Venetian informant, she had embarked—in what capacity was uncertain—on one of the two galleys of Venetian volunteers that city had actually dispatched to take part in the Papal fiasco. The ships were now anchored in Ancona's harbor, and my first move on arriving at the port had been to locate and question some of their sailors. These told me that no woman, high-born or low, who answered Helen's description had been aboard either ship. Having offered the seamen gold for confirmation of her presence, I was compelled to believe their regretful denials.

"Holy Father, I have come alone. But I bring you greetings from King Matthias. He regrets that vital affairs of state prevent his joining this most sacred enterprise, but he is praying most earnestly for its success." That seemed a safe-enough message to put into the King's mouth. Certainly Matthias would have welcomed a successful Papal foray against the Turk. But already the true Crusades were centuries in the past. Matthias fought the Turks because they were on his own doorstep, but no Christian prince in the late fifteenth century was going to spend years in a military campaign far from his own domain, exhausting his treasury and army in the process, while schemers at home worked to relieve him of his throne. Eleven years of relative stability had dulled the shock of terror sent across the continent by the fall of Constantinople. The Turk was for the time being more or less contained, even though the Ottoman Empire pressed up into Europe to the Danube and beyond.

As I spoke, the Pope gradually let himself sink lower among his cushions. He was greatly disappointed by my words, and his lips moved in silent prayer. It was hard to tell, now, what this man had looked like in his youth; I had heard that he had spent it largely in debauchery and riotous living, that only in middle life had he turned to God. But what he had once been like no longer seemed to matter. The aged, wasted, dying tend to look all the same. I could see that he was holding one hand lightly clenched, in order that the Fisherman's Ring might not slide off his diminished finger.

His weary gaze moved out through the open doorway of the tent, vainly questioning the sea-horizon once again. Then it returned to me.

"Yet you are here. It must have taken great courage for you to come alone, my son. I have heard of you."

And had written about me, too, the damned compulsive old scribbler, repeating for posterity all the vile gossip transmitted from Buda by his loquacious legate Nicholas. But at the time I did not know that Pius was a writer, and I pitied him. I said: "You have probably heard little to my credit, Holiness."

He sighed. "Yet you are here, when Catholic kings have turned their backs. Your sins will be forgiven you. I would like to give you my blessing."

Lacking the heart to explain to that sad old man the truth about my presence, down I went on my knees again and bowed my head. He yearned to lead an army, to see the banners fly, to smite the unbeliever, to retake Constantinople. But he had trouble getting the attention of one of the monks to bring him a pan to piss in. That old man, though, bestowed a blessing on me which I remember still. I suppose it must have been the last he ever gave.

Together we watched darkness slowly cover the horizon. Neither of us had the least idea how wide the oceans were, or that America lay undiscovered somewhere in their midst. Side by side in the harbor rode the two Venetian galleys, twin lanterns burning, their captains probably already in private conference deciding how soon they might be able to give up the farce and sail for home. The Pope's breathing was growing louder and more labored. I remained in the tent, unchallenged and almost unnoticed, as physicians and prelates, recalled from God knows where in that small town, began to gather.

A final time Pius beckoned me to his side. "You will be going far, my son. To a strange, long life, in distant lands. You will be going farther than . . ."

I bent over him, trying to hear more. But the rest was lost in the struggle of his old lungs to breathe, in a chanted dirge the monks chose that moment to begin. Pius died near midnight, and the ranking churchmen on his staff scrambled away in an excited effort to be first back to Rome.

Five

Travel by automobile was not something that Mr. Thorn enjoyed. In fact—except for flying machines of all types, which he liked immensely—complex machinery of any kind had always impressed him as perverse and unreliable. He detested, for example, firearms. But he could get along in an uneasy coexistence with mechanism when he had to; and recently he had been brought to the reluctant conclusion that the advantages of being able to drive oneself about in one's own automobile outweighed the attendant irritations. Thus it was that two evenings after Mary Rogers had splashed her Hollywood blood on Ellison Seabright, and one evening after her visit to Thorn's hotel, Thorn was alone in a rented vehicle, on his way to see the Magdalen again. Or so he hoped.

Persistence on the telephone had finally paid off, and he had wangled for himself an invitation to the Seabright mansion. Persistence, and a ploy of passing along for Mr. Seabright's ears some hints of information that Thorn guessed the most recent purchaser of the supposed Verrocchio would be unable to resist. The guess was evidently right.

The house lay in what was probably the wealthiest suburb of the metropolis. The high wall enclosing its several hectares of grounds was constructed in large part of real adobe; looking at this wall, Mr. Thorn thought that some segments of it, near the house, were possibly old enough to have seen forays by hostile Indians. He knew little of the history of this part of the world, but meant someday to study it, an effort he suspected would not be easy. History, unlike machinery, he always found interesting; but he had seen too much of history to have any faith in the official account of anything.

As soon as the drive leading to the house parted company with the curving public road, it passed under an iron gate, now closed, in the old wall. Just outside the gate, Thorn stopped his Blazer—having seen what a high proportion of the natives elected to use four-wheel-drive vehicles, he suspected they had some good reason and had followed their example. A gatekeeper, a Spanish-looking man, appeared now inside the ironwork, which opened itself on electric tracks as soon as Thorn rolled down his window and announced his name.

Inside the gates the graveled drive curved to and fro through spacious lawns now enjoying their evening sprinkling from an automatic system. Citrus blossoms blessed the air. From behind a mass of greenery the house came into view—for its time and place, quite an impressive villa, though it was not like some that Mr. Thorn had visited. Like its surrounding wall it was eclectic, with some good old sections that looked especially venerable. Additions over a number of decades, some quite recent, had made it very large.

As Mr. Thorn parked his Blazer and approached the sizable front portico, there sounded from somewhere on the other side of the building the thrum of a diving board, followed by the trim splash of a lithe body entering a pool. It was, somehow, a definitely female splash; and Thorn, with no more than that to go on, immediately visualized the dark and slender woman who had been with Seabright two evenings ago. Stephanie Seabright, bereft of her only child just two months past. Stephanie who did not seem to mourn, but yearned. And swam, too, evidently; though Thorn could not really be sure from a mere splash that it was she.

At the front door Thorn was met by a butler, who resembled physically the bodyguard who had attended Seabright at the auction room. This man was a little slimmer and younger, though, and therefore presumably a little faster on his feet.

"Come in, sir, you're expected. Right this way, please."

"Thank you." To Mr. Thorn, the simple crossing of any house's threshold for the first time was always something of an event; and in this house he had a special interest. Once inside, enveloped by air conditioning, he was led across a wide entry floored with Mexican tile into a sort of manorial hall that made the house seem even larger than it had looked from outside. The ceiling of this hall, at about third story level, was supported by wooden beams so gigantic that the whole effect reminded Thorn of nothing so much as the passenger concourse of the Albuquerque airport, where not long ago he had spent part of a long bright afternoon between planes, beseiged by sunlight, squinting through sunglasses and changing his place in search of deeper shadow. He had in his time been inside private homes that had rooms bigger than this hall. But not many such homes, and not much bigger.

Pushing open a massive door of carven wood, his guide stood deferentially aside. Halfway down the length of the booklined study thus revealed, Rodrigo Borgia rose up from behind a desk, all red smears cleaned away, and dressed as for a leisurely safari.

"Mr. Thorn, glad to see you again," Ellison Seabright boomed. "That's all, Brandreth," he added in an aside to the butler, and then came forward as to some old friend, extending one great arm for a handshake. "Too bad we didn't have more of a chance to talk the other night." In fact they had never talked at all. "That damned woman . . . you'd like a look at the collection, right? Of course you would. So let's go downstairs and do our talking there." Seabright had a light, homey, completely American voice. Mr. Thorn could easily imagine him reading the ten o'clock news, getting high ratings on the job.

Thorn murmured something in the way of a response. The easy voice of his host chatted on, while a massive hand on Mr. Thorn's bony shoulder guided him out of the study again and back across the baronial hall. At the far end of the hall a small elevator opened its bronze door and without a groan accepted the combined weight of the two men.

Of the several levels indicated on the elevator's control panel, two appeared to be below ground, and Seabright pressed the button for the lowest. During the brief descent he chatted with Thorn about the Arizona climate, and the importance of always maintaining the proper atmospheric conditions in rooms housing a collection. As he talked Mr. Seabright kept eyeing his guest steadily. It was a gaze not quite offensive, but still it would have been found intimidating by almost any visitor. The elevator eased itself to a stop meanwhile, surrounded by deep silence. Scream down here, thought Mr. Thorn, amusing himself privately, and no one will hear you.

"Ah, Stephanie!" Seabright exclaimed, taken by surprise as the door opened. The lift had delivered them to a perfectly cooled lounge or game room, of a size and elaborateness appropriate to the house. At one end of the room was a bar, and on one of the bar's six chrome stools perched the dark lady of the auction room, the lately bereaved mother. In a few more years she would have to give up brief bikinis such as she was wearing now—but not for a few more years, and she was making the most of the time left. Over the shreds of cloth she wore as symbolic cover-up a translucent short cape, some hybrid perhaps of cloth and plastic. Behind the bar, Thorn noticed at once, there was no mirror, but a mural of youths and maidens, pseudo-Greek and semi-porn, and Stephanie had to turn her head to see the men. Her dark hair as she looked round at Thorn was almost wet enough to drip, and her face bore the practiced smile that he remembered from the auction room. At Stephanie's fingertips on the bar, a tall glass held a little dark liquid and some ice.

"Mr. Thorn, my wife. Steff, you probably remember seeing Mr. Thorn, of Chicago, at the auction room night before last? That damned woman."

Thorn took the lady's tanned hand when it was offered as if he meant to bow and kiss it, but did not go that far. Stephanie's eyes rested perturbedly on his. On the skin her hand was cool, but there was a faint, heated trembling underneath. "My heartfelt sympathy, madam, on your dear daughter's passing."

"Thank you. Everyone who knew Helen says

what a remarkable girl she was." It sounded like a rehearsed line. Probably it had been used very often in the past weeks and months. Stephanie's eyes would not hold Thorn's directly for very long. Common enough. But he knew she was still wishing that she was somewhere else. Somewhere, perhaps, that did not exist outside of her own imagination.

"Anything to drink, Thorn? Then let's go take a look at a few things. Right through here."

Just as he was leaving the lounge, Thorn was granted a last unexpected glimpse of the swim-damp lady, in a mirror that had been almost concealed, for some reason, in a niche. She was still on her stool, eyes gazing back with vague puzzlement at the same area of reflective glass. Perhaps she noticed that the mirror bore no image of the lean man who had just pressed her fingers in a way that could be taken to mean something if she wanted to think about it.

More likely, Thorn considered, the oddity of what was lacking in the glass escaped her. Experience had long ago proved to him that people usually accepted such accidental non-perceptions without thought, or sometimes rejected them completely as being caused by momentary aberrations of their own senses. Of course there was a chance that the mirror had been placed there deliberately, and Seabright might have looked into it to check out his guest. Thorn himself, of course, could tell a vampire without any such subterfuges; but even the wisest breathing folk might have difficulties sometimes in doing so.

Fortunately for him.

Meanwhile the two men had walked through an

odd little curving tunnel, with white curving walls, and had entered what looked like a miniature museum. All white walls and new brown carpet. As far as Thorn could tell, Seabright's mind was still firmly on things other than vampirism.

"Some of the things in this room are mine," the big man intoned, sounding quite satisfied. "Were mine, I mean, even before last night's auction. Never seem to have room in my own house in Santa Fe for all my stuff. What do you think of this?"

It was a graceful silver ship, intricately modeled, standing alone on a low cube of furniture. Thorn chose not to see his host's generous gesture inviting him to pick it up. If he touched it the non-reflectable quality of his fingers would be very plain in the curve of argent hull. Instead he bent his head and walked around the object on its low stand, looking at it carefully.

"German . . . almost certainly sixteenth century. It is some time since I have seen a nef of this quality in private hands." Well, the piece was not really all *that* impressive; but it did not seem likely that a little judicious flattery would do any harm.

It seemed that he had passed the examination, or its first question anyway. Seabright, a little more relaxed now, chatted some more. Still probing, doing what seemed his best to probe cleverly. Finding out, as he must have thought, a fair number of things about Thorn without giving away much about himself. Thorn inclined more and more to the opinion that the mirror in the game room-lounge had been completely accidental. He doubted more and more Mary Rogers's estimation of this man as a Machiavellian murderer. Seabright simply did not seem bright enough to carry off any such scheme successfully.

The portion of the Seabright collection here visible contained a couple of really respectable things, not to mention the one in which Thorn was really interested and which they had not come to yet. Also it contained some that verged—no, more than verged—upon the pornographic. Those two young ladies under the oddly rumpled coverlet had their eyes closed but were enjoying more than sleep; the sculptured monk standing close behind the choirboy was, on second glance, not really intent on music. These examples and others more explicit appeared to be for the most part underground Victorian imitations of earlier masters. Maybe the porn things were all Ellison Seabright's to start with, for he discussed them roundly and seemed to take an extra pride in their display. They were not really to Mr. Thorn's taste, but he could be polite.

The walls of these underground rooms were thick, Mr. Thorn knew, inside their earthen envelope. Even with only interior surfaces visible he could sense the thickness all round him, virtually impenetrable, like the walls of a bomb shelter or a bank vault. Faultless air conditioning, that even Thorn could barely hear, maintained a good museum's silence, coolness, balanced humidity.

Yet there were soundless echoes of murder and violence in the air down here. Death not all that old. The much-publicized Seabright murder-kidnapping, of course. But Thorn had got the impression from the news accounts that all those scenes had been in the upper levels of the house.

Trading opinions, some of which may have

made sense, about the Rennaisance, the two men presently moved farther into the gallery. Mr. Thorn came to a halt. He saw with a pang the well lighted, centrally located space on a wall where the Magdalen should obviously be. She was not here, though she must have been. The empty place of honor was marked by the very faint outline of her frame.

He hoped, but did not immediately ask for, a quick explanation of where she was right now. Feeling more disappointment than was entirely reasonable, he continued his expected admiring commentary on the lesser works surrounding him. A few of these he could recognize as having been at the auction room. They had been brought back here afterwards, but she had not.

At last he stopped talking, to stand gazing pointedly at that central gap.

His huge host gestured, with selfconscious drama. "That's where the Verrocchio was, of course. Naturally I'm curious as to just what you meant when you mentioned the question of its origins to my secretary on the phone. I hope you're not going to try to cast any doubts on its authenticity? I'd hate to think that my confidence in that painting as an investment has been misplaced."

Thorn smiled. "Oh, by no means. It is extremely valuable."

"I'm glad you agree. I *will* take your opinions on art fairly seriously, you know, now that we've had this little talk. Though frankly some of the ideas you have on the Renaissance seem pretty farfetched, no offense, I'm willing to concede there may be areas where you know what you're talking about." Seabright emitted a calculated chuckle.

"You mentioned the painting's origins. I've already heard one crackpot theory on that subject, which I hope you're not going to endorse. But there, I'm sure I do you an injustice, Thorn. You must have something sensible to say on the subject. Possibly with evidence to back it up?" The big man paused, in an attitude of hopeful inquiry, of generous expectation that he was going to be told something that made sense.

Thorn hesitated. "I do have some ideas on the subject, as I told your secretary. As for evidence . . . before I begin, Mr. Seabright, would you mind telling me how long the painting has been here?"

"In this room? Why not? Since 1953. That's when my brother brought it home from Argentina. Some Nazi who evidently saw the end coming sent it there from Europe in 1944. During the war one of the collecting teams working for Goering had evidently liberated it, shall we say, from a chateau in Normandy. How long it had been at that particular chateau, or where it had been before that, we were never able to discover. Only a tantalizing hint or two . . . these things, the great ones, tend to have remarkable histories, don't they?" Seabright ran a hand back over his suntanned brow.

Thorn glanced at him, then back at the blank wall. "Indeed they do. They also have a habit of being stolen."

"Had you ever laid eyes on it, yourself, before two nights ago? I don't suppose you had the chance."

"On the contrary. I saw it several times. Some years ago."

That had not been the answer Seabright was

prepared for. The big man swung his heavy arms, like a furniture salesman getting bored on floor duty. "You saw it here? Ah, I see, you were acquainted with my brother, then."

"No, I regret, I did not know him. Or that he had the painting here . . . it was in Europe."

Obviously calculating years, moving his lips very slightly as he counted, Seabright gave a little shake of his head, whose thickness seemed to be becoming more and more apparent. "You must have been only a child."

Thorn had turned, was leaning with his arms folded against the blank space on the wall, staring at things on the far side of the room. "Yes . . . yes, I suppose I was. An ill-tempered child. Though at the time I was quite sure of my own power and wisdom, and there was no lack of people willing to humor me. But then—this painting—"

He came to a halt, not knowing how much he ought to say in the presence of this fool. Talking to Seabright was helpful, in a way, as talking to a child might be. But who else might be listening?

"The painting," Thorn went on, "acquired for me some special associations. Special meanings, that even now I find it difficult to explain. Yes, even difficult to explain to myself." He looked closely into Seabright's uncomprehending face, and for the first time the big man drew back a little. Thorn added: "For a long time I have wondered where it was." Then, more mildly, with a smile: "My own collection runs heavily to the Renaissance."

"Oh." Seabright blinked. "Then our tastes are alike in that, at least. Forgive me, Mr. Thorn, but I continue to find it somewhat odd that your name has never come to my attention before now. I had thought that all the world's important collections in my field were known to me."

"Almost all of them are, I'm sure."

"Almost. Yes, I see. My brother and I never cared for a lot of publicity either. And I am sure your collection must be important."

"Thank you, yes, I believe it is. And you are right, very little known. And also, regrettably, incomplete."

Seabright let out another chuckle, this one gross and uncontrolled, the laughter of a man who cares nothing for what he sounds like. "What real collector is ever satisfied? Tell me, are your things in this country?"

"Very few of them."

"I see. Well, I have no wish to pry. But I am always on the lookout for genuninely valuable articles. As investments, even if they do not match my own tastes perfectly. I prefer to deal confidentially whenever possible. I needn't talk to you about taxes and so on, you understand those matters, I am sure. There are possibilities of barter and exchange as well as purchase. I even, sometimes, have things that I wish to sell. Well, Stephanie. Join us?"

She had entered the gallery on bare and silent feet, still wearing her tiny swimsuit and her beach cape. Her dark hair was uncurling quickly in the dry air. Almost without looking at the two men she came to stand, in a model's pose so practiced as to be second nature, before the dim scar on the wall showing where the large painting had been removed. Her liquor glass had been left back at the bar.

"I miss that picture," she announced. "Isn't it foolish, with everything else . . . but I do miss it."

"You have good taste, then, in painting," said Mr. Thorn, pausing ever so slightly before the last two words. Stephanie's eyes turned from the wall to him.

"I myself," said Seabright, "prefer something more sensual than Verrocchio."

"A matter of taste," said Thorn. "So, you have paid a fortune for a supposed Verrocchio that does not really suit your preference?" He was still looking at the lady. *Help me*, her eyes seemed to be broadcasting. *I would like very much to get out of this. Sometimes it seems that I can wait no longer.*

What is it that are you waiting for? Thorn would have liked to ask. But there was no way to put the question now. He could be patient.

Seabright was answering him: "An investment, my friend, remember? But 'a supposed Verrocchio'? Aha, you are going to have some supposed revelation concerning the painting to offer me after all."

Thorn turned back to his host and asked him bluntly: "Is it being brought here today? I look forward to seeing it again."

"Here?" Seabright tried to sound surprised. "Why no, it isn't being brought back here at all. I'm taking it to Santa Fe, to my own house." He consulted his wrist watch. "In fact it's en route right now, on my own plane. Most of this other stuff is going to follow in due course. I'm having another room built on. But I wanted the Verrocchio there right away."

Thorn stood up straight, no longer leaning on the wall. "Ah," he said slowly. "Then I must hope to be able to see it there someday. In Santa Fe." He had the feeling of just having been checkmated. But not by this great fool, surely, nor this preoccupied woman. He felt a certain bewilderment. His real opponent, it seemed, had not yet even come in sight.

"Why not?" said Seabright, jovial and insincere. "If you're ever there, give me a call. It's been a real pleasure to converse with someone who knows what he's talking about. Now what was this idea you had about the painting's origin?"

Mr. Thorn had nothing to say on that subject now. Anyway he would not have had much chance to talk. He could hear the sound of the elevator door opening, back in the lounge, followed by the agitated approach of one person, a young man, and worried, to judge by the sound of his busy feet.

A figure to match the calculated image appeared, almost dancing through the white curve of the tunnel, garbed in white shirt and necktie, topped with a neat haircut. His face, that Thorn had never seen before, bore an expression eloquent of disaster. Thorn was conscious of calamity, like a compact cloud of darkness, hanging somewhere just above.

"Mr. Seabright, sir? Santa Fe just called."

Seabright rounded on the perturbed aide, turning his broad back on Thorn. "Well, what? Spit it out."

For a moment the young man sputtered, as if trying to take the order literally. Then he managed speech. "The plane is almost three hours overdue now, sir. And they can't contact Mr. Gliddon on radio."

Six

During the fifteenth century, for good and sufficient reasons, travel across most of Europe was considered hazardous. In one or two geographical areas this rule had happy exceptions, about which more presently. But in general one did not set out alone on a journey of any length, not if trustworthy or only moderately dubious traveling companions could be found. So before leaving Ancona, I attached myself to some Medici traders who were on their way home to Florence after successfully completing a mission in the south of Italy. Helen had last been reliably reported in the northern portion of the boot, and I could think of no better place than the City of Flowers, that nerve center of every type of communication, in which to try to pick up further news of her. As for the merchants, when they had looked at the letters of identification and introduction that had been given me by my king, they were glad to have my sword added to their escort. One crime of which I have never even been accused is brigandage. If my reputation had reached my fellow travelers' ears, and if they recognized me despite the letters' ambiguous treatment of my name, the recognition must have made them more rather than less eager to have me in their company.

On the second day of our journey north from Ancona we encountered another party of honest merchants. They were southward bound, their wagons freighted with rolls of Florentine cloth. These men had from us their first word of the

Pope's death, and we received from them in turn some news that my companions considered at least equally momentous. It made the good merchants of my own party look at one another grimly, and issue orders to their servants to prepare for a forced march. Cosimo de' Medici, head of the great mercantile family and the de facto ruler of the city-state of Florence, had gone to his own reward, in the manner of a stoic Christian by all reports, and just thirteen days before the passing of Pius in his lonely tent.

My traveling companions were not really surprised by the death of their master Cosimo, who had been ailing for a long time. Their concern, as we remounted and pushed on, was over what might be happening now. What was the effect going to be on business? The southbound travelers had told us that in Florence it was considered certain that Cosimo's middle-aged and eldest son Piero, called the Gouty, was going to take over his father's position as head of the family. This meant that Piero would probably also become the untitled but practically unchallenged ruler of Florence. What effect this change on leadership was going to have on the city and on the world it was difficult to say, and at the same time imperative to find out as soon as possible.

Being myself anxious to waste no time, I willingly went along with the forced march, and in a few days more had my first look at Florence. The city burst upon us as a splendid, nearby spectacle as we topped a hill. It was then one of the largest metropolises in Europe, enclosed by three miles of defensive wall, the high stonework of which was reinforced by sixty square towers. When seen as we saw it from the nearby hills, the city was truly impressive, its interior dotted thickly with church spires, with here and there the palaces of the wealthy rising amid acres of lesser construction. The Arno made a lopsided bisection of the city, and its waters, half mud, half rainbow, flowed out of it bearing all the colors of the Clothmakers' Guild, as well as the sewage of seventy thousand people. As we passed inside the walls I saw that the Guild artisans with their dyes and fabrics seemed to occupy all the banks and bridges of the river. The streets of Florence stank, like those of any city of the time; but there was also splendor in the air. The population was still much reduced from the pre-plague days of more than a century before, and considerable tracts within the walls had been denuded of buildings by fire and decay, had become gardens in which a million flowers grew along with plots of vegetables and fruit.

Just as foulness and beauty were mixed in the city's water, and stench and perfume in its air, so its mansions and hovels stood cheek by jowl in what appeared to me at first as a total confusion of society. Actually there was a logic. By tradition each Florentine family, however wealthy or poor it might become, still dwelt in its ancestral quarter. There was no enclave of the rich, no slum to confine the poor. The larger and finer houses contained within their walls their own storerooms, stables, and sometimes shops—none of this city's upper class disdained the touch of money or the business of buying and selling. These facilities would be of course on the ground floor, with gardens, halls, and courtyards added when there was room. The preferred living quarters were on the level just above. A floor or two above that dwelt poor relations, guests of secondary importance, and servants, in cramped apartments more exposed than those on the first floor to summer's heat and winter's cold. On the day of our arrival in the city the weather was still quite warm, and my companions had been wondering aloud whether the chief men of the Medici clan might not be found in one of the family villas that were scattered through the surrounding Tuscan hills, rather than in town. But as matters turned out we found them in the city palace, still working to master the turmoil of business matters brought on by the death of Cosimo.

The Medici palace was, as it is today, a massive stone building near the church of San Lorenzo, rectangular as a modern apartment block on the outside, and decorated with great art to which I at the time was almost indifferent. The outer walls of the ground floor were of simple, roughly dressed blocks of stone; the masonry of the second level followed the Doric pattern, and that of the third, the Corinthian. But as I say, such niceties were at the time quite lost on me, a rude barbarian soldier. Once inside the first courtyard, my fellow travelers dismounted and hurried at once into a private room to make a confidential business report to some official of the family bank. After I had goggled at the statuary for a while I too got off my horse and was courteously conducted to another room, where I presented to another officer my letters of introduction and credit from King Matthias. I realized that if my project was to thrive in Florence, I had best get off on the right foot with the Medici.

The preparations at Visegrad for my mission had been as thorough as they were secret, and the letters were in several languages, including of course Italian. In those of that language I was named rather ambiguously as Signore Ladislao—a fair translation of my Christian name—and all the letters promised the royal gratitude for any assistance given me.

The merchants who had traveled with me had doubtless speculated among themselves about my unspecified mission for Matthias, but had accepted the letters with little open comment. Now the Medici official, after a first reading, borrowed the documents from me, politely enough, and gave orders that I should be provided with suitable refreshment after my long journey. The weather being quite warm, I was led to a shaded table set in an open courtyard.

At any given time in that house it was more likely than not that some group of folk were banqueting. And though my interest in most kinds of food has long since waned, I can still remember . . . to gorge oneself whenever it was possible to do so was then the European standard of behavior. But not in mannered Florence. It was in Florence that I, the rough soldier, first saw a table fork, though that was on a later day. On that first day I dealt forkless with sausages, slices of melon, boiled capon, and pastries of whose elegant existence I had never before dreamt. I fell to with a will.

Presently some of the men who had shared the road with me appeared, smiling, to join me at table. While they were busy answering some of my questions concerning the city's history and customs, a young man I did not know came into the courtyard. He was dressed in new, rather simple clothing, cut of the best cloth. In a grating voice, and with a sad-faced courtesy and gravity beyond his years, he addressed me as Signore Ladislao and made me welcome to the house of his family. He was introduced to me, between mouthfuls and without ceremony, by one of my former fellow travelers. This youth was of course Piero's eldest son, Lorenzo, later to be called the Magnificent; and when his own hour came for subtle rule in Florence, he would wield more power than many an anointed king, and his patronage of art would markedly surpass even that of King Matthias.

On that day in the late summer of 1464, however, Lorenzo de' Medici was only fifteen years of age—though there were moments when his swarthy face, with its grim eyes, shave-resistant stubble, and the natural beginning of a furrow in his brow, looked thrity-five. Already the elders of his family had begun to trust him with minor diplomatic work. Beside him at my table now stood his little brother Giuliano, only ten, but already an apprentice Medici and at the moment sober as a German count. In those days childhood was a rare thing, for people of any class.

Lorenzo, however precocious, had not recognized my name. He had seen my letters, though, and could identify importance. He sat down at table and munched a piece of fruit while like a seasoned diplomat he killed time and sounded me out with a discussion of relatively neutral topics: the death of the Pope, the sad state of Italian roads. Then presently Lorenzo's father hobbled into the courtyard to join us. Here was the ruler, certainly, and I rose to my feet; but Piero's gnarled hand waved me to sit down again. Leaning on the table for support, he handed me back my letters, and bade me stay as a guest in his house for as long as I might choose.

Lorenzo too had sprung up with alacrity, that his father might have the seat at my side. And Piero knew who I was; I could see it in his eyes as at last, he settled himself on the bench beside me with a groan.

"Is it possible, Signore Ladislao, that we have met before? Have you lived in Targoviste, perhaps?"

My old Wallachian capital. I doubted, though of course I could not be sure, that Piero himself had ever dragged his gouty frame that far from home. Medici merchants had certainly been there, though. Where in the known world had they not been? I admitted cautiously that I had once lived in that city.

"Then perhaps," continued Piero, "you were there some eight years or so past, when an incident occurred that caused one of my family's most dependable trading representatives to bring back a strange report. Despite the man's good reputation, some found his story difficult to believe.

"It seems that this merchant, through a chain of the most unlucky circumstances, found himself alone and unescorted on the road, and carrying a great amount of gold coin, so that the first robber's eye to light upon him must have meant at the very least the total ruin of his life's work.

"He had just entered the domain of the young warlord Drakulya, said by some to be a prince of unparalleled ruthlessness and ferocity—I do not know the truth of those stories myself. But at any rate our exceedingly fearful merchant, perhaps never having heard the worst of the stories, dared to approach Drakulya himself, pleading that the prince assign guards to protect the traveler's property whilst he was passing through Wallachia.

"The prince only stared at him coldly. 'You say, then, that my good people are thieves?' 'Great prince, there must be some thieves in any land.' 'Not here, I do not tolerate them.'

"The merchant, having seen the skeletons of impaled brigands at roadside—or at least skeletons labeled as guilty of that crime, among others—was not going to argue. The upshot was that the prince commanded him to pick out a dark street corner at random within the capital and to leave all his goods, unguarded, piled there for a whole night. The merchant of course had no choice but to do as he was ordered. Then, resigning himself to ruin, he spent a sleepless night in a room of the prince's palace. In the morning, expecting nothing but the worst, he returned to where he had left his gold. In the daylight the bags looked like just what they were, bags of coin, unguarded by any visible presence. But not one had been touched. People of every degree, rich and poor, going about their morning business, were walking round them, giving them a wide berth as they passed." Here Piero paused, looking at me with inquiring eyes.

"I have heard the same story," I replied, "when I lived in that city . . . of course it is possible, Signore Piero, that you have seen me before and do recognize me, but on the other hand I am sometimes confused with a great rogue who is presently imprisoned in His Majesty's palace at Visegrad. It is of course not to be expected that such a man would be sent on a confidential mission for His Majesty; yet so strong is the resemblance that it sometimes causes me embarrassment."

Piero smiled his understanding. "Say no more, good Signore Ladislao; the farthest thing from my intention is that you should ever be embarrassed in my house. Say no more." And he stood up, and bowed to me; and with that the offer of hospitality and friendship was sealed.

When I had satisfied my appetite for food—which I moderated somewhat in conformity with what seemed to be the local custom—I was shown to what was to be my room, a sizable chamber on the first floor above the ground. Left alone in it, I blinked about me, wondering by what witchcraft these folk of common blood had managed to commandeer a royal palace. By comparison, my former palace in Targoviste was a savage barracks. Here, the bed was of inlaid wood, its covers and canopy and cushions all green velvet. A Byzantine mirror, its gilt frame wrought with cherubs, hung on one wall, reflecting a fresco of great beauty painted on the opposite. I stared at my lean, dark soldier's visage in the glass—incompatibility with mirrors was some years in the future still—wondering how many similar or even richer rooms were in the vast house, and wondering also at how little I seemed, after all, to know about the world.

How can I, even now, describe what the house of Medici was then? I cannot. Still, I will relate a thing or two. In a sense the place was like a luxurious, or I should say aristocratic, private hotel. There were merchants of other companies lodging there during my stay, along with religious of several ranks, agents, bankers, soldiers, travelers of every respectable kind coming and going daily. Of course Cosimo's recent death must have done something to augment this traffic, so that I probably saw it at its peak. But though I was a welcome and even pampered guest, I was only one of I know not how many.

Yet I was given what seemed to be special consideration by my hosts. Among the local people invited for dinner that evening was a man whose name I recognized as that of King Matthias's official ambassador to the official government of Florence, which was a council whose deliberations passed for the most part without great public attention. Shortly after Mersino and I were introduced, we were politely given a chance to converse alone. And as soon as he had the chance, the ambassador began to question me delicately about my mission. It seemed that he, as well as his fellow Hungarian envoys to the several Italian states, had received secret instructions from the king to the effect that a secret agent of his would soon be in Italy on urgent business. The ambassadors were not told what the business was, though some of them may have guessed; but they were strongly enjoined to give me all the aid they could.

There is a time for tight secrecy, and another time when full candor is required. I judged that the latter epoch had now arrived, and told Morsino plainly that I had been sent to find Helen Hunyadi, the runaway younger sister of our king. I did not discuss what I meant to do with Helen when I had found her, and Morsino did not ask. But he at once expressed his relief that I had arrived. Four days earlier a rumor had reached him, from two independent sources, of the presence in Florence of a woman who spoke Italian with a heavy accent that might well be Hungarian, and who had supposedly told someone that she belonged to the high Hungarian nobility. And if the stories regarding this woman's disreputable behavior were even approximately true, and if her family in fact had even a clerk's pretensions to respectability, then that family whoever they might be were in for trouble.

What disreputable behavior? I naturally asked. Morsino glanced around to make sure that we were quite alone. As he had heard the tale, a young and attractive girl of diminutive stature had recently arrived overland from Ravenna, in the company either of a troop of strolling players, or an itinerant artist, or some low company of that kind. (As Morsino admitted, he had been somewhat infected by the notorious Florentine freethinking attitude in matters of social standing. Still, even in Florence, there were limits.) On arrival in the city, the woman had reportedly engaged in business as a prostitute. And before Ravenna, so one version of her story went, she had been aboard a Venetian galley, traveling mistress of some adventuring scoundrel or other, perhaps one of the foreign mercenary soldiers who in the fifteenth century lived on the body of Italy, as numerous as fleas on a dog. Whoever he was, this man had grown nervous and rid himself of her when he had happened to learn her true identity.

"And in your opinion, Signore Morsino, does she belong to the Hungarian nobility?"

"I have not seen her. And I do not know how much truth is in all these stories . . . but the truth is, Signore Ladislao, in the form in which the story came to me, what scared off the adventurer was the woman's claim to be none other than the legitimate sister of our blessed King Matthias himself."

"He must have found that claim convincing."

"Evidently so."

"And where is this young woman now?"

Morsino shrugged. "That I cannot say. But I suppose it likely that she is still in Florence. Of course as soon as I heard these rumors I asked my local agents to quietly find out all about her. But they have not been able to pick up her trail."

I then asked the ambassador how far he thought we should take the Medici into our confidence. He considered, then gave his opinion that I ought to tell them as much as I felt I possibly could; the woman might be able to hide from Morsino and myself in Florence, but if she were anywhere in the city there was no way that she could hide from them. Even if she were here no longer, they might well be able to learn where she had gone. The goodwill of King Matthias would certainly be important to such far-traveling traders and bankers, and there was no reason to think our hosts were anything but well disposed toward our cause.

Later that evening I had a chance to talk privately with Piero and Lorenzo, and took them almost completely into my confidence, telling them that the woman I sought was a relative of the Hungarian royal house, and that I had been sent to locate her with as little publicity as possible. Piero nodded thoughtfully and agreed to help. But when he asked me what the young woman looked like, I found myself at something of a loss. Matthias's elder relatives, in the process of reading Helen angrily out of the family, had somewhat overshot the mark, unwisely burning the few existing portraits of her as well as effacing her name from all the written records they could reach.

"She is short of stature, Signore Piero, and of a slender figure. Her face is said to be beautiful, her coloring moderately dark." Piero looked at me, perhaps revising downward his estimate of my intelligence. But beyond that I had been given no real description, and could offer none.

That very night, searchers were sent discreetly out. And in the middle of the next morning the report came in of what would now be called a solid lead. A young woman speaking a language that was very possibly Hungarian had been seen three days ago, modeling in the workshop of a rising young artist named Verrocchio—a man who could be expected to co-operate fully with me in my search; his career was blooming chiefly as a result of Medici patronage.

I held a quick conference with Morsino, in which we decided it would be better if he did not accompany me to Verrocchio's workshop. If we were able to avoid giving notice of official Hungarian interest in the woman, so much the better. But Lorenzo volunteered to come along, and it was perfectly natural that he should do so. He was already known as a budding patron of the arts; he had visited the place before, and was well acquainted with its master. As far as anyone but Verrocchio himself might know, Lorenzo and I would be visiting only to inspect and possibly purchase some of the shop's output. The subject of the Hungarian woman, whether she was still there or not, could arise for discussion as if by accident.

We went through the streets on foot and with-

out escort, which seemed to be the ordinary way
for the Medici to get about in town, though Piero
with his gout frequently used a litter. Every few
paces, or so it seemed to me, Lorenzo was greeted
by someone high or low, and as often as not he
paused to exchange good wishes and bits of gossip.

"Do you think the woman we want is this artist's mistress?" I asked him when we seemed to
have a moment clear for private conversation.

Lorenzo paused in the middle of a narrow way,
smiling and gesturing with an exaggerated
flourish for an elderly woman carrying a market
basket of vegetables to go ahead of him. I had been
told again and again that this family of wealthy
merchants who were my hosts were also the virtual dictators of Florence; never before had I seen
dictators who behaved in such a fashion.

"I do not think so," he answered me when we
were alone again. "I know Andrea's tastes . . . no,
I think not."

The workshop was a smaller, poorer place than
I had been expecting. One large room, well lit by
skylights and windows, took up most of the interior space in a building rudely constructed of
planks and timbers. Off this large room a few
doors led to smaller chambers in the rear, and to a
yard. All was primitive as a stable, or very nearly
so. Verrocchio its master was rough-looking too,
a stocky man of about thirty with a gross face,
dressed in workman's clothing covered with various kinds of stains. He greeted Lorenzo with
warmth, and told us that his poor house was
ours—then grew nervous when Lorenzo whispered in his ear something of the true purpose of
our visit.

In the middle of the big room, under a roof panel open to the clear Florentine sky, an old man with rheumy eyes was posing in loose Biblical-looking garb while a single unshaven apprentice sketched him in charcoal on a prepared panel. After stammering some shy greetings to us, they both went on with the job. The door to one of the rear rooms stood open, revealing an elderly female domestic scrubbing at a pot.

Lorenzo and I sat at one side of the studio for a while, playing the role of customers while its master spoke with us about current projects. Or, rather, the tough-looking artist spoke with his young patron who rather resembled a Mafia don of a later century, while I listened and tried to look as if I understood them or at least was interested in what they talked about. Then, with a hint from Lorenzo to guide my taste, I purchased a small, newly-wrought gold chain.

Lorenzo then said that he had an important commission in mind; for the supposed heavy business discussion Verrocchio conducted us into the privacy of what must have been his own bedroom. The chamber was small, its walls heavily decorated with paper sketches. As the elder guest I was granted the single chair; Lorenzo perched on a chest, and Verrocchio sat on the rumpled bed, the only other article of substantial furniture available.

Yes, signori, about that girl, of course. She had been gone for the last two days, and Verrocchio did not know where, any more than he knew from where she had come. Some weeks ago one of the apprentices had brought her in, saying that he wanted to use her as a model and that she was willing to pose for others also. So she had been, even posing naked without protest, which had convinced Verrocchio that she was a whore. A good model, though. He had given her food, a place to sleep with the female servants, and a little money once or twice. She had spoken Italian badly and with an odd accent—certainly not the Greek accent so common in Florence since the refugees from fallen Constantinople had swarmed in; but outside of that, and a certain odd beauty in her face, he had thought her no different from any of a hundred other vagrants and runaways who could be picked up in the streets and taverns. Yes, somewhat better looking than most of them, that was all. Here on the wall were a couple of sketches of her made by his apprentices, if we would like to see.

I naturally looked with interest, but only one sketch showed the model's face at all clearly, and it had distorted her features into such an artificial expression of heaven-sent rapture that I thought it would be useless for identification. I made no comment.

Verrocchio talked on, nervously. He had had vague plans of posing the girl himself—yes, there was something truly lovely about her, *signori*— but the next thing he knew, she was gone, no one knew where.

I asked: "Which apprentice was it who brought her round? That stubbly fellow out there?"

"Yes. Would you gentlemen like to talk to him?"

We went out into the large room again, where Lorenzo with his usual good humor approached the dark-cheeked youth. Would he settle a small bet? That young woman who was here until a few days ago, what language did she really speak, besides her bad Italian?

The pseudo-prophet with the rheumy eyes got a chance to rest from posing. The apprentice put down his tools. He dropped things and was upset at being questioned. He stuttered that he really didn't know, he didn't think that he could tell us much.

I demonstrated what Hungarian sounded like. Yes, said the nervous youth, that might have been it. But he wasn't really sure. He had never talked to the girl much and didn't know her name. True, he had picked her up in a tavern, and brought her here for some modeling, but you gentlemen know how that goes—excuse me, perhaps you don't —but a man doesn't always learn their names. No, he didn't know where she was now. She had seemed unhappy—she had gone off—

It seemed to me that there was more to be learned from this man, but he was not mine to question as I willed. He was probably a valuable worker here. Perhpas later, I thought.

"Let us talk to the servants, then," said Lorenzo, still effortlessly maintaining the pose of a small bet to be settled. "And to the other apprentices."

The few servants were soon casually processed. I allowed them to get away with knowing nothing whatsoever, at least for the time being. As for apprentices, Verrocchio informed us that he presently had only three. The second, a somewhat younger and handsomer lad than the one we had already spoken to, was called in from the yard where he had been mixing pigments. This one, acting not too bright, only giggled slightly and glanced nervously at his master when I asked him how well he had known the woman; he did confirm, though, that my Hungarian sounded like the language the young woman had muttered to herself in when she was upset.

"What was she upset about?"

The youth made an eloquent gesture with both arms, that seemed to take in all of life.

"I have only one more apprentice, gentlemen. He lives at home, but is due to arrive here at any time now. Will you honor me by waiting?"

"It is we who are honored by your company, maestro," said Lorenzo, and sat down again for some more leisured conversation about Art. The staff went back to work. Presently the lad we were waiting for appeared. He looked to me no more than about twelve years of age, though quite tall and strong for his years. He was better dressed than either of his older colleagues.

Lorenzo, beginning to put a question to him, paused in mid-sentence. "Stay, I think I know you. Your father is Ser Piero the notary, is he not? Yes, of course, and how is he?"

"Father is well, signore."

Again we went through our list of questions. This time Lorenzo, as an acquaintance, did most of the talking.

"The girl perhaps talked to you about herself? Your good master here says that you spent more time drawing and painting her than any of the others did."

"Yes, she modeled for me many days. But we did not talk very much."

"Perhaps," I put in, "you have a drawing, at least a sketch, some good likeness of her that you can show me?" I realized that our fiction about the bet was by now too tattered to be of any other further use. "Since you say you put in so many hours at it. Can you draw well?"

The boy looked at me. There was something intrinsically cold, withdrawn, about him. "I can draw. I threw some of my sketches away, but I think there is something. I will see what I can find." He turned away.

"Stay," commanded Lorenzo. "The important thing is, do you know where she is now?"

"Yes, signore, I think I may know." We all stared at him. "In the palazzo Boccalini."

This obviously meant something to Lorenzo and Verrocchio, who exchanged looks. Then the master of the studio demanded of his young apprentice: "How do you know this?"

"I saw her on the street, two days ago, arguing with two young men of that family. They were starting to pull on her arms, and laughing. She was not laughing. And she has not been back here since."

Verrocchio looked all about him, as if calling on witnesses to this strange behavior. "Yet you said nothing to anyone here about this? Why?"

"No one asked me about it, until now."

Verrocchio glanced at us, then waved the youth away. When he was gone, Lorenzo said to me: "The Boccalini are no friends of my family. And what the boy said may be true, for they have a bad reputation of taking advantage of undefended young women. If she went with them, it may well have been unwillingly. I believe the older men of their family are still at their summer villa, leaving the young gallants unsupervised in town. We will do what we can to find out for certain whether she is there."

Verrocchio, chewing on his lip, had moved a pace or two away; he was not anxious to take part in these intrigues. At this point the young boy came back, lugging a fairly large wooden panel. "The little sketches are all gone," he said laconically.

His master took the painting from him and held it upright on a table, in good light. A twelve-year-old has done *that*? was my own first reaction, even untutored as I was in the difficulties of the art. For once, I think, Lorenzo's judgement was the same as mine; he scowled intensely and murmured something. Verrocchio, who must have seen the panel before, still sighed faintly with what sounded very much like envy. He snatched up a small brush from the table, and hastily flicked in his signature across a lower corner where part of the background had been finished.

He sighed again. "Yes, this is she, Signore Ladislao, an excellent likeness. From this you may know her. If she is where the boy says she is, I pray Jesus and San Lorenzo that you may bring her safely out. If that is what Your Honor really wants to do."

Lorenzo was still marveling at the painting in silence. Then he asked: "The boy really did this?"

The master nodded. "Indeed he did, Signore Lorenzo. I watched with my own eyes."

What impressed me most, at my then primitive level of artistic judgment, was of course the marvelously lifelike character of the face, which like most of the figure was completely finished; parts of the background, as I think I have mentioned, were still not done. With this face before me, I felt I must know the model at once if ever I saw her in the flesh. And this suggested to me another point: such a perfect, breathing likeness, if allowed to remain here, might someday serve as evidence in the hands of King Matthias's enemies, proof that his sister had indeed once been here and posing.

"I would like to take this painting with me," I said, reaching for my purse once more. "What is its price?"

But this time the master of the shop would have none of my gold. "Please, signore, you will honor me by accepting this trifle as a gift." Verrocchio made the offer quickly and easily; I am sure he calculated that in the long run he would not lose by such a gesture, which ought to bind him closer to the Medici in friendship; and, anyway, the gift was not all that expensive. Not in 1464, though within only a few decades the value of ready-made art from Florentine studios would increase tremendously.

"It is only the work of a novice, signore, though he is gifted beyond—" Verrocchio broke off, catching sight of the boy still standing nearby, silently attentive. "Back to your work now, Leonardo."

Seven

So.

It may be that some of my readers, equipped with good memories or else forearmed by a fortuitously recent reading of some art history, anticipated the little revelation at the previous chapter's end. But before these readers congratulate themselves too heartily, let them consider why none of those supposedly expert folk involved in the art auction uttered that most potent name. Why, barring one hint by Ellison Seabright, there has not been even the most tentative suggestion along that line. Two points awarded for the correct answer, and more on the subject later. For the moment let it suffice that the reader has now caught up with Mr. Thorn in this much at least: that Magdalen was definitely not a Verrocchio, worth perhaps the quarter of a million dollars or so that Ellison Seabright paid for it; it was instead a genuine Leonardo da Vinci, heretofore unknown to the experts as such, but if its origin could be verified worth easily twenty times that much.

The announcement of the missing aircraft caused Mr. Thorn to cut short his visit to the Seabright mansion as soon as he politely could—which, under the circumstances of confusion prevailing there, was not long. He took his leave without offering his host any further revelations of his own about the painting. He had not been about to provide that gross, half-clever criminal with any very truthful revelations anyway.

The two of them vaguely agreed that they would talk to each other again sometime and with that matters between them were left hanging.

Driving his rented Blazer back into the more plebian regions of the city, Mr. Thorn felt unhappy for several reasons. First, the painting was once more out of his reach, gone again, somewhere, where he could not even look at it. Second—or perhaps really first—it is always a painful experience, that dawning realization that one has underestimated an opponent. That first moment when the placidly grazing prey turns suddenly, baring its own fangs, unsheathing its own sharp claws . . . and, perhaps thirdly, perhaps worst of all, is the suspicion that one has finally grown old, become ineffectual through overconfidence.

Mr. Thorn, still determined of course to have his painting, but denied it, and realizing now that he did not even know who his true adversary was, would have liked to go back in time two days, and start over again in the auction room. That being impossible even for him, he decided to do the next best thing, which was to come as close to starting over as he could.

Sighting a public phone booth, he stopped and made a call. Twenty minutes later he was ringing the front doorbell of a modest house on an anonymously modest Phoenix side street.

Robinson Miller, eyes full of subtle suspicions, appeared inside and let Thorn in. At Miller's feet a small dog, on getting his first whiff of the visitor, yapped once in extreme surprise, and then was still. Behind Miller in the living room was the sofa that Mary once had mentioned, looking indeed as if it might have spent part of a long and adventurous career inside a Salvation Army store. Mary herself was just rising from its sagging cushions. Tonight her jeans had been replaced by shorts, revealing legs quite as attractive as Thorn had expected them to be. She wore a blue vinyl vest, doubtless because there was no bra beneath her blue T-shirt. With her usual eagerness for any new development, she greeted the visitor more freely than Miller had. "This is a surprise, Mr. Thorn. Glad to see you. Something's happened, hasn't it?"

"Yes. Though I am not sure exactly what." Thorn took the offered armchair, a place of honor that got the main benefit of the laboring window air conditioner. He declined well-intentioned offers of coffee and beer, and looked calmingly at the small dog who was edging close to offer worship. To the humans he related the essentials of his visit to the Seabright house.

Mary was quite as upset as Thorn had been to hear about the missing plane, though her disquiet had a nobler basis. "Then the plane is really down? That's bad. How many people were on it?"

"Oh, I am sure that by this time it is down, somewhere. I gather that it carried only the pilot, a man named Gliddon. A search is to be started in the morning."

"Gliddon," said Mary, and made a face. "I didn't like him." Still her dislike hardly seemed to make any difference in her concern over the pilot's fate. "When I lived at the house he was always in and out, though I never knew what he did. It must have been some kind of work for Ellison."

Robinson Miller said to Thorn: "Do I understand you to mean that you think the plane didn't really crash?"

"Correct me if I am wrong," said Thorn, "but I believe that the land between here and Santa Fe is somewhat sparsely populated?"

Miller nodded. "Five hundred miles of nothing."

"Mountains, deserts, some forests," Mary amended. "Late last spring two Air Force planes from the missile range at Alamogordo were lost. They crashed right out in the open and in spite of a big search it was months before the wreckage was found. At least it's not winter now. I suppose if Gliddon survived a crash in the mountains he's got a chance."

"Somehow," said Thorn, "I have little doubt that he survived."

Mary looked puzzled; she didn't get it yet. Miller said: "I suppose Seabright was having a fit. Though not over the missing man, of course."

Thorn nodded. "He was going through the motions of one who is, as you say, having a fit over some lost property. Barking orders, phoning hither and yon, demanding explanations, demanding action. But I . . . have had some opportunity of observing humanity under various kinds of stress. And I am sometimes able to see through efforts at deception. And—this is why I have come to talk to you tonight—I think Mr. Seabright was not truly surprised by the news that his masterpiece and his aircraft and its pilot were missing. Indeed, I suspect that one reason I was invited to his house tonight was to provide him with a neutral witness, able to testify to his surprise and his dismay."

Some of Mary's old fierce delight quickly returned. She thumped the arm of the battered sofa. "I believe you!" she cried. "He's pulled another trick! He's getting away with it again!"

But Miller was frowning, shaking his head. "The suggestion being, I suppose, that Seabright is somehow spiriting the painting away into hiding by faking a plane crash. But he's just bought it and paid for it. Why the hell should he steal it from himself?"

Thorn had his ideas on that subject. But he said nothing for the moment.

"Insurance money!" Mary pounced.

Her lawyer was still shaking his head. "No, I don't think so. That kind of thing isn't easy to get away with—"

"Neither is murder, but he got away with killing Helen and Del."

"—and *anyway*, since the painting was being carried on his private aircraft I doubt that any insurance coverage on it would be in force." Miller's gaze focused suddenly on Thorn. "You're not from some insurance company, are you?"

"No," Thorn said patiently. "I am a collector, as is Seabright."

A few feet away, in the kitchen, the telephone began to ring. Miller got up to answer it.

"Mary." Thorn looked at her intently. "Why did Delaunay give you that painting?"

His gaze did not bother her. "Why? I told you. Out of gratitude, for my helping Helen. He was that kind of a guy, I guess. He knew I'd sell the painting, I'm sure. He just wanted me to have some money to use, helping other kids."

"You say you think Ellison knew about this gift? How can you be sure?"

But Mary was looking toward the kitchen doorway. Miller was standing there, rather like some interviewer with a microphone, holding out toward Mary the yellow telephone receiver on its helixed cord. But the look on his face was that of a man in shock, and Thorn got to his feet.

"Who? What?" asked Mary vaguely, standing also.

Miller licked his bearded lips. "She says . . . she's Helen."

There was a pause in which no one did anything. Then Mary sprang forward. In a moment she was holding the phone pressed against her disheveled hair. "Who is this? If this is supposed to be some kind of a joke, it isn't . . ."

A feminine voice at the other end of the connection had begun to answer. It was a quiet voice, and its tones were mottled and distorted by an imperfect connection somewhere, and at first Mr. Thorn could not make out the words. But Mary could, and they had an immediate effect. Her face lost color, and her hand holding the receiver slumped a little. "What?" she asked weakly.

The voice at the other end made itself louder. Now both men standing by in the kitchen could hear it well enough to distinguish words. "Mary, this isn't any joke. It's me. I can't come back now, it's too dangerous. Anyway, I don't really want to. Everything's fine for me the way things are. But I wanted to talk to you. You're my best friend, Mary." Mr. Thorn, listening hard, thought there was a certain dazed quality in the voice; a disconnection from present reality, as if it might be reciting lines learned for a play.

"Helen? What do you mean, dangerous?" Mary's own voice now sounded no less dazed.

"Why? Where are you?"

"You know why, Mary, if I come back *he's* going to try to kill me again. Look, I wanted to tell you, Mary, I'm sorry about running away again, after all your work with me and all. But there was nothing else for me to do. Please don't try to look for me again, this time I'm gone for good."

"Baby, if this is really you . . . you tell me not to look for you? How can you call me up like this and say a thing like that?"

"You always said you wanted me to have a happy life someday. So now I'm going to be able to have a happy life. So let me alone."

Miller stood beside Mary where she sat in a kitchen chair. He was slowly bending over her, getting his ear closer and closer to the phone in her hand; and meanwhile his eyes squinted, as if he strained to see something in the far distance. Thorn waited motionless in the kitchen doorway, and he also was listening very carefully.

Mary was starting to recover from her first shock. "Listen, if this is Helen speaking . . . if this is Helen, tell me who was killed? Whose body did I stumble over in the dark?"

"There was a girl you didn't know about in the house that night. A girl named Annie, just a runaway from somewhere, she didn't count. Only Uncle Del knew that she was there, and he was killed too . . . but Mary, I don't want to talk about all that any more. I've found someone who I thought was lost to me forever. We're going to do real things, and it's all going to be okay. He's going to put me in real movies. Someday."

"Real movies? What do you mean, you've found someone? Who? Where are you? Helen, this can't be you."

"It's me, Mary. Remember what you once told me, about something you said you'd never told another soul? About you and your boy friend in Idaho? Want me to play that back to you now?"

"Oh my God." Mary turned still more pale. "My God, it is you, baby."

"Not your goddam *baby*." The distant voice turned petulant. Still a poor contact somewhere in the wires distorted it. "Just let me alone, please. Oh, Mary, I'm going to be so happy."

Mr. Thorn, listening, had doubts.

"Helen? Tell me where you are?"

"Goodbye, Mary." It was a lament, a ghost's farewell.

"No, Helen. Wait. Where are you? Helen?"

A click; what connection there had been was gone. Mary talked into nothingness for a few seconds, and jiggled the switch at her end of the line. After that she could only hang up too.

Then she lifted a dreamer's face to the two men. "You heard her. It was her. What do we do now?"

Miller appeared unconvinced. "It did sort of sound like her voice," he admitted. "Not that I ever talked to her that much, but . . ." He had to pause to clear his throat. "If that really was her, if Helen's really still alive, do you know what that means? That masterpiece that Ellison Seabright just paid for is really still her property. In the legal sense, I mean," he hastened to add when Mary looked at him.

"Even if Seabright has paid for it?" Thorn asked.

"Absolutely. No question about it. There'd be a devil of a legal and financial mess to untangle. But the painting would have to be held in trust for Helen, as per Delaunay's will. Assuming *he's* really dead. Wow," added the lawyer, looking at Thorn. "And the painting was on that plane."

"The matter of the missing plane," said Thorn, "is now perhaps explained."

Miller nodded slowly. "If Helen is still alive, and Seabright somehow found out about it, he'd then have a good motive to get the painting out of the way. Maybe sell it secretly; there are collectors who would buy."

Mary for once was not delighted to discuss villainy. She slumped in the kitchen chair, not looking like her usual self. "Rob, shall we call in the police and tell them about the call? How are we even going to start looking for her if we don't do that?"

"Indeed," put in Thorn, "how are we to start looking in any case, whether the police are notified or not?"

"Then you advise against calling them?" Miller was fumbling nervously for his pipe.

"My advice is that we first take thought. What exactly can we tell the authorities, and what will they believe? All three of us heard someone on the phone, but which of us can swear convincingly that it was Helen? Certainly not I, who never heard Miss Seabright's voice."

Miller, having found his pipe, held it in his hand forgotten. "I did—a few times. But I couldn't honestly say. Mary?"

Mary had her face down in her hands now. "Maybe . . . I don't know. Maybe it could have been someone else. I saw Helen lying on the floor in the Seabright house, dead. All shot to pieces."

Thorn asked: "You recognized the victim's face?"

"Her mouth was almost gone, her lower jaw. I

never realized till then that guns did things like that. Her hair . . . it looked like Helen's hair. I assumed it was Helen. Everybody did. It never entered my mind that it might not be her, because I never had any idea that there could have been another girl in the house. 'Annie.' Whoever it was on the phone just now said 'Annie'. Did you hear?''

Thorn and Miller both signed agreement. Mary went on: "It's crazy. I don't know any Annie, and I don't believe there could have been another girl. Dressed in Helen's robe?''

Thorn prodded: "But is it not possible? Some runaway, perhaps, being given shelter? That only Helen and her uncle knew about?''

Mary hesitated. "Delaunay would've told me, if he'd been doing that. Let me think about it. It's not absolutely impossible, I suppose.''

Miller was now inspecting his pipe as if it were some interesting alien artifact. "Assume we went to the authorities with this phone call, and could get them to halfway believe us. Then ordinarily, you know, a court order could possibly be obtained, the body in question could be exhumed, a certain identification made. Fingerprints, dental records, and so on. But Helen—if she was the girl who was shot—was cremated.''

"That's right,'' murmured Mary. "It was the family tradition.'' Rotating her head as if to ease weary neck muscles, she looked at the men. She seemed now to have pulled herself essentially together. "But—oh, this is awful—the more I think about it, the more I feel sure that it must have been Helen on the phone just now. That dead girl in the house . . . she could have been someone else, although I don't know who. But the girl on the phone mentioned something, a thing that happened to me in Idaho." Mary sighed and looked at Miller as if asking to be forgiven. "Something that I know I've never talked about to anyone but Helen."

"But that Helen might have talked about," said Thorn.

"Well . . ."

Thorn went on: "The girl on the phone said 'he' would try to kill her again if she came back."

Neither of the others wanted to comment. There was a short pause. Then Miller said: "She—whoever it was—said something else that I thought was strange. About being put into 'real movies', if I heard it right."

"You did," said Thorn. "And mentioned reunion with someone she had thought 'lost forever.' Who had Helen lost forever, Mary?"

Mary did not reply at once. Miller had put away his pipe and was massaging the back of her neck, her shoulders. She leaned back in the chair, yielding to the motion. "I don't know," she murmured at last. "She's run off . . . it'll be a rerun of last time, I'm afraid."

Thorn asked patiently: "What happened last time?"

She looked up at him, her head bobbing with the rhythm of the continuing massage. "Helen ran away and got as far as Chicago. Some jerk there had her acting in porn movies. She wasn't basically like that at all."

"I see. And do you think that this jerk, as you call him, is the long-lost lover she has now rejoined?"

"Oh no. Not him, never. She doesn't hate herself that much. But she did talk to me about some-

one else she met on the road, a boy who meant
something to her. She told me his name was Pat. I
don't know if he was involved in the porn factory
thing or not, but she must have known him at
about the same time."

"Pat was a runaway too?"

Mary thought. "I got the impression from Helen
that he was older, a little older anyway. Not a
runaway any more, an independent adult. No,
independent is not the right word for what adults
are like when they've grown up that way, on the
road. I've seen a bunch of them. Lost, usually.
Isolated. That's what they tend to be like when
they manage to grow up at all."

Miller said: "Come to think of it, I do seem to
remember hearing Helen once mention someone
called Pat. With a kind of wistful look in her eye."

"O'Grandison, that was his last name!" Mary
had suddenly come up with it. "Oh, Rob, that
must have been Helen on the phone. Oh, my poor
baby. I remember now. She used to say Pat had
talked to her about making good films, wishing he
could help make them, something like that."

And here, unexpected by either man, came
tears. Miller, still rubbing Mary's neck tenderly,
tried to react lightly. "Mother Mary," he joked.

"Don't laugh at me."

"I'm not." He squeezed her neck muscles firmly
again and looked at Thorn. "What do you think?"

"I think," said Thorn, "that in the matter of
making vile films in Chicago, and in the matter of
this Mr. O'Grandison, I may be able to learn something. I repeat that I am not an official investigator
of any kind, but in the course of an active life one
forms connections."

Eight

My Medici connection was going to be of no direct help in learning whether the woman I sought was in fact within the walls of the *palazzo* Boccalini. In fact if the alliance became known to the Boccalini it would have the opposite effect, for the two families were rivals, at odds in all sorts of Florentine affairs. My friends the Medici were of course the stronger, but I could not expect them to use their power too nakedly. Their rule in the city was a subtle thing, based on the maintenance of harmony among factions; and although King Matthias's gratitude would mean much to them as traders, it would not be worth upsetting a Florentine political balance already teetering with the impact of Cosimo's recent death. Lorenzo assured me of his family's continued help, but also made sure that I understood its limits. If I was willing to be patient, in a few days a Boccalini servant could doubtless be bribed, a spy perhaps planted in their household.

But my nature was impatient to begin with, and anyway it did not seem to me that I had time to spare. If Helen was not after all with the Boccalini, I was wasting time; on the other hand, if she was, not only might her life be in peril but her identity could be exposed at any time. In view of this I told Lorenzo that speed was necessary; and, within a few hours of leaving Verrocchio's workshop, my young benefactor and I had agreed upon another scheme.

At that time there was in Florence—I think the

building may be still standing, near the Mercato
Vecchio—an inn known as the Tavern of the
Snail. This snail was much frequented by the adventurous young bloods of the leading families,
the Boccalini in particular. Therefore we felt safe
in gambling that one or two Boccalini youth
would approach the place that very night, or at
worst within the next few evenings. As events
turned out, our most optimistic hopes were justified.

Lorenzo had three or four reliable men
stationed in ambush, along the route our game
would most probably take. The scion of the
Medici did not, of course, place himself among
the ambushers. He could not afford to have his
involvement in the affair discovered, and in any
case his skills were not those of physical violence.
My own part was to wait as patiently as possible
in concealment nearby. As soon as the pretended
robbers had sprung their trap I was to bound out,
crying for the watch, and rush upon them with
drawn sword.

As I have said, we were lucky on the first night,
and carried it off well enough. One of the paid
ruffians, playing his part with cheeky skill—there
is nothing easier than to ruin a plan of this kind by
a lack of convincing effort by all concerned—
offered me resistance, whereupon I ran him
through the arm, a touch of authenticity he had
perhaps not been expecting. After I had drawn
blood, there was nothing more to be seen in the
dark street of the attackers, and nothing heard of
them but their fast-flying footsteps in retreat.

My eyes had had a long time to grow accustomed to the poor light, and I could get a fairly
good look at the two Boccalini. They had man-

aged to get their backs against a wall, side by side, and were now slumped down somewhat in that position. Both had weapons drawn, both were panting and cursing, and one was bleeding in a minor way. Besides ourselves the street was now deserted, the hour of curfew long since past. As a rule curfew received little attention from young hell-raisers like these, of good political connections. Nearby dogs were ravening bravely at our recent dueling noises, their canine courage fortified by stone walls.

Warily I moved a little closer to the two dim figures. "Are you hurt, gentlemen? The pigs have taken to their heels."

The Boccalini snarled, grumbled, groaned, at Fate, at the world in general, at their attackers, at me. Then the smaller of the pair stood up straight and offered me at last some words of gratitude. From Lorenzo's briefing I thought I could recognize him as the eldest brother of the younger generation, Sandro.

We all three sheathed our blades, and introductions were informally exchanged. It was apparent that Sandro's younger brother Giulio was bleeding from his wrist rather more than could cheerfully be disregarded. An attempt at bandaging the wound with a strip of clothing failed to stanch the flow sufficiently, and the two young men decided that the tavern could wait, and that a retreat to their home was in order. It may have been in the minds of both brothers that assassination rather than robbery could have been the motive for the attack. Their family was certainly not without enemies, and assassins would be more likely than footpads to have a second try. At any rate, I was invited to go with them, and accepted with inner jubilation that I had not had to spend hours with them in the Tavern of the Snail before the invitation came.

Their house, no great distance away, was as Lorenzo had described it to me, a smaller, older, less well-built version of the Medici palace. A great barred door was opened to our shouts and pounding, and at once there came a rush of startled servants to care for Giulio. I followed the excitement through halls and a small open courtyard to a room where there was a soft couch for him to lie upon. On the way I kept my eyes open and took note of several girls and young women, dressed differently than the regular servants, in a gaudy style suggestive of the bordello. Though I looked sharply at each face, I could not recognize my Magdalen.

No sooner had we laid Giulio on this couch than with another rush we were surrounded by three more young men of the family, the brother and two cousins of my street companions. For the next hour things were operatic. Mighty oaths of outrage and revenge rang in the stone rooms. Shouts and gestures expressed extravagant grief and rage. Sword-wavings were directed at the unknown dastards who had done this deed; but they were absent and the naked blades imperilled only the help. It was unanimously agreed, a number of times over, that a punitive expedition must be launched into the night as soon as Giulio had been properly bandaged—a purported physician who lived nearby had now been sent for, and spiderwebs were being gathered as a coagulant. The correct target for this retaliatory raid could not be agreed upon, however, and all the talk came to nothing, as I had surmised it must. In the morning the young men of the family were going to have to take the practical step of informing their elders at their suburban villa; at present, though, there was really nothing to be done but to make sure that all doors and windows were secure, and then get on with the nightly debauch. Giulio, once the doctor had tied his arm up properly, was not so badly off that he would be forced to abstain from this. And of course I, as their heaven-sent ally and savior, was hospitably invited to take part.

Looking back, I see that perhaps I have not made it clear enough that from my first entry into the house, even with all the other things they had to shout about, my young hosts made me welcome with thanks and praise and every courtesy, extravagantly expressed. Like their greater Medici rivals in the Bankers' Guild, the Boccalini were often dependent for success on foreign men who lived by the sword, and the family habit of politeness to such had been ingrained in all its members.

"Have some more wine, Cousin Ladislao—you don't mind if I call you that? You have shown yourself more than a cousin tonight. Wine, and how about a woman or two? There are plenty here to choose from."

Indeed, I could see there were, all of them young and well-formed if not all pretty. Drawn by the excitement, ten or a dozen of these girls were nearby, a couple petting Giulio, others lounging about, chatting idly among themselves in a manner that showed they could not be ordinary servants. Some of them had managed to acquire rich clothing, and their confinement here, if such it was, appeared to be on quite lenient terms. Doubtless for all of them life here in the *palazzo* was a definite improvement over what it had been on the streets outside. I saw no one who looked like an unwilling kidnap victim. But neither had I yet seen one who wore the face of Magdalen.

"By the beard of St. Peter," I commented, "there are more women here than in the tavern, I would guess." I reached out a hand to squeeze a passing buttock, whose owner paused briefly to give me back a nervous smile. I drank some wine—not much. "But I am a hard man to please, gentlemen. Without meaning the least disrespect to your hospitality, I must admit that these wenches look to me like so many cows filled with milk. To a man like myself these are as nothing. I want fire." At this point I emitted a loud, completely un-Florentine belch; and I must confess that it was a deliberate attempt to express bold worldliness.

My hosts averaged about fifteen years younger than myself, and I was still far from an old man. They were duly impressed, and exchanged glances.

"It is something more fiery than these that you require," mused Sandro.

"Something different, at least." I waved a haughty hand.

A fat genuine cousin, Allessandro, raised his brows, hiccuped, and offered a suggestion. "There is a stableboy here, I am told, who plays the part of a girl quite—"

"Bah!"

Sandro was coming visibly to a decision. "Nay, old cousin Ladislao, come along with me. If it is fire you want, real female fire, then I think that I can promise you a treat."

The others, understanding what he meant after delays corresponding to their several states of

drunkeness, hiccuped, shouted, and belched
their approval. Sandro rose, and with a flourish
took up one of the candles from the table, signing
me to do likewise. Then with another great gesture he bade me follow him.

We went up one flight of stairs after another, to
a cramped top floor where some of the heat of the
past day still lingered in the roof whose beams
forced me to duck at almost every step. I counseled myself as we climbed that if this rare treat
proved not to be the one I sought, I had better
enjoy it anyway, or appear to do so. If I stayed on
good terms with the Boccalini, sooner or later I
would find out what had happened to Helen. If
they had really taken her. With my luck, I thought,
she was probably at that very moment on her way
to Naples, or to England, or the Sultan's court.

But my luck was not that bad. We came to a
heavy, crude door, from which Sandro took down
a bar. Then, having to duck his own head at this
point, he went in ahead of me with his candle. The
room was small and windowless, meaner than my
own cell back in the Tower of Solomon, and
ovenish with heat. A girl lay on the floor. Her face
was in shadow and she appeared so small my first
thought was that they were offering me a kidnapped child. But as she sat up on the strawed
floor I saw the soft proportions of a grown woman's body under the rough shift that appeared to
be her only garment. I noticed now that one of her
ankles was secured with a fine, bright, elegant
pet's chain to a vertical beam supporting the low
roof.

My guide held up his candle, that I might see
the captive better. "She has been here two days,
continually insulting us," he explained, rather

like a physician detailing the symptoms of a mysterious illness to a visiting specialist. "She will have nothing to do with us willingly, gentle though we are."

The girl's face, when at last I could see it under her fall of darkly matted hair, was bruised as well as grimy. Yet I was certain of it at first glance. "Why then did you bring her here?" I asked.

Either Sandro did not hear the question, or he preferred to let it pass. "Two nights ago she was scratching and biting like a wildcat, my brothers and I can all testify to that. All the fire anyone might want, my friend. Myself, I haven't been up here since then—maybe she is a little weaker now, I don't think she has been fed much."

The girl's eyes, that at first had blinked and squinted even in the weak candlelight, were steadily open now. She had the self-numbed, withdrawn look of a brave prisoner. With gentle caution I put a hand under her chin and raised her face more fully into the candles' glow. "She'll nip you," Sandro warned. But she did not.

Yes, beyond doubt my first impression had been correct. This was precocious Leonardo's model—but a Magdalen who now looked as if she had lapsed from divine forgiveness. She would indeed have liked to bite me, or to spit at me at least, but she no longer quite dared to do so. The Boccalini, not trying very hard, had taught her that much in two days.

I set down my own candlestick on the floor. "I thank you, cousin. This is what I wanted. I will see you in the morning."

"I wish you a sound night's sleep," laughed Sandro. And with a bow my benefactor left, taking his own candle with him and leaving the door ajar.

I could hear him starting down the stairs. As far as I could tell the girl and I were now the only people on the whole upper floor of the great house. With a tired sigh I sat down on the dusty boards beside my candle, and then in afterthought turned and bawled after Sandro: "Send up some water and wine! And food!" There came some unclear words in reply.

Waiting, I sat looking at the girl and thinking about her in silence. She was holding her torn shift together with both hands, and leaning against the wooden post to which her chain was fastened. She was looking back at me rather as if I were some inanimate tool with which she was going to be hurt.

A small padlock held a loop of the chain around the wooden post. Another similar lock bound another loop round her tiny ankle, which was certainly smaller than my wrist. The little room stank. In one far corner was a crude clay chamber pot. A dish and cup for food and water, both empty now, waited on the floor closer to the door, through which a little air had now begun to circulate.

In a few minutes a slave girl, one of the working servants, came up with the provisions I had called for. As soon as this servant had left the two of us alone again, I pushed the silver utensils within Helen's reach and sat back. After a quick glance at me she grabbed up the bright cup and drank thirstily, then began to eat the biscuits and sausage. She kept what must have been a half-starved appetite under careful control, like one who has had experience of what a sudden load of food might do to a shrunken stomach. Between measured bites, she cast at me more calculating looks than before.

The pauses in her eating began to grow longer, and I helped myself to a portion of the remaining food. Helen sat back on her haunches and looked at me steadily. "And now?"

She had spoken in her bad Italian; I answered in her native Hungarian: "Now you are going to come away from here. With me."

It was a shock. Until that moment I do not think that she had seen me as anything but another rapist to be endured somehow. But now she started. Her expression changed rapidly, as surprise was followed by the beginning of understanding, and that in turn by relief—a relief mixed with bitterness, but still a great liberation for all that.

She said in Hungarian: "Our Lady be thanked, for she has heard my prayers. I will certainly go to my brother, even, to get myself out of this."

"I should think you would." I did not tell Helen that returning her to Hungary was not one of the two options allowed me by her brother's royal command.

I moved close to Helen now, and drew my dagger. The bright links of the chain had scraped her slender ankle sorely where she must have tried to force it off. Holding her ankle and the chain against the floorboards, I could feel a delicate trembling in her leg, in her whole body. My dagger, a crude northern weapon, bit silently through the links when I leaned my weight upon it. It took me another moment to cut the other end of the chain free of the lock that held it round the post.

The blade went back into its sheath. Helen was still trembling, with the relief of the strain of fear. She told me later that she had been utterly convinced that the Boccalini were never going to let her go alive after what they had done to her against her will. Probably she was right. No one would take very much notice, or remember it for long, if a street waif simply disappeared. On the other hand a survivor telling stories would have been at least somewhat detrimental to the family's standing in the eyes of business associates and of the church.

"He is not really a savage man," Helen told me, rubbing her freed ankle, and at first I thought that she meant Sandro. "But he is king." Her eyes lifted, and for a moment I saw a spark of her own royalty in them. "And your name?"

"Here I am called Ladislao. But at His Majesty's court, Wladislaus." I could see at once that the name suggested nothing in particular to her. All to the good, I thought. Had the lady known me by reputation, my task might well have been still further complicated.

As it stood, it was quite demanding enough.

One of the options allowed me by the king was to report back to him that with my own eyes I had seen his sister safely and anonymously dead. For me to take that course would mean at least that the family name was guarded from any further damage. And it would be possible to hope that in time the scandals already generated might be forgotten.

The only other alternative I had been given by Matthias was to try to civilize the girl—which would of course require that first I take her to wife.

Startled though I had been when the king first

broached this plan to me, I had now been able to
mull it over long enough to appreciate the reason-
ing behind it. I had been forced to conclude that
from the king's viewpoint it had merit, the advantage of making some positive good at least a possibility.

Consider. For Matthias to somehow put an end
to Helen's escapades was imperative. They put
him in danger of becoming an international
laughingstock, and a king who has that happen to
him is lucky if he retains his crown, let alone such
a position of world leadership as the ruler of Hungary was grasping for. So he had to either kill the
girl, tame her, or send her to a convent—and having had one bad experience with such an estab-
lishment already, His Majesty was not disposed to
favor them as instruments of policy. To tame the
wench into a public asset was a much more attractive idea—Matthias was never one for wasting
people who could still be used. Helen as my wife
would bind me to his service, and might even
produce strong nephews to aid the royal cause in
later years. And, again, Helen's re-emergence into
public life as a lady of importance would tend to
give the lie to the extravagant stories that must be
already in circulation regarding her behavior.
Whereas her permanent disappearance would
tend, if anything, to confirm them.

For my part, I had wit enough to see that such a
marriage must be a mixed blessing for me at best,
despite the royal alliance that it entailed. Like an
awkward military position, it might have to be
defended constantly, not to mention the time and
effort that would probably be required to manage
the woman herself.

"Should you choose to wed her, Drakulya, then

I will not have you put her away again, do you understand? For as long as she lives, once you are married, she must appear in public as your devoted wife, honored by all and worthy of honor. Any more scandal I will not tolerate. In time I mean to have you both back at court—when time has proven that the arrangement works."

On the other hand, killing the girl quietly and quickly here in Florence would present me with no serious problems—no immediate ones at least. If the Boccalini came up to the attic in the morning and found her dead, they might disapprove—but not very loudly or strongly. They would certainly see to it that any killing in their household was effectively hushed up. In time the Medici would doubtless learn about it; but as long as King Matthias sent them no anguished inquiries about his sister, they would keep the matter quiet too.

So what held me back from instant murder? Was it only my own daring ambition, my wish to get ahead by presenting my lord king with the best possible solution? Was there no pity in me for Helen's helplessness? Looking back through the centuries at myself I believe there was, though I was not known for pity, and it was in general a hard and ruthless age.

And was I not attracted to Helen's beauty, which hard usage had not yet destroyed? Again, yes, I was—and, yet again, I think there was still more.

I had a feeling for what Matthias in his heart of hearts must really want, however firmly he had empowered me to kill his sister on the spot as soon as I could find her. Oh, he really meant it when he told me I could do that. Doubtless, if I reported to him that I had seen her dead, he would reward me for the favor. But then, afterwards . . . aye, forever afterwards. What would such a monarch always feel for the loyal servant who had carried such an order out? I had been a brother myself, and a prince too, and I could guess. Sooner or later a good use could be found for such a loyal man right in the forefront of a battle. And if the Black Army did not actually retire from him, and he survived—well then, later there would doubtless be something else again.

And still, besides all these reasons to spare Helen, I think there was yet more. My mercy in that little attic room had purpose yet unfathomed.

I had spoken earlier to Lorenzo about the possibility of a wedding. Seasoned intriguer that he already was, he had offered no comments and asked no questions but had obligingly set in motion some necessary arrangements. All I need do now was to get Helen out of the Boccalini house and to some place of safety, without overt Medici help.

While my unknowing bride-to-be prudently consumed the last crumbs of food from the silver plate, I wondered silently what would be the reactions of my adopted cousins if I simply strolled downstairs with her and asked to have the front door unlocked. Opening that door would not be something that we could do casually for ourselves; I had seen how they barred and chained the place up like a fortress for the night. And if Sandro should decide that he did not want me to take the woman away . . . well, I would not be able to manage either violence or bribery on the scale required to gain my way.

I stood up and stretched as well as I could under

that low roof, then looked out into the corridor. All was dark and I thought there were no listeners nearby. Doubtless none who could speak Hungarian, anyway.

"Can you still walk, Helen?"

"'Yes." She got to her feet, stretching too, but not as I had. Her movements were furtive and sinuous.

"Can you run?"

Still holding the wretched shift together with one hand, she tried walking for a few limping steps, then paused to look at me. "If I must, I can. Then all has not been neatly arranged? I am willing to try anything to get out of here, but I must know."

"Arrangements have been made. Perhaps not neatly, however, and not with the people of this house. These people we are going to have to surprise. Bend your knees, swing your legs, loosen them up."

She did as I bade her, exercising as well as the tiny space allowed. "I can run."

"Excellent. Now, I am going to chain your hands together—that is, I will wrap the chain around your wrists, but so you can shed it at will. After that we will go downstairs, and, I hope, out into the street. If there is any argument about our going out, pretend you are reluctant to do so. And move slowly, as if you can hardly walk—yes, that's fine. Then when we are outside, as soon as I tug twice on the chain, slip it and run hard. Right into the darkness, in the direction I will have you facing. Helpers should be waiting for us." So I hoped it would be; so it had been tentatively planned. "Run, run till you are caught, and pray Jesus it will be a friend who has you then."

Nine

The bored male midwestern voice at the other end of the long-distance line informed Mr. Thorn that Lieutenant Keogh was busy right now on another phone, and would he like to hang on? When Thorn submitted that he would, he was left to do so with a minimum of courtesy and a mutter of subdued office noise to keep him entertained. During this lengthy interval it crossed Thorn's mind that he might have made this call last night, and caught the good lieutenant at home instead of during business hours; but then, last night Thorn had himself been quite busy.

At last the receiver in Chicago was picked up again. "Lieutenant Keogh." The voice was familiar to Thorn, but at the moment it carried a load of official boredom he had not heard in it before.

"Yes, Lieutenant. This is Jonathan Thorn, calling from Phoenix, Arizona. Regarding that merchandise you were trying to trace, I believe I will have the information you need very soon now. If you could call me back, at your convenience, here at my hotel?"

At the other end there was a silent pause, concluding in a sigh and followed by a muttered vulgarity. After this a footstep, and then the shutting of a door which effectively cut off the office background.

When the lieutenant's voice returned it sounded no happier than before, but at least all traces of boredom had been effectively expunged. "We can talk now. This is something really important, I take it?"

"Of course, Joe, of course." Thorn smiled and lay back on the bed, letting his lean frame relax. A white plastic bag as long as a mattress and as narrow as a cot had been unfolded on the rich green spread. This bag was thin enough to be folded into a suitcase, and it was sparsely stuffed with something that crunched faintly as Thorn's weight came onto it, sounding for all the world like dried earth.

"Of course," he repeated into the phone. "Neither of us would call upon the other in a merely trivial matter, is it not so? Your wife's family did not summon Dr. Corday from London, after all, until the situation warranted. By the way, how is the lovely Kate? And how are her fine parents?"

"Fine, fine." The distant voice remained wary. "Her brother and sister are okay, too. By the way, if you're looking for Judy, she's away at school. But I guess you must know that." The comment was tinged with a certain fatalistic disapproval.

Thorn made his own voice soothing. "Say hello to Kate for me. No, Joe, I am not looking for Judy. Nor do I want anything from you that might be embarrassing to you officially. My dearest Mina would be unhappy if I did anything like that with anyone in the family. By the way, I am somewhat surprised—pleasantly, of course—that you continue on the force."

"I like to work, and I'm too young to retire." Joe's voice showed no sign of relaxing yet. "Anyway, Kate's busy a lot with volunteer work, and her old man respects me more for being self-supporting . . . so, tell me what you want."

"I would like whatever information you can give me about two people. The first is Mary Rogers." Thorn recited a brief description. "Mary tells me that she was a nun, or at least a postulant, in the Chicago area, where she did charitable work with runaway youth. She—"

"Wait a minute, wait a minute. Mary Rogers rings a bell. Wasn't she a kidnap victim, a hostage, in that double Seabright killing out there in Phoenix?"

"Yes. I was about to add that."

"Ho. Wait a minute. Ho, ho, ho. You're mixed up in that?"

"My present concern is not with that sordid crime directly. Of course if I should come upon anything that might aid in its solution, then you in turn shall hear it from me. As from an anonymous and confidential source. Is that to your liking?"

"Well, yeah, of course I'd appreciate any kind of a tip. If you'd rather send it my way than tell it to the locals, and it worked out, it wouldn't do my career any harm. Who's your second person?"

"A young man. Patrick O'Grandison." Thorn gave the spelling that seemed to him most likely. "As I understand it, this youth is somehow involved in making films, quite possibly pornographic ones. Probably in Chicago during the last few months. I should like to find and talk to him."

"What about?"

"A personal matter."

"I know what some of your personal talks can be like. Listen, I wouldn't want to help you find this guy, assuming that I can, and then hear later that he's missing some parts or something."

"Joe." Thorn sounded reproachful, almost hurt, a wounded uncle. "I have said that I mean only to talk to him. Of course what he tells me may conceivably change my attitude. But at the moment I bear him no ill-will."

"On your honor?"

The question had sounded grimly serious. And it was taken seriously, as Joe Keogh must have known it would be. Lithely but slowly Thorn arose from his crackling bed of rest, to stand with squinted eyes fixed on some point in the burning sky outside his tinted window. "Yes, on my honor, Joseph."

"All right." The distant voice reluctantly gave in. The scratch of some writing implement told that Lieutenant Keogh was making notes. "I'll see what I can find out. Give me your number and when I have something I'll call you back."

"I shall be waiting for your call. Oh, Joe, one more thing. You might try to learn whether the young lady has ever been in Idaho."

Thorn put down the phone, then picked it up again and dialed the front desk. "Have there been any calls for me?"

"Yes sir, there was one, as I recall. About half an hour ago. A lady, but she didn't leave her name."

"Thank you." Half an hour ago he had been asleep; more than asleep. Waiting now, in no hurry, Thorn strolled to stand at the high windows and confront the daylight world through slotted blinds and tinted glass. An inferno of sun out there; he peered at it as into a blast furnace. Later in the afternoon he would rest more, and then go out again at sunset. Right now the high view made him think of flying. It helped to take his mind off certain things in the far past, things about which nothing could now be done. Nevertheless they were lately coming back, for some reason, to bother him. Most likely because he had again seen the painting at long last. He watched the smoggy landscape until even the filtered light began to make a dull pain behind his eyes. Then he drew the drapes shut and turned away.

Why should it bother him, irritate him so much, that the identical Christian name had been borne by two runaway girls half a millenium apart? A million other runaways down through the centuries must have borne it also, in aimless flight, great unsung migration, across Europe and America and God alone knew where.

Apparently there had even been a certain physical resemblance between the two . . . also shared with more other girls than even God could count. No, he told himself sharply, stop this now. Helen, your second wife, is dead, has been for five hundred years in some unknown grave, and only on the Last Day, if then, will you see her again. Or hear her voice. Leonardo had not known how to record *that*.

The voice on the phone had certainly not been one that he, Thorn, had ever heard before. He could be sure of that, at least. As sure as one in this sad, mad world could ever be of anything . . .

God and damnation. He had walked into an auction room, and had simply stood there, surrounded by strangers, and looked at an old picture. And there had been *tears* in his eyes. In *his* eyes. What next?

A reminder, anyway, that not even he was immune to change. Though he had known for some time that he was not.

It could not have happened to Helen as it had to him. It could not. He would have known, must have known, centuries ago. After all that had been between them in his breathing days, he must, he must have been aware centuries ago of her altered but continued life. He had no reason to think that anything of the sort had happened to her. Only to one in ten million or a hundred million did such change come.

But he was changing. Doors were opening around him, and he was trying to read the symbols on them.

Last night he had spent hours prowling secretly inside the Seabright house. There he had slid past real doors and tried to discover real things. He had watched the occupants while unseen himself, and had listened to them while remaining unheard. In most of their private actions they were as banal as everybody else. Despite all his alertness and his new readiness to discover subtle meanings, he had been able to find out surprisingly little.

The people had been asleep most of the time he watched them, servants and masters alike, and he had listened to their incoherent mutterings as they slept. Listened and watched carefully, though he had known for ages now that the secrets of the bedroom were for the most part very dull, like those films made by scientific researchers whose excruciatingly patient cameras dutifully record the writhings of pajamaed volunteers in semipublic sleep, the sleepers now and then twitching and generating brain waves with the onset of dreams.

He still had dreams himself. Not many who knew his true name would have guessed that he himself, here this very afternoon in this very hotel bed, at about the time when some unknown woman was trying to reach him by telephone, had seen an infant nursing at the breast of Mary Roggers, an infant girl who had turned to look at Thorn with Helen Hunyadi's five-hundred-year-dead eyes. And then he had seen Giulio Boccalini, suffering with sword wounds and calling himself Gliddon, had helped Mary Magdalen to carry a small wrecked aircraft down a steep and pine-grown mountainside . . .

Dreams could sometimes be of real help. But Thorn had no reason to think that this afternoon's had included anything at all veridical.

He sat down near the phone again, waiting patiently for Joe's call. Age taught patience. In his solitude Thorn made no effort to look like anything but what he was. His chest performed no breathing motions. His eyes stared, blank and unblinking, staring perhaps at nothing. No part of his body moved, except for the fingers of his left hand, which played gently with the worn gold ring on the third finger of his right.

Last night, prowling alone through the Seabright mansion, Thorn had come upon a locked, plain, heavy door adjoining the subterranean art gallery. Naturally he had investigated, and had discovered beyond the door a rather extensive laboratory facility. He was no scientist, or technologist either, but had been able to identify in a general way a mass of photographic and video recording equipment. There were concealed see-throughs leading to the lounge-game room, so whatever went on there could be secretly recorded. The lab held other scientific equipment also, the purpose of which Thorn could not immediately fathom. It looked vaguely medical to

him. There was a small, almost cell-like anteroom
to the concealed laboratory. This anteroom contained a metal cot, folded now as if for storage, a
simple table and a chair. A toilet and shower were
in an adjoining cubicle; neither had been used for
some days.

A large wall safe in the laboratory, concealed
under a large but very minor painting, had room
enough inside to contain Thorn's whole body
once he had altered form enough to let him flow in
through the almost perfect sealing of its door.
There was no real light inside, but enough in-
frared radiation to let him see essentials. The safe
stored mostly cassettes of video tape, and canis-
ters of film. He opened one of the latter and
examined, as well as possible under the circumstances, the reel that it contained. He could
see enough frames of film, all showing nude figures in full color grappling orgiastically, to be
sure what kind of film it was.

Well, a Seabright porn factory. That was no real
surprise, after he had met Ellison. A private operation, no doubt; this family would hardly be in it
for the money.

Thorn stood outside the safe again, leaning a
newly resolidified hand upon the wood frame of
its concealing painting. The precautions seemed
somewhat exaggerated, in this day and age, to
hide mere porn. Was there some other angle, purpose, to the concealed records? Blackmail? But
that too now seemed rather outmoded. There was
something here that deserved thinking about. He
could come back later, if he decided it was important, and look again.

Right now he closed his eyes. Like the rest of the
house, these laboratory rooms had had many

people in them at various times in the past. He could not be specific about a number but he had the feeling that the number was surprisingly high. People had been paraded through here, he sensed suddenly, one at a time, several days or weeks or months apart, for a period of years. Most of them had been young, he thought. A certain flavor of the house of the Boccalini . . .

Upstairs in the mansion again, he prowled the silent hallway, which was lit by a backwash of outdoor security lights coming in through curtained windows on one side. He stopped at one closed bedroom door after another, trying to get a feeling for which room had been Helen Seabright's. He thought he could detect the aura of Mary Rogers' past occupancy in one bedroom. Ellison Seabright's gross snore obviated any need for subtlety in telling where he slept.

Here . . . in this room some young female, but not Mary, had spent a good deal of time a few months past. Thorn went in, through the crack of the closed door. The room had been stripped of almost all furnishings, but some things remained. Traces of young merriment, and fear . . . and considerable unhappiness . . . and just a touch of old perfume.

The occupant was certainly no one Thorn had ever known before. And she certainly had not been a vampire, either.

He found another room, one that had certainly been Delaunay Seabright's before the night of kidnapping and murder. This room too was now unused. Thorn stood in solid form in the center of its floor, mulling over in his mind the few photographs of the former occupant that had appeared at the time of the kidnapping and murder, when word of the painting's existence in the private Delaunay Seabright collection had first reached public print. Those pictures had shown Delaunay as having a fairly strong resemblance to his half-brother Ellison, though Ellison was ten or fifteen years younger.

The bedroom's furniture remained, perhaps because it was so massive, grandly antique. But the picture hangers on the walls were all empty now, and faint marks in a light layer of dust on some shelves showed where other objects had lately been removed; Ellison must be already scavenging. Any material object that might have helped Thorn to grasp the late owner's personality had, it seemed, already been removed. And this personality seemed harder to grasp than that of the dead girl. About all that was left was a little dust, some large impersonal furnishings, and shadows.

Thorn passed down the upstairs hall again, rather like a shadow himself, and silently entered the bedroom of Ellison Seabright. It was a guest room, really, but Ellison had made it his own. A snoring mound of body, clothed in an eastern garment of silken decadence, floated quite alone in a vast waterbed. Thorn did not gaze long upon this spectacle, but turned promptly to a door that connected this bedroom with another. With an anticipatory quickening of the pulse he entered the chamber he had been saving until last.

Stephanie Seabright's rumpled bed was empty. She sat nude in a soft chair before a softly lighted triple mirror, looking at her multiple images in the glass, and for a moment Thorn thought that she understood, had sensed his presence, and was waiting for him. Almost, he began to resume man-form. But he delayed a little, watching; and presently he understood that her attention was focused wholly on herself.

A luxurious robe was crumpled on the white carpet at Stephanie's feet. A small glass that smelled like pure vodka stood on the dressing table before her, bottle at hand to match.

Stephanie stood up suddenly, chair toppling behind her, and Thorn saw that what gripped her was fear. Not of him. She still had no awareness, conciously at least, that he was there. It was not a sudden fear, but one that had been growing, and still grew. Her attention was still on her own reflections.

Age was the terror.

Age, abetted by too much sun in some careless summer not too many summers past, was beginning to make the skin wrinkle. Here at the armpit when the arm was down, there at the corners of the eyes. Time soon to consider cosmetic surgery and all its implications. The shape of the breasts, even though they were small, hinted at sagging; the flesh on the thighs was no longer of perfect smoothness, but had begun to be slightly mottled with subcutaneous fat . . .

He could have appeared to her, a dim male figure standing or sitting in a pose devoid of menace, an apparition so gentle that she would not scream. He knew exactly how he might have done it. Experience rather than pride assured him that the seduction would be easy, and he could foresee its every move. Within an hour he would be able to taste her blood . . . she would perhaps begin to understand the centuries of youth that he could offer her . . . and she would tell him all she knew about the painting . . .

Which, unfortunately, would probably not be much.

Did his unknown opponent know him? Had it been calculated by that invisible but unavoidable foe that tonight Count Dracula would seduce Stephanie Seabright?

The man now calling himself Thorn could perceive, not far ahead of him in time and space, some blunder he must not make, a tripwire he must never touch. A life of half a thousand years well stocked with perils had taught his inner senses a great deal about danger, and had also taught his conscious mind to trust such inner warnings when they came. He must be careful, very careful now. He could be no more concrete about it than that. But the danger was vital. A trap, whether consciously set for him or not, lay there, not far ahead, and he had to identify it, move around it somehow, before he could advance. The phantom tripwire held him back, prevented his approaching Stephanie, prevented also his returning to the adjoining room and bluntly, brutally interrogating Seabright about the missing painting.

He waited long minutes in Stephanie's room, invisible, watching, waiting for a sign. Until weariness and vodka overcame her, and she clothed herself again in the rich robe that lay on the floor, and fell back, weeping, into her solitary bed.

Now, in his own solitary room at the hotel, Thorn played and replayed in memory the singularly unrewarding visit. Thoughts came and went, all of them discouragingly impractical. He had watched and listened to the news, and there was no word yet on the missing plane. A massive search was underway but everyone knew success was doubtful.

The tripwire was still there, he could feel it. Immunity to personal fear often made personal danger stand out with precise cold clarity when it came. And danger there was, in the near future, though just where and when he would encounter it he did not know.

Or could the instincts of half a thousand years be wrong for once, and he was confronting nothing but shadows? If a painted image could wring tears out of his eyes . . .

When the phone rang at last, Thorn roused from reverie with a quite human start. Outside the high windows the fires of day had dimmed considerably. Looking at his watch, he saw that hours had passed.

He lifted the instrument. "Thorn here."

Joe Keogh's voice said: "I found out from the archdiocese that Mary Rogers did work here in Chicago as you described. She's never had anything in the way of a criminal record in this state or any other. We'd know if she did, because she was so heavily investigated after the Phoenix killings. Everyone connected with that affair was. And you asked about Idaho; she did live out there in a convent for a couple of months, about two years ago. That's all I've been able to find out."

"I see. Thank you. And Mr. O'Grandison?"

"Well, he's something else, not exactly what you'd call a winner. He does have a record here in Illinois: marijuana user, cocaine user, no evidence that he's ever done any dealing. He's twenty-one now, according to our records; been in and out of juvenile homes and mental hospitals since he was twelve. No connection with illegal porn is shown; doesn't mean there couldn't be one, of course. Six months ago he was charged with contributing to delinquency—girl about fifteen years old who gave the name of Annie Chapman. But this girl disappeared from a detention home somehow before the case came to court, so it had to be dropped."

"Annie Chapman."

"You know her?"

"I do not think so, Joe." *A girl named Annie, just a runaway. She didn't count.* "Pray continue." The tone of Joe's voice had suggested to Thorn that news of importance was still to come.

"All right. I've talked to an officer on the force here who remembers O'Grandison. And he says O'Grandison was in the right time and place to have met Helen Seabright when she was here on her runaway. No evidence that he actually did, but he was on the scene or very near it."

"Annie Chapman too?"

"We don't know where she came from, what she might have been involved in, or where she went. There was some mixup at that juvenile home, evidently; they just let her walk out."

"Joe, you are sounding interested. Almost excited."

"That's a very big case out there, the Seabright thing, and now the missing treasure. I hope you meant it about giving me a tip when you can."

"Hmm. And where is Patrick O'Grandison now?"

Caution returned. "Why do you want to talk to him?"

"Joe, Joe, I have said that I mean him no harm."

Thorn smiled, very slightly. "Have I ever told you a lie?"

"Yes, goddam it, you have. Don't treat me like a kid."

The smile went away. "Have I ever lied, after pledging my solemn word?"

There was a sigh in the distance. "No, I'll give you that. Also I know you saved my life once, and Kate's . . . all right. My informant said he thought little Pat was still in town here. Are you coming after him?"

"Perhaps later, Joe; not immediately. Consider my word pledged on that much, if you like. I am busy with other matters."

"Listen." Joe's voice had altered. "Kate's told me that Judy's out there in the Southwest, for a summer school or camp or whatever they call it, near Santa Fe. Mountains, horseback, opera under the stars, and so on. I mention the fact only because I assume you know all about it already. I don't suppose there's any use my trying to talk to you about Judy, how young she is."

She had, as a matter of fact, recently turned eighteen; Thorn had sent a discreet birthday gift. (Ah, Mina, you must understand. He could do no less, seeing the family resemblance over four generations, seeing so much of you in her.)

"You are a truly moral man, Joseph." Thorn called him Joseph only rarely. "Thank you, you have been most helpful."

He hung up the phone. What Joe, like many other breathing people, failed to appreciate was how young all breathing women were—those utterly enticing creatures!—when seen from the viewpoint of an age of five hundred plus. Certainly differences exist between eighteen, say, and thirty-six, and again between thirty-six and seventy-two. But they are not really such great differences as breathing males seem to think. Delightfully subtle dissimilarities, rather, with the elder blood having its own bouquet, the blood of full womanhood its own of course, and of course in the young the sweet elixir of youth itself . . .

Still, Thorn thought dutifully, looking out the window into the burgeoning night, eighteen is rather young in these modern times, and actually Joe is right. He tried to make himself think solemnly about the problem.

Sometimes he thought that he would never live long enough to bring his own life under a proper measure of control.

Ten

Coming downstairs from the attic of the Palazzo Boccalini, Helen walked in front of me. Her hands were behind her back, her wrists looped with the thin chain, whose free end rested lightly in my grip. Her torn shift perforce gaped shamelessly. She looked as if she might be on her way to execution.

On the second flight of stairs we met the fat cousin, Allessandro, on his way up, candle in hand. He stopped at once, eyeing us inquisitively; evidently he had been impelled upstairs by curiosity as to just what games I might be playing with my gift.

"I have thought of a sport that needs some room," I told him, answering his quizzical look.

"In the courtyard," he suggested.

"Not room enough." It was not the Medici palace. "We will need the street."

Allessandro looked doubtful at that, but said nothing as he followed me down again. When we reached the ground floor I hailed the first male servant who came in view and gave bold orders for the front door to be opened. The masters of the house were already beginning to gather round, and looked at one another doubtfully. Watching them, the servant hesitated. But Helen was right on cue, displaying alarm at the prospect of being taken outside—the tall foreigner must at least have hinted to her, upstairs, what this new sport was to be like—and my adoptive cousins immediately warmed to the idea.

"Come on!" I roared. "Bugger the watch and the curfew. You don't mean to let them cheat you of some fun?"

Once I had put it in those terms, there was only one reply red-blooded youth could give. So far, at least, everything had been almost too easy. The night outside in the street was dark as tar, except for one feeble torch in a servant's unenthusiastic hand. "More lights!" I demanded, wishing for a distraction, and for some delay to let whatever Medici agents might be watching get themselves ready for action.

A manservant went back into the house for lights, reducing the odds minimally. I did not wait for his return; as soon as I had Helen facing the dark street in the direction I wanted, where there should be running room at least, if no active help, I gave two quick tugs on her chain. In a moment she had slipped her hands free of its loops and was off at top speed, running in desperate silence.

Watching the startled faces of the men around me, I tarried for a quick count of three and still got off in pursuit ahead of any of the others. My intent was to appear to be chasing Helen, at least until it became necessary to do more.

Helen ran with better speed than I had counted on, her white figure staying a little ahead of me in the darkness, maintaining a lead my long legs did not overcome. My drawn sword in my hand slowed me a little. I had taken off belt and all on entering the house, as a twentieth-century visitor might have doffed his hat, but then had routinely buckled the weapon on again as I came out.

Before I had run ten strides, shouts shattered the night behind me. A great alarm was going up, drunken voices, in which merriment was still the dominant tone, bawling for more torches. But not everyone, unfortunately, insisted on waiting for more light. Two pairs of feet were pounding after us, and one of these pursuers was already getting uncomfortably close. Meanwhile, ahead of me, Helen's first burst of speed was faltering. Fear indeed lends wings, but chaining and hunger are not the best of training regimens.

No use trying to delay what must now be done. I stopped and turned abruptly and cut at the nearest sportsman, aiming low for the legs. My blade bit bone, and with a loud cry he went sprawling. My second pursuer was drawn and ready for me when he came running up. He was evidently an armed professional retainer of some kind, and managed to delay me in masterly style, our swords conversing almost invisibly in the near darkness, whilst he bawled for help. But his allies behind him still dawdled, clamoring for their precious torches.

At last I got home with a thrust to the midsection, and was able to turn and run away again. Behind me the cries of my latest victim went up alarmingly, mingled with a new uproar from dogs safe behind stone walls. There was no hope now of avoiding a pursuit in deadly earnest. But of course I very soon had to slow my flight, begin to grope my way slowly, meanwhile calling the girl's name loudly as I dared. I added in her own language such assurances as I could think of, and prayed that she had had the wit and nerve to stop and wait for me, or else that some of the Medici men had come to her aid.

There were actually, as I later learned, no Medici men on hand. Their sole spy on the scene had stayed prudently where he could keep a good watch on the Boccalini. But fortune and the saints smiled upon us anyway. Helen's voice, a ghost-whisper of softness, replied at last to one of my more urgent hisses, and presently her small hand came reaching out of darkness to touch mine. I sheathed my sword and took it. "Can you find the way," I whispered, "to the workshop of the artist called Verrocchio."

"Yes." She paused as if surprised. "Yes, I think so." A moment more to get her bearings, and she tugged at my hand and we were off. Helen had been in the city longer than I had, had walked in it much more, and so had greater knowledge of its streets. More dogs awoke behind the walls surrounding us; but behind us the enemy were still organizing, perhaps suspecting some trap, at any rate not ready to dash recklessly off into the dark.

We turned corners; the sounds of their preparations fell behind us and disappeared. I began to breathe a little easier.

"Why are we going to Verrocchio?" The king's sister was not shy of asking questions.

"They know us there, and are friendly. It has been arranged."

Helen said nothing more at the time, but led me through alleys and narrow ways, until we emerged upon a broader street almost at the painter's door, having met no one en route. It took a minute of rapping with my dagger hilt to get any answer at all from within the studio, and somewhat longer than that to get the master of the house roused and brought to the door. Then, however, it was opened for us promptly enough. Verrocchio, candlestick in hand, alarm showing in his heavy features, his gross body wrapped in a fine robe, motioned us hastily in; we were already past him. After one last fearful glance into the darkness, he closed the portal quickly behind us.

"Send word at once that we are here," I ordered him, thinking it unnecessary to specify to whom word should be sent. Then turning to the gaping servants and apprentices, I demanded: "Bring decent garments for this girl at once." The help all stumbled away hastily under my glare, wrapped in whatever oddments of bedcovers and clothing they had grabbed when the alarms began, the younger apprentice tugging the bearded one by the arm to get him moving. Leonardo, who slept at home, was of course not in the group. Helen meanwhile stood quietly at my side, waiting for whatever might happen next.

"What happened?" Verrocchio blurted to me, then looked as if he did not really want to know. He turned his head and called after his retreating staff: "Perugino, there is a message you must carry!"

I took the candle from the master's shaking hand, and set it on a table, and seated myself there. I did not bother to answer his question. Helen, at my gesture, seated herself next to me.

The bearded apprentice was back in a few moments, fully clothed. As he was unbarring the front door again, ready to go out, I detained him with some words of caution. If he should have the bad luck to be collared by the watch for breaking curfew, he was to say that he carried an urgent business message for the Medici, and demand to be escorted to their house; and if it should become necessary to tell the watchmen any more than that, he could add that the message concerned a painting of the Magdalen. He gave me a look of fear and desperation mingled, and hurried out as soon as I released his sleeve.

Verrocchio and I barred up the door again. When I turned back to the table, Helen was gone—into a back room to change her dress, an old woman servant assured me. I sat down again to wait. In a minute or two Helen was back, and as she re-emerged into the light of the candle on the table I rose unconsciously to my feet. What they had given her to put on was the very gown of the painting.

"It's all we have that really fits her, sir," muttered the old woman, a little perturbed by my reaction.

"Never mind . . . it is all right . . . it is beautiful. Now, bring us something to eat and drink. Biscuits, wine, whatever."

Again Helen, my unknowing bride-to-be, sat down with me at table. The dress that had appeared glorious in dim candleglow at the far side of the room was not as glorious seen close up. Faded, somewhat worn, a little dirty here and there, tired with the flesh of many models.

Paintings, stacked in racks along the far walls of the room, regarded us with dim eyes. Verrocchio, still nervous, joined us at table when I gestured. He was still wrapped in his fine robe. Biscuits and spiced and watered wine were brought, in fine dishes and crystal goblets that were doubtless used ordinarily only as artists' props. I sipped wine, but after all did not feel much like eating. Helen, after days of hunger, was not going to let any opportunity pass. Noting her appetite, I counseled myself that tomorrow I should begin to limit her intake; I had no wish for a fat wife.

Only after my drowsy thoughts had reached

this banal conclusion did I realize that I had decided a matter of considerable importance, without ever giving it full conscious thought.

"Why are we waiting here?" Helen asked me, between measured mouthfuls of her second biscuit.

"For some friends to join us." I wondered how much more to say, and sighed. She was going to have to be told at some point, and the telling really could not be put off much longer. "Including one who is a priest."

At that Helen looked bewildered. I glanced meaningfully at Verrocchio, who with apparent relief stood up and left the table and the room. The girl and I were alone with the dim-eyed paintings.

I met her darkly puzzled gaze. "The priest is coming here to marry us," I informed her.

Comprehension grew by degrees in Helen's eyes. Never shall I forget how she looked on that first night we were together, sitting at that rude table. (Mina, my beloved, you will understand.) The model's gown, begrimed by use like all the women who had worn it, yet held some glory in its rich brocade. Her hard, small fingers, crumbling a biscuit. Her beaten, hunted, haunted face, so young. Her bare feet worn with the stones of Florence, with the hard roads of half of Europe. Her wild and filthy hair. Leonardo should have been on hand *that* night, and so should Goya.

As understanding grew in Helen's eyes they shifted from mine, to go staring past me at the wall. She raised a dirty hand and bit its thumbnail. Looking for the moment even younger than her years, she slowly began to weep, tears streaking down her cheeks.

Now this was a reaction that I could scarcely

take as complimentary. But it was obviously no calculated insult either, and somewhat to my own surprise I was not angry. I had understanding enough to realize that she wept for her whole ruined life, in which my portion was so far quite a minor one. So I only waited, silently, till she should be ready to talk to me again.

At last the tears stopped, and in a little while the silent sobs. Helen's eyes came back to me, and when she spoke again her voice was under good control. "Matthias allows me no alternative." Though stated flatly, it was really a question.

I shrugged. "Of course it is nearly always possible to kill oneself. But I think that if that path held any attraction for you, you would have taken it ere now." My first wife had in fact traveled the route under discussion, in a fit of madness two years earlier, her point of departure being my castle roof. I thought that I had learned to recognize the signs; I saw them not in Helen.

My blunt comment had made her look at me in a new way again. Now, you must understand that it was not my intention to be cruel. Cruelty I understood; I was, alas, already expert in inflicting pain, as well as undergoing it, and I could have been much more fiendish than that if I had tried. No, my apparent callousness was really intended to be helpful; and I still think it helped her more than if I had tried. or pretended to be kind. For Helen I was a hard rock rearing up suddenly out of the treacherous bog of life, a rock that as not going to be put aside for her own purposes. But, on the other hand, this stony intrusion offered firmness and support; she could cling to it, for long enough to catch her breath at least, without fear that it was going to sink. Nor was it going to attack her treacherously; it would never turn harder and crueler than it looked.

Helen's eyes fell to the table, to the bread and wine that had come to her through me. She looked up at the rustic but sturdy roof-poles of the shelter that I had brought her to. She rubbed the chain-sores on her ankle, and pulled the worn and gaudy gown a little more closely round her body. "What has the king promised you, in return for marrying me?"

"Nothing specific. That I will have an honorable position somewhere is implied, understood between us." At least I hoped that the king agreed with my understanding on that point.

"And what about me? Am I to be put back into the convent as soon as we are wed? Or what is the arrangement?"

"No convent. And there is no arrangement, except that you are to be my wife." I looked her over thoughtfully. "The ceremony will be here. Directly afterwards we will proceed, with some kind of protective escort, to a gracious house not far away. There you will have a bath." (Bathing, contrary to popular belief in the twentieth century, was as well thought of in that day as in this, at least among the well-to-do.) "And I expect we will remain in that house for a day or two, being hospitably entertained, if I know anything of our hosts."

Helen was looking at me with a measure of disbelief. I went on: "After that—well, what comes after that has yet to be decided. But I can promise that as my wife you will be treated with respect. And I think I can promise that from now on you will be well fed." There were a few more things, of great importance, that I meant to say to

Helen; but I judged that the saying of them could wait till after the ceremony was over.

It was my turn to be judged by her; a king's daughter and a king's sister looked through the grime. You are of good birth, then. Yes, I might have known that my brother would not marry me to a churl, whatever else . . . well, my lord Wladislaus the Romanian, or whatever I should name you . . . but that is not a Romanian name, is it? I hope you gain the reward that you are counting on for all these efforts and sacrifices to please my brother."

Her manner implied her doubt that I would gain much. And the king's sister looked long and boldly into my eyes, trying to puzzle me out. I continued to study her, with the same object. For whatever reason, the feeling grew in me that my decision had been correct. When at last Verrocchio peeked into the room again, I signed to him that we no longer required privacy, and he hesitantly rejoined us.

But before he could cough up any of the questions that must have been troubling him, horses were stamping in the street just outside his door. Presently another dagger-hilt came rapping on the wood. This time I answered the knock myself, and a moment later was joyfully letting in Lorenzo. Helen had been in Florence long enough to recognize the young tycoon on sight, and her eyes widened.

Immediately young Lorenzo, smiling, fresh, and good-natured at an hour that would now be called three in the morning, took me aside and heard from me privately the full story of our escapade. He did not trouble to hide his glee when I came to describe the street fighting; that several of his rivals in business had been pricked with sharp weapons did not grieve him in the least. As soon as this brief confidential talk between the two of us was over, he went back to the street door and opened it again. In a moment we were joined by a sleepy friar, just dismounted and scratching his backside. Ten or a dozen horses were gathered outside the door, and I could hear the low voices of other men; Lorenzo would never have come on such a mission in the dead of night without a good escort.

The friar asked few questions and showed no surprise, being evidently experienced in matters of intrigue. As evidence of Medicean forethought he had come armed with all necessary holy dispensations, civil permits, writs, blessings and the like, enough spiritual and bureaucratic armament to have wed two Barbary apes on short notice had such a union appeared desirable. Only on one point was he in the least anxious, and I hastened to assure him that the formalities of my own conversion from the Eastern to the Roman Rite had been accomplished ere I left Hungary.

The bearded apprentice had managed, somehow, somewhere, to gather an armful of flowers in the middle of the night, and came to present them to Helen. She appeared quite touched. The younger lad had at last found her a pair of respectable shoes that almost fit, for which I thanked him. Verrocchio did not seem to know quite what he ought to do about a wedding gift; if he would keep his mouth shut afterwards, I thought, that would be quite enough. In the end he gave each of us a gold ring, making sure Lorenzo saw the gesture. And so finally my bride and I were standing before the friar, the menials all dismissed, a wor-

ried Verrocchio as one witness, and Lorenzo-
the-Magnificent-to-be, nodding benignly, as the
other.

Helen was taking it all quite well, I noted with
cautiously increasing optimism. At least she
spoke the required words in a firm, clear voice: "I,
Helen Hunyadi, of the household and family of
Matthias, King of Hungary—"

Then it was my turn. "I, Vlad, son of Vlad
Drakulya and of his household, Prince of
Wallachia—"

I had surprised Helen one more time. Without
taking my gaze from the priest I saw her face turn
up to me.

Eleven

"It's very nice of you to help out," said Mary Rogers, her blue eyes looking up trustfully at Thorn as he unlocked and opened for her the right-side door of his rented Blazer. Her strong legs in worn blue jeans swung her athletically up into the vehicle. "Robby had to take the Ford," she added, when Thorn had gone round to his own doorway on the driver's side and was climbing in.

"I understand." Thorn first secured his seat belt properly—his sometimes ferocious conflicts with machinery were never *his* fault—and then put the key into the ignition. Presently he was driving down the swooping ramp from the hotel garage, squinting through sunglasses as he pulled into the city street awash with the molten daylight of late afternoon. The sun itself, he had made sure, was safely behind some buildings. It would not be getting any higher today. Robinson Miller, whose more-or-less-gainful employment was with the local Public Defender's office, was working late this evening, visiting on his own time with clients said to be in great need. And a couple of hours ago Mary had received a phone call from the Seabright house. A woman on the staff there, a Mrs. Dorlan, who Mary had apparently got to know during her residence at the mansion, had told her that her remaining belongings were ready to be picked up.

"She sounded sort of in a hurry. Why they're all of a sudden in such a hurry to get rid of the stuff, I don't know. Cleaning house, I guess. But I feel

more comfortable going over there if I have someone with me. And you did volunteer earlier."

"I assuredly did." That of course had been before his first visit to the mansion, when he was
still looking for an invitation of some kind, any
kind, to let him cross the Seabright threshold. But
now he welcomed any good reason to be alone
with Mary.

She said: "I suppose they'll just have the stuff
piled out on the porch. There isn't very much."

Thorn snarled faintly at an errant Volkswagen.
"I take it you have not yet told Helen's mother of
that strange telephone call?"

"Stephanie's not much of a mother. A nasty
thing to say but it's true. Anyway I don't think
she'd talk to me. I could write her a note about the
call but she'd never believe it."

Thorn did not argue that. "Then I suppose you
have not informed the police, either."

Mary was studying him. "No, we haven't. You
said something about an official connection that
you have. I'd like to know what you found out
through that."

"Not much. Confirmation of things you had
already told me. No hint that Helen might be still
alive." The last sentence seemed to echo in his
mind when he had spoken it. But he had settled
that.

"Damn." She was obviously disappointed. And
worried. "Well. Whoever it was, she didn't sound
like she was in any immediate danger. So if it was
Helen, I guess she can call home for herself any
time she wants to. If it wasn't . . . I can't imagine
who it might have been. Or why they'd want to
play such a trick."

The rest of the ride out to the wealthy suburbs

passed for the most part in silence. This evening no one was manning the mansion's great iron gates. But still the gates were locked.

"I don't understand. They knew I was coming out tonight."

Half a minute of intermittent horn-blowing at last produced a smallish man, in yardworker's clothes, hurrying over the lawns from the direction of the tree-screened house.

"Oh," Mary said. "It's Dorlan." She waved to him through the gate.

The little man, peering from inside, seemed to know Mary too, though he offered no real greeting. "Didn't recognize the car," he mumbled, and set about unlocking the gate and rolling it open by hand.

"Mr Dorlan, this is Mr. Thorn, a friend of mine. He just came along to give me a hand with the things."

Dorlan, who had not been visible on either of Thorn's previous visits, nodded grudgingly. "I'll just ride up to the house with you and let you in."

"Let us in?" Mary echoed in an uncertain voice.

"They've all moved out," replied Dorlan. There was a kind of grim shyness in his manner, and he did not look directly at either of his visitors. He left them momentarily to shut and lock the gate again, after Thorn had driven the Blazer in.

"Moved out?" Mary asked him blankly when he came back.

"Me and the Missus are the only ones left. We're leaving in the morning. The rest of the staff all got paid off. Mr. and Mrs. Seabright are gone to Santa Fe."

Thorn made a faint hissing noise, almost a sigh. Otherwise he made no comment. The Blazer rolled along the graveled drive with Dorlan perched in the small rear seat. Mary looked vacantly at the house as it appeared from behind the screens of palms and citrus. The portico was empty. "My things?"

"Still inside, up in your old room. They told me to get 'em out on the porch before you come, but I ain't had time."

Thorn stopped near the front of the house. Sunset was still lingering in the second floor's west windows. "The move is permanent?" he asked.

"Far as I know. They want all their mail forwarded. This place is being closed up. Though I hear Ellison's the owner now."

Mary opened her door and hopped out briskly. "Well, I'm just as glad. I don't want to look at him again. At any of them."

Thorn got out too, followed by Dorlan, who was now looking intently at the taller man, as if fascinated despite himself. Dorlan yawned suddenly. "Damn tired," he complained. "Worked all day. No friggin' air conditioning this afternoon. Power's off in the main house already."

"Very tiring," agreed Thorn. "You will be glad to get to sleep." He extended a hand, palm up, while Mary watched in growing puzzlement.

"I'll say." Dorlan fumbled a set of keys loose from a chain at his belt, and handed them over. He yawned again, and tottered to the portico, where he leaned against one of its imitation Doric columns. A moment later he sat down. His eyes had closed.

"*Oh dear*," said Mary, and fell silent, forgetting whatever comment she had been about to make. A large mastiff had just appeared at the corner of the house. From her days in residence she remembered the beast as an unpleasant and dangerous watchdog. It was staring at them intently and a low vibration of warning issued from its throat.

"Quiet," said Thorn softly. Mary had no doubt that he was talking to her, but instantly the dog's growling trailed off. It leaned forward, as if about to charge, or topple, in their direction. Then somehow there was a change of plan. The great head, ears askew, turned away from them. The dog sniffed the gathering dusk. Then it turned round twice in place, scratched at an ear, and lay down peacefully.

A faint snore arose from Dorlan, who sat leaning against his post. Mary looked from one phenomenon to the other, and seemed to be trying to think of some suitable comment. She was evidently unable.

Keys jingled briskly in Thorn's fingers. "Come. I should like to see the room you occupied." He unlocked the great front door and pushed it open, and like some old courtier bowed Mary in ahead of him. She found herself accepting the bow as something perfectly natural.

The house was filled with what felt like an unnatural heat—it was only the day's heat that had crept in through fallen defenses, Mary realized, but it felt strange in rooms where she had never known anything but cool comfort. Out of habit she flicked a light switch in the cavernous great hall—nothing happened, of course. But enough daylight remained to see that a start had been made at covering up furniture, getting the place ready for some extended period of inoccupancy.

With Thorn at her side Mary crossed the great, silent hall, heading away from the study and the elevator, toward the foot of the broad main stairway. But when she reached the stair she stopped. "I haven't been back here since—that night. Oh, I came back once with the police, re-enacting what I could remember for them. But . . ."

"But it all comes back to you much more strongly now."

"Yes, you're right, it does." She shivered.

"Good. Very good. Shall we go up?"

Mary wanted to protest that it was not very good at all, that she was growing frightened. But she would not be a coward. She would get her property that she had come here for, and then she would leave, if possible before the darkness thickened any further. She started up the shadowed stair. Thorn's feet, closely following, were inaudibly light.

As I was going up the stair
I met a man who wasn't there . . .

How did it go? Something like that, anyway. Actually she was quite glad for his tall, silent presence. It was not this man she feared. She hadn't realized, or had lately forgotten, that when she lived here she had felt real fear of certain other people in the house. In her imagination she could see Ellison Seabright now at the head of the stairs, as he had been standing on that night, looking down at her . . . and behind Ellison, another and truly terrifying figure that came and went before Mary knew who it was, and maybe she didn't want to know . . . even only in her imagination . . .

She half-stumbled near the top of the stairs, and Thorn's hand came to support her elbow neatly. "Thank you," Mary murmured. "God, yes, you were right. How it all comes back . . ."

"Your bedroom," said Thorn, interrupting a silent pause, "must have been down this corridor, on the right."

"Yes. But how did you know?"

Thorn was pacing slowly away, not answering. He reached a door and pushed it open, and stood in the hallway inspecting the dim interior thoughtfully.

"That wasn't mine."

"Delaunay's."

"How could you have known?" She came up beside Thorn; the room he was gazing into was so dark it was impossible to see anything. "Oh, of course, some of the magazines published plans of the whole layout, didn't they? There was so much publicity. I'm glad that's finally beginning to be over."

"What was Delaunay like?" Thorn was looking into the room as if to read its very shadows.

"Oh . . . big. Not quite as big as Ellison, and five years older, but there was a fairly strong resemblance. Physically, I mean, of course, that's all. Del was a kind old man, shy of publicity. He was always kind to me, anyway. He came here from Australia when he was very young. He still had something Aussie, as he called it, in his speech at times. He and Ellison had the same father, different mothers."

"How was the family wealth amassed?"

"I'm really not sure. Somewhere a couple of generations back, I guess. Del built up the fortune even more during his lifetime. He never seemed to me to be the tycoon type, you know, mean, agressive, a go-getter. But I guess things could have been different when he was young." Mary seemed about to add something but then decided against it. Thorn thought that for once her mouth closed prematurely.

"What?" he prompted. .

"I . . . well, I shouldn't say it. But sometimes I wondered about him."

"Oh? In what way?"

"Well . . . just that I didn't think he could have been as nice to everyone as he was to me. He was just a little bit too good. Oh, that's a rotten thing for me to say after he was so generous to me and all. But you know what I mean?"

Thorn nodded encouragingly. "Perhaps I do."

Once over the hump, Mary plunged on. "Look, I've known one or two people, in religious orders, who I thought were really saintly. It's not all that common there, believe me. But there were one or two who I wouldn't be surprised if they were canonized someday. They were really good. They had a, a kind of joy about them. Well, I never felt like that about Del. He went through all the motions of being very good, with me at least, playing the role of this extremely nice old man. But . . ." Mary, with a helpless gesture, despaired of saying it just right.

"But," supplied Thorn, "he could have been acting."

Mary sighed and moved away from Del's room, going down the corridor, her steps picking up briskness as she went. "It's wrong of me to talk like that. He really gave me that Verrocchio."

"Did he, indeed? Then where is it?"

But Mary had been distracted. Halfway to her old room, walking the thickly padded, silent carpet, her steps moved irregularly to one side, as if in some involuntary reaction.

Thorn took her again by the elbow, gently stopping her forward progress. "Where did you find the murdered girl?"

Mary had backed up against the wall and was staring at the floor just in front of her feet. Now her voice was a mere whisper. "Her legs were stretched out in this direction. Like she had been running, and then was shot from behind, and just fell forward, you know? But she must have been turning her head to look behind her just as she was shot, because her face caught it. The whole front part of her head was . . . I couldn't have identified her face, no one could. But otherwise it looked like Helen. She had on a white robe of Helen's, and there weren't any other young girls around. At least not as far as I knew."

"Annie Chapman?"

Mary tried to read Thorn's eyes; he had taken off his sunglasses at last, but the dim light made it hard. She said: "That's the name that . . . the girl on the phone mentioned. I swear to you I never heard of any Annie Chapman, not until we got that crazy call. I've been racking my brain trying to remember, and the name means nothing. But since then I've been thinking . . ."

"Yes?"

"Well, maybe Delaunay wasn't as good, as perfect, as he let on to me. And I know he was involved with trying to help runaways; or he told me he wanted to get involved with it anyway—"

"What are you trying to say, Mary?"

"Well. Maybe—ordinarily he'd have told me, or Helen would have told me, if they were giving shelter to some other kid. But maybe, well, maybe he—just had a girl in his room for the night."

"I suppose it would not be terribly surprising." Thorn sounded faintly, fondly amused. "Men of good repute have done even stranger and more wicked things than that."

"I know," Mary agreed uncertainly. She was looking down at the carpet again. "She—the girl, whoever it was—was lying right about here. Somehow they've cleaned up all the bloodstains. The white robe she was wearing had fallen open, and I could see she didn't have anything underneath it. Helen told me once that she had taken to sleeping that way, in the raw, ever since she'd been on the road."

"Mary, I would like to hear your story of that night from the beginning. According to the news accounts—were they at all accurate?"

"Pretty much, I guess." Mary's brashness had been fading steadily. Her voice was now almost a child's.

"According to them you heard noise, ran from your room, and came upon the dead girl. What happened next?"

"I—it's hard for me—"

"Go back and start again, Mary. You were asleep."

The pattern in the carpet before her eyes was being melted by the onrush of night outside the windows, disappearing into darkness. She didn't want the fixed pattern to go. She held onto it desperately, resisting the voice of Thorn.

"I want you to go back and start again, Mary. Go back—"

In sudden fear, Mary turned toward him. Her hands folded themselves like the hands of a woman praying, or diving into deep water, and in a moment she had completed a soft lunging motion that brought her face into secure hiding against his chest. "Hold me," she murmured.

His hands held her, and they were warm. But his voice was inexorable. "Go back. You were asleep."

I can't do it. Her protest was silent, but vehement as any shout, and she knew that it was heard.

"I will help you. You are under my protection now. I would not ask it if it were not important. Will you not help me to find out the truth about Helen?"

Mary dared not open her eyes. If she looked up her eyes might meet his.

"Go through it all. Once more, with my help, through it all, and that will make an end to it. An end to the bad dreams that now plague you almost every night."

Surprise tricked Mary into looking up. "How did you know that?"

His eyes were hard to see. But it was hard to look away from them again.

"No," Mary said once more. But she knew that the force of her protest was failing.

Mary was sleeping, something she still did most comfortably and deeply in her old nun-pajamas. And even as she slept it seemed to her (though with some fitfully active portion of her mind she simultaneously knew better) that Thorn was unreal, that his talk in the dark mansion with her was nothing but a fading dream. A dream from which she would presently awake, to find herself in her own sunlit room, the bedroom next to Helen's. When Mary awoke it would be cheerful morning, and she would be surrounded and defended by all the safe wealth of the Seabright house . . .

. . . and into her sleep there tore a fist of shot-gun noise. The roar slammed against her bedroom door from the outside, jarring Mary instantly awake. Her eyes flew open to register dark mid-night, only accented by the pale dial of the bed-side clock.

Whatever that slam of sound had been, it must mean that something was terribly wrong. Adrena-lin propelled Mary out of bed, grabbing in reflex for the red robe that lay as usual over a nearby chair. One arm in a sleeve of the robe, struggling to sleeve the other, she flung open her bedroom door and ran out into the hallway. Here the dark-ness was less intense; as usual some muted il-lumination was coming in through the hall win-dows from the security lights that ringed the ex-terior of the house. Somewhere out there now the mastiff, and another watchdog, were raging futilely.

A few steps down the hall, a white bundle lay on the floor. Mary ran to it, and stopped when one of her bare toes touched warm stickiness on the carpet.

Vaguely she was aware of sniffing the unfamil-iar stink of burnt explosive. She could see the white thing on the floor quite plainly now, but in a state of new shock she was still trying to make sense of the world in which this white murdered thing could have existence. There were urgent human voices, not far away, saying—Mary could not quite make out what. She hardly raised her eyes. She still had not moved when vague figures walking the darkness, two coming from her right, one from her left, closed in to bracket her. A ski-masked man standing at her left was pointing a

long-barreled firearm of some kind right at her
midsection. Mary's belly shrank toward her
backbone.

Delaunay Seabright, also in robe over pajamas,
slippers on his feet, was standing at Mary's right.
Another ski-masked man was holding the muzzle
of another, shorter weapon against the back of
Delaunay's head.

"Mary," Delaunay said. There was only a small
tremor in his voice, which was basically calm and
careful. "Mary? Do what they say."

"Oh. Uh."

"Mary. Listen to me. Keep control of yourself."

To this at last she gave some kind of an assent.

As if he had been waiting to see what her reaction would be, the masked man holding his gun at
Del's uncombed gray head now spoke for the first
time: "Move along."

The other gunman gestured and prodded Mary
ahead of him, toward the descending stairs. Turning briefly, a few steps down, Mary saw that Ellison and Stephanie had come out of their rooms
and were watching. They had stopped as if the
first sight of the gunmen had petrified them in
their tracks. One of the masked men had turned
round too, and was motioning silently for Ellison
and Stephanie to follow—keeping them, Mary
thought, in sight, away from telephones.

As Ellison obeyed, advancing slowly, he moved
into a patch of security light from one of the hall
windows and Mary got a look at his face. It was a
good look.

She was prodded again, and turned, proceeding down the stairs.

At the foot of the stairs, on the floor of the great
hall, some of the household staff were assembled,

as for a called meeting. Not pausing in his slow descent, the man who was pointing a gun at Mary raised his voice, including them all as he recited a small speech.

"You'll be hearing from us about Delaunay Seabright. Getting him back is gonna cost you a lot of money. But this woman here"—a gun barrel poked Mary's back—"is just insurance. Now get this clear. I don't want to see police cars following us—we'll leave her brains on the pavement for them to run over. I don't want to see or hear no choppers overhead—they'll see us put her out of the car doing eighty. We got high explosives out there in our truck too—if worst comes to worst we'll go that way, and take both these people with us. We got all the cards. That girl on the floor upstairs is there because she ran, she panicked, and to show that we mean business.

"Got all that? Remember? Don't forget to explain it all to the pigs when you call 'em in."

Mary had turned her head slightly again. Ellison Seabright understood, all right. All too well, as Mary saw. Oh, Ellison's face was controlled, but Ellison's face *knew*. He was frightened, perhaps, but neither surprised or terrorized. When one of the masked gunmen looked at him, he nodded, twice, and that was the only objective sign of his complicity in the plot that Mary had been able to name to the police later. Other people probably nodded, too. But as she watched him there grew in Mary the incommunicable certainty of his guilt. He had known all along that his brother was going to be kidnapped tonight, and Ellison was very glad beneath his fright.

Mary and Delaunay went helplessly the rest of the way down the stairs, passing among the motionless, helpless servants to the great front door. Now in an alcove at the far side of the great hall one man of the household staff was observed in the act of trying to pick up a phone.

"Put it down, you, put it down! Or we kill her right here, and take one of you in her place."

The butler put it down.

Then Mary, Delaunay, and the two kidnappers had passed through the front door and were outside. The great dogs were still savaging the air with their noise, fenced away (by sheer accident, it was later testified) where they could not get at the marauders. The night was a warm one for so early in the spring. On the gravel drive there waited in darkness a late model pickup truck with an elongated cab containing a rear seat. The vehicle was tall as a Blazer, with high road clearance, standing on grotesquely rugged all-terrain tires. Mary was prodded up into the back seat, then pushed down into a crouching position on the floor between the front seat and the back. Her whole body was forced into the narrow space where people riding in the rear seat would ordinarily have some trouble fitting in their legs and feet. The cab was broad, the front seat evidently had plenty of room for three, big Del included. A burlap cloth, under the circumstances an effective blind, was thrown over Mary. Doors slammed. Then one of the abductors, leaning back from the front seat in what must have been a strained position, dug a gunbarrel joylessly into her elevated rump.

"No jokes, Seabright. You understand that? I'll blow her ass right off."

"I understand."

The truck's engine roared. Gravel flew up from

the drive to bang the fenders. In moments they were on paved road, having passed through a front gate that was obviously being held open somehow. Almost from the very start of the ride, Mary lost track of where they were. Different types of pavement roared under the rough, speeding tires, but she could not think coherently to tell what the changes signified. Now they must be on some main highway, for speed was constant. The heavy-duty shock absorbers in this off-road vehicle made even the highway ride a relatively rough one, kept death's obscene metal organ jiggling against her body. From time to time there was a little talk of some kind among the three men; Mary could hear murmuring but in the roar of rough tires and racing engine she could not understand a word.

With heartfelt fervor she recited prayers, and fragments of prayers, that yesterday she would not have been able to remember. The ride remained continuously fast; there was little traffic to contend with in these lost hours of the morning, and as far as Mary could tell there were no pursuers either.

In Mary's original experience the ride had been mercilessly long, containing lifetimes of terror. But duration in this reliving was somehow modified, her time in the back seat cut short. Moving cautiously in her cramped, aching position, she registered the fact that at some recent time the gunbarrel had been removed from her flank. She tilted her head under the burlap, enough to see that dawn had begun to filter into the cab. By now the truck had slowed somewhat from its headlong highway rush. It seemed to be jouncing at thirty miles an hour or so over an unpaved road.

The vehicle, without slowing, turned rather sharply. It slowed down, then, and turned again, with a shifting of gears. The men in front had been silent now for a long time. Now Mary felt a perceptible tilting. The road must be climbing rather steeply. Turning, climbing, shifting, went on for another unmeasurable time. Mary was taken completely by surprise when brakes brought the vehicle to a halt and the engine was turned off.

She didn't try to move immediately; she wasn't sure she would be able. The door behind her opened, and cold air rushed into the cab along with the new day's light. Now her burlap cover was pulled off. Groaning, she tried to rise on her numbed arms and legs.

She was alone in the truck. The men had got out already and were standing together just outside. Del's head was bowed, his gray hair disheveled. The vehicle had been parked on a steep slope, so it looked almost in danger of tipping sideways. It stood on a segment of primitive road, whose ruts were cut so deeply as to be impassable to an ordinary car. On all sides grew tall trees, the vague shade of their needled branches dimming the predawn whiteness of the sky. One of the masked men, standing just outside the downhill door, reached to take Mary by the arm as soon as she had risen halfway on her deadened limbs. He half-helped, half-pulled her out.

The other gunman stood patiently pointing his long-barreled weapon right at the midsection of Delaunay Seabright, whose hands, Mary now saw, had been bound behind him. Del had raised his head and was looking at Mary. Across some tremendous gulf, as it seemed to her. The man who held her arm dragged her away from the

truck. Her legs were barely functional. They
crossed a space of thin tree growth that could
hardly be called a clearing, and approached a
small, weathered cabin that Mary did not see until
it was only twenty feet away.

"Mary," Del called after her in a hollow voice.
"Chin up. You'll get out of this."

She glanced back at him, but could think of
nothing to call out in return. One of her bare feet
trod on a patch of hard-frozen snow. They were
somewhere high in the mountains, toward
Flagstaff. The cabin was almost invisible under
the tall pines and fir. Its door squeaked loudly in
the still mountain air as the man with Mary
yanked it open. Darkness still ruled inside, and
when the door shut again behind her, full night
had returned. There seemed to be no windows in
the rude shack, no openings at all besides the
single door. She stumbled ahead across an earth-
en floor, trying to make her legs start working
properly, rubbing her arms. Near one wall her feet
found stones suggesting the remnants of a hearth.
She bent, groping, to discover a fireplace of sorts,
a chimney. The aperture was much to small for
her to think of trying to force herself inside.

Suddenly the door behind her was opened
again, letting in some light. One of the masked
men, wearing a holstered pistol and carrying a
hunting knife along with some lengths of cord,
came in. He said nothing. Repressing an urge to
struggle, to scream pointlessly, Mary let him tie
her hands behind her back, her ankles firmly together.

When the job of binding her was done, tightly,
the man went out again and vanished from sight
somewhere, leaving the door open. Standing in

the middle of the cabin floor, she could see just
the rear end of the truck, protruding from behind a
thick double tree-trunk. Delaunay was standing
near the large tree. His robe was open in front, so
he must be cold in his pajamas. His hands were
still behind his back, and his ankles had been tied
now too, so that when he turned toward Mary and
the cabin the movement was an awkward shuffle.
The second masked demon was still looking over
Del's shoulder from behind.

"Mary?" Del called again. "Are you all right?"
The real concern in his voice was plain.

"So far," Mary managed to get out. It seemed
that under present conditions such trivia as
wrenched joints, numbed limbs, chills, and nervous exhaustion did not deserve notice.

The man standing behind Del poked him with
something, making him sway forward. Then he
inched a little closer to the cabin in his bound-
ankle shuffle. He cleared his throat. "Mary, they
tell me the plan is this. You are to be left here,
tied up but unharmed. They'll phone the police
and tell them where you can be found. Returning
you safely in this way is meant to show that I'll be
safely returned, too, as soon as the ransom's paid.
Details about the ransom will be passed along
soon. Right?" Del turned his head to ask the question; the mask behind him nodded.

Del went on: "Neither you nor I have seen these
men's faces, Mary. We've hardly heard them
speak. Neither of us will be able to identify them.
So, I believe them when they say they'll let me go
as soon as they're paid. Now I want you to em-
phasize that, to everyone, when you're set free.
Will you do that?"

Set free. Set free. Mary could hardly hear or understand another word beyond those two. Del was staring at her strangely. With a great effort she finally managed to make her brain function, and her tongue. "Tell everyone you believe you will be released. If the ransom's paid. Yes, yes, I will."

"Please do, Mary. They also say they'll kill me if the ransom isn't paid, and I believe them about that, too. Is that all?" The two masked men were both standing with Del now; he looked at them, one after the other, and received a single nod.

Del nodded toward Mary. "You're going to have to do something to protect her from the cold. It'll be hours."

One of the men moved away, toward the half-visible truck. A truck door opened and closed. He came back, bearing an armload of blankets; rough, brown, army-surplus-looking things. He draped them wordlessly round Mary's shoulders, front and back. As long as she did not move much, they should remain. Then he went out of the cabin again and with his companion took hold of Del.

They dragged him off among the concealing trees, out of sight toward the truck. The last words that she heard from Del were: "It'll be warmer, Mary, when the sun gets up. Hang on. Help will come."

Could it be that she had never said goodbye to Del at all? Had never given any last words of encouragement to that old man who had done so much for her. She had heard the truck doors opening and closing, once again. And then, moments later, the totally unexpected blast.

Mary had collapsed onto the earth floor, groaning, at the explosion. Something terrible was happening again, though she could not at first grasp what. The brief thudding of debris upon the cabin roof kept her crouched down. One piece hit so hard that dust and fine fragments fell from the inside of the crude roof. She huddled there for an endless time, in a dazed state approaching madness.

Light grew slowly outside the cabin door, which had been blocked open with a piece of branch. Day had come officially. Birds started to sing at last. Mary could smell the burning, and she could hear the faint crackle if she listened. The woods were wet, almost dripping, branches decked with late spring snow, or else they might have gone right up. Gas burned, rubber burned, other things burned and she could smell them when the breeze blew some of the smoke toward the cabin.

When finally she began to try to look out of the cabin door, she could no longer see the pickup anywhere as an integral object. Only debris, unidentifiable pieces of this and that, lay within Mary's field of vision outside the cabin.

After a time she painfully dragged herself, losing some blankets in the process, over to the door. From there she could see more. There lay a fender. One of the truck's wheels had come to a stop against the cabin wall.

After another time she raised her eyes. On the other side of the semi-clearing, Del's robe was draped between two high branches of a Ponderosa pine. The robe sagged like a laden hammock. There was no sign of Del's head or hands or feet, but the robe was certainly not empty . . .

. . . and the scene of the cabin and the wreckage began to vanish. This vanishment was a process as intermittent as the disappearance of the lights of a house passed on the road at night behind a long screen of trees.

On the road at night. Driving a lonely road, while slowly and surely things seen passed away.

Driving, riding, along a desert road, with her head slumped on a shoulder that gave her, oh, such a marvelous feeling of security . . .

She was back in the jouncing truck again, but no it was not the truck this time thank God it was the Blazer, and Mary was upright in the right front seat. Ahead of her the headlights speared continuously along a curve of high desert road, narrow unpaved road with bear grass and cactus along its sides. There were no other lights to be seen, in all the midnight land about.

She had gone to the Seabright house, to pick up her things, with Thorn . . .

Thorn.

He was driving, and he glanced sideways at her for a moment, mildly, as the weight of her head came fully up off his shoulder.

She drew a hard breath.

"Softly, Mary. Gently! It is all right. You were remembering some unpleasant things."

"I was . . . I was right there . . ."

"No, you were not there tonight. I had started to drive in the direction of the cabin, the place where the explosion happened. But it proved unnecessary to take you there. Everything worked, you were able to tell me all en route. So we are now heading back toward Phoenix—that pleasant glow in the sky ahead is from the city's lights. We shall be there in a couple of hours."

A couple of hours. She yearned for the lovely city. She felt weak inside, as though recovering from an illness. Loneliness and night and disorientation overcame her. She had never felt so far from home in all her life. She had never understood before how runaways must really feel.

Weakness turned her back toward childhood. She was a bad girl, and she wept now, for all the sins of her past life. For infatuation and sex in Idaho. For broken promises. For living with Robby, endangering his immortal soul. Was it really his idea or hers that they should not get married?

Thorn glanced at her again. "Ah. You are experiencing a common reaction to the experience you have just been through. It will pass. Presently you will feel much better."

"What experience have I been through? What have you done to me?" The words came out in a snuffle.

"What have I done? Very little. Ah, here we are. I must obtain some petrol."

In half a minute the deep invisibility of the night gave forth a small, almost abandoned looking gas station into the headlights. Thorn could hardly have seen the place before the headlights picked it out; he must, thought Mary, vaguely be familiar with this road. Anyway, the place was certainly closed, utterly dark and still.

Thorn pulled in, though, and up to the gas pumps, and turned off his engine as confidently as if he had seen some of those television-commercial attendants cartwheeling out to give him service. When the headlights went out, Mary saw that a thick crescent of desert moon had risen, to make the setting a ghostly stage.

"I shall be only a moment," Thorn said from just outside the vehicle, and slammed the door carelessly behind him.

Mary was not going to offer any comments on the practicality of trying to get gas here tonight; not now, and not to Thorn. With great relief, though, she found some of her mental strength returning. All right, she had done some things in her life that were wrong, but nothing all that terrible. Even when she closed her eyes again, Thorn's face seemed to hang before them. It wasn't his fault that she felt lousy. He understood. And he didn't want her to cry, to suffer.

For some reason, what Thorn wanted had suddenly become important to her. Even more important than—than—was it really love that she knew with Robby, after all?

She opened her eyes again, just in time to see her companion vanish beside the silent station. Yes, vanish was the right word, though the building was near, and the moonlight fairly bright, it seemed that he had just disappeared.

Mary waited quietly, wondering if the owner perhaps lives somewhere in back, and had heard the car door slam—

And Thorn was back again, even as he had gone, standing now beside the gas pumps with keys jingling in his hand. He was rattling them impatiently against a pump, with a muttering of what sounded like Latin oaths.

Mary said, through her partially rolled-down window: "You hypnotized me, didn't you? We were at the house . . ."

"Your property that we went to retrieve is all in the rear seat. This damnable device will not . . . ah."

Very faintly, there came the sound of small motors, electricity.

Mary turned to look into the rear seat of the Blazer even as the dim figure outside began to pump gas into its tank. There were here familiar string-tied boxes, one of them unopened since Chicago. There was the small, battered spare suitcase that she had all but forgotten. Things she evidently didn't really need. All her essential stuff was now at Robby's house.

"Thank you," she called out softly, turning back to the window.

"It is I who should thank you. You have been of considerable help."

"How?"

He didn't answer. The desert here was high enough so that the night had grown quite cool. Mary breathed deeply of its coolness, meanwhile listening to a distant owl. Her thoughts were ready to go with the bird, fly through the night. Sadness was rapidly being replaced by a fierce though quiet elation.

When Thorn had finished filling the tank, he came like a conscientious attendant to treat the windshield with a squeegee no one had bothered to lock away. That task complete, he vanished again in the direction of the building. This time Mary made a more intense effort to watch closely. But this time too Thorn simply disappeared.

Then abruptly he was standing at the driver's door again, opening it to get in. I don't believe this, Mary thought, feeling delighted, as by some stage magician's cleverness.

"You had to go back in to return the keys," she remarked cheerfully.

"And to leave payment." His voice seemed to chide her gently for having omitted anything so important. "Not, of course, at the outrageous rates listed on these signs."

"'Oh, of course not." Was this really her, so eager to be agreeable?

He was now seated beside her, with the door closed. Looking at her. But for the moment he made no move to start the engine.

Something in the way he looked at her made Mary sigh faintly and lean back in her seat. "You were right," she said. "It was hard to go through that, but now somehow I feel sure those dreams aren't going to bother me any more."

"I trust that they will not."

The moonlight was silver and strange. Mary had the feeling that she had never really looked at moonlight closely before.

Again she was the one to break the silence. "I have the feeling," she announced, "that when you kiss me I'm going to enjoy it very much."

One of his eyebrows went up. "Then I must seem churlish indeed to delay. But I would like to find a better place than this."

Thorn turned the key in the ignition. He was immune to personal fear, but not to horror. And he supped full on horror in the next moment, when he heard the strange reaction, and sensed the hellish fire of the bomb blast, blowing backward and upward at him from the engine.

Twelve

Our wedding night, or wedding morning rather, was spent at Careggi, the beautiful Medici villa which lay only a few miles outside the walls of Florence. Lorenzo praised that country retreat to me extravagantly as we rode out through the silently opened city gates before dawn, and told me that much of his childhood had been spent there. I was on my own stallion, Helen at my side on a docile young white palfrey that Lorenzo had begged her to accept as his own wedding gift.

We reached Careggi just as the sun brightened the Tuscan countryside. Piero, gout and all, was waiting for us on the grounds, seated on the rim of one of the great stone fountains near the main house. The head of the Medici family rose to offer us greetings and congratulations, then led us to what would now be called a debriefing session, in the guise of a wedding breakfast at which the men and women of course sat down separately. The questioning was very polite and very smooth, and accompanied with intervals of real celebration; but in the course of an hour my hosts had managed to extract from me more information than I had been aware of carrying regarding the Boccalini and their affairs. When I was finally milked dry and yawning, Piero made flowery apologies for the delay, presented me with a jeweled collar and a warhorse as my own wedding gifts, and released me to join my bride. The sun was fully up by now, the day already growing warm.

The women had finished their own breakfast

somewhat earlier. Helen had been bathed and perfumed under the direction of the ladies of the household, and was already installed in a second floor room that in years past had served, so I was told, as a bridal chamber for members of the family. I was now, amid some merriment, conducted thence myself.

Closing the door of this room behind me with a weary sigh, I turned to the great bed to discover my new wife fast asleep. I hardly needed a second look to make sure that this was no coy bridal ruse, but only the natural result of great exhaustion. I did not intend to wake her; I myself had had almost no sleep during the past two days, and at the moment rest felt more attractive than any other sensual delight. Yet when I had undressed and turned back the covers, I paused to look. Nightclothes of any kind were still the rare exception rather than the rule, and my bride's whole inventory of physical charms was available for inspection. The wholesale removal of rags and grime had left visible a number of bruises I had not been able to see before, along with a few half-healed scabs. But it was a young body, basically healthy and of a trimly attractive shape. I seemed likely that it would give me considerable pleasure, and might bear me strong, healthy sons as well.

Pulling a cover over us both, I let my head fall back in weariness upon a pillow. But the finely woven bed canopy above was bright with morning, my mind was full of a hundred concerns, and sleep refused to come at once.

That there should be an unfamiliar, girlish breathing at my side in bed was in itself no strange phenomenon. But it was strange, very strange, to reflect that this particular sound would not only grow familiar, but it could nevermore be lightly put away.

At least she did not snore.

It was approximately mid-day when I awoke, with my right shoulder gently going numb under the steady pressure of a smallish head covered with brown curls. I needed a moment to identify the head with certainty. The hair looked much different since it had been washed, and there was also a delightful difference in the smell; my slowly awakening senses discovered some essence of the flowers of the Tuscan countryside.

The girl was still in a deep sleep. She was not clinging to me, exactly, though she lay with one arm across my chest—again I got the impression rather that I was the rocky protuberance upon which she had been cast ashore by the storms of life.

Gently I eased free my deadening arm, drew open the bed curtains, and looked around the room. Someone had been in while we slept— bedroom privacy was not valued then as much as now, and anyway the curtained bed provided it. Fresh clothing of fine cloth and the latest cut had been laid out for us both, upon a pair of great wooden chests that served both to decorate the room and provide storage.

Atop a third such chest leaned paneled Magdalen, her back propped against the wall. I considered her presence, and understood from it that all my few possessions must already have been brought here from the Medici house in town. From this in turn I understood that my wife and I would be expected to avoid the city, at least while the affair at the Boccalini house was still fresh. Which seemed to make obvious sense.

Shortly after being dislodged from my shoulder, Helen had moved voluntarily in her sleep, turning on her back and pulling the cover up close under her chin. She lay with pretty pink lips parted to reveal surprisingly good teeth. Reclining with my head propped up on one hand, I studied her. I found myself turning my gaze from her flesh to the Magdalen's freshly painted face, and back again. As I have mentioned, the painting was still unfinished, but the work remaining to be done consisted of details of the woman's dress and of the background. As far as I could see, the modeled face was nothing short of absolute perfection. It was Helen, and yet was not—it seemed rather that the living face beside me had somehow failed to reach its own ideal.

That I, Vlad Drakulya, now had possession of both breathing flesh and painted image, was a fact; and the more I considered this fact the more momentous it grew, the more pregnant with a significance whose nature I could not grasp at once. Like other men of the fifteenth century, I was usually more than half ready to see omens, hidden meanings, wonders spiritual and supernatural. Even in the warm sunlight of midday.

Helen, this girl of hardly more than half my size or age, stirred in her sleep beside me. Then she turned on her side away from me, and a moment later snuggled backward till her soft flank touched me under the light cover. I forgot the painting, and moved to accomplish the one thing still necessary to seal our marriage completely in the eyes of God and man. Helen, only half awake at first, resisted me mechanically—but then, as she awoke fully, she relaxed, and even gave some evidence of enjoyment.

As soon as the first dance was over, I pulled some pillows into better position for both of us, and we lay there side by side, regarding each other and the world from a nest of greater physical comfort than either of us had lately been accustomed to.

"My bride," I meditated aloud. There was a grave expression in those dark young eyes now fixed on mine, and I was trying to fathom what might be going on behind them.

"Yes." The one-word answer somehow conveyed, I thought, her willingness to accept brideship as a starting point and to see where it might lead. And I was cheered by the fact that she did not seem to be a heavy talker. Reticence by day and a lack of snoring by night would count for much.

A light warm breeze was stirring the fine gauze curtains at our open window. I could hear gardeners at work not far outside. They were digging, snipping branches, scraping at the earth. A good male voice rose lightly in Italian song. We were a floor above ground level, secure against casual observation from outside, but from where we lay much greenery was visible. The grounds at Careggi were quite as impressive as the house. When I sat up fully in our bed and pulled its curtains farther open I could glimpse graveled walks, distant lawns being smoothed by grazing sheep, and beds of massed flowers. There was a fountain, studded with statuary and rimmed by concentric rings of masterly stonework. All shimmered in late summer's warmth.

"Ah," said Helen, in a new tone. I looked and

saw that she had just discovered the painting. Next moment, without pretense of modesty, she had slipped out of bed and gone to inspect it at close range.

"I wish my face was truly so," she said at last.

"But I think the artist has accurately caught your beauty." I was an experienced husband, you will recall.

"But no, this is really a marvel. I never had the chance to take such a good look at it before—I was always on the other side of it, you know, when I was posing."

"I agree, a marvel. Too bad it is unfinished."

Without turning, Helen gently waved one hand in my direction, dismissing that objection; and, certainly, the painting was essentially complete. "I think," she said in Italian, "that boy has been touched by the good God."

But my mind was turning elsewhere. The two of us had important matters to talk about, and I judged the time had come. "Helen."

A hand on one bare hip like Donatello's *David*, she turned her head at the new sound in my voice, and probed me with her eyes. Then slowly she returned to stand beside our bed. She took the hand that I extended to her, then paused, fingering its ring. The circlet was then still fat with gold. Helen looked at it, and at the untanned groove worn by it into my finger underneath. "You have been married before, my lord," she said.

"It will please me for my wife to call me Vlad. Particularly on such private occasions as this. Yes, I have been married. My first wife is now two years dead."

"I will pray for her soul."

"Thank you." Sooner or later, I supposed, I

would be called on by Helen for some explanation of her predecessor's leap from the parapet; she would learn something of that tragedy from others even if I never brought it up. But right now I was not going to mention it.

"And you have children?"

"They are staying with relatives at present." I sighed; another subject that could wait. But Helen's question had brought back to me my grief for the son I had loved most. He was a love-child indeed, born to a favorite concubine. He had been riding with me, before my saddle, when I began that last ill-fated retreat from the Turks, the withdrawal that had degenerated into a desperate flight, and had ended for me only with my personal surrender to Matthias. During that fiasco my son had been lost, and when I spoke to Helen on that morning at Careggi, I thought him dead.

"Helen. There is a matter between us that I wish to dispose of now. I intend to speak of it this once, and then never again. Nay, let me put it this way—in future I will not even have this subject mentioned in my presence."

Of course she knew what I was bringing up; she must have known that it was coming sooner or later. Her eyes were withdrawing from me as I spoke, though they still looked in my direction. Her royal chin was lifting.

I went on in a businesslike tone: "I mean of course these shameful escapades of yours during the past few years, since you broke off your betrothal to the Sforza. The whoring and debauchery."

"You say whoring?" Some sparks flared up; she pulled her hand free with a jerk.

I let her break my grip. "If 'whoring' is the

wrong word," I answered coldly, "then pray instruct me, what should the right one be?"

With that I expected for a moment that she might try to strike me. But then her body sagged in weariness, and she sat down on the edge of the bed, not touching me. Curls of dark hair hid her face.

Finally she spoke. "Men, as you know, have taken me by force. And, yes, at times I have sold myself, for food, for survival. And yes, I have known lust for men." Helen paused, still looking away from me. "That is all I care to say."

"It is enough. More than enough, indeed. Understand that I demand no apologies, confessions, explanations, for anything that you have done up to now. All that is over, finished, wiped away completely, and I shall never reproach you with it." I drew breath. "What I do demand concerns your conduct from this moment forward. It must be that of a model wife of exalted birth: virtuous, modest, obedient. In every detail beyond reproach."

Helen had lifted her face enough for me to see her eyes under the dark hair; but I could not read them. She gave me an inspection that went on for what seemed a long time, and still I could not guess what she was thinking. When she spoke it was only to ask a question that seemed to me insultingly irrelevant. "How long do you mean for us to stay here, in this house?"

My hand seized her wrist; if she had not been Matthias's sister, it would have taken her by the throat. "Have you been listening to me, woman? I want to know that what I say is understood." My voice was still not loud; I have never been one for shouting much.

Helen gasped and leaned forward, easing the pressure on her forearm. "Yes, my lord Vlad—I have heard and will obey. I meant my wedding vows—every bit as seriously as you meant yours." When I released her arm she sighed, and closed her eyes, and rubbed it gently.

"Then I will gladly proceed to answer your question. I believe our hosts will be happy to entertain us here for a day or two. Meanwhile some other arrangements will doubtless be made. It will be suggested that we might like to travel, leaving the region of Florence, at least for a time, lest our presence here become known and be an embarrassment. The news of our wedding is doubtless already on its way to your royal brother—our royal brother, now. Perhaps we will go to Pisa, or Genoa, and wait there for a while to know his pleasure."

"But I thought . . . you mean it is possible that we will not soon go back to Hungary?"

"It would please you to remain in Italy?"

She hesitated. "Yes. Yes, it would."

"I would say that it is more than possible." And Helen appeared relieved to hear this news.

As I had predicted, the two of us spent the remainder of that day and all the next as honored guests at the Medici villa. We rested, and did what newlyweds in all times and places are supposed to do. Our hosts called upon me to demonstrate some tricks of fencing, for which they offered appreciative applause. We joined them in conversation, the skills of which I believe I first began to appreciate when in that household; and in games, and music, and in listening to the poetry of Lorenzo and others. On our first evening at Careggi I had the pleasure of meeting the beautiful Lucrezia, Piero's devoted and intelligent wife, who looked much too young to be the mother of grim-faced, beard-stubbled Lorenzo. You can see her beauty still, in the face of Ghirlandajo's St. *Elizabeth*.

I remember Lucrezia talking alone with Helen, at great length, while I was telling Lorenzo as much as I could about King Matthias's artistic patronage. In particular Lorenzo wanted to hear more of the royal book collection. Later that night I could see that Helen had been weeping; but I chose not to question her about it. Experienced husband or not, perhaps I made a great mistake.

On the morning of our third day at Careggi, as I had more or less expected, my bride and I were cordially invited by our hosts to visit a house they owned in Pisa. Pisa was a small city at no very great distance from Florence, and at the time under Florentine—and therefore Medici—political domination. We were loaded with more presents, and furnished with an escort for the journey.

The house, when we reached it, proved to be no more than a comfortable cottage; no doubt it looked smaller than it was because we came to it from the opulence of a palace. Yet I was content with its modest comforts, considering it only a way station on the road to power and glory; and it seemed to me that Helen was content also. She had recovered from whatever had made her weep, and was playing the role of devoted wife to my fullest satisfaction.

A few weeks later, when autumn was well under way—it was an extremely lovely autumn in Italy, as I recall—a message at last reached me from King Matthias. The royal blessing was pronounced upon our union—rather perfunctorily, I thought, at no great length and with no special warmth. Then to business. I was to join the king and his army in Bosnia as soon as I could possibly do so, and that was that. Reading between the lines of this missive, I felt sure that the campaign was not going as well as had been hoped. In fact it seemed likely to me that a military disaster of some magnitude might have been in the making when the king wrote; fine considerations of peace and harmony in the officer corps no longer prevented his using another good field commander.

Well, I was ready. A honeymoon idyll in flowered idleness now and again was enjoyable, but I was basically a soldier. I made immediate plans for my departure for the distant front on the morning after the letter arrived; and, following a terse hint in the king's message, for Helen's departure from Pisa on the same day as mine. She would go back to Florence, where she would remain under Medici care. Eventually she would be sent under escort with some traders to Buda, there to remain till I should be free to join her.

On what was to have been the morning when this planned temporary separation began, I was awakened by a servant crying that something was amiss. Helen was already gone, though not with any Medici escort. On the pillow beside mine, my own bare dagger had been laid, its point aimed at my head.

Thirteen

Thorn in his timeless mode of horror had no choice but to watch the centimeter-by-centimeter progress of the wavefront of the blast as it rose toward him along the steering column. The shockwave of it was so intense that it distorted vision like thick glass. He could watch it coming, but he could not get away in time; not even he could move that fast. Nor were his extranormal powers able to dissolve his solid flesh to mist quickly enough to allow him to avoid the onrushing pain and shock. He could think, and, thinking, doubted that the blast was going to end his life; it was too artificial a thing to be able to do that. He would survive, though with what injuries he did not know. Yes, he would survive.

As for Mary . . . if he could not save himself, it was even more hopeless that in these first microseconds of the expanding bomb blast he should be able to do anything for her. He had not even time to move his eyes for a last look at her, much less reach out an arm in even the feeblest gesture of protection.

The only thing that he could do, he did: willed himself to change into a form intangible. He did this with all possible speed, yet the change did not even begin until his feet and the lower portions of his legs had already been engulfed by the blast-wave. A fraction of a microsecond after his eyes reported the immersion of his feet, his vampire's nerves already had brought the pain of the fire and force enveloping them to eat at his brain like acid.

The dissolution of his solid shape began to ease the pain, though not before it had risen as far as his lower torso. Something hard and mechanical, yes, the steering column itself, came spearing, raping its way right through his melting abdomen, reaching for his fading spine. His last clear sight of the blast through solid human eyes showed him the walnut-grained instrument panel exploding with an awful velocity toward his face. *It is not real wood,* he had the time to think. *It cannot kill me even if I am not fast enough to get away.* But he was gone before the panel struck.

Ten yards outside the vehicle, the blast-wave already past, and the first surge of secondary flame beginning, Thorn gathered his mist-shape back into that of man. He reformed his body as quickly as he could, despite the renewed pain brought by the recreated nerves, and the consciousness of real injury done to his feet and legs. In solid shape he could see more clearly, and act with greater force.

When his vision cleared, the roof of the Blazer was completely gone, as was the hood, with new fire blooming where they had been. Some portion of the explosion directed downward had lifted the front of the heavy vehicle clear of the ground, and it was now in the process of falling back. Debris still sang like shrapnel through the air around Thorn's ears.

Before the blasted wreck had fallen back again on its four burning tires, Thorn leaped toward it. His motion began on two feet and ended on four, beside the wreck; instantly a second bound on wolf-fast legs bore him, armoured in thick fur,

straight through the flames where doors and windows had once been.

Mary was no longer there. Her mortal form, or
what was left of it, had been blown clear of the
vehicle on its far side.

A wolf's teeth closed on her hair, and on what
was left of the collar of her shirt. She was dragged
away from the fire, to a distance where its flames
were no longer hot enough to burn.

One of Mary's arms was gone, off at the shoulder. Both of her legs were twisted, lying at wrong
angles like those of some great discarded doll.
Still her eyes were open, and alive. They were
blankly blue, familiar eyes in a blasted face from
which most of the lower jaw had been ripped
away. In man-form again now, Thorn crouched
over her. He must have looked half-dead himself,
with his clothing blown to rags and his skin covered with the black residue of the explosion. But
though his nervous system still rang with pain he
could tell now that his own injuries were minor, a
result of organic matter in his own clothing im-
pacting his body under the force of the blast: the
leather in his shoes, the cotton in some of his
clothing. His wounds would quickly heal.

But Mary.

It was obvious from the first look at her that she
was not going to survive.

Unless . . . there was one desperate chance to
take.

Thorn closed his eyes, and willed the double
fang-growth in his own upper jaw. Then he
crouched lower over the girl, bending till his lips
touched her charred flesh. In a moment he had
tasted of her living blood. Then, kneeling erect
again, he ripped open the burnt remnants of his

own garments at the chest, and with one taloned fingernail nicked his own blackened skin. Then he lifted the girl like a nursling babe toward his wound.

He tried, tried desperately, to give Mary his own vampire's blood to drink. With her jaw gone, her own blood drowning her, it was impossible.

She never drank the blood that might have given her a chance for a transformed life. Yet still it took long minutes for her death to be complete.

"Who's it from, Bill?" Judy Southerland followed the back of Bill Bird's blue shirt through the sunlight of highland New Mexico, along the pine-needle path that led from her cabin, past the schoolroom-studio where Bill taught and worked at sculpture, to the lodge that housed the school director's office.

Bill turned his head back briefly. He wasn't handsome, not by Judy's standards anyway, but very nice. "He said he was your brother-in-law. But then he said to be sure not to scare you, that the family's all okay."

"I see. Thanks." But Judy was sure she would have felt it had there been something serious wrong with Mom or Dad or Kate or Johnny; she felt things like that, even at a distance, and always had. There had been a bad dream last night, she suddenly remembered. She frowned, but the content of the dream escaped her now.

Brown-haired, sturdy, never in her young life a runaway, she walked wearing jeans and plaid shirt into the director's office. The outer room was otherwise unoccupied at the moment, maybe so she could take what sounded like an important call in privacy. The walls here, as in most of the other camp buildings, were of thick logs, the interior surfaces cut flat, heavily and neatly chinked. After that the walls had been sealed with a glossy finish through which the wood shone yellow. With walls like these it was possible for life indoors to be as civilized, as cultured, as anyone might wish, even amid mountains verging on wilderness. The fanciest interior furnishings did not look out of place. Fritz Scholder prints hung here in the office, along with the obligatory Navajo rugs.

Judy picked up the phone, meanwhile smiling reassuringly at Bill, who had remained hovering just in the doorway. "Hello," she said. Outside the screened window, open on this warm late spring afternoon, tall pines waved in a breeze.

"Judy? This is Joe. Kate and everybody here are all okay, it's nothing like that."

"So Bill said."

"But there's something I still thought I ought to talk to you about."

Judy glanced at her watch. Mid-afternoon in Chicago, one time zone away. Joe must be calling during his duty hours at the station; for him to do that, it must be something important indeed. She knew now who it was about; the feeling, though not the manifest content, of last night's nightmare came back in full force. She felt no surprise; as if, on some interior level, she had already known. "I didn't think it was the family, Joe."

"You see," said Joe's voice through the long-distance buzz, "I got a call just a little while ago from the Phoenix police. A vehicle was blown up with a bomb out there in the desert last night, and at least one person killed."

He can't be dead, I would have known at once if

he were dead. "I follow you."

"They were trying to trace the man who had rented this vehicle. He had also occupied a certain hotel room out there, from which room a long-distance call was made to me here in Chicago. Judy, I think you know which man I'm talking about."

"Suppose I do." Bill was still hanging in the doorway; no doubt courtesy was urging him to leave, but something he saw in Judy's face was evidently compelling him to hang around. As soon as the call was over he would offer to try to be of help.

"Don't be defensive, Judy, I'm trying to help."

"I know you are, Joe."

"Have you seen him, since you've been out there? Have you heard anything from him? It could be very important."

It certainly could, to me. "Why? Are the Phoenix police after him?"

"Not in that sense. At least I don't know that they are. They're naturally trying to find out where he is, after his car blew up, and a young woman who must have been sitting in it was killed. There could be some possible connection with that Seabright murder and kidnapping case out there a few months ago. You've heard of that."

"I've heard of that. And about What's-his-name Seabright's missing painting just the other day. They haven't found the aircraft yet. But I haven't heard from the man you're talking about."

"Good. I didn't have any reason to think you might have, just a hunch. For your sake, Judy, I just don't want you to get involved in any way."

"I see." *Why was she so angry? Joe meant well.*

"Now if he *does* contact you, for any reason, will you please for God's sake just give me a call?"

"I suppose I could do that." She could hear her own voice still chilly and upset. She was really angry with herself, Judy supposed, because she had almost missed completely being aware of how much trouble he was in. Might he be badly hurt? She couldn't tell. Once before when he was hurt, to the point of death, she had been able to help. Now . . . the contact between them had evidently faded, without her being aware of it.

Phoenix. But at the moment she had no feeling for where he was.

Bill still fidgeted in the doorway, watching her. Good. Maybe she would need some help from someone. She smiled at him.

Joe's voice said: "I didn't tell Kate I was going to call you on this. And of course I didn't tell your folks."

"Of course." Judy's parents and brother had no idea of the truth shared by Joe and Kate—that vampires existed, and that Judy had had one as a lover.

"I just thought it was my duty to make sure that you don't get involved in this. You being out there in the same part of the country and all."

"Oh, damn it, Joe!" Judy never swore. "Are you sure you wouldn't like me to drive a stake through his heart if I get the chance?" Only after the words were out did she remember Billy listening. But Billy would take them as metaphor of some kind; odd, how easy it was for some kinds of truth to remain hidden.

"Judy, Goddam, Judy." Joe on the other hand tended to swear a fair amount. The phone now made his anger tiny. "I'm just trying to look out for your own best—"

"It seems to me that *he* once let himself get involved in some pretty serious trouble that *we* were having."

For a few moments the long-distance buzz had the line to itself. Joe's voice when it came back was decently troubled. "I know, we owe him a lot. After what he did for Kate and me, I'll stick my neck out. But how do we know what he's involved in? I'm just trying to get *you* to stay clear, kid, for your own good. This other young lady who was blown up and killed in his car was probably on good terms with him too, and—"

"Thank you." Judy got the two words out in an acceptable voice, and then quickly hung up the phone. She hoped Joe heard them and really appreciated that she understood and was grateful for his desire to help. Joe really did mean well. It was just that right now Judy was too mad to talk to him any longer.

Billy was still in the doorway, with concern for Judy's troubles written all over him. She smiled at him again. She didn't want to involve anyone else in anything dangerous. But she would, if necessary.

Her hand still on the cradled phone, Judy closed her eyes. Feeling guilt, and love, she tried for contact. As soon as she really tried, it came. The man called Thorn was still alive, she was completely sure of that. Somewhere to the west and south of her, at some considerable distance.

She thought that he was now asleep. But even in the sunny log room she trembled. She was frightened at her perception of his pain and rage.

Fourteen

The servant whose howls had wakened me was a weepy old woman, her past scarred, as I now suppose, with tragedy of one kind or another that must have driven her half mad. She was diligent about the house, but given at times to supernatural fantasies. Her cries continued in the middle distance as I sat there in my bed, I know not for how long, looking at that dagger on the pillow and fatalistically pondering its meaning. I did not require the noise of the ancient seeress to convince me of disaster.

The only logical conclusion I was able to reach regarding the dagger was that Helen had considered killing me with it before she fled—already, somehow, I had no doubt that she was gone—but had then for whatever reason decided against my murder. Still, she wished me to realize that the topic had been under consideration, and she had left the dagger so aimed to symbolize the fact.

Besides this vaguely humiliating and cryptic communication, no message from my departing wife could be discovered. As matters turned out, the old woman was screaming for no more occult reason than having been told of her mistress's defection by one of the grooms. This unusually unintelligent lad, while about his morning chores an hour or two earlier, had chanced to see Helen leaving. He reportedly belatedly how she had ridden off into the predawn mists on her white palfrey, a thin roll of clothing with a few other belongings tied up behind her sidesaddle, and accompanied by a cloaked male figure astride another horse.

The lackwit groom stuttered and stammered this story again to me, adding that it had never occurred to him to raise an alarm when he saw this. It meant nothing to him, he asserted, that his mistress should have decided to go for an early morning ride. Herein he was mistaken; it meant in fact that I paused to slit his nose for him before I took to the road myself in a frantic effort to pick up my lady's trail.

It turned out that there was no trail, at least none that I could find. In a state of rage that grew ever colder and more pure, I rode at a good speed for an hour along the road that led in the opposite direction from Florence, but caught no sight of the one I sought. Nor would any of the folk I questioned in passing admit to having seen Helen ride that way with her secret lover, with that faceless, unidentifiable figure in the groom's stammered story, a man who would be glad to settle for losing part of his nose when I caught up with him.

As for what I meant to do to Helen . . . I do not remember making any specific plan of vengeance then. But it was well for her that morning that I could not find her.

Of course I might well be pursuing in the wrong direction, and after an hour I turned round. It then naturally took me another hour to get back to our Pisan cottage. I had sent some of the servants I considered most trustworthy to scour the neighborhood in other directions, and these were back before me. They trembled when they announced that they had nothing helpful to report. Their fear was wasted, for when I looked at them I believed that they had really tried.

What was I to do? Missing spouse or not, honor
and wisdom alike forbade me to postpone by so
much as half a day the start of my long trek to
Bosnia. The king's orders had been explicit, and
the urgency of his need apparent in them.

I did what little packing I had to do, and concluded the business of closing down the small
household. In all this I was surrounded by servants who moved in a desperate, counterproduc-
tive hurry. My servants in my homeland had
sometimes tended to be that way also. Whenever
I glanced at these folk or spoke to them they
dropped what they were carrying, or shook so that
their fingers could not tie a knot. Matters were not
helped by the gurgling moans, drifting in from the
stables, of the groom with the runny nose. Once or
twice I was on the point of going out to quiet him.

A quick inventory disclosed that Helen had left
behind the greater part of her new wardrobe, including items I had bought to please her, as well
as the lavish gifts of the Medici. I directed that the
servants should share these out among themselves, which acted as a tonic to their morale. As
far as I was able to determine, my fugitive wife
had taken with her no money, or very little; and no
jewelry or gold of any particular value. There was
no telling, of course, what contribution of wealth
her mysterious escort might have brought to the
escape.

At last my eye, searching the vacated rooms for
any bits of important business left unfinished, fell
again upon the painting. My first impulse at that
moment was to draw my bloodied dagger and
hack the thin panel into splinters. But a moment's
cool thought held me back from any such rash
demonstration. Not for a moment had I consi-

dered permanently giving up the search for Helen. When eventually I should be free again to look for the woman who had so basely used me (as I then saw the case) and then deserted me when her fortunes had improved, such a close likeness could very well, I thought, prove invaluable.

So, I delayed the start of my own long journey enough to send the painting back to Piero in Florence. Along with it I dispatched a brief written explanation of what had happened, and a request that he should keep the picture for me until I either returned or sent for it. To this I added a plea that the Medici use all their powers to try to find the woman for me whilst I was away at war; and that, should they succeed, Helen be held in some secure convent against my return. To some degree I shared my king's misgivings about convents; but given the society we dwelt in, no better alternative was apparent. Also it galled me, as it always has, to have to ask anyone a favor—but again I could see no better course available.

All this was quickly done. Before midday, a few scant hours after my wife's desertion, I was on the high road out of Pisa, in the company of a few mercenaries I had recruited locally, still growling oaths into my mustache as I rode.

My plan was to go overland, passing the Alps before snow flew. I wanted to avoid the uncertainties of taking ship upon the Adriatic at that season. And besides, if it must be admitted, I had then and have now no particular liking for the sea. Unfortunately for my plans, the first snow of the season reached the high passes simultaneously with myself and my small escort; it cost us a slow and dangerous struggle to get through.

What with one delay and another, I did not

reach the scene of the summer's and autumn's fighting until almost midwinter, by which time military operations were nearly at a standstill, King Matthias had withdrawn himself and much of his army to Buda. On the whole, the campaign had gone better than I had expected for the Christian cause. Mohammed II, in personal command of sizable forces, had invested the fortified town of Yaytsa early in the fighting season, but the timely arrival of the Black Army with the King of Hungary at its head had soon broken the seige. Historians, if there be any quick ones in the present audience, may wish to note that the generally unreasonable preference shown by European rulers for mercenary troops during the following few decades can be traced back to this victory by Matthias's well-trained hirelings.

I had missed all the glories of this warm-weather campaign, such as they might have been. But I was not too late, while carrying out a mounted reconnaissance, to take part in a snowy skirmish of more than ordinary stupidity against a Turkish patrol similarly occupied. From this brawl I escaped with my honor and my life, my horse and my sword, the dagger which had once been left on a pillow aimed at my head—and a slow-healing thigh wound that temporarily made any further martial activities on my part out of the question.

I rested in camp until I felt able to sit a horse again, then set out for Buda, progressing by slow stages through a landscape that grew more familiar as I went. I had not been invited to present myself before the king; but then I had not been forbidden to do so, either. Indeed, I had heard nothing at all from Matthias since my leaving

Pisa. So I judged that some kind of a personal report was necessary, though I did not look forward to delivering it.

It was already the early spring of 1465 when at last, still hardly able to stand, I appeared before His Majesty in his palace. Matthias looked older; kingship and the Turks were aging him rapidly. He received me in private as before, but with a lack of warmth that was immediately noticeable.

"Where is she, Drakulya? Word reached me months ago that you had lost her."

It was I who had sent him that word, of course. "I do not know where she is, sire." I tried to explain the circumstances as best I could.

He cut me off with a gesture. "I see you have a wound there that prevents your fighting. But you can travel, or you would not be here. So take yourself to Italy again, and find her. It would have been wiser for you to have stayed there last year and seen to the matter. She is your wife now, and I hold you responsible."

Such are the ways of kings, and the difficulties of trying as loyally as possible to serve them. We dissolve now to a shot of me galloping madly right-to-left over the Alps. No, of course in actuality it was not that quickly done. This time the king was not so eager to provide me with letters and with gold. But eventually he had to admit that if I were to go, it were best that I succeed; and if he wanted me to succeed he had better give me all the help he could; and by the time he was convinced of this my leg was better, well enough to try the mountains.

Officially, you understand, I was all this time still imprisoned in the Tower of Solomon. And in truth there were a few moments during this epoch when I might have been tempted to settle for a return to my comfortable cell. But in fact, by the early summer of 1465, I was again on my way south to Italy. This time I was traveling as an officially nameless member of a delegation from Matthias to the new Pope, Paul II. Leader of the delegation was Janus Pannonius, who was what is now called a humanist, and also a poet, of about my own age. Pannonius and his uncle Janus Vitez had long been on good terms with their ruling kinsmen, the Hunyadi family. In a few years both Januses were to be entranced by an ill-starred conspirator into a revolutionary intrigue, and Matthias was going to have them killed; but in 1465 their prospects were still bright.

By the summer of that year, Matthias had somewhat revised his earlier thinking on the subject of papal crusades. If he, the King of Hungary, was going to have to make a career out of fighting the Turks anyway, then he might as well have all the help he could scrape up, well organized or not. Pannonius and his delegation were in fact going to Rome to plead for a new Crusade.

Having gone to school in Italy as a youth, Pannonius spoke the language well, and with his help I brushed up on my own Italian during the journey. En route our leader entertained the rest of the party with songs of his own devising, verses about the difficulties of politics, the perils of dealing with the infernal Turks, and the pains of life's personal tragedies. When he warbled about a cuckolded husband, he seemed oblivious to the fact that I gave him close attention, and so I wisely restrained my reactions, judging that my own history was not known amongst my companions. All in all, Pannonius blended show business and

politics in a way you might have thought star-
tlingly modern, could you have heard and understood his yodelings. For my part, at the time I was
little in sympathy with either art. And my mind
was filled with affairs more personally important.
When at last our little party reached Florence, I
quietly dropped out.

Piero had grown a little goutier since I had seen
him last, and a little older under the burden of his
new responsibilities as head of Medici Enter-
prises. Still he welcomed me more warmly than
my own liege lord had at Buda. I think it was
during this second trip that I first began to fall in
love with Italy. And the merchant chief listened
sympathetically to my problems. Yes, he had been
instructing his people to keep their eyes and ears
open everywhere they went. But unfortunately he
still had nothing to report of Helen's where-
abouts. She had perhaps, he though, gone very far
away this time.

I had to agree, though in the past she had demonstrated an affinity for Italy. And perhaps, I
thought to myself, this time the Medici were really not so very interested in trying to help me
find her. Well, they could scarcely be blamed.
They had done much for me already, and they
certainly had plenty of other projects to keep them
busy, for example trying to make a living, and
keeping a complex city-state going in a difficult
world. It must have been plain to them that my
marriage was a lost cause, even if my bride could
be found again; and that Matthias was unlikely to
be pleased however the situation turned out now.

As he strolled beside me through the cavernous
rooms of the *palazzo* Medici, Piero gripped my

sleeve in a friendly way and gave it a little shake. "Have you spoken to Morsino yet, friend Ladislao? It may be that he has heard something that we have not."

"I doubt it. But I will talk to him. And one thing more, Signore Piero, if I may try your patience. Remember the painting that I had sent to you from Pisa? Would it be possible to have some of your people look at it before they depart on trading missions." I said this partly, I suppose, to impress Piero with my unflagging determination.

He nodded vigorously, as if pleased to be bothered with still one more request. Probably he had little intention of honoring it anyway. "The painting is very beautiful, and I thank you for its loan. I have kept it where my eyes can fall on it every day." And with a little beckoning gesture he led me into another room and showed me the Magdalen above a fireplace. We both regarded it for a few moments in silence.

Then Piero went on: "I will have it moved to your room, if you like . . . of course you are going to stay with us, while you are in Florence."

"Thank you, Signore Piero. Your hospitality and generosity are more than a poor soldier like myself deserves." I was about to add that I had no wish to find the painting gazing at me each morning when I awoke, when a new idea struck me, what I considered to be a really clever thought. "And yes, I would like it in my room. Though I trust that my stay will not be long."

To implement my new brainstorm, I paid a visit that very day to Verrocchio's studio. This time I went alone—Lorenzo, I should perhaps explain, was out of town on business at the time.

The studio had been transformed in the year

since I had seen it last. There were at least half a dozen apprentices in sight, all of them busy shoveling sand, mixing and grinding pigments, hammering boards together into a platform, sweating and sending up a haze of dust from all the drudgery that lies behind serene fine art in metal and stone and paint. None of these youths recognized me, nor I them. But one went promptly to inform the master of my arrival, and returned in a moment to lead me to another room.

The very structure of the building had been changed considerably during the last twelve-month. A neighbor's stable had been taken over, and built into the growing complex. Raw timber walled some rooms completely new. But though the place was much enlarged, it was still crowded by its new production; business was booming tremendously.

I was conducted to where Verrocchio was at work, in one of the newly added rooms. The master, who had not changed noticeably, was not really glad to see me, though he made me welcome with effusive words. *Here comes trouble*, the expression on his fleshy face proclaimed. He was at work sculpting a clay figure, about half life-size, whose model, a sturdy lad wearing only a leather apron and some token bits of ancient-looking armor, stood on a small stage under the usual skylight. At a second glance I recognized this youth, altered by a year's fast growth, as the very one that I had come to see.

"Messer Verrocchio," I began, "I suppose you have seen or heard nothing of the Hungarian woman since the last time I was here?"

"Nothing. Well, that is, only that she . . ." Verrocchio broke off, looking embarrassed.

"You mean you have heard of my marital difficulties with her, and that she has run away again."

He nodded.

"Be sure and let me know if you hear more. You know where I can be reached. But it is really a painting that I have come to see you about today—a painting, and this young fellow who did it."

Verrocchio proved willing enough for me to hire away his apprentice and model for what I said would probably be a few days' work. He probably thought that his powerful patrons were still more interested in helping me than they really were, and I did not trouble to enlighten him. And so that very afternoon I was standing with Leonardo before the Magdalen in my small guest room at the *palazzo* Medici.

"It is only the face that I really want, you see. As many copies as you can make, drawing well, in the time that you can work for me. Here is the painting. And you must still have the woman's face in your mind's eye, as she spent a long time posing for you."

The boy was handsome, but there was something inhuman, almost, about his eyes. If I had met him armed in the field, I should have expected him to be extremely dangerous, for reasons having nothing to do with size or training.

He said only: "Tracings could be made, if we had thin paper."

"I can get you paper, or give you money to buy some. What I must have are good likenesses of this woman. I want a man who has never seen her to be able to recognize her when he does, once he has studied one of your sketches."

Leonardo was pinning up a small sheet of paper on the small easel he had brought with him. "Yes, I think I can do that, provided the man who looks has good eyes to see."

He began to draw. I, having learned how sometimes good artisans were bothered by close observation, moved away to look out of the window into the courtyard.

"Have you ever seen the woman again in the flesh?" I asked, as casually as possible. I had not forgotten that only this young artisan's tip had enabled me to locate Helen the first time around.

"No, signore," the boy answered. But there was something in his voice that made me turn back to look at him. I found him regarding me in that calculating, almost robotic way of his. Then he added: "But I have seen Perugino since then."

"Perugino." It took me a few moments to recall where I had heard that name before. Yes, Verrocchio had spoken it, at some point during at least one of my visits to his place of business a year ago. "Perugino was the bearded apprentice, in your master's studio last summer?"

"He had shaved, the last time I saw him."

"And where was that? And when?"

"I saw him here in Florence. About six months ago. But since then I have heard that he has gone to Rome, to paint some murals in a church there. Which church I do not know." Leonardo looked at me for a moment longer, then turned back to his work.

I turned back to the window again. I found one hand, knuckles white, wrist shaking, clutching my dagger's hilt. Dolt that I was! not to have known. But still I could not believe that a king's sister could have left me for a mere artist . . .

Before my eyes in imagination, I brought the face of the bearded one, clear as my memory could focus it. Now I could remember how that countenance had looked when I first brought the rescued Helen into the studio—the very place where he had first brought her to be a model. Confused, stunned, displaying a strange mixture of emotions. Somehow I had got the impression that Perugino had first met her in some Florentine tavern. But what had Morsino said? . . . *an attractive girl, of diminutive stature, recently arrived . . . in the company of a troop of traveling players, or an itinerant artist, or something of that kind . . .*

And Matthias, earlier. Something about an artisan. How his sister had actually run off with one. If she could do such a thing when a Sforza wedding was in prospect, then why not as the bride of a Drakulya?

. . . and again, just after the wedding ceremony, Perugino handing her an armful of flowers. How had he looked, then? Could I trust my memory to tell me? And she . . .

It was still almost impossible to believe. I turned away from the window again. "Leonardo," I called softly. In my greatest angers I maintain full control of myself and my behavior. "Be plain. You are telling me that she ran off with this Perugino."

"It is nothing to me, *signore*. I do not wish to become involved. But yes, I think that is what happened."

"I see. And has this matter been discussed at the studio?"

He hesitated. "Not really. Not much. I think we all guessed, last year, what had happened.

Perugino quit the studio a little while after you left for Pisa. But you were gone. There was no way to tell you anything. Signore Lorenzo did not come round again to the studio for a long time."

"I see." No one wanted to get involved, really. I supposed that that was natural enough.

Now I thought that the youngster was suddenly afraid of me, perhaps wishing that he had kept quiet. Still his hand sketched steadily enough. He unpinned one paper from his easel and put up another. He was working quickly, already there appeared to be several finished preliminary sketches.

I was about to speak, when I glanced down at them. To study the topmost paper better, I picked it up. It showed the essential lines of the Magdalen's face, angellically done, the key to the face captured, just as I had wished.

Again I was about to speak when the corner of another drawing, at the very bottom of the small pile, caught my eye. I pulled it out. It was every bit as well drawn, but a grotesque.

It was a male countenance, set in an expression, almost a mask, of insane rage. I needed a moment to realize that I was holding a caricature of my own face.

Fifteen

Rage augments strength, and sometimes cunning and the will as well. If one can harness it properly, and take the time to seek out tools, and improvise means, then eventually if one has eyes that see in virtual darkness, in a matter of only a few hours perhaps, the door of even a heavy wall safe can be seen swung back, with its great lock reduced to hanging wreckage. Success had been greatly aided by the ability to work on both sides of the door alternately. And now the cans of films and containers of tapes could be brought out. It was something to do, somewhere to start; and it had become necessary now to make a start at once.

Electric power to the Seabright mansion had recently been shut off, a difficulty overcome by some attention to the main. Dorlan and his wife had also departed by the morning after the bombing, which was a help.

The laboratory tucked away in the mansion's lowest level was equipped with projection devices of all kinds, and these when sworn at properly in medieval tongues were at last persuaded to function properly. The private show, sans titles, soundtrack, or any other frills, began.

At first glance the star of the show, an enormous fat man who cavorted naked with adolescents of both sexes, as in some gross parody of more conventional porn, appeared to be Ellison Seabright himself. At a second look it did not appear to be him. The monumental man in the film looked as big as Ellison and resembled him facially but was even older, with a fringe of white hair round his massive head. Now and then he could be seen casting a look toward the hidden camera that must have done the filming through one of the concealed ports in the playroom wall. It was recognizably the playroom-lounge of this very house where the action was going on. The huge old man knew without a doubt that the camera was there. He was intending to watch himself in action later, evidently thus doubling his enjoyment of these acts. Here we did not have your common garden variety of senior citizen. Mr. Thorn, no stereotype of the golden years himself, had no doubt at all that he was beholding the image of Delaunay Seabright.

The broken safe had yielded up perhaps a dozen cans of film in all, with an equal number of videotape cartridges. A sampling of three, four, five, six of these containers showed no essential variation in content, though the supporting cast appeared to be always different. With one exception. Several times the same lean, dark man of thirty or thereabouts appeared—otherwise the players were all quite young and interchangeable, coming and going like seasonal flowers in a vase.

After the sixth sample, Thorn turned off the projector and sat in darkness trying to think. He could feel that sunny daylight had come, aboveground, but that did not concern him here. His course of breaking into the safe, despite its first feeling of instinctive rightness, was proving to be of no apparent help. The sad secrets of the safe seemed to have nothing to do at all with Mary Rogers or her death. Nor did they explain why Seabright or anyone else would have any reason tó want to eliminate Thorn. Nothing here to tell Thorn who was guilty, where to start a search . . .

A faint sound, aboveground, out of doors but near the house. A car had stopped.

Someone else was coming to the mansion.

There was no hurry on this job, no need to be furtive. As former butler-bodyguard in the house, the man called Brandreth still had a set of keys. If the police or the FBI or reporters should be watching the place this morning, he could tell them he had been sent by Ellison Seabright to check on things, and Ellison Seabright would back him up.

Brandreth eased his car to a stop outside the iron gates, and got out to unlock them. Even before he stopped, he had noticed the other car, parked a little distance away on the other side of the road. Whoever was watching the place from over there wasn't trying to be very subtle about it. Brandreth of course would go on in, the perfectly respectable servant doing a job. Only when he was in the house and sure, very sure, that he was alone, would he get on with his real job and go to open the small hidden safe that Gliddon had told him of . . .

A couple of hours earlier, about dawn, Brandreth had met Gliddon in a small town in northern Arizona, to get keys and instructions. Brandreth had been at the door of the dingy hotel room, leaving, when Gliddon called him back. "And, listen, if you ever get any ideas about seeing what's on those tapes and films and putting them to use yourself—"

"Not me, boss. Not me."

"—then you can go right ahead and try. They're

not *worth* a cent, get me? I'd go and take care of them myself if that was the case, even if I am supposed to be missing. They're just something that could mean trouble for whoever is found in possession of them, and Seabright tells me he wants 'em out of the house. So get 'em and dispose of 'em, and I mean thoroughly.''

"I will. I—"

"How are you going to do it?"

Brandreth, with an inward sigh, leaned his large body against the doorframe. Gliddon's stare always unnerved him and he tried to take a relaxed pose in order not to show it. "Want me to bring 'em here?"

"All the way up here? No. I won't be here anyway, I have to disappear again. Just tear them up, burn them, scatter the ashes. Then stay in Phoenix, where I can get hold of you by phone. I may have another job for you soon."

Brandreth looked a question.

"No, I don't think it'll involve wasting anybody, this time. Never can tell, though."

"I did all right on that Blazer, huh?"

"I guess." Gliddon looked meditative. "It just bothers me that the guy we were supposed to get wasn't in it after all. Maybe we shouldn't have been so cute, using delayed timers and all."

"That was your—"

"I know, my idea." Gliddon spoke very patiently and reasonably. "I just didn't want your thing going off in the hotel garage, injuring innocent bystanders and all. Too much heat gets generated that way. It's bad publicity. Well, it looks like maybe we got rid of Thorn anyway; he may still be running. And I don't think our employer's really unhappy either that we blew up that bothersome broad. Teach her to go out with strangers." And Gliddon had smiled.

Brandreth, watching, felt something like a shudder, purely internal. Even if Gliddon was not as big, and a queer besides, Brandreth was afraid of him.

Now, several hours later, Brandreth going calmly about his butler's business had just got the iron gate unlocked when he heard a car door from across the road. He looked up and saw that a lone man had just got out of the vehicle, an ancient sort of wreck, that was parked over there. The man was walking across the road toward Brandreth, approaching tiredly, almost reluctantly. Not a cop, probably not a reporter either, although there was nothing specific about him to rule out either possibility. He had long brown hair and an unkempt beard, and looked as if he hadn't slept all night.

When the man got close he said: "I was just watching, wondering if anyone was home over here."

"The house is vacant now, sir." Brandreth was wary, but confident. He had several inches and about thirty pounds on the other man, not taking into account the pistol in his belt under his jacket, if this turned out to be a game of some kind. "I'm one of the staff. I just come round periodically to check if everything's all right."

"Oh." The other considered this, with vacant sadness. He put his hands in his pockets and brought out a big-bowled pipe and put it away again. "I'm Robinson Miller. Mary Rogers was . . . was a good friend of mine. She used to live here once. Maybe you knew her."

"Sir?"

"Mary Rogers. The girl who was blown up with a bomb last night. I've been at the morgue, looking at her, trying to find out something from the police. You ever look at anyone in a morgue? Who's been all torn to pieces by a bomb?"

Brandreth had to bite the inside of his cheek to keep from smiling. Talk about coincidence, this was good. Gliddon would get a chuckle out of this one when Brandreth told him—or would he? "I'm sorry to hear that, sir. There was something on the radio about someone being blown up in a car."

"She was out here, at this house, last night, you see. With a man named Thorn, the one the car was rented by. Did you know that?"

"No, sir, I had no idea she was here last night." Brandreth found the impulse to smile completely gone. He was watching this dazed man very carefully and at the same time trying to think. "Dorlan, he's the regular caretaker, would have been here then."

Robinson Miller wasn't really listening. "You see, I talked to the police at the morgue, but I didn't really say anything important. I wanted to think things over, first. Like I might have an idea of who was behind the bombing. It was these people here, this Seabright bunch, who killed her, one way or another. Oh, I don't blame you, you just work here. There was a man named Gliddon who worked here too, and he's supposed to be dead now but he's not."

"He's not?" Brandreth had no trouble at all in sounding surprised.

"No he isn't. Thorn told us that and they killed him, or tried to. Mary knew it, and they killed her."

This sounded like it might be too serious to let it

get by without taking action. "Sir? You really don't look well. Would you like to come into the house for a moment? I can get you a cup of coffee, or a drink, or something."

Miller sighed. He rotated his head, and rubbed the back of his neck in weariness. "That's good of you. Maybe I will, if you're sure they're all gone. I wouldn't want to face them just now. I don't know what I might do."

"They're all gone, I'm sure. Listen, there might be a thing or two I could tell you about the Seabrights, if you're interested. I don't want to get involved, though."

Miller suddenly looked somewhat more awake. "A thing or two? Like what?"

"Oh, not about bombings. Nothing like that. But . . . look, sir, why don't you just drive your car in through the gate, and park near the house? There's been some problem lately with vandalism in the neighborhood."

"With my car, it doesn't matter," Miller said. But then when Brandreth looked anxious he trudged back across the road and started up his engine. With the gate standing open, they drove both cars in; then Miller waited in his while Brandreth locked up the gate again. Then he followed Brandreth's car up to the house, where neither car would be visible from outside the gate.

As he led the way up to the main door, Brandreth looked the place over carefully. The house looked tightly closed up, all right. But as soon as he had unlocked and opened the front door, he stopped; an overhead light just inside was burning, and he had thought that the electricity was supposed to be already turned off. Well, things might go a little easier on this visit if it wasn't.

Like a good butler Brandreth switched the overhead light off now, then gestured deferentially.
"The bar's downstairs, sir. If you'd like a drink."
Downstairs was more certainly private, if things
should happen to take a turn for which privacy
appeared desirable, as Brandreth was beginning
to feel sure they would.

"It's morning, but—hell yes, I want a drink."

Since the power was still on, Brandreth led the
way toward the elevator. Once he had his guest
down in the rec room at the bar, he filled an order
for Scotch on the rocks, and then tried to reach
Dorlan on the intercom that communicated with
the caretaker's quarters. No one answered. Evidently the man and his wife were gone, and the
dogs with them, as Gliddon had said they would
be. All satisfactory, the place would be lonely as a
tomb.

Brandreth flipped off the intercom and gazed
across the bar at Miller, who already looked like a
lonely drunk. Half the Scotch was gone. Brandreth asked: "Did I understand you correctly, sir?
That you have some reason to think Mr. Gliddon
is still alive?"

Miller looked up, though not as if he really saw
Brandreth, or heard him. He chewed his brown
mustache. "You know, she just wouldn't leave it
alone. She wouldn't. She kept harassing Seabright, and threw that stuff on him, and then she
went off with Thorn to cook up something more. I
don't know what, but . . . I guess she never really
understood how dangerous the world can be."

"Sir, I can make you another one of those if
you'd like."

Robinson Miller looked down at his glass for a

fairly long time. "I don't know," he said at last.

"Excuse me, sir, I just want to check on something in here." While Brandreth was waiting for his man to get drunk and/or talk some more spontaneously, he thought he might as well do the job that he had come here for in the first place. Switching on more lights as he went, he walked off into the white tunnel and through it to the laboratory area just off the museum. Here a white panel in the wall came loose, just as Gliddon had said it would, and the small safe hidden behind it opened properly for Brandreth when he used the combination Gliddon had provided. He closed up the safe again and started to walk back to the lounge. All the valuable art had already been taken out, of course, and everything looked—

What was that wrecking bar doing, lying beside the inner laboratory door? Brandreth detoured a few steps and stood looking down at the tool. He thought he recognized it as one that was customarily kept in a shed near the caretaker's lodging.

He had broken into houses himself in his time, and he had a feel for when something was going on along that line. The lab door was locked, but it took Brandreth only a moment to find the right key in his bunch. With gun in hand he opened the locked door, to behold ruin—a big wall safe, one Gliddon hadn't even mentioned, yawning open. The door of it had somehow been cracked, with parts dangling from their steel roots in the concrete-reinforced wall.

Someone was behind him, and Brandreth spun, brandishing the gun. Miller had doubtless been approaching innocently, for he was carrying his

drink in hand. At the sight of Brandreth's face and
weapon he recoiled, and seemed to come fully
awake for the first time.

Miller started to say: "You've got to be in on—"
before he caught himself. Then he tried again,
lamely: "There's been a robbery."

"Brilliant, cocksucker," said Brandreth, and
raised the gun. He had been surprised and upset at
a moment when he thought himself in control of
the situation, and when that happened he sometimes tended to lose his head. Miller turned, cow-
ering away, trying to protect his head. Brandreth
brought the gunbarrel down, cracking on a
forearm, bringing a yelp of pain. Then he laid the
second blow alongside Miller's hairy head, not
too hard. Miller pitched forward on his face, and
lay there groaning, trying to move.

"Now, son of a bitch," said Brandreth. "You're
gonna tell me—"

He reached down, meaning to yank the smaller
man to his feet. But something that felt like a
gorilla's paw closed on Brandreth's own left
shoulder. His reaching arm was stopped. Then his
whole body was yanked into the air, as it hadn't
been since he was pint-sized and in the orphan-
age. Now he was being thrown. The room spun
round him with his flight, and smashed him with
its far wall, almost hard enough to knock him out.

He wasn't that easy to take out, though. Gun
still in his right hand, he got himself up on one
knee, ready to use it on—

—on one thin man in dark, burned-looking
clothes. A man with a pale, half-familiar face,
calm now as an utter lunatic. Thorn, God yes, it
was Thorn. Brandreth, when playing butler, had
one day answered the front door of this very house

to let him in. He must be a black belt in judo, to throw a man of Brandreth's weight like that . . . but Brandreth held the top card in his own hand now. As his head cleared, he smiled, even though his left shoulder still wasn't working, and was going to begin to hurt like a bastard in a minute.

The situation, and Thorn's burned clothes, made Brandreth smile again. "Holy shit," he remarked. "You must have been standing right beside the car." Then he made a preemptory motion with his gun. "Who else is in here?"

"No one," the singed man said calmly. "We three are quite alone."

"You blew that safe? I guess you're pretty good in the trade yourself." Brandreth could see, in the far corner of the room, Robinson Miller getting slowly up to his hands and knees. A drop of blood dripped from Miller's head to the carpet. But this time it wasn't going to be Brandreth's job to clean up anything.

Thorn inquired: "In the trade?"

"You know. Making things go bang. I'm pretty good at that myself."

At last there came a change in Thorn's madly cool expression—a relief for Brandreth, it had begun to make him nervous to have someone look back at him like that from the wrong end of a gun.

"Then it was you," said Thorn, "who planted the bomb . . .?" He had no need to finish. He could read his answer in Brandreth's face. "How fortunate," he added in a softer tone, and came walking forward.

"You're better off dead, you lunatic," said Brandreth, and fired. Twice.

And somehow missed, both times. How could he have missed? And fired again, and—

The grip this time came on the arm that held the gun. Brandreth screamed, feeling the bones go.

When he came out of it, or at least out of it enough to know where he was, he wished he hadn't. He was sitting propped up in one of the chairs inside the laboratory, which was almost dark. In front of him a projection screen had been rolled open, and Thorn stood nearby, fussing with a projector. Beyond Thorn the door was open to the small room with the cot, and Brandreth could see that Robinson Miller was lying in there. Miller's face looked pale in the dim light but he was only sleeping, for his chest rose and fell.

Thorn lifted his head from what he was doing, enough to glance at Brandreth from the corner of an eye. He inquired softly: "What is on this film that you were carrying?"

"Honest to God . . . I don't know."

"We shall soon see, in any event. Why did you come to this house today?"

"I—I was the butler here. Just checking up—"

Thorn put out a hand and touched him on the arm. "That is a half-truth, and not acceptable. Ah, if screaming will relieve your feelings, pray continue. I feel sure that those who scream down here are never heard outside."

The next time Brandreth's senses cleared, Thorn was bending over him again, but only speaking very gently, pointing to a frozen image on the screen. "That is the face of Delaunay Seabright, is it not?"

"I . . ." Brandreth tried his best to see the screen clearly. He was still slumped in his chair, groggy with shock, bathed in a cold sweat. His left arm wouldn't work and his right felt as if the bones might be about to poke out through his coat sleeve. He didn't want to know if they really were. "I dunno." His voice was pitiful. "I never saw Delaunay. Honest to God. Ellison's the one who hired me."

"And Gliddon?"

"Gliddon was already working for the Seabrights. I take orders from Gliddon. He passes on what . . . Ellison wants." Brandreth drew a deep, shuddering breath. Once he had been seriously afraid of Gliddon. But now he understood more fully what it could mean to be afraid. "Gliddon's supposed to be dead now. But he's not."

"To be sure," Thorn said soothingly. "And it was Gliddon who sent you here to get this film?"

Brandreth nodded. He could feel another faint coming on now, and tried to fight it back. He knew that if he fainted now he was going to be revived. But he didn't know how.

"And what were you to do with it?"

"Destroy it. The film and tape both. Just the ones in the little, hidden safe. Gliddon said there were more in a big wall safe somewhere, the one you blew I guess. But he didn't care about those. Why these are so important I don't know. Something big is going on here that I don't know about . . . I don't ask questions. I need help with this arm. Or I'm gonna pass out."

"Who helped you with the bombing?"

"I . . . do all that on my own. Gliddon just told me to do it."

"Not Ellison Seabright?"

"It was supposed to be what he wanted done. I

dunno. I hardly ever talk to Ellison. He's supposed to be in Santa Fe now. As far as I know, he
is."

Thorn turned away, to the projector. Brandreth
let out a sighing groan. In the next room, Robinson Miller mumbled something but did not wake
up. Now the screen darkened, then brightened
again with a closeup of Delaunay's face, talking.

"This will be Session Thirteen," Delaunay's
bass voice said, addressing the camera. He was
filmed sitting in the laboratory. He was wearing a
turtleneck sweater under an expensive sport coat,
and looked vastly more competent, somehow,
than his half-brother ever did. "Session Thirteen,
on the fourth of April. I think we made real progress yesterday, and I hope for more today."

Darkness again, and when the scene came back
there were two people sitting in the lab. In a soft
reclining chair facing Delaunay and what was
probably a hidden camera sat a teenaged girl with
brown hair, small and slight, demurely dressed.
Delaunay was also fully clothed, and it was soon
apparent that both participants were likely to remain that way.

The girl was gazing, dreamily, at a small instrument on Delaunay's desk that sent a rhythmic,
gentle, flashing light into her eyes.

"—sleep," Del was intoning gently as the scene
started. "Deep sleep. And you will not wake up
until I tell you. You will be able to hear me perfectly, and follow my instructions, but you will
not awaken until I tell you . . . Helen? Are you
asleep?"

"Yes," the girl answered in a calm, remote
voice. Her eyes were now closed.

Delaunay brought his hand out from under his

desk, where it had perhaps been on a hidden control that served to turn hidden recording devices off and on.

In Brandreth's ear Thorn whispered: "Who is the girl?"

"It must be Helen Seabright. The one who was killed. It looks like her pictures. I never saw her."

Thorn stood up straight, emitting a faint sigh.

"The last time we talked, Helen," Seabright was now saying, in the voice of a chatty psychiatrist, "you told me that next time you'd tell me why that painting fascinates you so."

"I don't want to talk about that, Uncle Del." It was a prim, calm voice, the voice of a young lady who knew her mind.

"But next time is now, Helen," Seabright prodded gently. When he got no response he tried again. "I'll make a bargain with you, if you like. How's this? I'll leave the painting where you can come and look at it anytime. And in return—what, Helen?" The girl had said something, very low.

"I said, it was really Annie who liked the painting anyway."

"Oh yes, of course. But you can like it too."

"And Annie's dead now."

"No more Annie. That's quite right. And do you miss her?"

Helen frowned.

Seabright said softly and with great certainty: "Annie was always running away. She had no home, no family, no love. Always and forever on the run. Don't you think it's really better that she's dead?"

"I don't miss her, really. She's really better off . . . but sometimes . . ."

"Yes. All right. Now, as I started to say, Helen,

I'll leave the painting out somewhere, where you can look at it. And in return you, now don't frown, you don't have to talk about the painting at all if you don't want to. Only about some other things, that happened to you when you were . . . much younger than you are now. How does that kind of bargain sound?"

The girl was troubled. Frowning, she shook her head, and mumbled something.

"We don't necessarily have to go back very far in the things we talk about. Not right away. Suppose we began with that night when, how shall I describe it, that night when Annie was here for the first time? Would it bother you—I see it would. All right. All right. You needn't do anything that you don't want to do. Not at all. Not for Uncle Del. Would you rather talk to me about the painting, then? It's a nice, fascinating old thing, isn't it?"

"Yes. Oh yes, it is." And Helen's agitation, that had been growing, eased somewhat.

"Who painted it, my dear? Who do you think did?"

Brandreth, somewhat surprised at himself that he still hadn't passed out again, heard a small, strange sound from somewhere nearby. From Thorn.

Delaunay Seabright's image explained: "You see, my dear, some people think it may have been done, long years ago, by a famous painter called Verrocchio. Have you heard of him?"

"Yes."

"Now don't say you have, don't say anything just to please me. You really did hear of Verrocchio, before I mentioned him?"

"Yes."

Seabright paused, as if hopeful that the girl might say more. When she did not, he went on: "Others, on the other hand, think it barely possible that a certain young boy did that painting. A boy who became quite famous in later life. Most authorities believe the boy was too young when this was painted, that he hadn't yet started to work in Mr. Verrocchio's studio. Now I wasn't there myself and I don't know. But I'd like very much to find out. If—"

The girl was toppling forward in her chair. Seabright moved quickly for all his bulk, to catch her, ease her tenderly back into a sitting position. Her face had gone completely pale, drained-looking. "All right, Helen. All right, that's it for today. You are feeling fine. You are going to wake up soon, when I tell you, as from a deep, refreshing sleep." It took another minute of careful coaxing and urging to bring the girl back into what appeared to be her original hypnotic state.

"I'm going to wake you up soon, Helen. First, though, would you like to give Uncle Del his big hug for the day?"

The girl's eyes opened for a moment, then closed again. She arose, dutifully, and walked to the man's chair to bend over him and hug him, gently, almost formally, like some shy distant niece. The huge man patted her back with one hand. His other hand went to the hidden control beneath his desk. The screen went dark.

The ringing phone jarred Chicago police lieutenant Joe Keogh out of sleep. He was lying in his and Kate's bedroom in their condominium apartment on the North Side, just off Lake Shore Drive. This was not one of the supremely expensive towers down close to Michigan Boulevard, but an older building of modest height, somewhat farther north. The place had large rooms, from the days when they built them that way, and hardwood floors and a fireplace. Joe would have been hard pressed to make the mortgage payments on his pay unaided, let alone trying to furnish and decorate the place the way Kate had. He found it really pleasant to have married into money.

He rolled his spare, muscular body over in the wide waterbed, establishing waves, and lifted the phone. "Hello, who's this?" At home he used a more guarded answering technique than the efficient response that was his habit at the office.

"Joseph, I have some information for you."

Joe was fully awake in an instant. He switched on the bedside lamp, and at the same time glanced over his shoulder toward Kate, as if for reassurance that she still slept at his side. He could see, between a mounded blue blanket and a white pillow, a familiar mass of honey-blond hair and the curve of one naked shoulder. For a man with his job, middle-of-the-night phone calls were nothing out of the ordinary, and in six months of marriage Kate had already schooled herself to sleep through most of them.

Joe was sitting up straight now, running a hand through his sandy hair. The waterbed was no scene for serious drama; it wobbled gelatinously, gently rocking his body and his wife's. "Are you hurt?" he asked the phone.

"No, Joseph, not seriously. I appreciate your concern." The voice sounded much as it had on the comparatively few occassions when Joe had heard it before: precise, slightly accented in a vaguely middle-European way. Good-humored. Still good-humored, after a bombing, oh my God.

Joe found himself sweating slightly, and turned back the covers a little. "Go ahead, then."

"First of all I would like to confirm what I have heard about how it could have been done; how the bomb could possibly have been planted where it was."

"Yeah, the bomb. I heard about that. They called me about it. Were you near the car when it blew up?"

"I was in it."

"Oh." Good God. "And you're . . . who do you think planted the bomb?"

"On that I believe I now have information that is accurate, if incomplete. The technician was a man named Brandreth, acting on orders from a man called Gliddon. The very same, I believe, whose aircraft was supposedly lost not long ago."

"Ah. That business about the painting. And where are Brandreth and Gliddon now? And how do you spell Brandreth?"

"Gliddon is probably somewhere in Arizona or New Mexico; I have no precise information. And Brandreth can be found in the Seabright mansion in Phoenix. The place is otherwise unoccupied."

"He's in—"

"You need make no hurried calls, nor be concerned to write down his name. He will be there."

"Oh."

"Now about the bomb. By the way, Joseph, is your home telephone secure?"

"I guess. Internal Investigation doesn't tap it any more, if that's what you mean. Since you were here in Chicago they've given up. They don't want to know what's going on with me."

"Then let us discuss the bomb. No one, I think, could have planted it in that vehicle between the last proper functioning of the starter and the explosion."

"Okay, I have a couple of ideas. Sometimes I talk shop with a friend of mine who's on the Bomb Squad. It's possible to use a detonator that doesn't function until the second or third time the starter's used. Or to use a timer. A timer could be set for a specific time, or else not to start running until the engine did."

"I see. Yes, that confirms what I have been told. Thank you."

Joe glanced again at Kate. She hadn't moved, and he thought it probable that she was still asleep. He said: "The Phoenix police told me on the phone that it looked like a real professional job. See, your hotel there had a record of a call from your room to my number at the station here in Chicago. So naturally one of the first things Phoenix did in their investigation was to call me."

"Naturally. I suppose they named no suspects? Did the name of Ellison Seabright arise at all in your conversation?"

"No it didn't. I wouldn't have expected them to name me suspects even if they had some. You think he was involved too?"

"Gliddon works for the Seabright family. Or he did. Much is still obscure to me. And there are matters involved that I find personally troubling. I want to be certain about Ellison before I move against him."

"Please do."

"And what," the distant voice inquired, with casual brightness, "did you say to the Phoenix police about me?"

Kate had moved. She was facing Joe now, and at
least one of her baby-blue eyes was open, regarding him over a mound of pillow as she waited
calmly to find out what was going on. Maybe she
had already heard enough to know, or guess, who
he was talking to.

Still watching Kate, Joe cleared his throat. "I
told them that a man calling himself Thorn sometimes phones me and gives me information. That I
had no idea of this Thorn's real name or where he
lives or where he calls me from. That's not as
crazy as it might sound. There actually are infor-
mants who behave like that, and sometimes they
give useful information."

When the other end of the line remained silent,
Joe went on: "Of course the next thing they asked
was what you had been calling me about from
Phoenix." He paused again here, thinking carefully. If ever it should come to a choice between
getting himself into legal trouble, police trouble,
and making an enemy out of the man now on the
phone, he knew which choice he'd have to make.
Kate's family could afford the best in legal help,
but a lot of good that would do him if— "I said
you'd talked to me about a possible lead on the
missing painting that's been in the news, but that
you hadn't given me anything definite on it at all.
Is that all right?"

"Yes, Joe, that is quite all right." A soothing
tone.

"Of course they quickly discovered that there
isn't any Oak Tree, Illinois. And since your home
address was a fake they'll probably assume that
the name Thorn's a fake too. So most likely they're
stuck as to where to look for you next. Since your
body wasn't found with the car, they'll assume

you weren't in it. Maybe they think you planted the bomb yourself. By the way, there were parts of a pair of man's shoes, pretty well destroyed, found in the wreckage."

"I am not surprised to hear it. Brandreth's shoes fit me tolerably well."

"They thought the woman's body was lying on the wrong side of the vehicle for her to have been in the driver's seat. It was the Mary Rogers you were asking about, I assume you know that. Say, was she a friend of yours? If so, I'm sorry."

The long-distance hum of equipment. "We had not grown to know each other well," Thorn replied at last. "Still, I think a certain rapport was beginning to grow between us. We might have become good friends. One has few good friends even in a long life, and one loses even them. Yes, her death grieves me."

Kate reached out to touch Joe's arm with one finger. When he looked at her, her lips formed a silent, one-word question: Judy?

Joe shook his head minimally. He had no reason to think as yet that Judy had come into it at all. Then he asked the telephone: "What about that O'Grandison you were asking about, is he connected with this in any way? None of my contacts here seem to know where he is. They say they haven't seen him for a while. Have you reached him yet?"

"I have not. I know no more about him now than when I spoke with you last."

"Okay. Do you want me to tell Phoenix that I've heard from you again? That you blame the bombing on Gliddon and this Brandreth or whoever he is?"

Thorn took a moment before answering. "If in

return, when you hear anything about the where-abouts of Gliddon, you are willing to tell me—then yes, you may tell them that."

"On second thought I guess I won't have to mention Brandreth. But I'll tell them that you called again, and that you claim Gliddon's still alive. How's that?"

"That will be fine. . . . Joseph."

"What?"

"Do not worry, about me. I mean that I am an old friend of Kate's family, which is now yours. I know that you are my friend, and mean well. And I am not all that greatly concerned about what you tell or do not tell the police in Phoenix or any-where else. Trouble with the law does not mean much to me, ultimately. Take care of Kate, and of yourself."

And with a distant click the line went dead. Joe had the vague sensation that his ears were burning. As if he had been caught out in cowardice.

Slowly he hung up the phone, and looked at Kate. He said: "I was going to tell you. I did call your little sister, earlier, trying to warn her not to get involved in this. She got a little angry at me, but I think she knows I'm right."

Kate looked doubtful at first. Then she looked worse than doubtful. "I don't know, Joe. You say you made her angry? Were you issuing orders?"

"Come on, give me credit for a little more sense than that."

"Still, I don't know. She's quite grown up now. Maybe even suggesting what she ought to do was a mistake."

"I figured she must have heard in the news about the bombing. I don't know if she knows that now he's calling himself Thorn. I don't have any idea when they've seen each other last, to tell the truth."

"I don't know either." Kate sighed. "Maybe it's all over. And her school *is* at least five hundred miles away from Phoenix."

"I don't think it's all over for her. She got angry. But as far as I could tell she wasn't really planning to do anything, like go to Arizona. She's anything but a wild kid, usually." Then Joe paused, listening to his own words, what he was saying about a girl who had had an affair with a vampire, however brief.

Husband and wife lay looking at each other, exchanging hopeful and supportive thoughts. At least Joe was trying to make the exchange hopeful, and he could see that Kate was doing the same.

"Well," Joe added at last, "we could call her again in the morning, and tell her that we know for sure now that he's still alive."

"She must know that much at least," Kate said positively. "There's still at least that much contact between them, if there's any relationship left at all."

"Yeah, I suppose. That's spooky." Joe knew that Kate knew more about the subject than he did.

"Give me a hug, Joey."

Joe rolled away from Kate to turn the light off. Then he rolled back again. Kate hugged his face against her bare breasts.

The telephone rang again.

For a moment, as he floundered his way back over the quaking mattress to pick up the receiver, Joe's imagination flickered with a truly horrible suggestion. Suppose, just suppose, that Thorn had been deranged somehow by the bomb's concussion, and turned into a crank phone caller. To imagine *him* gone mad, driven out of the state that with him passed for normality . . .

"Hello, who is this?"

In the next moment, puzzlement and fear had a new tangent. It was a woman's voice on the phone, one that Joe had never heard before. It sounded young, and, of all things, vaguely British. "Yes. Am I speaking to Mr. Joseph Keogh?"

"Lieutenant Keogh. Yes. Who is this?" It didn't sound like long distance this time.

"Sorry, lieutenant, of course, of the police department. I don't suppose you would recognize my name. I should like to communicate with Mr. Jonathan Thorn. Have you any idea at what number I could reach him quickly?"

Sixteen

Pat O'Grandison was heading west again. From northern Indiana he thumbed his way through Chicago and right on, following Route 66, or Interstate 55 as they called it now. His intention was to find Annie, the girl he really liked.

He had missed Annie, he had to admit it to himself, more than he could remember ever missing anyone before. They had met—well, never mind where they had first met, but they had spent days together in Chicago some months back. Then Annie had dropped out of sight and Pat had just assumed that she was gone for good, like everything else good that had ever happened to him. Then bang, gosh, one night in Calumet City, Indiana, she had shown up again out of nowhere. At least Pat was almost sure she had. Not really *absolutely* sure, because next morning he had been having a bad time with his mind again, and the morning after that he woke up in the looney bin again.

He stayed in the mental hospital for a few weeks and was then discharged, with all the usual bullshit about commitment to a sheltered care program and a case worker and so on, and on that same day he sniffed the air and decided that the warm weather was far enough advanced to hit the road. And headed west.

Damn, but he missed her. Annie was the only girl, the only female, practically the only person of any kind that Pat could remember feeling anything like this about. Almost the only person he could remember ever really liking. And what made it even stranger, was that as a rule he could get along okay with girls and women but he didn't usually seek them out, or care for them as close associates. For a companion, a partner in bed or on the road, he generally felt better with another male. Preferably a bigger and stronger male whose presence could afford at least the illusion of protection; as almost any boy, by the time he was half grown, was bigger and stronger than Pat, that particular condition was not too hard to fulfill.

But now he just kept on thinking about Annie, the girl he really liked. She had told him once, just before they took her off to the juvenile home in Chicago and got ready to put Pat on trial, that her last name was Chapman. A lot of the people that Pat met had changed or were changing their names for one reason or another, so he tended not to take names very seriously—he wasn't always completely sure what his own real name ought to be, if it came to that. But he was sure that he liked Annie, whether Annie Chapman was her real name or not, and he needed her as much as he had ever needed anyone. She was all girl, nothing dyke about her, and yet she still had an air about her of being able to offer protection. Small as she was, no bigger than Pat himself, there was this hard core in her that he sensed he could lean on. And even if the protection she offered was not physical—well, maybe there were kinds of protection even more important.

In bed she did some kinky things, at least as far out as anyone else he'd ever known. And he had known a few. And the coupling of his body with hers had given him more than he'd ever got before, with man or woman or girl or boy. And maybe, Pat thought in a corner of his mind now that he was on the road again, maybe he had better convince himself that it was just the good sex with Annie that was making him look for her now. Because, if he thought about it, he was almost sure that there was more to it than that; and somehow it bothered him deeply that there should be more.

It could be that one of the things that had him out on the road again looking for her was the simple fact that Annie liked him. She had talked with Pat, stayed with him when she could have chosen to go off with someone else, had gone out of her way sometimes to do little things that she knew would make him happy. Very few people ever did that. Most people of whatever age or sexual orientation did not like Pat for long, once things between them had got beyond the elementary first stage in which they simply admired his more-than-half-childish good looks.

So here he was, hitchhiking southwest on the interstate out of Chicago. And how many times had he come this way before? He didn't really know. More than a couple. He wasn't at all sure how many. One of the problems with being periodically insane was that things in the past always tended to get blurred.

But, on the other hand, what you might have thought would be a difficult problem, that of locating Annie, didn't really bother Pat at all. Because he now had a strong feeling for where Annie ought to be. Where she had to be, in fact. He couldn't name the place but he could tell where it was. Roughly southwest of Chicago, and at some distance considerably more than a day's drive.

This was another thing that could be scary if he stopped and let himself think about it much. He knew it wasn't normal to have this kind of a strong hunch for where another person was. But then there were a lot of things about himself that were abnormal, as he had known for a long time. A number of doctors and other experts had found different words to tell him so. If you looked at it in that light, one more abnormality didn't seem all that worrisome. Besides, he had figured out that his hunch could have a logical explanation. Annie might have mentioned to him sometime that she intended to head for some certain place in the Southwest, and maybe Pat had been stoned or drunk or half asleep or a little crazy, or all of the above, and what Annie said hadn't registered properly with his conscious mind. But on some deeper level he had heard, and remembered.

On the first day of this present trip, going southwest through Illinois and then Missouri, Pat told the people who gave him rides that he was headed for California. Each time, as soon as he had told someone where he was going, they wanted to know where he was coming from, and each time he said that he had just left home. To questioners who tried to pin him down more closely, he answered that home was in Chicago— it was a big city, as good a place to be from as any other. He never mentioned his just-concluded stint in the Indiana mental hospital, or any of his previous stints in similar institutions elsewhere. Pat knew he was crazy, but he had never been crazy enough to tell a benefactor that.

As evening approached at the end of his first day's travel, Pat hiked himself down off the main

highway. Spring was far enough advanced so that
he wasn't going to freeze to death overnight no
matter where he slept, but he hoped to somehow
get inside. He thought he would be able to manage
that. Enough trips on the road, and you developed
a feeling for such things, when things were likely
to be easy, and when hard. Here the crickets were
out as darkness fell, and it was almost like summer. Pat liked deep summer best.

On the outskirts of Joplin, Missouri, he found
himself hiking past a deserted-looking house. No
other houses were very near. A look around and
another quick sniff of the air decided him that he
was not likely to find a better prospect. He went to
a side window and checked out the house. No
furniture. It was not only deserted but seemed to
have been standing vacant for some time. Pat
broke a window in the back and climbed inside.

He put his knapsack on the floor for a pillow
and covered himself with his light jacket, the best
he could do toward keeping warm. As for food,
the last people to give him a ride had bought him a
sandwich, too, out of pity, and that would have to
do for food until tomorrow. Pat was used to not
eating a lot. Though it was still early in the evening he fell asleep almost at once, stretched out on
the bare floor.

At first he knew that he was asleep, and shivering a little. Then he began to dream of Annie. In
Pat's dream, she was asleep, stretched out also
upon boards, but her boards looked like the floor
of an attic somewhere. She was wearing a non-
descript pullover shirt and jeans. Then Annie in
the dream opened her eyes and looked at Pat, and
smiled at him, and he knew beyond any doubt
that in a moment she would reach out her arms to

him and they would make love. Instead all that happened was that he woke up, uncomfortable on the boards after having got used to a hospital bed again, and shaking a little more with cold than he had been before. Well, life was usually like that.

Late next morning, when he had got as far as Oklahoma, Pat began to have serious doubts about California as his real destination, though he continued to use it as an answer whenever he was asked. Everyone more or less expected that a young drifter would be headed for the Coast. Whereas if he had said that he was bound for somewhere in Arizona or New Mexico, that would be an interesting answer; people would wonder why he was going there, and ask more questions, and think about him some more. Or so it seemed to Pat. As a general rule, the less other people wondered and thought and talked about him, the happier he was.

As the day went on a little, he began also to have a feeling that he didn't want to go to Arizona. He wasn't sure why. But he certainly hoped it would turn out that Annie wasn't there.

A few of the people who gave him rides asked him what he meant to do when he reached California. He answered that he meant to get a job there making films. Whenever he said this, his questioner looked at him again, and chuckled to himself or herself in one tone or another, and immediately became patronizing. Because they could see he wasn't joking. But in fact his answer was quite sane and realistic. He would have got a job making films if he had been going to California. Not Hollywood movies, no, which the people assumed he meant. But there were a number of people in other towns out there making a lot of other movies of one kind and another, and during the past few years Pat had already been connected with several of them. In matters having anything to do with movie-making he was an authentic genius, though totally unpublicized, usually unemployed, and practically unpaid.

Sometimes the people who gave him rides asked him how old he was. They were beginning to have plans for him, at least tentative plans, of one kind or another, when they asked that. Pat's answer would vary, depending. If he thought the tentative plan was to hand over poor young Pat to the juvenile authorities somewhere, for his own good, he could answer with the truth. To the best of his own belief he was actually twenty-two, though he had to overcome a certain inner reluctance to admit to himself that he was that old. And he could document that age with a driver's license that bore his photograph, if the discussion ever got that far.

In cases where the plan did not involve turning him over to the cops, he often varied his answer downward. No one as far back as he could remember had ever doubted him if he said he was sixteen. If he said he was seventeen, they sometimes still doubted, believing him to be certainly younger than that.

To the truck driver he was riding with when he reached Albuquerque, Pat had said he was sixteen. The truck driver had then responded with: "First time away from home, huh?"

"Yeah."

"I got a long drive ahead. We'll keep going all night," said the driver, and squeezed Pat's thigh, and smiled.

It was still early afternoon. Pat smiled back and

made no protest about the hand on his leg. The driver was surprised and chagrined when just a little later, at a truck stop near the junction of Interstates 40 and 25 Pat announced that he was getting out, for good.

"Hey. What the hell. I thought ya wanted to go to California."

Still smiling, Pat slid down from the cab to stand on the sunstroked pavement. He stretched. Mountains whose name he had never learned, though he had come through this way going east or west so many times, rose barrenly a few miles to the east. He had chosen a good place for his announcement; a truck stop surrounded by a city, with a fair number of people about. The jilted trucker was not going to be able to do anything, or even to argue very much.

"Hey. Kid."

Pat did not even turn, but simply walked away. His feeling for Annie had altered suddenly. West was no longer the right direction. Now she had to be somewhere to his right, somewhere to the north of here. He could tell that she was out of walking distance still, but now she was no longer anything like a full day's drive away.

Interstate 25 going north out of Albuquerque was a new route to Pat. But one highway was not all that different from another; he was really at home on them all. Hiking the shoulder now, going up an entry ramp toward the northward traffic flow, Pat felt a certain relief. Not only at leaving that particular trucker behind—sadistic tendencies there, experienced instinct whispered—but at not having to go on to Arizona, which was the next state west.

There had been a bad scene out there in

Phoenix, once. Real bad. Pat couldn't remember it consciously. But the stink of it still came up to conscious memory, like something dead and too shallowly buried. A warning: Don't dig here.

Pat topped the entrance ramp and kept on moving, hiking, looking over his left shoulder at a burst of speeding cars that passed him. Like an accomplished athlete or an old actor going into an old routine, he only needed to use half his attention in trying to flag a ride. Meanwhile he could use the other half on the question of what he ought to do when he reached Annie.

He could tell where she was, in a general way that seemed to get more particular the closer he got to her. But he couldn't tell what she was doing. For all he knew, she might be home, reconciled with her parents; or maybe in some other situation that she wouldn't be anxious to leave, just to hit the road again with Pat. So he ought to have some kind of hopeful proposition ready for her, something really attractive to suggest.

He would talk about—what else?—getting her into movies of some kind. Every girl liked that idea, and Annie was quite good-looking enough to make it credible. In fact, now that he thought of it . . .

Now that he thought about it, making movies with Annie was suddenly the one thing Pat wanted desperately to do.

Sure. Of course. There would be some way. Why not? Almost forgetting to work at picking up a ride, Pat hiked excitedly along the shoulder. The mountains to his right were forgotten, as was the intermittent roar of traffic at his left elbow. He would find Annie, and they would go off somewhere and make films, and everything in his whole screwed-up life might fall into the right place for once . . .

He remembered now how he had been talking with her in Chicago once, and she had been fascinated by some of the stories of movie-making that he'd had to tell. She seemed to understand that he was telling her the truth . . . or maybe it wasn't in Chicago. Somewhere. She *had* been with him somewhere else, before Chicago, now that he came to think of it. Or was it after?

Somewhere else. A place he didn't want to think about right now. But she had liked him, and it had been so good, that special way that they'd made love . . .

A movie with Annie in it was certainly a great idea, and if he wasn't crazy he would have thought of it before now. Could he really do it? Could he really at last straighten out his own life that much? The idea, when put in those terms, scared him a little.

He knew he could handle the movie itself, if he ever got the chance. He would pick up Annie, and they would go somewhere where he could get a job with some film-maker. Maybe even right here in New Mexico. There were bound to be people here somewhere making films, and some of them had probably heard about Pat from people out on the Coast. When you were good, word got around.

Porn was by far the easiest kind of work to find, for Pat at least. Particularly when they found out that he was ready, willing, and able to double as an actor. He did well in front of the camera as well as behind it, though acting or performing of any kind wasn't really what he liked to do. His androgynous good looks were in demand, for straight, gay, or free-style porn. There was only one kind of thing he'd never touched, and never would. So he took part in the filmed sex smiling like the madman he sometimes was, faking the sex as much as possible, meanwhile continuing to keep himself happy by thinking how he would do the lights and the camera work and time everything differently if he were put in charge. Of course there was a dreary sameness in all porn, or almost all. But there were an infinite number of ways to disguise the sameness, if you knew what you were doing. Pat never doubted that he did.

But very rarely had he ever been allowed to take charge, to show what he could really do, though sometimes his suggestions on specific points were taken, by filmmakers who were always gratified with the results. The equipment and the space had always belonged to someone else. Nowhere, as far as he knew, was there a complete film of any kind that he had made. Once he had been allowed to take complete charge, at some real madman's house in Mexico. And once, another time, in this mansion with giant roof beams they had been going to let him take over, but . . .

. . . something had happened. And now here he was, hiking north on Interstate 25 and trying once more not to think about Phoenix. Today for some reason was a day for struggling with that problem. Maybe just because this was the first time he had returned to the Southwest since . . .

. . . someone had brought him into that rich guy's mansion out there, someone promising what they called a party. And Pat had thought he understood what that entailed . . .

His thought recoiled now, twisting, from a half-vision of blood. The memory faded, like a dying dream, almost as quickly as it had come. It left behind it no new knowledge, only a wash of sick fear. What he couldn't stand was the fear that that time he had been maneuvered into working on a snuff film.

Real torture on film, and real death. That would be for Pat an ultimate profanation, a blasphemy. He would have no part in it at all, though what exactly was being profaned, he could not have said . . .

His inner thoughts had become a burden, and it was a great relief when a car stopped for him at last. A new yellow Pinto, stopping cautiously, well ahead. Pat hitched his small backpack higher on his back, and trotted. The face peering back at him from the window on the driver's side was that of a middle-aged man with steel-rimmed spectacles, alone in the car. A fatherly type, it would appear. Perhaps genuinely so. As soon as they were under way, the man would begin to wonder aloud just why a young kid like Pat was hitchhiking alone; didn't he realize it could be dangerous?

"Hi, young feller, you going up to Santa Fe?"

Something about the name sounded reasonable. "Yeah," said Pat, and climbed in on the right. Santa Fe was one of those towns whose name everyone had heard, but he had never seen the place before. Right now, though, it sounded congruent with Annie.

The car was rolling, easing cautiously off the shoulder onto pavement, picking up speed. The man asked: "You got some family up there?"

Pat not-answered, as he often did. Looking out the window, he pretended that he hadn't heard. The man cleared his throat but did not repeat the question. Later on he would. A small roadside sign announced that they were entering an Indian reservation. God, what could even Indians do on land as barren as this? Raise sheep? But there were none in sight.

You could make movies, of course, you could do that just about anywhere. Pat visualized a line of Indian dancers a thousand strong, their line stretching away over the yellow-brown plain. Make it ten thousand, the line would still look small. A camera in a low-flying aircraft, skimming just above their heads . . . tell them to show no expression on their faces . . .

The Pinto sped in scanty traffic. They kept topping long brown hills, one after another. Annie was getting close. In the distance, on every side now, more mountains reared. Somehow the highway had shrunk, it seemed too narrow here to be called an Interstate. Pat hadn't been watching the signs. The man, after his first attempt to talk, was unexpectedly going to be silent. Who knew what went on inside people's heads? No one did. No one. It was all right, silence was okay with Pat.

After they had driven for the better part of an hour through virtual nothingness they topped a final long hill. Now, miles ahead, some kind of a town or city came into view, looking as if it had been dropped at the foot of the tallest-looking mountains around. Their peaks still showed white that Pat supposed was snow.

The man cleared his throat again. "Whereabouts can I let you off?"

Pat brought his gaze back into the car, shifted his position in the seat. Annie was near. "Somewhere around the center of town is fine. If you're going that way."

"The Plaza?"

Pat didn't know what The Plaza meant. "That's fine. Anywhere around there is fine."

The man stopped the Pinto twenty minutes later to let Pat out in the midst of a minor traffic jam in narrow streets. Slanting afternoon sunlight warmed low buildings covered with what Pat would have called beige stucco; they put him vaguely in mind of pictures that he had seen of Indian cliff dwellings. And here were some Indians, real-by-God Indians, with their blankets spread on a roofed sidewalk to display pots and jewelry for sale. Above their heads the rough ends of unfinished logs stuck out of the edge of the building's roof.

"Thanks for the ride." Pat flashed a merry smile as he got out. He always liked to do that, no matter what. Maybe he hoped that the people would remember him.

The man huffily not-answered as he drove away.

Annie was somewhere around here. That way. Within walking distance now, or almost. Pat started walking.

On the rear patio of his huge house near the northern edge of Santa Fe, Ellison Seabright was trying to get his wife posed properly to paint before the light changed any more. They were out on the rear patio, overlooking a spectacular scene of what was almost wilderness. Only a few other houses were visible, around the edges. Ellison had given Stephanie a supposedly genuine seventeenth-century Spanish shawl to put around her while she perched on the low stone balustrade that rimmed the patio. Just behind his subject, a slope of sandy earth and sparse wild grass, punctuated with dwarfish juniper, fell unfenced and almost untrodden for a hundred yards to end in the bottom of a sinuous ravine. Somewhere down there was an unmarked line where Seabright land ended and national forest land began.

Beginning right with the steep opposing slope of the wild ravine, the Sangre de Cristos mounted to the north and east, claiming the sky in one great rounded step above another. The highest and most distant shoulder of the mountain, blue-clad in distant fir and pine, hid behind it the bald snowcapped peaks projecting upward beyond timberline. Almost all the land in view was government land, unsettled and unpeopled. The mountains went up a mile or more in altitude above the seven thousand feet or so of the patio; a thousand years, Ellison thought, or maybe more than a thousand, back in time.

Ellison vaguely enjoyed thinking about the mountains, and liked knowing that they were there as a subject for his own painting, whenever he got around to it. He seemed to be chronically pressed for time, and rarely felt he could take time out from business to pick up a brush himself. But today, at last, he had Stephanie at home with him. And a few hours without people or business to interfere.

Stephanie, sitting on the balustrade, had at last got the shawl arranged to Ellison's satisfaction. She smiled into the lowering sun, as if she enjoyed its warmth.

"You're in a cheerful mood today," Ellison commented, getting some paints out of the box.

"Why shouldn't I be?" Her voice was lighter and easier than he had heard it in some time.

"No reason. You're basically a lucky lady." Except for Helen, of course, a few months back—but if Stephanie could start to forget that now, Ellison wasn't going to remind her. "But last week in Phoenix you were worried about the sun, how it aged the skin and brought on wrinkles. You said you weren't going to pose for me any more, out in the sun."

"The sun here isn't as hot."

"And you've stopped imagining you have wrinkles, I hope."

"I don't intend to get them. I know you divorce your wives when that happens, and look for someone younger. You've done it twice before."

Ellison looked at her. She gave him back a smile, enigmatic, Mona Lisa. "Shall I cross my legs?"

"No," he said, pretending patience, wondering what was going on. "We have the pose all settled. Let's just concentrate on keeping it." A change in his wife lately, sure enough; he had thought it was only Helen's death, but it was more. Ellison squinted about the huge patio, all winey sunlight and bluish shadow, with more furniture than a small house. He was looking for his tube of titanium dioxide white. "Do you realize," he asked, "that's it's now been almost four years since you have posed for me?"

"Really? That long?"

"Since shortly after we were married."

"Surely it hasn't been that long."

"Oh, yes. I remember that Helen was hardly more than a little girl. She kept sneaking around to see what we were up to. In those days I generally had you posing in the nude."

The mention of Helen seemed to have had no effect. Something else was certainly on her mind.

"I wish you would have posed nude again today. Out here, against the mountains. I gave all the help the day off, you know."

"I know. But it's too cold today. Maybe next time."

"There. That's just the smile I want. Hold it for me, if you can. Just like that."

Ellison found that he was a little nervous about the painting. God, it was a long time, it must be a couple of years now, since he had really tried to paint anything at all. Would he really be able to do it now?

He suddenly spotted the tube of paint he had been looking for. It was on a small stone ledge not an arm's length from where he had set up his easel; now he recalled setting it down there. He picked up the tube and fidgeted with it and dropped it back into the paintbox. Then holding a stick of charcoal he looked at his model, and then beyond her to the mountains, where the changing sunlight made blue folds slowly appear and disappear. The light changing like that, and it was so long now since he had really tried. It was going to be hopeless.

"Are we going to talk about Del, sometime?" Stephanie asked him suddenly.

"What's there to talk about?"

"We both know that he's still alive. You don't have to be so cagey with me."

"Yes," said Ellison. He was not going to try to get the background in at all today. Only Stephanie. "Yes, well, don't you think it's wiser not to talk too much about the fact?"

"No one can overhear us. I just wondered how much you knew about the—details. I know you're handling business deals for him. Do you think anyone else knows he isn't dead?"

"I say it's wiser not to talk, even out here. There could be someone up there, behind any of those rocks, listening. Directional microphones have amazing capabilities these days."

Stephanie glanced behind her at the hillside, then resumed her pose without appearing to be convinced. "Someone? Who?"

"My dear, you must have some idea of how much that painting is worth. Whenever such amounts of money are concerned, a lot of people take an interest."

"Ellison, our phone might be tapped, but no one's hiding up on that mountain twenty-four hours a day watching our house."

"How do you know that?"

The sound of the doorchime came drifting cooly out through the open patio doors, from inside the cool caverns of the house. Ellison sighed, put down the charcoal stick, wiped his hands, and went to answer. Having all the help gone was not necessarily a boon. He supposed this would turn out to be some neighbor brat with Girl Scout cookies to sell.

The boy standing at the front door was undersized and shabby. He was a total stranger to Ellison, yet at first glance Ellison knew he was not selling cookies. Nor was his presence here merely some routine mistake. The young face waiting had something extraordinary about it; and not only extraordinary but wrong. This unusual wrongness Ellison accepted as a sign that the visitor knew what door he stood at.

"What is it?" Ellison demanded. In annoyance

he used the lordliest tone he could produce, even though he was already sure that there would be no getting rid of this lad that easily.

The young eyes, cloudy blue, looked back at Ellison. Most people would have seen in them a probability of innocence. But Ellison saw more, and worse.

"I want to see Annie," the apparition announced, in a voice whose boyish appeal seemed to have been practiced.

The name meant nothing to Ellison. He only looked at the intruder, willing without much hope that he should go away.

"Annie knows me. My name is Pat O'Grandison, I'm a good friend of hers. I know she lives here."

"No one named Annie lives in this house. Or ever has."

"You her father?" the youth asked doubtfully. "Maybe she's not here right now, but if not she'll be back soon. Has she run away from home, or something like that? If that's it, she'll soon be back."

Ellison heard a soft sound behind him, and turned to see Stephanie approaching. She came looking like a great Spanish lady, with the old shawl still round her shoulders. Her face was troubled as she stared at the visitor.

Ellison spoke to his wife while nodding toward the boy. "One of Del's old crowd, perhaps?" he mused. "But he never brought any of them here, to my knowledge. I thought all that went on out in Arizona, not here under my roof."

Stephanie only shook her head slightly in reply. Eyeing the visitor up and down, she asked him: "Who are you? Why are you here?"

The boy put out a frail arm to lean his weight tiredly against real adobe bricks. He scratched at one with a black-rimmed fingernail, as if he wondered what it was. "Can I come in and get a drink of water, please? It's all right, I really know Annie." Then he focused on Ellison suddenly; as if, Ellison thought uncomfortably, he might be trying to recall where he had seen the big graying man before.

"I think we'd better let him in," advised Stephanie. "He looks a little sick to me."

"On something, more likely."

"What's the difference?"

"Oh all right, let him in."

The boy came in and like someone near exhaustion dropped himself into the first handy chair. He was blond and undersized, dressed in travel-worn jeans with white road dust on them, and a plain T-shirt, once white. A small knapsack of fabric dull as camouflage lay on the floor beside his chair, one of its straps still resting limply in his slack right hand. His snub nose and beardless cheeks made him look no more than fifteen or so. But Ellison was sure that he was older.

Several components of Ellison's mind, one of them artistic, considered that young face with growing fascination. Here was one of Del's people, certainly. The face was beautiful. And, leaving aside whatever might be due to present tiredness, there was that inward something that was very wrong, that had told Ellison at first glance that the boy was here for some real purpose. His coming meant trouble, maybe, but there was nothing accidental about it. Ellison wondered: Did Del send him here?

He asked: "Have you been here before?"

"No." A hesitation. "Though I got the feeling that maybe I seen you someplace."

Ellison looked at him.

"I guess I'm mistaken. Hey, if Annie's not here, how about Helen? It just occured to me, maybe it's possible that you and I know this girl by different names? I mean, sometimes when people run away they'll use a different name?"

The blue eyes shifted from Ellison to Stephanie and back again. It was impossible to read just how much was truth in them, and how much guile.

Ellison looked at his wife, trying to get some cue from her, but he couldn't. She kept regarding the visitor very thoughtfully. At last Ellison said: "There was a girl named Helen in this family once, living in this house. She's dead."

The boy considered that. He had slumped down in his chair until his head rested on its padded back. The strap of the backpack had fallen free of his limp fingers.

Stephanie crouched down gracefully beside the chair. "Helen was my daughter. If we're really talking about the same Helen. It's true, she did run away from home once. And she is dead—there was a lot of publicity about it at the time. You must have read some of that? Seen it on television?"

Then visitor opened his mouth, then closed it again, evidently reconsidering whatever he had been going to say. "I didn't know she was dead. Sorry."

"Where," asked Ellison, "did you think that you had seen me before?"

"I dunno. Maybe I was wrong about that, too. Sometimes my ideas get all, all screwed up."

Stephanie straightened up. She was smiling

briskly, almost like a nurse, as she touched the youth on the shoulder. "You must be hungry and thirsty," she said in bright inviting tones. "Come along with me to the kitchen, and we'll see what we can find. What's your name?"

"Pat." And Pat got up out of his chair quickly, following Stephanie like a puppy entranced by a first kind gesture.

A few moments later, Ellison followed them both, keeping a little distance. Peering into the breakfast room, he could see the youth seated at table there, his back to Ellison, already chewing on something. Stephanie was pouring milk into a plastic tumbler for him. Beyond, in the kitchen, the sink was modestly stacked with dirty dishes from lunch. It would be tomorrow morning before any of the help came back.

Once the wanderer in his dirty T-shirt had been launched on a meal, Stephanie rejoined Ellison for a conference. "What do you make of this?" she whispered.

Ellison tugged her a little further from the kitchen, into the next room. "I don't like it," he answered in his own almost rumbling whisper. Then with a gesture he retreated further still, to where the boy had left his pack. Ellison bent and opened it. A dirty, lightweight jacket came to view, along with a few other items of spare clothing. In the bottom were some granola bars, their wrappers worn with a long time of jostling in the pack.

Ellison stood, grunting. "And I don't know what it's about. But I'm going to take whatever steps are necessary to find out."

Seventeen

Oh, I could regale you now with all the sights and sounds and smells of fifteenth-century Rome. But it would be misleading, insofar as my story is concerned. The truth is, that at the time of my first visit to Rome I was scarcely aware of my surroundings except as they affected my search for Helen. I was beginning truly to wonder whether I might be the victim of some enchantment, so obsessively had the woman's image, in paint and sketch and memory, come to dominate my thought. Of course I wanted revenge on her, and on her lover—but gradually I was coming to realize that I wanted something more as well. More than mere vengeance, however ferocious, would be needed to give me satisfaction. What exactly the other thing might be, I did not know. But I hoped I would know, in the first moment when I looked on her again.

From Roman church to Roman church I plodded like a pilgrim, searching for the artist Perugino. I had not imagined there would be quite so many Roman churches. At my waist was the dagger that had once been left on a pillow, aimed at my head. Folded into my purse was a small bundle of sketches by Leonardo da Vinci, likenesses of the sister of the King of Hungary. I was having trouble finding any places to dispose of these pictures where I might reasonably expect them to be helpful.

On the third day of my Roman search I found a small church where, one of its priests told me, an artisan named Perugino had been painting some murals a few months past. But the painter was certainly gone from the neighborhood now, gone completely away from Rome the priest thought, and his mistress with him if he had had one. The priest had never noticed any woman at all in Perugino's company, let alone one speaking Hungarian and bearing a resemblance to my sketches.

I thanked him, and took my search for Helen to one of the nearby taverns. There some local men said they thought they might have seen her—said it with an exchange of winks. They were sophisticated city-dwelling jokers, metropolitan wits who jested at the expense of the lovelorn barbarian on his fool's quest. Somehow it was not plain to them that I was seeking vengeance and not love. I left one dead, two wounded, and had to take my searching elsewhere. My best talents are not in diplomacy, nor in the craft of the detective either.

After I had spent another day in fruitless prowling about Rome I visited the precincts of the Vatican. There I located my former traveling companions, the Hungarian delegation come to ask for a Crusade; while waiting to see His Holiness they had taken lodgings near the old St. Peter's. In Florence, where I had dropped out, they had been joined by my old acquaintance Morsino. Now Morsino greeted me in friendly style; he looked grave, though, when I told him of my recent brawl, and he counseled me to make no further requests or demands for official help in any Italian city. King Matthias, Morsino thought, was no longer fully committed to the search. As long as Helen continued to remain out of sight, committing no more public scandals, that seemed to be enough for the king; and Morsino thought perhaps it ought to be enough for me as well. The idea seemed to be to let sleeping Helens lie where and with whom they would.

My own views, I promptly explained, were different. The king had sent me here with orders to search for Helen, and search for her I would, for my own honor as well as that of royalty. If he, Morsino, thought that he could organize the hunt in Rome more discreetly and effectively than I, well, he was welcome to take a hand. And this invitation the worried envoy at last reluctantly accepted.

I hung around St. Peter's environs for another two weeks, undergoing fits of restlessness that alternated with periods of almost immobile depression. Then Morsino's efforts at last bore fruit. An agent hired by him brought me a witness, a poor woman who swore she had once lodged near an artist and a Hungarian woman who had been living together in the neighborhood of the church where Perugino had done his painting. Shortly before their disappearance some months past my witness had heard the couple talking about moving on to Venice.

I am not going to write much in these pages about the next twenty months of my life. It was a period in which I did things that I am not proud of, and which there is now very little purpose in remembering. My leg was fully healed by this time, and I could ride and fight effectively. Good fighting men, and, even more, capable military leaders, were at this time very much in demand in Italy because of the ceaseless squabbling of the city-states and petty principalities, not yet forged

into a nation. I had not been many days in Venice
before I signed a soldier's contract with the emi-
nent mercenary Bartolomeo Colleoni. My funds
were running low; and I expected to retain
enough time to myself, and freedom of movement, to allow me to continue the search for
Helen.

Colleoni had then been for ten years the General
in Chief of all the Venetian armed forces. But, like
most of the other successful *condottieri* of the
time, he had as his ultimate goal the carving out of
his own personal domain. Some of his colleagues,
like the founder of the Sforza dynasty in Milan,
succeeded admirably in this enterprise. Many
others failed miserably; but, like Sforza and Colleoni, most had had but little to lose when they
began.

My new employer was famed for his vigor, both
marital and martial, at an advanced age; for his
ferocity (which was somewhat remarkable even
for the time); his collection of rare books (when all
books were rare); and for his pioneering efforts in
the development of what would now be called
field artillery. Whereas if he is remembered at all
today outside of a few history books, I suppose it
is only because of Verrocchio's titanic equestrian
statue of him, still standing in a square in Venice
. . . but I digress.

When Colleoni heard from me that I had lived
in Florence recently, he took it for granted that I
had served there as *condottiere* also. What else
would be expect a foreign soldier to be doing? He
promptly began to pump me for all the information I could give about the state of Florentine
military preparedness: How many in the militia?
How well were the fortified walls maintained? I

told him what I could, which was not much, and he evidently took my reticence as evidence of praiseworthy loyalty to a former employer. I did not trouble to disabuse him of this idea.

So it was that in the winter of 1466-67 I found myself serving as a company commander in Colleoni's nominally Venetian forces. I had under me about a hundred men—or, as the reckoning was usually kept then, thirty lances. In very early 1467 my troops and I were engaged in the investigation of the assassination of a Colleoni agent, the mayor of a village whose name I must admit I have forgotten but which could hardly mean anything to you now in any case.

The investigation was soon proceeding according to the standards of the time, which is to say that my men had taken a score of hostages, and we were on the point of beginning to hang some of them unless someone who knew something about the assassination should come forward. In fairness to myself I ought perhaps to be allowed to interject that the mayor had evidently been a good man, for his time; a good politician for any time, perhaps; and that I still think the assassins would fairly have deserved hanging if we had ever caught them.

Snow was in the village air, and misery was rife as usual among the populace. I found myself seated one morning at a writing table that might have belonged to some scholar, to judge by all the papers on it, in a house that was mine so long as I and my armed men chose to occupy it. I had sat down at the table to write out a report for Colleoni on the affair, and I suppose that those of my men who from time to time looked in at door or window assumed that the black frown upon my brow was

due to the difficulty of wielding a pen in such a
wise as to leave an intelligible message upon
paper. Alas, no. I was even then something of a
writer—I could at least set down my letters large
and clear. What was troubling me were things
more fundamental. I was grappling with matters
of Conscience and the Law.

Contemplating the last year's work of my own
hands, I found that it was not good. Oh, my activities had been legal, of course, or could be ar-
gued such, according to the contracts, the agree-
ments, that I had with Colleoni, and he in turn
with Venice. And there were the customs, tradi-
tions, treaties, oaths, and whatnot that established
Venetian dominance over these poor sheeplike
villagers I was oppressing.

All legal. Everything I did. And yet in the end it
came down to my setting the edge of a blade, or
the loop of a rope, against the throat of some poor
wretch. Then whatever I said was law; and whatever he said meant nothing, if it were not agreement.

As if I—I, Drakulya!—were no better than a
highwayman.

At home in Wallachia I had been Prince, and
there too my word had been law. But there I myself had been the anointed ruler, which justified
much—did it not?

The front door of my borrowed house creaked
open, and there came in white light from the
snowy day outside, and then a blurred human
shadow thrown across my papers. Glad of any
interruption, I looked up.

To behold Helen.

Eighteen

Eighteen-year-old Judy Southerland didn't know where she was going tonight. She knew only that the man who had been her lover appeared to be in desperate need, and that she had to try to give him what help she could.

Dressed in casual hiking clothes, which would fit in just about anywhere that she had to go in the Santa Fe area, she stood looking at herself in the mirror of the pine dresser in her one-room private cabin—Astoria was a very expensive school. She was wondering if the clamor of her lover's need, so strong in her mind, showed in her face; she decided that she couldn't tell if it did or not. Nor could she tell if she was thinking straight in her effort to do something about that need.

She wasn't even sure if the man she felt so bound to help was still her lover.

Judy had encountered him for the first time in Chicago, last December. The affair between them had begun then, and another episode had been added to it when she had visited Europe with her family in January. And then, after making love with a vampire, she had come home to live with her unsuspecting parents in a Chicago suburb, where somewhat to her own surprise she had resumed a life at least outwardly quite normal for a girl her age. Dating young men who never would have dreamed of drinking blood from her neck, and who, if she had ever tried to tell them the truth about it, would have thought that Judy was utterly—

And there had been some doubting moments, earlier this spring, when Judy had wondered that herself. Was it after all possible that she had imagined the whole affair? Or dreamed it, somehow, to go along with the bizarre problems that the whole family had been having then? But when she began to doubt, a word to Kate or Joe was enough to assure her that it had all been real. Judy could understand, now, why people who had had experience with vampires were never heard from on the subject.

The contact-at-a-distance with her vampire lover had been established at the beginning of the affair. At first it had been quite strong; anytime she felt like tuning in on him, and on several occasions when she didn't, there would come through a strong sense of his environment, and of whatever he happened to be feeling at the moment. With the contact she had had no trouble at all in locating him in Europe, nor he in finding her. But after the European episode, as the days of separation grew painlessly into weeks, Judy had begun to suspect that the goodbye he had murmured so lightly there had after all been meant as permanent. Come to think of it, no arrangements for another meeting had been definitely established, and a fading of the subconscious contact had set in. The fading had been imperceptible at first, and then there had been whole days, and then whole strings of days, in which the contact was not only absent but forgotten. It would come back, with a dream's vague aura of unreality about it. And then it would go again—

—and then the savage explosion, many miles away, had sent shockwaves of reality through a midnight dream to wake her. She knew at once that he had been hurt. Not so badly hurt this time as once before, when she had come to him and saved his life. But again he was alone and injured. He was beset by injuries, half-mad with wanting revenge for them, and driven wild by the theft of some object that he craved so much there had to be more to it than mere wealth, however great.

He apparently had no idea where this object had been taken. But Judy, who had a special kind of sensitivity of location, a sensitivity much heightened by her experiences, could see it a little when she tried. It was a painting, an old painting, and Judy thought its subject was a woman. The painting had been wrapped in rough cloth now, and it was leaning against a rough wall, some-where in darkness . . . somewhere . . . she thought it was not far from Santa Fe.

If she went to it herself, then the contact that he must still have with her would show him where the painting was. Words never came through the contact, nor did conscious thoughts, and try as she might she could think of no other way to help him, and to ease the pain that his need had in-flicted upon her.

Her image in the mirror looked perfectly solid. The pale surface of her sturdy throat was no longer marked by even the faintest remnant of the puncture-scars. Those scars had always been tiny and inconspicuous, and she was surprised to realize that she did not know herself on what day they had completely disappeared.

There had been times, last winter, when Judy had felt sure that the affair must go on to the conclusion that he had once or twice spoken of in warning. Becoming a vampire was not as quick or as simple as the foolish motion picture stories had it; but let them exchange blood enough, and Judy would be changed, and permanently. But he had never gone into detail about the change, and Judy had been left free to fill in the particulars with her own imagination. Would her mirror-image give warning days in advance, as it slowly went transparent? Or flick out like a switched-off light? And afterwards, would her shadow still be visible in reflection, adding one more complication to the mockery of science? Judy was unable to remember ever seeing *his* shadow in a mirror . . . she did remember his saying once that there could be photographs, at least those made with cameras that did not employ interior reflective surfaces to position image upon film. There could be photographs of him, but he didn't like the idea and so as a practical matter there were none.

Judy's eyes dropped to the note that she was leaving on her dresser, propped up against the mirror. If all went well she would be back here in a few hours, safely, before anyone else had come into the cabin and read it. But she had to admit to herself there was a pretty good chance that things were not going to go *that* well.

To Whom It May Concern:

Something very important to me personally has come up, and I am going to have to be away from school for a short time. It may be for only a few hours, or for a couple of days. I am leaving this note here on Tuesday evening.

I intend to call in to the school office within about 48 hours if I'm not back by then, and say that I'm all right. Please do not start any wide search for me before then, as I should be perfectly all right. If I should fail to call in within about two days, then you can search. But I don't think there'll be any problem.

Sorry, but I don't see any better way to do this. If it is felt absolutely necessary to call someone about my being gone, please call my sister, Ms. Kate Keogh and not my parents. Her number is on file in the office.

This is nothing terrible but it's necessary.

Judy Southerland

The salutation at the start, now that Judy read it over, looked somewhat grim to her, like the opening of a suicide note or something. But she wasn't about to take the time now to do it over. The sense of urgency, of need, grew ever more pressing, and she couldn't afford to let it go untended until she had to run around and scream or something.

She thought the message looked okay otherwise. If she wasn't back before the staff started looking for her they would come into her cabin and find it, and then it would probably be read over the phone almost immediately to Kate and/or Joe. That was all right; they would be able to guess something of what was going on, and when the police were called in, Joe could . . . well, it was too bad, but right now Judy had to leave.

She had money, a couple of hundred bucks, in her pockets, and credit cards. What else did she need? It was hard to say, since she didn't really know where she was going. But money in some form was all you really needed, as a rule.

Judy slipped into her windbreaker, turned out the lights, and went out into the spring night. After a moment's internal debate she left her cabin door unlocked; somehow that seemed to make her departure less serious, more temporary.

The next step, of course, was to arrange a ride of some kind into town. Once she got there . . . well, she would just have to see then where she was called to go.

Walking toward the cabin that served Bill Bird as combination studio and living quarters, Judy saw with a mixture of guilt and relief that the lights were on inside. Bill looked first pleased and then somewhat wary when he saw who was tapping so discreetly at his door.

"Judy. What can I do for you?"

"Something's come up, Bill. I absolutely need to get into town right away, and I wonder if you could give me a lift."

A hesitation. "Oh. Did you check at the office?" There was a prescribed system of signing out, and also one of pooling rides.

"Can I come in a minute?" And once inside the one-room cabin, much like her own, Judy pulled shut the door behind her. A crude female nude, about half life-size, stood under lights. The clay looked wet, and Bill was wiping his hands on a rag. It seemed he must have been working from memory; anyway there was no model in sight. "I'm going to level with you, Bill. There are reasons why I didn't want to do that."

"Oh? Something private?"

"Yes. And the truth is I don't know when I'll be able to get back. I want to—meet someone, in town or near town."

"Oh."

She wished he would stop saying oh. "No, it isn't anything like that. Just someone who desperately needs help. And there's nothing illegal wrong about it, but at the same time it's very private."

Bill opened his mouth, but failed to utter the anticipated word. Now Judy could almost see the wheels turning over in his head. Abortion appointment? Drug rendezvous? Or a friend of Judy's on a bad trip with some drug, or in some trouble with the law? Or simply running away from home? Bill asked: "Where are you supposed to meet this person?"

"It's not easy to explain. I'm sorry. Look, can you just give me a ride into town? If you don't want to, I'll understand and I'll figure out some other way of getting there. I appreciate that there's some chance of your getting into trouble here if you break the rules." *Is this really me,* Judy wondered, *willing to use someone in this way?* She thought that for the first time she could begin to understand how alcoholics, addicts, could be as ruthless as they sometimes were. The craving— dominated.

Bill was looking at her carefully. "It's all right, Judy. I'll give you a ride."

"Thanks, Bill. I mean it. I really do appreciate it, I can't tell you how much."

Waiting for Bill to take care of a few things and grab his coat, getting ready to go out, Judy leaned against the doorframe, groping mentally.

He, the man she sought, had been very recently in a great desert basin which contained a large city and a mass of warm air, almost hot air, fairly heavily polluted air. Names of course never came through the contact, but Judy had no trouble recognizing Phoenix. But Thorn, she perceived now, was there no longer.

. . . he was coming closer, moving almost

straight toward her from the southwest. His feet were running, racing at a terrible pace . . . four feet running, and all of them were his . . . this was a mode that she had never experienced before.

"What's wrong, Jude?"

She opened her eyes and pushed away from the doorframe, making herself stand up straight and smile. "Nothing . . . maybe a little headache."

Bill looked doubtful. But he was holding the door open for Judy now, and she went on out. Her own feet trod again the springy needle carpet of the forest path. Two human feet, hers were, in shoes, not like . . . the landscape around *him* had been momentarily clear to Judy. It had seemed to be bright moonlight there, though from here her merely human eyes could see that tonight's moon was only a dim crescent.

Those distant, running feet were coming closer quickly, loping almost directly toward Santa Fe. It would be hours yet before Judy could meet them. How many hours she could not guess.

They were in Bill's car now, a small Buick several years old, and he was starting the engine. As he turned the key Judy at the last moment knew irrational panic that a great bomb under the hood was going to go off and turn them both to jelly. So strong was the sensation that she had to bite her tongue to keep from crying out. Nothing happened, of course, and now he was driving over the rutted gravel of the parking lot toward the gate, which as usual this early in the evening was standing open. He asked Judy casually: "Where exactly are we going?"

Her conscience would not lie down quietly. "Bill, I don't want to get you into any trouble for doing this. Maybe you'd better not."

"Oh, just driving you to town isn't all that bad.
Bending the rules a little, maybe, but . . . oh, hell,
look, Judy. You're already in real trouble of some
kind. I'd have to be blind not to see that. I don't
know if it really has to do with some friend, or if
the friend in trouble is you—anyway I can see that
you need help. So why don't you just tell me
where you have to go? And on the way, tell me
what it's all about."

"Oh, Bill. You're beautiful." Suddenly near
tears, Judy reached to squeeze his bicep, which
felt surprisingly large and hard. "Bill, the trouble
is, I don't *know* anything exactly yet. Just that I
have to be there . . . maybe when I get into town,
things will be clearer."

"How is that going to help?"

"It's difficult to explain." Or maybe impossible.
Once when her brother Johnny had been in the
hands of kidnappers, Judy had been able to see, to
locate perfectly, the house where Johnny was
being held. Of course that time she had been hypnotized, by . . . maybe the trouble was that this
time she wasn't hypnotized.

"No, I don't think I want to drop you just anywhere." They were driving the camp road now at
a brisk pace, traversing a midnight aisle of trees.
"Tell me, Judy. Are you really intending to cut out
from school altogether? Or do you really mean to
come back tonight?"

"I *hope* to be able to get back tonight, Bill. I've
left a note in my cabin, just in case . . . but oh
God, I hope I can get back there before anybody
reads it."

Bill turned his eyes from the night road long
enough to look at her. He whistled softly. "All

right, this is very serious, I can see that. Is it all right if I ask what the note says?"

"It says . . . it's just meant to be reassuring. I'm trying to keep my parents from finding out . . . Bill, don't mind me if I act a little crazy tonight. I know I'm acting like I'm crazy but I'm really not. Do you know anything about the psychic?"

"Psychic . . . well, not really, I guess. But I like to think I have an open mind."

Nineteen

Helen was garbed in much poorer clothing than the elegant garments in which she had departed our Pisan cottage. She was shivering with cold, and her rags, like those of the traveling poor of any century, were marked with the dust of the road. Her face looked thinner than I remembered it, and her hair had returned to the condition in which I had first seen it. Otherwise her appearance had changed very little in the two years since her desertion. She was leaning one hand on the wooden doorframe now, and the knuckles of the hand were white, as if she felt it necessary to grip something to keep from turning and trying to run away again.

I remember that as I looked at her my first reaction was only a curious numbness: all right, she is here. I looked past her then, and nodded a dismissal to the soldier who had brought her to the house. He went out behind her, and closed the door.

"Come in," I said. But of course she was in already.

My wife and I considered each other in silence. I saw now that she had rags wrapped around her feet in place of shoes. Her shivering arms folded now beneath her breasts, she stood there waiting. I thought I could see in her face something of the same numbness that I felt myself.

"So." That was my next attempt to start. The truth was that in recent months I had no longer spent much time dreaming of revenge. I think

now as I look back, I really think, that the first
feeling I began to have was a simple, uncompli-
cated relief—that I could now settle the thing
between us, somehow, and after that I would no
longer have to stay near Venice and work for Colleoni.

Helen asked: "Have I your permission to sit
down?" She was almost swaying on her feet, I
saw. Certainly she sounded tired, or rather as if
she had just been beaten, though I could see no
bruises. Her voice had changed more than her
appearance.

I gestured, and she sank into a chair, hands
covering her eyes. "I am giving myself up into
your hands," she said.

"I can see that."

"Because I am too tired to run any longer. Too
tired even to try to bargain with you. Just giving
up, that's all."

"I see." But really I did not, and I puzzled over
the matter for a few moments in silence. "But
what is there to bargain about? And why come to
me at all? You are still young, still attractive.
Surely you could find some protector who would
take you in."

Helen at first slumped in her chair. Then she
straightened, raising reddened eyes. "All right,
Vlad. Maybe you really do not know. But I am too
exhausted for any . . . so I am going to tell you.
Perugino is one of the hostages your men have
taken here. Now maybe I have damned both myself and him to hell by coming to you. I don't
know. I can't tell any longer what I should be
doing. I'm too tired and weak and hungry to know
anything. I'm giving up."

"Ah. Perugino." I leaned back in my chair. The

name had a strange sound on my lips; it had been a long time since I had spoken it. Actually I had never really looked at the hostages, only glimpsed the huddled gray mass of them from a distance. I suppose I had not wanted to look at them closely. My men had informed me how they were being held, under close guard in an otherwise empty barn just across the road from my borrowed house. There were a lot of empty barns in the country now. And now I wondered if I would have recognized Perugino had I seen him. My memory could no longer give me a clear image of what he had looked like, and anyway he might well have changed.

Helen spoke again, in the dead voice that was now hers. "We have been on the move almost constantly. We have run from the soldiers, yours and others, and we have looked for work. Artisan's work, peasant's work, anything. From Rome to Venice, even to Milan. There I saw Sforza once, by accident. We were quite close, but he looked right through me without seeing, as if I were a ghost. Then we moved back to Venice again. Then out here. We have been living in the next village down the road." Suddenly she put out a hand to grip my writing table's edge; she looked pale, as if she might be about to topple from her chair.

"You will need some food," I said. And instead of calling in a servant, whose presence I did not want just then, I got up and began to look around for some myself.

"Yes, some food please. I need some. It was not easy for me to come here, Vlad. Vlad? I ask you to let him go."

In a rucksack I found some bread, and brought it to her. It was dark bread, and stale as I recall, having been for some time left in the pack forgotten. We soldiers had enough. Helen took a couple of bites with animal hunger. Evidently her teeth were still good. I sat down again and watched her eat. Whatever vengeance I decided to pronounce upon her and her lover, it would have been foolish to try to gloat over her with it as she lay on my floor in a dead faint.

Chewing, she asked: "The hostages are all going to be hanged, aren't they?"

"So it would seem. No one has yet come to us with the names of those who killed the mayor."

"Is that why the hostages were taken? We did not even know."

"Bah. You really expect me to believe that?"

"We in the next village, I mean. That is where Perugino and I have been living. The soldiers just came through, rounding up all the men that they could catch."

I looked at Helen closely, decided that she was telling me the truth, and made a small sound of disgust. The village I was in, now that I thought about it, did look small to have provided so many hostage bodies. I was going to have to take some disciplinary action, hoping to instill in my squad leaders some glimmerings' of intelligence.

Helen went on: "There is always hanging, butchery of some kind, going on in these villages. I wonder that the people manage to grow any food at all." When I did not answer, she was emboldened, and pressed on: "You could let him go. It will not matter to you, will it, if there are twenty bodies hanging, or only nineteen?"

I thought to myself that it was hardly going to matter if there were twenty or none at all. Except of course to the twenty themselves, and to their families. And to leave the men alive might work a benefit to the land at large. But my words through some bitter perversity followed a different path than my thoughts.

"Maybe," I said, "I will be doing them all a favor by hanging them now. If I let them go, they will have a few more years of suffering in this Godforsaken country and then die anyway. Will Perugino be better off or worse off if I let him go?"

"I don't know, Vlad." And I believed that she did not. But then she began to weep, sobbing so that she had to stop chewing on her bread. "I don't know. But let him go. Please, please, let him go on living."

"You still ask me not to hang him."

"If you put it that way—then you are going to do something to him even more horrible. Oh, I knew it, I should never have come to you." Yet hunger made her try to bite the bread again; she choked on it and went off into a fit of coughing. I got up from my chair again, to dipper some water for her from a pail.

"And suppose—just suppose—that I should let him go, entirely free? What would you do then? Assuming that for some reason you were given a choice."

Helen drank, and choked again, and drank a little more, and put off answering. Later she was to tell me that at this point in our interview she felt sure that I was only playing with her, mocking her, that at any moment the horrors would be announced, that I would call out for the torturers to enter. But I was not playing. I was much less certain than she was of what was going to happen next.

It occurred to me that what I really ought to do

was hang Perugino, who was demonstrably guilty of something, and let the nineteen innocent clods go free. But then the guilty man's troubles would perhaps be over—a church-painter like him would be sure to make his peace with God before he reached the gallows—whereas the nineteen would be doomed to who knew how many more years of suffering. Well, that was the kind of mood that I was in.

The reader doubts, perhaps. I have and had a bloody reputation. How is it possible to prove today that I did not torture a certain wretch to death in 1467? Well, can the reader himself prove himself innocent of all crimes committed in that or any other given year? But, the reader protests, in 1467 he was not yet born. Let him prove that, too, say I. If I can live so long, then why not he or she?

Forgive me, gracious Mina. I am overwrought, with reliving things that have more power over me than I guessed they would, when I sat down to write.

Let me put it this way. Though it was claimed even then that I had ruled too harshly in my own land, I had never gone so far as to hang nineteen men who were not even suspected of any crime. And if, in the time when I was Prince, some officer of my realm had reported to me that he was carrying on an investigation in such wise, depopulating my land of healthy industrious peasants to no purpose, his own carcass might soon have been observed in a position higher and more uncomfortable than that afforded by any ordinary scaffold.

Something in my face must have inspired Helen to new hope. "Vlad," she burst out suddenly, "I know that I have already made wedding vows with you, and broken them. But they were forced and I did not consider that they bound me. I will make them again, if you would have me still. The position you hoped to gain can still be yours—you will be the brother-in-law of a powerful king—if you will let Perugino go free. I will never see him again. I will, I swear it to you by whatever you like, be a faithful wife to you, whatever you choose to do to me."

Now it seemed to be an effort to think about her at all. I rubbed my face, and suddenly felt tired, and angry—an anger on the level of irritation, as if my wife had been nagging me for days. "Quiet," I said, and as if to demonstrate her new talent for obedience, Helen broke off some renewed plea before its first word was fairly out. I sat there looking at the papers on the table as if I were eager to get back to them, as if Helen's coming had interrupted some delightful task.

"Where did you first meet Perugino?" I asked her. "I have often wondered about that."

Helen was silent for a few moments, trying to compose herself. Then she said: "It was when I was in the convent—the first time, I mean, the convent near Milan. I was staying there while the final arrangements were being concluded by my brother, for me to marry the Sforza. Perugino was working in the convent chapel. He had been hired to make paintings on the walls."

"Which Sforza were you to marry?"

"Galleazzo Maria himself. The negotiations were all secret. Matthias badly wanted an alliance with Milan."

"Ah. Small wonder His Majesty was so angry at you when you thwarted him. Tell me more. I suppose the bridegroom-to-be was perturbed also?" If Galleazzo Maria Sforza's reputation has now fallen behind mine—I should say remained above it—it was not always so.

"There was a delay in the final arrangements. The Sforza was away on some business or other, I was never told what. So of course there I was, waiting in the convent, as the only proper place for me to stay. And in the chapel a young painter was at work. I was consumed with quiet anger at my brother, at what he was doing with my life for the sake of politics. As if I were only a soldier, to be used up in battle at the commander's will."

"That is the way of battles. And of life."

"I tell you I . . . not of my life. Or so I thought. It began, with Perugino, as a way of getting back at Matthias. But Perugino was the first man I had ever had, and it became . . . great love. The two of us ran away together. And we have been together ever since, as much as we could be. We thought we would be quickly caught, so at first we lived with a kind of . . . raging joy. Do you understand? To do just as we liked, to fear nothing. I wanted to leave scandal wherever we went, to get back at my brother and at the world. For what they had tried to do to me.

"Then later, it was . . . later it began to be no good. I have sold myself, to get food when we were starving. Again to get shelter, when Perugino was ill. When I was sick, he . . . I don't know what he did, but he stayed with me. Now to save his life I will do anything you like."

"Why did you leave that dagger on my pillow?" Helen did not seem to know at first what I was talking about. I drew it from the sheath at my belt and held it up by the tip of the blade. The steel was still lightly notched where I had used it once to cut through a small chain. "This very dagger, here."

At last she remembered. "That? It was meant to show you that I did not hate you, you were not my enemy. Otherwise I would have killed you before I ran away."

"I see." I looked at the weapon, and restored it to its sheath. "And where have you been living? Just now?"

"As I said. In the next village down the road."

I had one more question. "Does Perugino know that you have come to me now?"

Helen took thought, then shook her head. "I don't see how he could."

"I want to talk to him, before I decide anything." Helen wanted to speak, but I put up a hand and she was silent. "I am going to have him brought over here now. I want you to step into the other room, and listen from there. As you value his life, keep hidden and silent, no matter what you hear, until I tell you to come out."

Perugino's beard, if he had ever in fact shaved it as Leonardo had once informed me, had long since grown back to greater length. There was gray in it now; though he was still in his twenties, probably a decade younger than I, his face was already becoming that of an old man. Still, I was quite sure that I would have known him, had I ever gone to look closely at the hostages.

"I recognize you, Perugino," I announced, when the soldiers who had brought him had gone out of the house again, leaving the two of us together. "Do you know me?"

I honestly do not believe that he did know me,

at first. He was shivering worse than Helen had
been, and I believe a good part of his shivering
was due to fear.

"Come. In your position you have nothing to
lose by admitting it. You know that we met at
Verrocchio's studio."

Gradually it dawned on him. He almost met my
eyes, and then would not. His hands were bound
behind him, which made it hard for him to find
the least refuge in a pose, or in gestures.

"Well, speak up, man. Answer."

"Yes, signore, I think I do know you. I'm sure of
it, in fact." Perugino's voice was so low that I
could scarcely hear it. There seemed to be no
resistance of any kind left in him; there had been
some in Helen, despite her continued claims that
she was giving up.

"Good," I said cheerfully. "Good, I am glad.
Then the chances are that you remember my wife
as well."

Despite the cold, Perugino stank of sweat. Old
sweat, fear-sweat. The stink grew now a little
fresher. His face sicklied over with an attempted
smile. He shook his head a trifle, not knowing
what I wanted of him, how much I knew, or what
if anything he ought to try to say.

I tried to imagine him impaled on a high stake.
He would stink even worse that way. The image
brought me nothing but disgust. I sighed. It was
hard to imagine that this creature before me had at
one time been truly young, and good-looking, and
brave enough to play at games with the betrothed
of Galleazzo Maria Sforza inside high convent
walls.

I said: "I am in no mood to play games with you,
man. I know that you and she have been together.

The thing is this. We have taken some women hostages, too, at the next village. And it happens that Helen was among them."

Perugino's expression hardly changed. Perhaps he had no extremes of reaction still unused. It was at this point that I finally decided what I was going to do.

"Now, are you listening to me, artist? I have orders from Colleoni to hang thirty people here, to make an example of this place. But I find that some of my soldiers cannot count too well. The total of hostages, men and women included, is now thirty-one. Are you following me?" The lies came to me quite easily as I went along, and they were of a kind to be readily believable to any inhabitant of that region. As for Perugino, I think I could have told him that the key to the pearly gates was in my pocket, and he would only have nodded agreement with that same sickly, insanely hopeful smile.

"Listen to me further, wall-painter. I tell you that I have sworn a great oath—never mind why—that my vengeance shall not fall upon both of you, but on one only. Therefore I am compelled to set one of you free. I will then hang the other—after some preliminary punishment. Now the question is, which is it to be? The guilty wife, or her seducer? Which goes free, and which one suffers?"

I think, looking back, that I was wasting my inventive powers. I think that of it all he heard and understood almost nothing but those two words, "goes free." The moment I was silent, he fell on his knees in supplication.

"You will set me free? Lord, sire, you are a great lord, a blessed man. My aged mother will bless you. Her prayers and mine will go with you from this day forward, to the hour of your death . . . I swear that I will never bother anything of yours again. My gratitude will be eternal . . ."

I do not remember now the whole catalogue of these absurdities he babbled. But it went on and on, perfectly disgusting. I cut it short: "What of the woman's fate? Does that mean nothing to you at all?"

"The woman. Ah. You will know best about that, sire. I swear to you that I am never going to look at her again. I swear . . ."

I was as good as my word to Perugino. A few minutes later he was walking out the front door of my borrowed house, his hands cut free of their bonds by my notched dagger. His pass with my signature on it was in his hand, and one of my soldiers was with him to escort him to the edge of town.

Now I can hear the gentle reader murmuring again. What would the infamous Dracula have done, had the man proved as self-sacrificing as the woman? Well, it is my theory that Helen in coming to me was really not all that altruistic— she was tired, as she said, and took what she saw as the best chance, obeying an almost suicidal impulse—to get out of an intolerable situation even if it should mean death. On the other hand, if Perugino had proven himself ready to sacrifice himself for her—I did not think he would, but if he had—well, I should probably have taken him up on the offer.

As matters actually went, I walked into the room as soon as Perugino was gone. I stood there silently confronting Helen, who had sat down on my bed.

"But he is no longer a brave man," she murmured, staring at my boots. "If he ever was. So much has happened . . . what did you expect?" Then her eyes lifted. "Tell me, are you going to have him killed now after all? Stabbed to death somewhere down the road? Tell me now if it is so."

I had considered some such plan, but had decided against it. I half-expected that the fog of war was likely to carry out the postponed execution without any active effort on my part, local conditions being what they were. This was a faulty expectation, as we now know; Perugino's lifeless paintings done after 1467 are still to be seen covering a great deal of wall space in a number of Italian churches.

"It is not so," I assured her. "I do not mean to have him killed—unless he should come near you again. Then I will kill him, but only as an annoyance, not as a matter of honor. Do you understand?"

Helen tried to look agreeable, but I could see that she did not understand. She could not, perhaps, or she did not care.

So I explained it to her, once. "That man is already dead."

Twenty

Pat O'Grandison was dreaming again, and again the dream was of Annie, and in this dream she was naked. She and Pat were in bed together, and the sheets were satin. There were paintings and statues all about, watching. Pat was enormously aroused, but even more important was the secret that Annie was about to whisper into his ear.

Before he could hear a word of it, he awoke with a small start. It was dusk, and he could not immediately remember whose great house this was or how he came to be in it. He was lying on his back on a sofa in an unknown, luxuriously furnished room. His shoes were off, and his knapsack was under his head where he had put it to make a pillow against the sofa's wooden arm. He was beginning to remember now.

A brown-haired, slightly built girl was sitting at the foot of the sofa, looking at Pat. She wore jeans and a loose pullover shirt.

"Annie?" Pat was fully awake in an instant, and his body jerked up into a straight sitting position. At first glance he was sure this girl was her. The sense of Annie's presence was very strong. But as soon as he got a good look he could see this wasn't Annie's face, though this too was a face he ought to know. He had been asleep, and there was certainly a resemblance, and the lights in the room had not been turned on as yet.

"I'm Helen, Pat," she said, in a voice that was certainly not Annie's either. "Annie's friend. You saw a lot of me in Chicago. Don't you remember?"

"Oh, yeah. Sure. Gosh." *Gosh* popped out in Pat's speech fairly often, part of a general plan, never deliberately thought out as such, to remain as young or at least as young-seeming as he possibly could. Sometimes this plan worried him and he wondered at its purpose.

The girl took hold of his foot in its dirty sock, squeezing it absently, as if she were petting a small child. Her fingers were strong. "Pat? You know Ellison has just been on the phone, talking to someone about you. He was very guarded in what he said, but I'm sure you were the real subject of what they were talking about."

"Ellison?"

"My stepfather. He owns this house. The big fat man who looks a lot like Del."

"Del?"

The girl sighed faintly. "Del is his older brother. You don't remember anything about that night in Phoenix, do you, when you and I first met? That was at Del's house."

Pat pulled his feet free from her near-caress and swung them to the floor, where he started fumbling them into his shoes.

Helen told him: "I wouldn't be a bit surprised if Ellison is making plans to get rid of you tonight. I don't know why else he would have let you sack out in his house like this. He doesn't like boys the way Del does sometimes. He just wanted to check with Del first, or with Gliddon, about what they want to do with you. Maybe they'll want to find out how much you know."

"Oh my God. I'm gonna split." Somehow Pat doubted that the girl was making any of this up, just for fun or just to get him out of the house.

There was something about that huge old dude, her stepfather, that made Pat believe he could be capable of murder. Anyway, even if Helen was making it up, it wasn't a situation Pat wanted to prolong.

But even now he couldn't just leave without trying once more. "Helen? Tell me where Annie is. I know she's right around here somewhere."

Helen shook her head, and appeared to be annoyed. But then she reached over and with cool fingers touched Pat on the cheek. It was almost like the way that Annie had used to reach and touch him sometimes. "Pat, I know you liked her, and she liked you." Helen paused there, looking at him with strange eyes in the dusk. "She was there on that night in Phoenix, too. She met you the same time I did. A lot of things got started on that night."

"I don't really give a shit about that night in Phoenix any more." Pat was jerking on his shoelaces to get them tied. One lace broke, and he just let it go. He stood up. "Where is she now?"

"I was trying to tell you." Helen, sounding irritated, stood up too. Pat could see now that she was barefooted; still she stood a little taller than Annie. "The bad news about her. She was just a runaway from somewhere, and she didn't count for much. Anyway, you see there was another real bad night at the house in Phoenix, a few months after you were there. I mean the night when Del was supposedly kidnapped. Something went wrong with the scheme and Annie was killed. Almost everyone thought that I was the girl who died. Just as they thought that Del was dead—he wants everyone to think that, of course. But really he had another body ready, the body of a fat old man, that would look enough like Del after it had been blown up in the truck. And he even faked dental records and everything, just in case. You can do a lot, when you have as much money as Del has. And—"

"I don't wanna know about all that, I wasn't there. I'm gonna leave."

"Sure. You'd better get out of here now. But what are you going to do, just walk the roads? You'll be picked up, that way."

Something in the way she said it made it a special warning. "Picked up?"

"I don't mean just by the law. Look, Pat, I'll give you a ride somewhere, okay? I know Annie would want me to look out for you if I could. She thought you were something special, you know. She talked about you quite a lot."

"She did?"

Helen didn't answer, but moved away. His backpack dangling from one hand, Pat followed her on tiptoe through several darkening rooms. They came to a heavily grilled back door, where Helen bent to do something to the lock.

"Where are your folks now?" Pat whispered near her ear.

"Sometimes they don't seem much like my folks," she whispered back. "They're around. Be quiet. Here now, I've got to hold this—you go on out."

The door swung open to a small patio. Pat had been in mansions before, enough to know something about alarm systems. He went out quietly. Helen delayed behind him, doing something to a mechanism attached to the heavy door, then closing it carefully behind her when she was out too.

After that she led Pat along the side of the

house, over a brick walk, to an outside entrance to
the garage. Again there was a brief delay, while
she used keys and stealth for a tricky opening.
They were inside the garage then, where it was
very dark. Helen led Pat past two cars to a third
smaller one and unlocked the right door for him.
When the dome light came on he could see he was
getting into a Subaru, one of the small station
wagon models that he thought usually came with
four-wheel drive.

Helen walked around and got in on the driver's
side. It was cold in the garage. The engine purred,
headlights came on, a garage door rolled itself up
ahead of them, and now somewhere an alarm bell
was ringing stridently.

"Now they're going to wonder what's going
on," Helen said, a certain satisfaction in her voice.
The Subaru leaped into the night.

She drove Pat in a direction that must have
taken them away from the center of town, for the
roads remained up-and-down-hill gravel. You
might have thought you were already way out in
the remote countryside, except there were so
many mailboxes along the road, and gravel
driveways curving away from the road uphill and
down. There must be a fair number of houses
tucked just out of sight. In the dark it was hard to
tell.

Gradually the driveways and mailboxes thinned out, then finally ceased to appear at all. They
were really getting out into the boondocks now.

"Where we going?" Pat asked, beginning to get
curious.

Helen didn't answer right away. "There's something I think I want to show you," she said at last.

A lot of road was going by in the lonely headlights. Traffic, that had never been heavy, had thinned out now to nothing. Pat wondered, and couldn't tell for sure, whether or not they might be driving in some great circle, and it was all a hoax, a joke on him.

"Sometimes," he said, to be making talk, "I feel like I been on the road a hundred years."

"Don't talk like that. I feel that way too much myself."

"You?" He sighed. "Actually you've just tried it once, right? With Annie to Chicago? And now you're home again."

Helen turned on the car radio. Rock music came in. But then almost at once the music began to fade, as if they were far and getting farther from the station. At last she said: "Yeah. Just that once."

"And that's where I met you. Right?"

"No." Now her voice was remote, and there was something in it that frightened Pat. "I told you where we met. It's no good just trying to forget what has happened, Pat. You can't change things that way. You met Annie and me both that first night in Phoenix. Uncle Del was giving a party— that's what he liked to call it, anyway. You were invited. I mean Gliddon brought you in, along with a few other road-kids that he collected somewhere. He's good at collecting. And he likes that kind of party too."

"Helen? Maybe you could just take me back somewhere near the center of town, and let me off. I'll do okay getting a ride from there."

"But you got stoned so early you probably really don't remember anything. Dear Uncle Del and his parties. And that one was especially bad because someone got killed. And did you know, we were all in a movie that night? You're such a movie freak, I bet you remember that much anyway if you tried hard."

Pat had an inward feeling, terrible and indescribable, that he got usually when a bout of mental illness was about to strike. But he knew what was going on. No way he was going to be lucky enough to get out of that.

"Or most of us were in a movie, anyway," Helen amended, turning off suddenly onto an almost invisible side road. "On some of us it wouldn't take," she added obscurely. The car jounced violently. The road, or track, was badly rutted here and obviously little used. A branch dragged across the windshield. Then the bottom of the car scraped hard on a rock or graveled hump projecting up between the ruts. Helen drove on as if she hadn't noticed the noise. Apparently no serious damage had been inflicted.

"Was Annie in the movie?"

Helen didn't answer.

"Come on, Helen, tell me. Annie isn't really dead, I know that much. I got this feeling about her, you know?"

"She's dead!" Helen snapped at him, in a new and abrupt voice. She turned her eyes from the road to look at Pat, long enough so he wished she'd turn back and watch where they were going. Again low branches of some kind clawed at the windshield, and the car rocked in and out of ruts. So far the four-wheel-drive was pulling it through. Helen had to turn back to watch her steering. Angrily she said: "How can I help you when you keep on saying crazy things like that?"

"Sorry, I . . ."

A sign came unexpectedly into the headlights. It had been crudely improvised long ago, long enough that the wood and the white paint were weather-worn, the message barely legible. It said, simply enough: BRIDGE OUT.

"Helen, you sure you know where we're going?"

Helen rounded one more curve, and then slowed down some more. Not for a sign, though. The headlights had now fallen upon what at first appeared to be a wreck—an old car slewed diagonally across what was left of the road, as if it had stalled in some attempt to back out or turn around. Standing near it and squinting back into the Subaru's headlights were a pair of young people, a dark-bearded man and a brown-haired girl. Pat knew another moment of spurious recognition; but this girl was obviously too big and sturdy to be Annie. The man with her was bigger still; both were dressed casually but well.

"Shall we stop?" Helen asked abstractedly, as if she were conversing with herself. Actually there hardly seemed to be a choice, given the blocked and narrow road. A moment later they had come to a halt, a few feet from the stalled car. The man on foot, trying to shade his eyes with one hand, approached the Subaru warily on the driver's side. But before he reached it the girl, her eyes now freed of the headlights' glare, was looking in through the window that Pat had just rolled down. She looked at Pat, and at the young girl driving, and relaxed.

Helen was saying nothing, so Pat spoke. "Can we give you guys a lift somewhere?"

"Sure," said the girl. "I'm Judy Southerland, this is Bill Bird. We got stuck."

The young man, also somewhat relaxed now, was looking in at Helen, who had finally rolled her window down. "We'd really appreciate it," he said with feeling. "I guess it was kind of crazy, our trying to get through here, especially at night. Where are you guys headed?"

"Just riding." Helen sounded cool and remote. "I'm Helen, this is Pat. Actually there was something I wanted to show him, out this way. You want to come along?"

The young man called Bill was silent, as if he didn't quite understand. Pat could hear a night-bird somewhere. The thin moon was down by now. He could see about a million stars, but not a man-made light in sight other than the one pair of headlights.

"Sure we will," said the girl called Judy. "Or I will, anyway." She looked over the top of the car at Bill, and something passed between them.

He shrugged. "Okay." And he moved to open the Subaru's back door.

"No," said Helen, surprising them all. "From here we walk."

"Walk?" All three of them said it.

"It isn't far. Come on." And she turned off the car's lights and engine and got out. She seemed to Pat to be perfectly calm and serious. She moved to the uphill side of the road and paused, evidently waiting for the others to follow.

Pat and the others exchanged puzzled looks, as well as they could by starlight, then he moved to Helen and the other two followed. In single file they began to climb.

The ground was rough and pathless, but Helen moved as if she knew her way. Pat looked down at her feet and realized with a chill that they were still bare. She *had* to be crazy . . . he didn't know whether he should appeal to the newcomers for support, demand they call a halt, or what. He himself was crazy, that much he knew already. As if there were no other choice, he kept quiet and let himself be led.

The hill at least wasn't high. Soon they were going down its other side, now completely out of sight of cars and road. Then partway up another hill, and along its twisting flank.

Judy wondered aloud: "Does anyone think we'll be able to find our way back? Where are we going, anyway?"

"You don't know?" asked Bill.

Helen paused calmly and turned back. "There's a sort of settlement where we're going. They have a phone there. I know you can't see it from here. But it's just over this next hill." Her voice sounded completely reasonable.

"Oh," said Judy. They went on. Pat had lost track of how far or in which direction they had come. He kept on, following Helen's soundless feet. He hadn't thought, on first seeing her this evening, that she was high on anything—Pat could almost invariably tell—or that her head was screwed on wrong. But now he was dead sure that something wasn't anywhere near right.

Once he paused, turned back, almost determined to call a halt.

The girl, Judy, walking close behind him, shook her head minimally and pushed him gently on. Her eyes were focused past Pat, on the darkness ahead where a low mass of shadow now seemed to indicate trees. She knew, on some level, what she was doing.

He turned again, and walked, one foot loose in its shoe with the broken lace.

"Here," said Helen quietly, turning long enough to utter the one word, then pushing on. And the way began to slope down, the ground underfoot smooth enough to indicate a path. The sound of running water drifted upward, very faint at first. There was at least a respectable trickle.

They came in among the first trees, and darkness deepened. Judy asked: "What is this place, anyway?" Pat could now see buildings of some kind, faintly visible in tree-shaded starlight.

"There used to be a mission here," said Helen. She came slowly to a halt, looking ahead into blackness.

"But you said there was a phone. Didn't you?"

"There is. It's a radiophone of some kind. I guess some special, secret kind."

"What?"

"We'll ask Gliddon if we can use it." Helen's voice was still dream-calm.

"What? Who?"

A new voice, harshly male, said: "Don't move. All four of you freeze, right where you are." And light sprang at them, a blinding beam of it from each side. Pat, as soon as he could begin to see again, made out the ski-masks and the shotguns; and he devoutly wished that he could immediately go mad.

Twenty-one

I rode with Helen, across a countryside infected with war as with a plague. Before we had ridden two hours toward Florence, a small band of brigands appraised us, then let us pass by, though we two were quite alone. Colleoni's soldiers were behind us in the village, where before leaving I had ordered all of the remaining hostages released; I hoped that some of those peasants at least would have wit enough to abandon their homes and flee with their families before whoever was appointed my successor took control and rounded them all up again.

To have thus breached my signed contract with Colleoni did weigh somewhat on my conscience. I was not one to break any solemn agreement lightly, though it was common for mercenaries of the time to do so and change sides. But my conscience found relief in an excellent argument, namely that my loyalty to King Matthias must take precedence over any such temporary pact made for money; and so, by extension, must my duty regarding the king's sister and my wife, now that I had located her again. As to exactly where my duty with regard to Helen lay, I had not yet made up my mind. Certainly, I told myself, it was not the kind of problem I wanted to deal with offhandedly, whilst I was distracted with carrying out some lunatic persecution of the poor.

Helen, mounted on a spare horse that I had commandeered, rode beside me and just a little to the rear. The storage chests of the scholar's house

had yielded up enough women's clothing to afford her an air of respectability, though the garments showed as ridiculously too large when she
dismounted. She said little as we rode, but
watched me almost continuously. I knew she
could not believe that I was not plotting some
utterly fiendish revenge. Tonight, or tomorrow,
she was thinking, I would contrive somehow to
serve her Perugino's faithless heart baked in a pie.
And as soon as she had partaken thereof I would,
with a maniac's cackling, tell her so; and then I
would spring upon her, and get on with whatever
torments I meant to use to end her life . . .

Oh yes, I admit, I did play in the back of my
mind with some shadowy plans along such lines.
But somehow my heart was not in them and they
never took on substance. Where Helen was concerned I had no will for tricks like that. On the
other hand my honor would certainly seem to
demand that I inflict some serious punishment
upon her for running off with another man. But
what was the punishment to be? I could not decide.

Meanwhile I counseled myself that while I was
making up my mind I ought to lead her into trust-
ing me, by pretending that all had been forgiven. I
would play the model husband, that when the
hour for vengeance struck at last, it would be all
the sweeter and more exquisite. And the delay
would give me time to plan and prepare revenge
carefully . . . eventually, I told myself, I was
bound to hit upon a plan for which I could feel
some enthusiasm.

Our road wound among silvery-green olive
groves, past cypress that looked dead with winter
and war. Snow lay scattered on the Tuscan earth

that summer would once again make lush with
greenery. Still, after only a day's ride, the land
was starting to look less like one of Goya's later
portraits of war. Peasants and some other natural
creatures of the earth were once more to be seen,
behaving normally.

"This is the road to Florence, my lord." At last,
it seemed, I was to have some conversation.

"And is there any reason why we should not
take the road to Florence?"

"None. Oh, none. I am willing to go wherever
my lord wills."

Though I offered no explanation then, I had
decided to go to Florence because in all that tur-
bulent land there was no other place where I
could be so sure of a welcome; I brought with me
detailed news about a powerful enemy's plans
against that city, as well as a strong sword-arm to
help oppose those plans.

The journey took us several days. There were no
haystacks to sleep in, but plenty of abandoned
buildings. My lady appeared to welcome my hus-
bandly attentions inside these, as once she had
inside a palace. On our last day of travel, when we
were almost at our goal, we passed that very place,
Careggi. I rode to the gate and gained admittance.
But the great country house of the Medici proved
to be unoccupied in winter except for a caretaker
staff. Some of these goggled at my companion,
making me suspect that news of our coming
would precede us to the city, even though we
headed directly on to Florence after only a brief
pause for refreshment.

The palace on the Via Larga was even busier
than I had seen it before. Yet again the leading
men of the Medici family welcomed me, and

greeted Helen, almost without twitching an eye-
brow. They were used to wonders, in that house.
And yet again their welcome had a different tone.
The first one, more than a year ago, had been
strongly tinged with curiosity; the second, last
summer, polite. This third reception had in it the
wholehearted enthusiasm of men who are being
given needed reinforcement on the brink of war. I
quickly discovered that Colleoni's plans of con-
quest were already known here in broad outline,
though the details I could provide might well
prove invaluable.

Lorenzo listened appreciatively to the version I
gave him of events since I had seen him last—
according to which Helen and I had merely gone
through a lovers' quarrel, and she had been living
with me almost continuously since our separate
departures. Doubtless he did not believe it, but
understood that it was to be taken as official. By
then Piero had rounded up his military advisers,
and closeted himself and me with them, to study
greedily the lists of material and drawings that I
was able to set down pertaining to the Venetian
war machine. Interest in Colleoni's new model
firearms was intense. While we were relaxing a
little later, both men amused me with the account
of how Lorenzo had saved his father from assassination in 1466, outwitting ambushers hired by the
rival Pitti family. I found out later that the Medici
vengeance for that attempt had been prompt, precise, bloody, and discreet.

Helen and I were domiciled in one of the visitors' rooms. There the painting was again
brought in to stay with us, as if it were some
antique Roman household god. On the first full
day of our stay, the Duke of Urbino arrived at the

palace. The Florentine Council, who governed the city generally under instructions from Piero, had found the Duke available and currently an enemy of Venice, and had placed him in charge of preparations against Colleoni's expected onslaught.

I respected the Duke's military reputation, and found him an impressive figure. He was already dressed in light armor, though by most calculations combat was still some months in the future. Listening as he chatted with our hosts, I was surprised to realize that he too was a serious book collector, or at least aspired to be one, in the same league as the Medici and King Matthias. I thought to myself that the world seemed to be changing drastically. No longer, it appeared, would fighting, praying, and the maintenance of honor be all that were required of a successful man. Very well, I thought, I am going to have to learn to think as well. I have always been able to manage great changes in my lifestyle when necessary.

One day in the palace, with a group of officers pondering Colleoni's field artillery, I was sketching the weapons from memory as best I could, when some man entered the room where we were gathered but then immediately withdrew. This made me glance up, just in time to recognize the retreating back of one of the Boccalini.

"There will be trouble, Lorenzo," I said to my young friend a little later.

Lorenzo had been in the room also, and had noticed the near-encounter. "Perhaps not," he soothed me now. "We will try to prevent it. There are others, too, who, shall we say, do not work well together. Yet Florence must be defended. If the Boccalini and the Pitti can work with us, they can tolerate you as well."

"Even when we meet face to face?"

Lorenzo furrowed his swarthy brow, considering. Already he looked forty. "I suppose that you, my friend, are going to take an active part in the fighting, and will be going out into the field shortly?"

"Yes. The Duke has already asked my help in training and organizing new troops."

"That is good, because the Boccalini will be staying in town. Meanwhile I advise you, not that you need any such advice, to guard yourself."

Shortly thereafter, whether because of the Boccalini or for some other reason, it was delicately suggested that Helen and I might want to move out to Careggi, which was now beginning to be occupied by other military guests of rank; and yes, the painting came with us once again. From Careggi I presently departed for an advanced camp in the field. Helen appeared to be concerned as she bade me farewell. My own feelings about leaving my wife behind were fatalistic; I did not ask the Medici to put her into a convent, or to set a watch upon her whilst I was gone. What would be, would be. Somehow I had never got around to deciding upon a suitable vengeance for her earlier trangressions, and now . . . now other decision were more demanding.

In the spring, under the direct leadership of the Duke, we mercenaries and the more valiant citizens of Florence met the more numerous forces of Colleoni at the town called Molinella, roughly halfway between Florence and Venice. The land there was marshy, and horses slipped and fell in mud, and some of the wounded drowned. What we fought was certainly not a great battle, by the standards of those combats that have changed the world. But for some hours we fought in earnest, which was not always the case when one mercenary opposed another. The fight began near midday, and went on, with pauses, until after dark, and the dead totalled six or seven hundred on both sides. Colleoni's new cannon served his cause well, until I managed to lead a squadron of cavalry into his rear, where we overtook a pack train carrying his reserve of gunpowder. After the ensuing fireworks he was unable to make headway. By nightfall the Florentine forces had been worn down, but so had the Venetian; still, it would have been senseless for Colleoni to advance against our fortified city walls, whilst our army still remained in the field against him.

Successful condottieri were nothing if not practical, and did not care to squander today lives that could still be useful to them tomorrow. With much practiced torch-waving, and shouting back and forth, a preliminary truce was worked out, though night had already fallen, making communication difficult. Then by torchlight the Duke and Colleoni embraced each other, exchanging congratulations on their personal survival.

I was suspicious of treachery, but those with more experience in these parochial wars laughed at the idea; and in the morning both armies indeed retreated, as had been agreed.

A few days later, I returned to Careggi. As I approached the villa, I found it difficult to maintain my fatalistic attitude on the subject of my wife. If she should be gone again—I had difficulty in trying to think beyond that point. But I recognized in myself the signs of inward rage.

To my surprise Helen came running to meet me, in the yard near the stables, having evidently observed my approach from the window of our upstairs room—this time we had not been granted the bridal chamber.

Before I had dismounted, she was at my stirrup. "You are alive," she said. Her eyes had a look I could not remember seeing in them before.

"It pleases you to see me so, madam?"

"Pleases me? Pleases me?" Helen sounded the words. Evidently she would not have thought of putting her feelings just that way. "But you are all I have."

Twenty-Two

The half-ruined building into which Judy and her three companions were urged at gunpoint was evidently very old. The door was shielded on the inside with a blackout curtain, in the form of a sheet of dark plastic; once that barrier had been passed, Judy, Bill, Pat and Helen emerged blinking in the white glare of a Coleman lantern set on a rough table. They were standing in a large room, walled with old brick in bad repair. Judy could recognize the soft-looking light brown that she had recently learned to identify as real adobe. Three temporary cots had been set up along one wall. More sheeted plastic was suspended overhead, to protect the beds and other contents of the room from the effects of what must be a leaky roof.

"Sit down. Here," ordered one armed man, pointing to the open space in the middle of the hard-packed earthen floor. "Hands behind you when you sit. Then nobody move."

The four of them sat down. And nobody moved, or spoke. One man passed behind them, tying wrists. He was quick about it. It was as if he had had cords ready for some job like this, and had been practicing.

Hasty glances to right and left assured Judy that her companions were looking pretty sick. She herself was not quite as scared as they appeared to be; she had an inner certainty that help of a most effective kind was on its way. Judy was sure that he now was aware, at least dimly, of her presence here, near the very thing that had already drawn him so powerfully, and he was coming, at great speed.

The trouble was that Judy could not be at all sure of how far he had yet to travel, or long it would be until he got here.

As soon as four pairs of hands had been tied, the tallest of the masked men, the one who gave the orders, got the prisoners to stand up again and then went along the line going briskly and impersonally through all their pockets, and dumping out Pat's knapsack as well. Judy could see from the corner of her eye that the searcher took no money from Bill's wallet. He appeared to be chiefly interested in ID's, which he looked at and then put back. But Bill's car keys did disappear into the tall man's pocket.

This quick search completed, their chief captor stood in front of them, looking at them for a moment. "Ralph," he said abruptly then, "better get the Jeep out." And he tossed one of his henchmen the two sets of car keys he had confiscated. "It'll take some towing to get both their vehicles around the hill and under cover, but we'll have to do it, now we've come this far. Ike, you go along and give him a hand. Cover up the tire tracks. I can manage here."

The other two men went out of the room by a side door that led into some sort of hallway. A minute later Judy could hear an engine starting, as if the Jeep the men had been told to use were parked in some attached garage or shed, with no closed doors between. Gradually the sound of the engine moved away.

"Sit down," said the ski-masked man who still remained. The four sat, a movement made awkward by bound hands. The Coleman on the table emitted a faint hissing noise, and sent out its glare. The masked man set down his shotgun, where he could reach it easily and at a careful distance from the others, leaning against a stack of crates that appeared to hold foodstuffs. Then he said: "Well, people. We've got some things to talk about, before I can let you go."

He certainly has no intention of doing that, thought Judy to herself. Whatever was going on here . . . had something to do with that painting. The painting, the old painting showing some woman . . . it was still wrapped in rough cloth. And now Judy could tell there was clear plastic around it too. And it still leaned against a rough adobe wall in darkness—within a few feet of where she was sitting at this very moment.

Judy opened her eyes with a start. But the sound she had heard was only the wind, scraping a pine branch lightly along the building's ancient roof.

The standing man had turned his head toward her at her motion. Now slowly he turned back to the girl who had introduced herself as Helen. She was the one getting most of his attention.

The man said: "A little bird tells me your name is Helen Seabright. How come you're carrying car keys but no license, no money, nothing else?"

Helen shook her head. She didn't look especially frightened now, Judy realized. Dazed, but almost eager, as if she would like to hear the answer to that question herself.

"I know you too," Helen answered. "You're Gliddon. I don't think anyone ever told me your first name."

"You called me by that name outside. I'd like to know why. Also, I want to know just what the *fuck* you're doing up here at midnight, talking about a radiophone."

Helen was unperturbed. "I know you have one, in this building. Back in the other room where the stove is. I've seen it."

Gliddon whistled softly under his mask. He said no more. He stood there looking at them all until the other two men came back from their task of moving and hiding vehicles. It took them the best part of an hour.

Galvanized when his household alarm shrieked that a locked door somewhere had been opened, Ellison Seabright jumped to his feet and hurried at once toward his bedroom, to check the master security console and to arm himself with a Luger that he kept there. Stephanie, with whom he had been arguing in the breakfast room, for once caused no interference, but fell silent and came along. She had to step lively to keep up with him. He could still move quickly, Ellison told himself, when there was good reason to do so.

Puffing, he entered his bedroom and switched on the light over the security console—the sun had gone down a little while ago and the house was full of gathering dimness. From a table drawer beside the bed he grabbed his weapon. Gun in hand, he saw the console's indication that the intrusion had been in the garage.

He grunted at Stephanie and started out of the room. She followed. They both understood that there could be no question of calling the police.

When Ellison poked his head into the garage, one of the car doors was still standing open to the thickening night, and the inside lights were on.

The Subaru was gone.

Ellison looked around, then closed the door to the outside and turned off the lights. He glared at his wife. "You—" he began, sure that whatever had happened was going to be her fault. Then he led the way at a quick walk back to the room where they had left the boy asleep. The young visitor, or intruder, was gone.

Ellison switched on another light. "He's taken our car," he said. His wife did not answer, and he glared at her. "Well, hasn't he?"

Stephanie gave him back a strange look. "I don't know. It may not have been him who did it."

"No?" Ellison was suddenly aware of the gun still in his hand, though it was hanging motionless with muzzle pointing down at the carpet. "There was no one else in the house." At that she looked more peculiar than ever. "Was there? Was there? Stef, why did you do it?"

His wife only sighed, a sound blending weariness and impatience. "Oh Ellison. Do what?" For some reason she had never adopted any diminutive or nickname for him. Sometimes in the past he had wished secretly that she would do so.

The gun like a great weight seemed to pull his arm down toward the floor. "Don't pretend to be stupid. You guided him out of the house for some reason—"

"I was with you when the alarm went off."

"—and you arranged somehow to give him the keys to the car. You may have done a lot of damage to important plans, plans that you don't begin to understand."

"I don't begin to understand?"

"Did it worry you so much, that I might decide

to have him killed? Your own daughter was killed and you got through that." Then Ellison thought to himself: I shouldn't have said that.

"Ellison. I didn't help him. I didn't know he was going to leave. I didn't want him to leave until it could be decided what to do about him. If he had any help it came from someone else. And you don't have to be so secretive, about your plans to sell the painting secretly and make a fortune, you and Del. Del's told me about that. Or your own bombing scheme. Del wasn't too happy about that one." She paused, sniffing. "Oh my God," she said.

"What?"

"Don't you smell it?"

"What?"

"Very faint, but it's there. The perfume Helen used to like to use."

"Stef, this is very stupid. You're trying to distract me. There was no one else in this house, and someone helped that boy to get away and steal my car. He couldn't have done it without help. Even if he'd found the keys, how could he have avoided the other alarms?"

"I'm not trying to distract you, Ellison, I'm trying to explain something. But I suppose I ought to leave it to Del. Oh God, don't you know anything of what's going on?"

That stopped even Ellison, for a moment. "Now just what in hell is that supposed to mean?"

"I wish you'd put that gun away. There are no burglars. It'll be better if Del explains to you himself. When was the last time you talked to him?"

"I haven't seen him since the kidnapping setup, and the last time he called was days ago. It bothers me when he calls, though he keeps assuring me that the phone here isn't tapped by anyone. How can he know that?"

"Oh." Abruptly Stephanie was almost smiling. "He now has ways of telling, about things like that."

"That's exactly what he said. I don't understand what it means, and I don't like it. He's taking too many chances."

"He *did* tell you that he means to come here tonight?"

Ellison was astonished. "Of course, he told me. I didn't know he'd let you in on it too. He talks too much. And that's another thing, his coming here. When I asked him how he knew the house wasn't being watched, he just laughed. He wouldn't even discuss it."

"If Del says it's all right, then it's all right, Ellison. Believe me."

"Why? Will you answer that simple question for me?"

"Del," said Stephanie, in a new voice. Ellison spent a moment trying to make sense of this as an answer, and then realized that it had been a greeting instead. She was looking over his shoulder.

Beyond a doorway, in the dimness of the next room, towered a figure as tall as Ellison himself, almost as broad. It certainly looked like Del, though Ellison could not at first make out the face in the dim light. It looked like Del, but something had been changed—but it was Del, it was so like him to stand there like that, listening, not saying a word until he was discovered.

Ellison cleared his throat. "I didn't hear you come in. How did you get here? How do you know the house isn't being watched? What if—"

The figure came toward them, moving with Del's walk into the light. Del's face, undoubtedly. But vastly changed, young, lean, no longer sagging in cheek and jowl, under a full head of crisp brown hair.

Del looked at least thirty years younger than when Ellison had seen him last. How? Plastic surgery? More than that. But what?

"Del. You're . . . you're . . .

"Ellison. You're you're you're." Del's rejuvenated voice mocked him, while Del's young face smiled. "You're you're you're. Still as much of an idiot as ever."

Then the smile, changing as it moved, was turned on Stephanie. "All this ringing on the radiophone would seem to indicate something serious. I was coming anyway, so I thought I'd just come over instead of answering." Del's manner was supremely confident. "What's it all about?"

Stephanie took a step closer to Del, reaching for his hand. "I'm so glad you did. There was a boy here. Ellison thinks maybe he was one of the kids you . . . who was at the house in Phoenix once. The boy kept asking for Annie. Said he knew that Annie was here, and he didn't want to go away. Now he's gone, and so is one of the cars."

Del's forehead creased in a mild frown. He glanced up quickly at the ceiling. "Did you—?"

"No, I haven't been up there. I don't know if she's there now or not. And I haven't talked to Ellison about her being there. I've been waiting for you to do that."

"A wise decision," said Del.

Ellison raised his voice. "Will someone kindly inform me what is going on here, under my roof?"

"Close under your roof, old man," said Del. His

young face looked so strange, so strange. It wasn't, it couldn't be, simply makeup or anything like that. It brought back authentic memories. This was really the way Del had looked, thirty, forty years in the past.

Del asked Stephanie: "Did this boy give a name? What did he look like?"

"Short, blond hair, very young." Ellison couldn't remember the name, but Stephanie did. "He said his name was Pat O'Grandison, something like that."

"Ah," said Del. "Yes. She talked about him, before she decided she was going to be Helen. I suppose she's gone with him. But I'll go up and take a look."

And with the last word, Del disappeared. Just like that, from the middle of a lighted room. Ellison found that he had raised his own arms, and like a sleepwalker was groping through the empty air where a moment earlier his rejuvenated brother had been standing.

And was standing again. Del's powerful young hand, materializing in mid-air, casually warded Ellison's groping arm out of the way.

"She's not in the attic now," said Del to Stephanie. "The earth and everything looks undisturbed." His light frown had solidified but did not seem to dent his confidence. "So the two of them apparently took off together. They're both crazy so I'm going to have to check up on what they're doing."

Stephanie said: "She was wearing Helen's perfume again."

"Oh, she's completely settled in as Helen now, in her own mind. I don't know how she justifies to herself sleeping in the attic all day, and occasionally flying out through the wall at night and enjoying a drink of blood. Not the way Helen should act, certainly not in Annie's dream of the home-sheltered adolescent. She may be five hundred years old, I don't know, but inside she's still a little girl wanting to be loved."

Ellison groped his way to a chair and sat in it. He looked at the gun still in his own hand and wondered for a moment what it was doing there. He tried to frame questions that he could ask and that would do him some good, but got nowhere in the attempt. The crafty suspicion suddenly sprang to life: his wife and his half-brother were conspiring to drive him mad.

The spark of suspicion had no sooner been ignited than it sprang up in a roaring blaze.

He looked up, keeping his face calm. Understanding seemed to grow. "You're not really Del," he announced his sudden insight. No one could shed, really shed, thirty or forty years. Stephanie had murdered Del, after all, and had found this young man who looked like him. Could Del have had a son who looked this much like him?

Del's young face looked at him, and away again, contemptuously. "I'll see you in a little while, then," the youth said to Stephanie. "Can you manage things here?"

Stephanie was clinging to him impulsively. "Don't go yet. Del, change me now, tonight. You said you would, as soon as you were changed yourself. Now you're all set. I don't want to go on like this, with him, another day. Not another hour if I can help it. You can't imagine what it's like. Take my blood once more. Change me."

"Oh, I can imagine. But, as I say, I'm going to be busy for a while. If she heads for the painting again tonight there could be problems. Gliddon's out there, and his men, and they don't imagine that there are any such things as vampires. I'm not quite ready to be rid of them all just yet."

To Ellison, listening, the whole conversation had become utterly insane, incomprehensible. Yet it was perfectly plain to him from looking at the two of them just what was going on. What had happened between his wife, *his wife*, and the giant young demon-figure that somehow looked like a young Del.

Now Ellison watched as the young man who looked like Del took Stephanie by both arms, and kissed her softly on the forehead. He said, in his perfect imitation of Del's young voice: "I will. I'll change you. You'll be young forever too. But you have to understand that when that happens, it will make a difference between us. No more lovemaking. It doesn't work between two vampires, you understand. Then we'll just be—friends. So I don't want to rush things. I love you just as you are."

Stephanie gave a wild cry. "You don't want me any more. I can see it. You're through with me now. And, my God, I gave you my daughter for your games. You've had both of us and used us up. Helen's dead, and I'm—now you want to leave me with this, this obscene old lump of fat—"

Ellison was not conscious of getting to his feet, or of saying anything, though he could hear his voice. And the gun in his right hand rose levelly and seemed to go off by itself. He had at last got Stephanie's full attention. She stood up very straight, and gazed at Ellison with wild and unbelieving eyes. Then her hand caught at the seventeenth-century Spanish shawl and at her breast beneath. And then she fell.

Ellison held the gun up higher now, and shifted his aim. And now he was looking straight down the long Luger barrel, at Del's eyes, excited but unfrightened, that gazed straight back at him.

"You haven't learned a thing, have you old man?" said Del. Ellison fired, but somehow Del was not falling, though he winced as if with pain. Anger and triumph were in his face and he was moving rapidly toward Ellison, reaching out for Ellison with young powerful hands. The Luger fired and fired again, and Del came on unharmed.

Twenty-Three

Fade in on violence.

If you have seen one tournament of jousting, you have seen them all. But then, unless you are after all, in tune with my jests, almost as old as I am, you have never seen even one, have you? Never mind.

There were church bells in my ears, when I knew that no bells rang. Angels swam round me in an alarming swarm; not, as modern legend has it, looking for the point of a pin to sit on, but rather to cluster before my eyes inside my steel helm, good and evil disputing for my soul.

I understood vaguely that my helm was being lifted off, by gentle hands, but the knowledge made things no clearer. I saw the totentantz; and I saw, as on a stage, tableaux from the old French story in which three living men meet their three doppelgangers all wrapped in shrouds.

"Is he dead, then, at last?" It was the voice of my dear wife Helen, and she was despairing almost utterly. "He is dead. I know that he is dead."

Someone else muttered something. If this was death, at least I did not fear it. The Angel of the Lord swooped near to me, dispersing the fog of lesser cherubs who were swarming in my eyes, and spoke to me. What the angel said to me then I may not yet reveal.

"He is not dead," said another, non-angelic voice.

I was lying on my back inside a jousting pavillion of fine white cloth, lit gloriously from

above by bright sunlight. My armor had all ben
stripped away, and my body, wrapped now in
white linen almost like a shroud, was a mass of
many hurts. I hurt no more, though, than was
seemly for one who had been knocked off a horse
by the brutal impact of a long, sharp-ended pole,
and had probably been trampled on by horses'
hooves thereafter. Meanwhile the Angel of the
Lord transformed himself into Helen, who sat at
my side dabbing with cool perfumed water at a
certain abominable lump upon my head.

Presently I understood that this wretched lump
was coextensive with my head itself.

"I feared for you, oh my lord." And Helen was
weeping softly. Dab, dab, oh so gently. Her perfumed kerchief of fine Florentine cloth was mottled red.

"That I was dead?"

"Yes. Oh, Vlad, your face was pale and still."

"Know then that I am alive." I raised an aching
arm to catch Helen's hand, whose dabbing minis-
trations had become more irritant than help; and,
to provide a sweeter reason for the catch, I
squeezed what I had caught, and brought it to my
lips. "And, even if I had been dead, to have such
an angel ministering to me would make me rise
again."

A non-angelic face in the background coughed
and grimaced at this remark. It was, I realized
now, a friar standing by there. Doubtless he had
come to anoint the dying.

"I would not have you jest about such things,"
said Helen. But I think what really bothered her
was her perception that I was not jesting. This was
in early 1469. By then we had been five years
married, and had lived long enough as man and

wife to begin to know each other well.

"Your good wife speaks wisely, my son," the friar chided me. "You have been near death today, but today it is God's will that you live. You should consider that one day He must will otherwise. Death will come to us all, or soon or late."

I considered the friar's long face, and liked it not. "Nay, father. Does it not say somewhere in the Scriptures, 'we shall not all die, but we shall all be changed'?"

The friar's face said emphatically that mine was not a proper attitude; but what could one expect from these foreign soldiers who were the bane of Italy? "It saith also, that the devil may quote Scripture when he likes." After that, sensing himself no longer quite welcome, the priest bowed out through the tent flap and took himself away.

"Vlad, do not sit up yet. Rest yet a while, and I will tend to you."

"I will sit up." For the moment, though, it was quite enough just to get my elbows under me and raise my shoulders. "And shortly I will rise, and walk. I want to see the progress of the tournament." There was a large roar, of many excited voices, not far outside. The pavilions had been set up in rows quite near the stands and the lists. Now there came groans, and loud prayers of alarm; again some shrewd blow had been dealt. "Who unhorsed me? Who dealt me such a devil's blow? I don't remember."

"I do not think I saw who it was."

"Nay, Helen, it is only a game, is it not? Do you think I am going to go looking for revenge?"

The great misbegotten lump that was my skull ached all the more mercilessly when I sat up. But evidently, despite all my interesting visions, I had

not been unconscious for very long. The brightness and warmth of the sun shining through the
pavilion top told me that the time was still near
midday, and the crowd's voice sounded as fresh
and enthusiastic as ever.

Again shouts of encouragement and triumph,
mingled with those of disappointment, drifted in.

"Who is winning?" I wondered aloud. And
without letting myself think about the problems
of movement, I got to my feet and began to dress
myself.

Helen sighed and let me have my way. "I do not
know. They say the grand prize will be awarded to
Lorenzo himself, whatever happens in the jousts.
It is his wedding we are celebrating, after all, even
if he is no warrior."

I grumbled reflexively at that. Not that I wished
for myself the fame of winning. I did not want to
be prominent in the public eye; I was still Signore
Ladislao in Italy, because I was still theoretically,
officially, imprisoned in Hungary by my brother-
in-law, and would be for another seven years. His
Majesty King Matthias was still wary, still uncertain of what reception I might be accorded were I
to appear in a place of honor at his court; and he
was, for somewhat different reasons, also unsure
of what Helen's reception would be there. Meanwhile I had been occupied with other things.
Some of these were tasks undertaken for Matthias,
and none of them have any proper place in this
history. But I was on better terms than ever with
the Medici, who ruled more firmly than ever in
Florence; and they would not take no for an answer to their invitation to this tournament and
wedding.

It was a celebration, a festive occasion, the like

of which had perhaps not been seen in those parts since the days of ancient Rome. Arm in arm with my wife (She was, I must admit, helping me to keep steady on my feet, though she managed to make it look as if I were the one supporting and assisting her) I presently walked out of my pavilion, which stood surrounded by a multicolored mushroom forest of other tents like itself. I was at once congratulated upon my quick recovery, by smiling gentlefolk nearby. Only a few yards away, the temporary stands held cheering thousands. In the middle distance the Palazzo Medici was strung with flowers from every doorway, window, and cornice, as were many of the other buildings in this quarter of the city, and even some of the many church spires in the distance. The land where the tournament was being held had been, only a few months ago, a wasteland of abandoned buildings, emptied decades ago by plague. At Piero's direction, all had been leveled and made smooth for a jousting ground to help in the celebration of the wedding of his eldest son to the lovely Clarice Orsini. Now, as I strolled with my wife, the prize seats of the grandstand came into our view, and I could see some of the Orsini delegation there now, the future in-laws of Lorenzo, ready to weld their elder dynasty to his.

"Shall we go and watch the fighting, Vlad?"

"No, I have changed my mind. I think I have seen enough of combat for one day." And I guided Helen in the opposite direction from the lists. "I prefer to seek more soothing entertainment."

Through increasing crowds, lively with celebration, we moved toward the palace. There was something strange about the crowd, and it puzzled me until I realized there were few hawkers; food and drink were instead being given to the masses free during these proclaimed days of joy. Musicians played on a small green, and some gentlefolk were in sport performing for the crowd, treading the stately old French *basse danse*. It reminded me for a moment of the old French story in my dream, or vision.

Helen must have seen me smile. For whenever I displayed good humor she was wont to bring up some topic she had been saving till I should be in a good mood.

"Vlad, you have been fighting so much these last few years. In these little wars, and tournaments. Do you mean to keep on fighting always, until one day when I think that you are dead it turns out I am right? Is it not time to let the younger men do their share?"

"Oh, am I old?"

"You are—mature. And there should be more to life than giving and receiving blows. And—Vlad, I tell you truly—on the day that I do see you lying dead, I think I shall go mad." She said it simply and without emphasis.

"I am a soldier."

"My husband, with your agreement, I am going to write a letter to my brother. He could end this farce of your supposed imprisonment at any time, and then we could go home. I think that by now I have demonstrated that I can be well-behaved. And you—you could be Prince again, in Wallachia. Matthias could install you there if he wanted to."

"I can see political reasons why he would not want to. Not now, at least. I think he will not agree to your proposal."

"Then I should wait for a time, and write again. You would like to go home? Such a change would please you?"

I looked around me. I had, as I have written, fallen in love with Italy. Yet it was not home. Then I looked intently at Helen. "It would please me very much," I said, "to rule in Wallachia again, this time with you beside me. Though you must realize that things there are not *always* perfectly peaceful. There have been moments, one or two in history, of unrest, invasion, murderous intrigue and treachery—a few upsets of that sort." I had to smile. "By St. Peter's beard, you worry about me in tournaments, and yet wish to see me on that throne again?"

Helen was distressed, but determined also. "Oh yes, I know there would be dangers at home, too. But there—how can I put it?—the dangers would have meaning. You would be defending our own homeland. That is what a sword ought to be for, and a cannon too."

"I think you have a woman's view of swords and cannons and war."

"Well, and if I do? A woman can be right. And if death came, in some great, just cause, then in death too there would be meaning. If you were to die so, perhaps I would not go mad to have you taken from me."

I did not know quite what to say, or think. "I have told you, wife. I mean never to submit to death without a struggle. The old scyther will have from me such a fight as he has not known in a long time."

Arm in arm we walked on, through celebrating

crowds toward the palace. I had heard that Leonardo was to be there this afternoon, discoursing of his art to those folk who loved such things more than tournaments.

Twenty-Four

It was after midnight when Gliddon finally heard Ike and Ralph returning the Jeep to its shed. Shortly after that the two of them came into the room where he was still standing over his prisoners. They described to Gliddon the Subaru wagon and the old Buick, and told him how they had searched through both without finding anything of interest. Both vehicles were now covered with old tarps, in a ravine where no one was likely to look. Ike said they had done a good job in getting rid of tracks.

Gliddon listened, and nodded, and presently gave more orders. He wanted his four captives disposed in four separate rooms for their interrogations. There were plenty of rooms, otherwise unused, in the old place, and Gliddon preferred to have four separate stories to sift through for the truth instead of one. He didn't anticipate any great trouble in getting at the truth, or at least the part of it that these four unlucky kids could tell him. But he could see that even when they'd told him all they could, plenty of problems were going to remain.

In his days of hiding out here Gliddon had wondered sometimes whether the many little rooms in the sprawling old building might have been monks' cells in the old days. Many of the rooms still had doors, though few had ever had windows. When Gliddon looked into the little earth-floored chamber where Helen had been put to wait for him, he saw that what had been a tiny window must have been blocked up earlier by Ike or Ralph, with chunks of wood and wads of plastic, as part of the general effort they had made to keep out some of the cold and to keep their lights from being visible. Anyway, Gliddon thought it a damn good thing that one way or another they weren't going to have to camp out here much longer. The deal for the undercover sale of the painting ought to be concluded any day now, according to what Gliddon had heard from Del Seabright on the phone.

Keeping his small battery-powered lantern aimed at the girl, Gliddon set it down on the floor. The old door of the room sagged half-closed behind him, and he let it stay that way. It was cold in here, even colder than out in the big room, and Gliddon in his heavy jacket was no more than comfortable. But the girl sitting on the floor was barefoot and without a coat; still she wasn't even shivering. Or very much frightened, either; the expression on her face as she looked back at Gliddon was half dazed, half arrogant.

She's on something, all right, Gliddon thought, staring back at her through the eyeholes in his mask. She's got to be. He could only hope that she was not too far out of it to do a little useful talking. Del's niece. Well, that was just too bad. Del might make a fuss, but Gliddon couldn't see any way to avoid wasting this girl, and the three who had come with her as well, now things had gone this far. Helping Del sell the painting his way had been an okay idea, but it wasn't necessarily the only way for Gliddon to go. He himself was no art expert; but experts could be hired when they were needed, as Gliddon himself had been hired, often enough, for his own specialty. Now he had the painting, and he had an airplane, and he knew one or two people down in Mexico who would be glad enough to welcome him there with his treasure any time he wanted to drop in. He understood he wouldn't be getting anything like full value for the painting that way, but still he ought to be able to turn a nice profit. And tonight things were looking more and more like that was the route that he was going to have to take.

He stood there looking down at Helen for a while, and her expression didn't change. That was a bad sign. "Well, girly. You and your friends have sure got yourselves into a bunch of trouble here. I mean a real bunch. Can you understand that? Am I getting through to you at all?"

Evidently he wasn't, for Helen still sounded almost cheerful. "My Uncle Del is going to be angry with you for this. He's going to be out looking for me. He loves me a lot, you know, just like I was his own daughter."

"Yeah, I bet he does. And in several other ways as well. I think I see how that goes, kid. But there's one thing I definitely *don't* get. You see, I really thought that you were dead. Just like everybody else, I thought so. Now it turns out you're not dead, and you've been hiding out with Uncle Del, and Mommy and Stepdaddy too, I suppose; so okay. But *I* should have been told that you were still alive. I mean, I was in on that snatch operation from the start, all the way, and *I* thought for sure that you were the one who was gunned down in that upstairs hall. We sure as hell shotgunned someone."

Gliddon paused, with a faint sigh. The sappy look on the kid's face didn't hold out much hope that he was going to learn much from her tonight.

Could he believe anything she said, anyway? But
it was important that he try—something was
going on here that he wasn't in on. Something
even deeper than the faked kidnapping and killing, and the faked loss of the painting. Something very important, no doubt about that. And he
hadn't been told by the Seabrights.

But wait. At last, as the kid considered what he
had just told her, her eyes were beginning to look
shocked. "That was my girlfriend Annie who was
killed," she whispered. "Did you do that?"

"You know, Helen, I think you've changed a
little since that night. Stand up for a minute, let
me take a look."

Obediently the girl stood up on her bare feet.
She managed the move quickly and without difficulty despite having her hands fastened behind
her back.

"I think you're a little taller now, Helen, than
when I saw you last. I can recognize you, but . . .
you've changed. How old are you, anyway?"

Helen tossed back well-cared-for brown hair
from her face. "When was that? When did you see
me before?"

"Look, kid, you've seen me before, right? You
were pretty sure about my name."

"That's . . . different."

"Yeah, sure. You know when we saw each
other," Gliddon assured her softly, "if you can get
your brain working. It was at your dear Uncle
Del's house in Phoenix. One night he had a special kind of party there, he used to have them
regularly, and I suppose the old fart still does.
This time he wanted you to play along, and your
Mommy wanted to make him happy and she said
you could. Either he didn't invite your Mommy

that time or else she didn't want to come. But I remember I was wishing she had, because she looked like a real good piece still." Gliddon paused. He was remembering what he had done with this very kid on that very night. But that had nothing to do with anything now, and the look on her face assured him that she wasn't remembering much of anything at all.

He went on. "Anyway, where we met doesn't matter all that much. The point is that I know you, and that I'm going to find out why you came out here tonight. How'd you know that I was here, and had a radiophone, and so on?"

The girl brightened; she understood now what he was talking about. "Your phone has some kind of a scrambler thing on it. So if someone else listens in when you talk to Uncle Del or Mommy or Daddy, they can't understand a thing."

"Uncle Del and Mommy and Daddy Ellison really tell you a whole bunch, don't they? I wonder why."

"Uncle Del does. I don't see Mommy much any more. Because I sleep in the attic a lot now. And Daddy thinks I'm dead. But he doesn't really care. He's only my step-daddy anyway." Helen giggled prankishly.

"I get it. Or maybe I don't. So I suppose you brought your friends out here tonight to show them the radiophone."

"Pat is the only friend I brought. I don't know the others, we just ran into them by accident. And what I wanted to show Pat was the painting."

Gliddon sighed. At this stage, he wasn't really surprised. "You can sit down again if you want to, Helen. Who told you about the painting being here? Uncle Del? Or was it your mother?"

Accommodatingly she sat down. "Uncle Del. He's always wanting to talk to me about it."

Well, people could get their kicks in an infinite variety of ways; Gliddon had understood that for a long time. Still there was something going on here that he knew he didn't yet understand. "Now look, Helen, what I'm going to ask you now is very important. You want to get out of all this trouble that you're in, don't you? How many other people have you talked to about there being a painting out here, and a radiophone, and all?"

"Nobody." And now at last, delayed, the sniffles started. "Just the kids who are here."

"Nobody else at all? You're sure? You're very sure?"

"Yeeesss." The word trailed off into a great sour violin-note of a sob.

Gliddon felt like slapping her, like killing her. But for the moment he wasn't rough. He was very seldom rough without calculation, and right now it wasn't called for by the situation. He found himself tending to believe the kid. If what he heard from the other three captives tended to confirm her story, then these four but only these four would have to go. Then maybe the operation of selling the painting as Delaunay planned could still go on.

He patted Helen gently on the head. "Just take it easy, kid. We're going to get this all straightened out, but it's going to take a little time. I'm going to have to keep your hands tied up for a while yet, okay?"

She was sobbing and didn't answer. Maybe he ought to talk to her again, Gliddon told himself, when she'd had a little time to come out of it. He picked up his lantern and went out through the sagging door, which almost fell off when he moved it. Ike, still ski-masked, was sitting at the end of the corridor like a guard in a prison, in a position to keep an eye on all the cells. Gliddon nodded to him, then turned away and went into the cell where they had put the boy he also remembered from Phoenix. Another Uncle Del special.

This one was obviously scared shitless. He sat on the floor in the corner as Helen had been sitting, but he had twisted to hide his face in the corner of the wall. He looked around with eyes squinted almost shut when Gliddon entered with the lantern.

Gliddon put the lantern down casually on the floor, and then took a relaxed pose, leaning with his back against the wall. "Kid, we got ourselves a real serious problem here. But I have hopes that we can straighten it out without anyone getting hurt. Does that sound to you like the way we ought to go?"

The boy nodded quickly. "Oh yeah. Gosh." Obviously he wanted desperately to believe what Gliddon had just said, about no one being hurt—but maybe he couldn't quite believe it. He made a little choking noise in his throat.

"On your driver's license it says your name is Pat O'Grandison." Gliddon's mind had had a little time to work on the name by now, and it sounded right to him, like he had heard it before and it really belonged to this punk he recalled from Phoenix.

"Yeah, that's right. We didn't mean any harm by walking around here, we just got lost. The bridge was out down there, and one of the cars was stuck. The girl said she knew where there was a phone, back this way."

"The girl?"

"The one I was riding with. She was just giving me a ride. I didn't want to bust in on anything up here."

"When you say the girl, you mean Helen Seabright?"

"Yeah. That's her. That's who she told me she was."

"Well then *say* Helen Seabright. I want to be filled in on all the details, so tell me everything you can. What happens to you from here on is going to depend a lot on what you tell me." Gliddon worked a cigarette and a match out of his shirt pocket and lit up. "Here, want a drag?"

"Sure. Thanks."

Gliddon held the smoke, let the kid inhale deeply. "Now, you say that Helen Seabright was just giving you a ride. You mean she just picked you up along the highway?"

The kid hesitated. Gliddon could see him wavering, and then apparently deciding to tell the truth. Yippee. "No, we started out from her place in Santa Fe. Her parents' place, I guess. Great big house. Gosh."

"And her Uncle Del was there with you, and you were all having a sort of party before you decided to take a ride."

"Party? No. I just came to the house looking for another girl."

"You like girls?" The boy was silent, and Gliddon went on: "Never mind. Who was this one you say that you were looking for?"

"Annie Chapman, her name was. Still is, I guess."

Annie Chapman. One name Gliddon was never

likely to forget. Not after that one party night in Phoenix, and what had happened afterward. Del's big secret, whatever it was, that Gliddon wasn't in on—it would have something to do with her. "All right. Then what?"

"Then . . . I kind of conked out on a sofa for a while. When I woke up this girl, Helen, was sitting there and she started talking to me. Also there was a woman in the house, and a man, an old guy, real huge. I don't know if he was her Uncle Del that you mentioned, or her father, or who."

"You never saw him before, huh?" He peeled off his mask. "How about me?"

The kid was immediately struck blank and hopeless. "I don't know. I don't think so. I don't always remember things too good."

"That's fine. Outta sight. Some things you're not supposed to remember. But when I ask you to remember something, you make a special effort, huh?"

"Sure. Anything you say."

"Now do you know who that big old man was?"

"No. I don't. Really."

"Okay. And the girl you started out looking for was Annie Chapman."

"Yeah, but they all swore she wasn't there and they didn't know her. You know her? She looks quite a bit like Helen."

Yeah, there had been a good resemblance. Gliddon pondered. Sisters, somehow? Nothing seemed to quite make sense. And this kid didn't seem to recall that orgy night at Phoenix at all. Gliddon himself had picked up both Pat and Annie on that night, one at a bus station, one on the road—recruiting for parties had been part of his job for Delaunay. Another part had been join-

ing in—Del liked to have a physically able and
trusted employee on hand in case things got
rowdy, as they often did. That night the group had
included Helen, Pat, Annie Chapman—and
what's-his-name, that muscular young drifter
who had followed Annie when she danced off
into the museum room, and had been killed by her
there. Gliddon could see it yet: the strong, naked
young male swinging the silver artifact, some
kind of model ship, right for Annie's head; and
Annie dodging and reaching up somehow out of
her crouch, grabbing her assailant by wrist and
ankle, and—and just flipping him somehow, so
that his long-haired head smashed on a marble
base, and blood sprayed on the white carpet.
Gliddon had seen a few fights in his time, but
never before a stunt like that.

And from that moment, Del had made Annie his
special project; he had wanted something special
from her, obviously. And Gliddon, looking back,
couldn't be sure that the special something had
really had anything to do with sex. Gliddon had
seen very little of her from that night on . . .

And then, on the night of the engineered kidnapping, it must have been Annie Chapman, running in panic through the upstairs hall of the same
mansion, who wouldn't stop when she was yelled
at and so had caught a charge of buckshot in the
head. Del must have known who the dead girl
was; but he had said nothing to Gliddon; and the
family had identified the dead girl as Helen, and
had cremated her.

Why?

Something to do with inheritance, with wills,
with who gets what. Gliddon didn't understand
all the legal angles of what happened when some-

one as wealthy as Del died or supposedly died. Del wanted to be thought dead, to disappear, while in fact retaining control over most of his own great riches. Gliddon could understand that; he was trying to do something like it himself. But he was more and more convinced that something else important was being planned by Del, and Gliddon hadn't been dealt in. Except, maybe, in some way, he was going to be set up to take a fall.

Damn the whole Seabright crew, anyway. They were trying something that Gliddon wasn't going to like when he found out about it. The way things were looking, more and more, they pretty well had to be.

The boy still sat on the floor, looking up at Gliddon, growing more and more frightened; he looked sick. "Listen," he pleaded now, "I gotta go to the toilet. Please."

"Okay," said Gliddon. He turned away and stuck his head out of the door of the cell. Suddenly he found himself feeling and thinking like a jailor, and it was amusing. "Ike? You got a client here. Take him for a walk and bring him back. I want to talk to him some more, later."

Judy could hear, down at the other end of the strange little hallway, the voices murmuring, sometimes rising a little in anger or in fear. The implacable man who had made them all prisoners, whose name apparently was Gliddon as the girl called Helen had said, seemed to be making his rounds like a doctor in a busy clinic, going from one treatment room to the next.

At least none of the patients were screaming. Yet.

Judy, to control her own fear, concentrated as

much as possible on something else—on that hurrying approach that only she could sense. He was coming, in an onrush that seemed utterly tireless. The difficulty remained, though, that Judy could not tell how far he had yet to come. With a great effort she tried to communicate her own fear and need to the one approaching, and after a while it seemed to Judy that his speed had become greater still. But no words, no plans could be exchanged, and she could not be sure. The landscape around him was still all wild and empty, she could perceive that much . . . but where were his running feet? Abruptly Judy realized that he was now wingborne.

A bright light against her closed lids startled her. She squinted open her eyes to see Gliddon, now without his mask, looking down at her over a small lantern. His face was more ordinary than she had imagined it. In one hand he carried a casual, half-smoked cigarette.

His voice was not unkindly. It might even fit the doctor she had imagined. "Let's see, your name is Judy Southerland, as I recall from your ID."

"That's right." Her own voice came out pleasingly strong. "I think you'd better untie my hands."

"Now just try to have a little patience, Judy. I didn't ask you to come here, you know. What are you people doing here, anyway?"

"I . . . any answer I give to that is going to sound pretty silly."

"Try the true one on me. That'll save time and trouble."

"I—no, I don't have to tell you anything at all. Except that you'd better let me go. Help is going to be coming for me."

The man set down his lantern carefully on the floor. Then without changing expression he drew back his arm and hit Judy open-handed across the face. Never in her whole life before had she been struck like that. Now she understood what was meant by the old expression about seeing stars. A moment later she tasted blood. And her tongue had become an odd, paralyzed lump that in a moment was going to hurt badly. It started to hurt.

She tried moving her jaw, and was a little surprised to find that it still worked. Then, speaking carefully around her tongue, she said: "You're going to be sorry you did that. Oh God are you ever going to be sorry."

Perhaps her sincerity made a momentary impression on the man, for he seemed to hesitate. Then he took a puff on his cigarette, and reached out to grab Judy by the hair. She saw what was coming, and uttered a little shriek. "All right! All right, I'll tell you the truth, if that's what you want. Don't blame me if it sounds completely crazy."

Her hair was released. "I'm listening."

"I just talked Bill into giving me a ride. Then we ran into these other two by accident. I have no idea what they were doing out this way. But our car was already stuck down there when they came along."

"I see. It was your idea for Bill to drive you out here."

"Yes."

"Why? You just like to take rides in the middle of the night? On roads like that one? If you just want a peaceful place to screw, you don't have to drive out of town this far."

Judy was silent. A hand rested on her head, and

here came the cigarette again, toward her face.
She yelped. "Wait! I'm going to the Astoria
School, you see. Up in the hills on the other side of
Santa Fe."

The approaching fire paused. "That's nice, tell
me more." Judy could feel in the man's hand on
her head that he was enjoying this.

"It has a bearing. Wait. Well . . . one of the girls
there was saying that her brother had been out this
way recently, deer hunting, and there were some
people living here in the old buildings." Judy
stalled there. Invention had flagged, because of
the way Gliddon was looking at her.

This time the cigarette came all the way. And it
didn't withdraw until she had screamed, twice.
"Deer hunting in the spring," the man said then.
He let her go, and leaned back against the wall,
looking at her thoughtfully while she sobbed.

"You know what I think I'm going to do?" he
said at last. "That young guy who gave you the
ride, as you say. I haven't talked to him yet. I think
I'll bring him in here and talk to him. As soon as
either one of you tells me another funny story, I'll
pop out one of his eyes. I have a way of doing it
with my thumb, just like this." Gliddon demonstrated in mid-air. "Then we can talk some
more about deer hunting in the spring, and I'll
take out the other. I'll use him up a little at a
time—"

"All right, all right! We know about the painting. I mean I know about it. Bill doesn't know a
thing."

Her interrogator sighed. It was an angry sound,
but Judy realized, slowly and with fearful relief,
that the anger this time was not at her. Gliddon
stared at the adobe wall for a time, as if he were

looking into the distance. Then his attention came back to her. "You were all at one of Del's parties tonight, right?"

Judy nodded agreement. She had no real idea of what she was agreeing to, only that agreement was the expected answer, the believable answer, the answer that would at least postpone more pain.

"I thought so. At Ellison's house in Santa Fe?"

Judy read the question as well as she could, and nodded her head again.

"Yeah, I thought so. And for once the old asshole got stoned himself and talked too much. One time when I wasn't there to look out for him. How many other people were there, besides you four that I've got?"

Judy paused. Thought, hoped, prayed. "No one."

"You know what I think? I think you're lying to me again."

"No. No I'm not. No."

Gliddon sighed faintly. Basically he believed Judy. Hurting girls was something that he enjoyed very much, but right now he had one more person to talk to. First, though, he meant to take a short break and grab something to eat.

For Pat, being left alone with his imagination under present circumstances was almost as bad as being worked over. Almost. He had been worked over seriously a time or two in his life, and he understood how lucky he had been to survive those occasions without permanent damage. He feared that this time he was not going to survive at all. When the man called Ike had taken him out of his cell, Pat had feared that he was going to be killed at once. Then when that hadn't happened, he considered trying to seduce Ike. But in Pat's experience in rough situations such efforts only tended to make things worse.

Back in his cell, crouched shivering again in his adobe corner, he could imagine the worst of everything that was going to happen to him. He almost welcomed the shivering that shook him and made his teeth chatter. Maybe if he was lucky he would freeze to death before Gliddon got around to him again.

To Pat it seemed now that he had always known that he was going to end something like this. There had never been any use in hoping for some other outcome. Life as he had known it had been basically like this all along. A few bright intervals here and there. But he seemed to have spent an awfully high percentage of his lifetime alone in the dark.

But this time he wasn't left alone in the dark for long.

After the glare of first Gliddon's lantern and then Ike's, it was hard to see anything in the dim cell. But as soon as Pat's eyes became accustomed to the gloom again he could see, or thought he could see, someone standing just inside his door.

He could have sworn the door hadn't been opened again, but . . . and then he saw that it was Helen. Her hands were free, and she was looking at Pat gleefully, like some small girl triumphant in a game of hide and seek. Pat knew a relief so great that it made him feel for a moment as if he were going to faint.

Helen put a finger to her lips—as if Pat might need any warning to keep silent. Then with an impish smile she stepped close to him and squatted down. "I fooled them," she whispered. "They thought I was sad because I was crying."

Pat wanted her to get to work at once on his bound hands. But she just squatted there. She added: "They're going to be mad—I already set Bill loose." She continued to look at Pat fondly, as Annie had used to do sometimes. But Helen was doing nothing helpful.

"Helen," Pat pleaded at last, in quiet desperation. "Help me get loose."

"In a little while. I want to kiss you, first."

"Not now, not—"

She was leaning toward him, and now her lips stopped his. Her lips—Helen's lips?—felt cool. In another moment Pat had recognized their touch, even before they left his mouth and moved down toward his throat.

"*Annie.*" His own whisper was still very soft. But it carried the astonishment of a shout.

"Hush, lover, hush," the girl murmured against Pat's neck. Her brown hair brushed his face. Only Annie had ever really bitten him in making love. And now he felt her teeth again.

It wasn't pain. But as he had known it with Annie a dozen times before, it had the intensity of great pain. Never, with anyone else, anything like this . . . it went beyond, unimaginably beyond, anything that he had known of sex.

Pat moaned. He couldn't help it if the sound was loud. He forgot his bound hands and even the threat of death. He couldn't tell how long it went on. He never could. He knew only that at last it ended, and that the moment Annie took her mouth from his throat and let him go the shivering came back, even stronger than before. Pat felt he wasn't going to be able to go on living in this condition. Something was going to have to happen soon to end it, one way or another. He felt so weak now that he wondered if he was dying. But the idea conveyed no fear.

He was miserable, colder than ever, very weak, but no longer afraid as he slumped back again in the angle of the wall. The adobe behind his back felt soft and crumbly. "Annie, don't leave me." As long as she stayed with him, he wasn't even going to worry about how she had managed for a time to look so much like Helen.

"You can call me Annie," her soft voice answered. "For you to is all right." She was standing up straight again, in the middle of the little cell, and despite the darkness Pat could see her a little better than before. "Poor Pat. You don't look good. But it's going to be all right, Annie knows what to do for you."

"Annie."

"Or you could call me Helen. I was Helen once before . . . a long time ago."

With crossed arms she grasped her loose pullover shirt at the waist. In a quick motion she slid it up and off over her head. Her upper body, completely uncovered, was slender and pale in the darkness.

"Annie . . . help me . . . get me out of here."

"Don't faint now, Pat. Don't, my lover. Here." And what the pale girl in the darkness was doing now seemed very strange; even Annie had never done anything quite like this before. With her left hand she cupped and lifted one of her small breasts, and with the nail of her right forefinger she drew a line just underneath. A short dark line appeared on the pale skin. Annie was bending over Pat, bringing the dark line closer and closer to his face. "Here, lover. This'll help. This'll help a lot."

He understood now what was expected of him. In a moment it no longer seemed strange at all, and his lips parted, hungrily.

A little later, when the shotgun fired at the other end of the building, Pat didn't hear a sound.

Twenty-Five

Gunfire and uproar brought Gliddon running, cursing through the fragments of sandwich that he spat out of his mouth, grabbing up his shotgun from where he had left it leaning against the stacked crates of food. At the far end of the building, Ralph reported to him that the prisoner as yet unquestioned, Bill Bird, had somehow got loose. Ike had seen him, with unbound hands, sneaking out a door and then making a break for it. Ike had fired at him, evidently missing completely; and then Ike had gone in hot pursuit.

"Get him!" Gliddon snarled, shoving Ralph toward the door also.

"He could maybe try something like doubling back, to get the Jeep—"

"I hope to hell he does. Get him!" And Ralph ran.

Gliddon drew a deep breath, let it out. Well, all right. He had pretty well made up his mind anyway that he was going to have to cut out alone, and probably tonight, sometime before dawn. So anything that got Ike and Ralph out of the way, kept them from raising any objections, might well turn out at this stage to be an actual advantage.

He trotted toward the shed where the aircraft was kept, at the other end of the building from the Jeep. Should he stop on the way and finish off the people left in the cells? No, first things first; it looked like there was a good chance of one witness getting away anyway. First make sure of the painting and the plane.

He reached the aircraft shed, which was attached to the north end of the building. He, Ike
and Ralph had built it carefully out of old lumber
so it wouldn't look strange from the air. Now at
once Gliddon dragged open the wide doors. In the
moonless night the section of abandoned road
which served as runway was vaguely visible. Lantern still in hand—now was no time to worry
about showing a little light—Gliddon then turned
back toward the deep end of the hangar-shed,
where he had stashed the packaged painting in
the middle of a stack of rotted lumber, studded
here and there with rusty nails.

And as soon as he had turned, he stopped. In the
beam of his lantern stood the slim young girl,
Helen, bending over the pile of old boards and
timbers. Her hands were free, and now she was
down to wearing nothing but her jeans.

"God," said Gliddon, speaking aloud but to
himself. "They're all loose." And any one of them
could finger him for kidnapping, at least.

"Don't you point that gun at me," the girl said,
straightening up and turning, a hand on one hip.
She put her other hand on a flimsy table that
Gliddon had brought into the shed when they
were doing some maintenance on the aircraft engine, as a place to set down tools and parts.

And Gliddon paused for a moment, struck by
her face. It was suddenly different. And her voice
. . . maybe he was starting to go crazy himself, he
spent so much of his life around nuts of one kind
or another.

She was starting to say, again, "Don't you—"
just as Gliddon fired. And at the same moment,
somehow, the table she had been holding came
flipping up into the air toward him. As if the girl

had tossed it, though no little girl could possibly—and the charge hit the table in mid-air and blew the middle of the table into fragments. The legs and various splintered parts of the top went flying everywhere. The thin wooden tabletop was not enough to save the girl, of course, not at close range like this. She went down at once. Gliddon shone the lantern briefly on the bloody mess, then set it down so he could rub his right forearm. One-handed wasn't a good way to fire a twelve-gauge, even if you did have a powerful grip. Anyway, he hadn't broken any fingers, though one had been torn slightly by the trigger guard in the recoil.

He set the weapon down too. Then it took him a minute to dig through the lumber pile and get the painting out, bulky and heavy inside its special protective crate and wrappings. Grunting, he wrestled the package over to the Cessna, got the cargo compartment open and worked the package inside. A tight fit; carefully planned by the Seabrights, probably, even as far back as when they bought the aircraft; give them credit for being planners. That was one reason Gliddon didn't want to ride with their plan to the very end, not once it had become obvious that they were keeping important secrets from him.

He reloaded his shotgun—he liked a simple double-barrel for reliability, two shots were enough if you knew when to use them and could put them where you wanted. Then he headed back into the building to finish off the two live witnesses he could still reach. In passing he glanced down once more at the dead girl. He thought she had moved amid the blood. Even so, there didn't appear to be any need to waste another shell on her, but he would check again on his way back.

Tonight everything was one surprise after another. Looking into the room where he had left the punk called Pat, he saw that the kid appeared to be dead already. Pat lay still, on his back, bound hands underneath, with open, unblinking eyes and some kind of bloody mess around his parted lips. Beside him lay the sweatshirt Helen had been wearing. Well, whatever, the kid looked dead. Making sure, Gliddon knelt down, felt a forehead that was already cold. No heartbeat under the shirt. He flicked an eyeball with a fingertip and got no reflex blink. No need to waste a shell here, either.

With a growing sense that speed was necessary, Gliddon turned away. He had to make sure that the last prisoner, the girl called Judy, was still where she was supposed to be.

Indeed she was, though she was working to get the door of her cell open when Gliddon got there. She was alive and still hand-tied, and satisfyingly terrified. It was reassuring to find at least one person behaving as they ought.

Gliddon would have loved to play with her for a while, but there just wasn't time. He set down his lantern and raised his gun and grinned. "Sleep tight," he said.

And whirled round, on nerves that had become hair-trigger, at the ghost of a small sound just a few steps behind his back.

The small brown-haired girl with the bloody torso stood there, seemingly ignoring her great red wound. In the reflected lantern-light the wound now looked more like scar tissue than like hamburger. Gliddon's eyes must have played him tricks a minute ago, the flimsy wooden table-top must after all have saved her life. Temporarily.

"Gliddon, Gliddon." She didn't even sound hurt. Her little-girl voice held a tone of soft reproach, and it appeared that she was smiling at him.

Gliddon's nerve might have held up, would have held up, if she had been yelling, or attacking him, or crying out in pain for mercy. But he couldn't take this kind of a reality just now. He fired both barrels right in her face. The girl's hair blew back in the wind of the blast, but her face remained untouched. The wall behind her cratered widely and shallowly, and a choking cloud of brown adobe powder burst into the air. The girl stood there with her lovely, smiling face untouched.

Gliddon dropped the emptied shotgun, grabbed up the lantern again, and at the same time drew his pistol. The lantern's beam shining through the cloud of settling dust showed him Helen's dazed and gentle smile. The great red scar along her ribs and belly looked almost superficial, like an old, half-healed burn or scrape.

"Gliddon, no, you shouldn't. Uncle Del's going to be awfully angry with you. He loves me, I'm his niece. I'm just like his very own little girl, he says."

Gliddon couldn't think any longer. He triggered his revolver at the figure, and behind it wood and adobe shuddered and burst, gave up flying fragments to the air.

There was something else in the air, at Gliddon's elbow. He sensed another presence, saw another human figure starting, trying, to take shape. He turned and ran, fleeing by instinct to the aircraft shed.

Judy, gazing at the new apparition, almost broke down in her near-hysterical relief. "You're here, you're here, thank God. I was . . ."

Her voice trailed off. The figure of the vampire taking shape before her eyes was not that of the man she had been expecting. She stared as the form solidified. It was that of a huge man, massively built. He looked quite young—she knew how deceptive that could be—and Judy was sure that she had never seen him before.

He was looking at Judy oddly. In a bass voice he asked her: "Who did you think I was?"

Before she could answer, another man's voice screamed outside in the night, a hundred yards or more away: "Ike! Gliddon! Help!"

Judy slumped, knowing behind closed eyelids a sudden vision: white teeth quenched in red blood. The help that she had waited for had come.

In the aircraft shed, Gliddon hurled himself into the Cessna's cabin. The engine would be cold, but he had kept everything as ready as possible. He was going to make it now. Mexico, here we come.

He grabbed for the electric starter. The engine caught on the first try . . . then coughed, and died. He tried again. The pale figure of the girl was following him. Here she came, walking toward the aircraft through the dim shed, and in the restored silence when the engine died again he could hear her softly calling.

Any moment now he was going to wake up. But no, this time the engine caught and held. He released brakes and grabbed the throttle, and now he was rolling for the doors . . .

The slender blue-and white figure of the girl in jeans came sleepwalking right into the path of the rolling aircraft. Gliddon could see the disaster coming but it was too late for him to do anything about it. Just at the moment of catastrophe everything seemed to be happening at once, and he had not even time to perceive it all, but he had the distinct impression that at that very moment there was yet another person in the shed. A dark-clad man with a pale face, standing near the girl and in the act of reaching for her with one outstretched arm . . .

. . . Gliddon's right hand had hit the switches, and was reaching for the throttle, but too late. The sound of the blow had elemental power, and Gliddon knew the wooden prop must have been sprung if not completely shattered. The aircraft shuddered with the impact, the engine dying finally in a great cough. Gliddon had a door open and jumped out of the cabin again almost before the Cessna had stopped rolling. Something lay on the floor, but he was not going to stop to decide what it was. If there had really been two people in front of the propellor, quite likely it had hashed them both.

Moving in desperate haste he wrenched open the cargo compartment again, pulled out the awkward package and ran with it, stumbling, arm muscles quivering, out of the shed and through the passage that led to the other shed where the Jeep ought to be parked. The Jeep was there. Gliddon wedged the encased painting into the back seat, then sprang into the driver's seat and started the engine with a roar.

The Jeep bounced out of the shed and away into darkness, following a route that twisted among dimly visible boulders and over tiny hills. Next Gliddon headed down into a breakneck ravine that took long minutes to work through, at walking speed, even with the four wheel drive. At the bottom end of this ravine a small stream murmured almost invisibly. Otherwise the night had grown quiet; so far, there was no pursuit. Tires splashed, and then the Jeep was working its way uphill again. Gliddon drove out of the rough at last on the old road, not far from the point where the punks' cars had been stalled. Only a few more miles and he'd be on highway. Then he'd head south. He had in mind a place or two where it ought to be possible to steal another plane.

He felt it was safe to use the headlights now. As soon as they came on they showed him a solitary figure ahead, walking along the primitive road in the same direction he was driving. This figure too was small and slight, but it had on a shirt, and its hair was light in color. As the Jeep slowly overtook it from the rear, it turned. The pale eyes did not squint in the headlights. Numbly Gliddon recognized Pat O'Grandison's dazed, childish face and bloody mouth.

But Gliddon had begun by now to regain his nerve. He was able to believe again that the world was manageable. If tonight's events hadn't beaten him yet, there was no way they were going to.

It wouldn't really be practical to try to finish someone quickly by running over them, on this twisting, humpy, low-speed road. Especially not on a night like this, when people who had looked finished kept coming back.

Calmly watching the Jeep approach, the kid stuck out his thumb, hitchhiking. Well, why not? Gliddon saw that somehow, and it was against all sense, the kid had even managed to pick up and repack the knapsack that Gliddon had emptied onto the earthen floor during the search.

Gliddon slowed the Jeep, meanwhile feeling with one hand for his pistol. It was gone. He must have dropped it somewhere. Never mind, there were plenty of other ways. But he'd rather not delay for a killing until he'd got a few more miles on his way.

He stopped the Jeep beside the waiting boy. "Want a ride, kid? Get in."

The kid didn't even appear to recognize Gliddon. "Thanks," he acknowledged, and got in quite calmly, just as if this were afternoon on the Interstate somewhere. He slipped out of his knapsack and dropped it on the floor, after noting that the back seat was pretty well filled with a huge package. "I'm headed for California."

"Me too," said Gliddon, and eased the vehicle ahead, tires gripping the edges of an old rut, scraping around a rock. Maybe, just maybe, his luck was starting to turn a little for the good.

In the weeks since he had succeeded in inducing the girl to transform him into a vampire, Delaunay Seabright had reveled in the new keenness of his senses, among other things; and he had discovered that they remained most usefully acute when he retained the form of man. Thus it was that he was walking on two human feet when he moved stealthily into the aircraft shed. In the

shed there was much more light than his eyes now
needed, an electric glare streaked with shadow,
spilling from a battery lantern that someone had
dropped and left on the dirt floor.

The Cessna was almost at the opened doors. It
looked wrecked, with its cargo compartment door
standing open and one blade of its wooden propellor broken to half its length. But Seabright gave
that little attention. Directly in front of the plane,
the figure of a lean man dressed in black, turned in
profile to Seabright, was down on one knee. The
man, head bent, was giving his full attention to
something on the earthen floor. Seabright could
not see his face at first, only his white and bony
hands, sifting the dry dust.

Even though Seabright continued to advance
into the shed, one step and then another, the
kneeling man did not look up. Surely anyone of
even moderate alertness would have by now
sensed his presence . . . then with a quiet shock
the realization came that the kneeling man knew
Seabright had entered the shed, but simply did
not care.

Seabright advanced yet another step. He now
had, or thought he had, an understanding now of
what his dark-garbed visitor was, if not of who.
For some time now Seabright had known it was
practically inevitable that sooner or later he must
encounter one or more of the Old Ones—that was
how he had thought of them, when in private
thought he had made his plans. It had taken him
years of research into the ancient and the arcane to
convince himself of the reality of vampires, and to
be able to recognize, however belatedly, that the
girl called Annie was what some of the old books
called *nosferatu*. He was not at all sure what the

others, when and if he met them, would be like. Surely they were not all mad, as the girl had been. In his heart Seabright expected that they would prove to be not all that essentially different from breathing people—manageable, for the most part, by someone like himself, once he had grasped what really made them tick.

He would not submit to being ignored, and now he moved forward yet another step. First he would make sure that his own credentials were established, and then . . .

The kneeling figure in dark clothing at last raised its face. And Seabright, who in recent weeks had imagined himself become totally immune to fear, found himself stepping involuntarily backward. The face was pale and thin, and on the surface it held nothing terrible, though it was marked with wooden splinters from what must have been the propellor's terrible impact against another body that was now nowhere to be seen. From one splinter in the forehead a trickle of dark blood ran down into one eye and out of it again like tears. Yet Seabright retreated another step, and yet another, until the adobe wall came against his back. One of the Old Ones. But he had never dreamed it could be so hard simply to confront one of them.

The figure straightened slowly until it stood erect. It was actually not as tall as Seabright, but from several yards away he got the impression that it was towering over him.

"I was a second too late," the man in dark clothing said softly, in precise and only faintly accented English. "A second too late, and she is dead. Already nothing but dust. That is how we old ones go."

With a great effort Seabright made himself push away from the wall, and speak out boldly. "Who's dead? Who do you mean?"

"You are Delaunay Seabright," the man said. "And you used her."

"You're Thorn," said Seabright, suddenly understanding a little more. "No wonder you . . . I heard about that bombing. No wonder you were able to escape alive." Trying hard, he made himself look closely at the other's face, and was astounded. Were tears mixed with the blood on those almost emaciated cheeks?

"She is dead," said Thorn.

"Look, I'm really sorry about that. Very sorry. She and I were lovers, you know. But she was more than a little bit crazy, and it's not my fault she—"

An invisible giant's fist closed down on Seabright. He was picked from his feet and spun through the air back against the earthen wall, with a violence that tore his clothing and his skin. Imposed force choked his outcries in his throat. Desperately he tried to change his shape, to melt his flesh to mist or nothingness for escape. But his own powers, that he had thought almost perfected, were infantile against the potency that held him now.

Delaunay Seabright sought to strike back at the dark man. But he could no longer even see where his opponent was. The vise-grip blinded his eyes, even as it crushed his ribs. Now he could feel the bones of his elbows, pinned to his sides, shattering in their sockets, and he could not even scream. Then, still capsuled in solid form, he felt himself being propelled helplessly through the air again, driven by what felt like the energy of a locomotive. His eyes were allowed to open, in time to see the ancient wooden beams of the building hurtling toward him.

Nothing prevented Judy Southerland from screaming, and scream she did. She knew that her long-hoped-for rescuer was now somewhere near at hand. But he had not come to her. And she could feel that something had happened, something terrible, something to drive him mad, though she had no idea what it was. Violence as shocking as a bomb was bursting, just on the other side of the building, while Judy, her hands still bound, could not get out of her cell, could not do anything to help herself.

Then, abruptly, came help in a surprising form. A woman Judy had never seen before, a young-looking woman wearing some kind of high-necked granny dress, was bending over her. There came sharp snapping sounds and the tough cord fell from Judy's wrists.

"And you must be Judy," the young-looking woman said. She strongly resembled someone Judy knew—yes indeed, she actually resembled the image that Judy still saw daily in the mirror. In the middle distance there rose a great cry, as of some huge predator in torment. "There now, he's making a great lot of noise over there, isn't he? And I must go to him, but I wanted first to have just a quick word with you. You see, you can't understand what has happened to him tonight—I understand it, a little bit, and I must go, and you must stay here quietly and not try to talk to him just now."

"Gliddon!" That was another voice now, a man's voice shrieking from not far away. "Gliddon, it's got me, for God's sake helllp—"

Judy stuttered: "I . . . he's . . .'"

"He's been your lover, yes, Judy, I know. He was my lover in the same way, but that was many years ago . . . my name is Mina, by the way. We shall meet again, someday, perhaps—but then perhaps not. In either case I wish you well. I must go now, to do what I can. He can be very dangerous like this."

The woman, or the vision of a woman, was gone. No, it had been more than a vision, for Judy's hands were free, the cords that had bound them lay snapped away like thread. And the door of her cell, that she had been trying vainly to force, now stood slightly ajar. Judy pushed weakly against it, then stopped, her eyes closed. Her contact with her once-beloved, strained by the burden of things that Judy had never imagined it might hold, had broken and was gone.

Or had it been deliberately cut, as by some seamstress' scissors?

For the moment she did not care. Freed hands, freed mind—for the moment it was enough, it was all that she could ask for, to enjoy both.

Then Judy's eyes opened, and she cried out again. Great wing-beats of throbbing sound were buffeting the roof above her head. For a moment she cringed from monsters. Then there was a glare of harsh electric light outside, and her own good sense came to her rescue. The light bobbed and probed with the throbbing roar, seeking a good place for helicopters to come down

Gliddon had at last maneuvered his Jeep as far as the highway. It was a dirt road, smoothly graded and two lanes wide, that could pass for a state highway in this part of the boondocks. Gliddon looked both ways into darkness, at zero traffic. He considered, then suddenly reversed the Jeep. A few yards back he had noticed a branching road, and now he found this again and backed into it for a few more yards, until he had reached a place that he was sure would be out of sight of the highway by day.

He stopped the Jeep there, and grinned over at his young companion. "Afraid this is as far as you go, kid."

"I'm going to California," the boy repeated vaguely. He rubbed at the dried mess around his lips, looked at his fingers, then touched one with his tongue. He appeared to be trying to remember something.

"Sure. This is Hollywood and Vine. Hop out. I'm gonna fix you up with a job in the movies."

"I'm going to get a job out there making films. My home's in Chicago." But the kid got out on his side, obediently enough.

As Gliddon stepped out of the Jeep on his own side, he remembered something else. "Hey, kid, you were pretty good that night in Phoenix. Better than any of the girls. I wish we could have finished good friends, the way we started." He walked through the beams of the headlights and put a hand on Pat's shoulder. "I wish we could get a little fun in right now. But I'm in a hurry." And Gliddon, remembering the wounded finger on his own right hand, drew back his left arm and with a practiced, lethal snap sent the blade of his hand with full power against the youngster's neck.

And Gliddon shouted, blinded by the pain and shock. It felt like he had struck a thick wooden pole.

Before he could begin to think of what to do next, the kid had taken him by the right arm. And somehow Gliddon, try as he might, could not pull free.

"Your finger is bleeding, gosh," the boy said. There was something in his voice that was not sympathy, and was certainly not fear either. Whatever it was, it made Gliddon look closely at the kid's face, and then try again to pull away. When Gliddon saw those dried stains around the childish mouth. And how Pat's teeth had changed. When the boy displayed them in a merry smile.

Epilogue

And then all at once the seat at Joe's right hand was empty no longer. For a moment he wondered if he had dozed off, and so given the young lady a chance to sit down unnoticed. But then he understood.

The brown-haired girl in the high-necked gown was smiling at Joe. She was quite attractive, and he at once caught the strong family resemblance to Judy. Glancing back at Judy briefly now, Joe saw that she was deeply asleep.

He turned back. He wasn't exactly used to this sort of an experience yet, but similar things had happened to him before and he could handle them. He returned the smile. "I think," he said, "that I spoke to you on the telephone once, Miss."

"It's Mrs. Harker, actually." Her voice was soft and charming, slightly British. "But please call me Mina. Vlad has told me a good deal about you, and I really feel we are already friends. And since we are sharing a ride tonight I wanted to say hello. And to reassure you, perhaps, on one or two points in connection with these recent—events, that have been so distressing."

A stewardess, passing in the aisle, looked vaguely unsettled by the sight on an unremembered passenger. But the stewardess naturally had plenty of other things to worry about already—there was no problem, really, with a pleasant-looking, undemanding young woman who simply sat chatting with a man. No need to concern oneself; and Joe's understanding grew of how the whole vampire business could remain a secret even while it went on and on and on.

"Well," said Joe, "I'm glad you say 'reassure'. The one kid, Pat O'Grandison, is still missing, and the painting also. And Mr. Thorn, of course. Otherwise there are just bodies all over hell, in mansions, in Jeeps, in garages and old adobe ruins."

"Yes," Mina agreed with a sigh. "It has been a terrible business. Just terrible." She looked at her nails, as any young lady might. They were neatly manicured, Joe noted, and not very long. Certainly nothing at all talonish, not at the moment anyway. She added: "And I don't think they are going to have any success in looking for the painting."

"Oh no?"

"It is my feeling that the real owner might by now have put it away safely somewhere."

"Oh." Joe turned his head to glance once more at Judy, who had not moved. "According to Judy, he was rather crazy, there at the end. She says it was very lucky that you showed up when you did. I was wondering . . ."

Mina smiled again. "Vlad's going to talk to you himself," she said. "Say hello to Kate for me. If you think it wise." She leaned back, and was gone. But the seat remained empty only for a moment.

Joe flinched, just slightly. He couldn't help himself.

If Thorn noticed that infinitesimal recoil, he gave no indication. He smiled lightly at Joe and patted him on the arm. "Thank you, Joe, for your support."

Joe tried to make his arm relax on the seat divider. "You're welcome. Er . . . ah . . . Mina told me there's no use out looking for that painting any longer?"

"Your sense of justice, Joe, may be soothed to know that for the first time in centuries, it is now in the hands of its true owner."

Joe didn't have to ask who that might be. He wondered suddenly if the painting, disguised somehow, could be cargo on this very plane. He wasn't about to try to find out.

"There is one more point, Joseph, on which I wished to speak to you. I mean the young man, Pat O'Grandison, who has disappeared."

"Oh. You're not through hunting yet."

"I detect a certain disapproval." Then in a sort of parenthetical action Thorn leaned forward in his seat and slowly reached past Joe toward Judy. With one finger he very gently touched the burn on her cheek, and her puffy lip. She was sleeping deeply, and did not stir. Thorn sat back. "Actually this particular hunt is one that I should think you might want me to conduct. The youth has not wronged me; I am not seeking revenge."

"Sorry. What, then?"

"He is . . . a runaway. In years, not a child any longer. But not a responsible adult. In fact he is intermittently mad."

"As I understand it, he's been like that most of his life. So are a hundred thousand others running around loose. So what's—"

"Joseph, you do not understand. Remember how the body of the man Gliddon was found."

Joe had heard about that. The state police had said it looked like Gliddon had been half eaten by some animal. "Oh. I thought that was . . . not that I would have blamed you, after . . ."

"Oh, I would have killed him, certainly. But his blood would have been carrion to me. Not to that boy though. That boy is *nosferatu*, now; or rather in a grotesque halfway state that may persist indefinitely. And he is out there somewhere, hitchhiking. If I were greatly concerned for the welfare of the breathing populace of this great nation, I would be anxious that he be found; I would concern myself about him. Of course, as you say, there are thousands of others—"

"What?"

"Oh, not insane vampires, not all of them, but just as dangerous sometimes. To themselves, if not . . ." Thorn's voice trailed off.

Joe stared into the pale face, and could see torture there.

"As she was," Thorn went on at last, whispering. "For centuries, it would appear. Since the day, perhaps, when she saw me fall to traitors' swords and thought that I was dead. Wandering the earth. Seeking to have a home again, and human contact . . . in, as I say, some kind of halfway state. Able to eat the food of breathing humans, to face the sun without distress, to find a kind of sleep anywhere on earth. But able to find real rest nowhere at all. They are mad, and they are outcasts from both worlds, and I do not know how many of them there are who wander the earth tonight. Too much happens to them in their breathing lives, and madness supervenes. Too much happened to me, but I was—very strong. Yes, very strong."

Impulsively Joe put a hand on the arm of the

man, the human being, who rode in the seat beside him.

Thorn looked at him. "It was she, though." He paused. "I am almost sure."